HIVE

FIRST EDITION
10 9 8 7 6 5 4 3 2 1
Published in May 2005
ISBN: 0-9759229-4-7
Printed in the U.S.A.

Published by Elder Signs Press, Inc.
P.O. Box 389
Lake Orion, MI 48361-0389
www.eldersignspress.com

HIVE

A Novel By Tim Curran

elder signs
press

2005

This is for Elaine Lamkin

PART ONE

OUT OF THE ICE

". . . there was one part of the ancient land . . . which had come to be shunned as vaguely and namelessly evil."

— H.P. Lovecraft

Antarctica was a graveyard, of course.

A subzero cemetery of high frozen monoliths and leaning tombstones of exposed, ancient rock. A burial ground of sunless wastes and biting cold, snow plains and ragged mountains. Gale-force blizzards sucked the warmth from a man and tucked him down deep in frozen tombs and covered his tracks with shrieking windstorms of ice crystals that blew just as fine and white as crematory ash. Like the snow and the cold and the enveloping darkness of winter, the winds were a constant. Night after night, they screamed and wailed with the voices of lost souls. A communal death-rattle of all those interred in mass graves of coveting blue ice and sculpted into leering, frosted death angels.

Antarctica was dead and had been for millions of years.

A wasteland, some said, where God had buried those things he no longer wished to look upon. Nightmares and abominations of flesh and spirit. And if that were true, then whatever was entombed beneath the permafrost, locked-down cold and sightless in that eternal deep-freeze, was never meant to be exhumed.

Nothing stays buried forever at the Pole.

It was one of those sayings they tossed around down there. Sometimes you weren't sure what it meant and other times you weren't sure you wanted to. But it was true, nonetheless: nothing stays buried forever at the South Pole. The glaciers are in constant motion, grinding and tearing at the primordial bedrock far below, and what they don't dig up, sooner or later the blizzard winds will blow clean like bones in the desert. So if Antarctica was a graveyard then, it was one in a process of perpetual resurrection, vomiting out those awful bits of its past it could no longer hold down in its belly.

This is how Hayes saw it on his darker days at Kharkhov Station when his poetic turn of mind began devouring itself one bite at a time. But he knew it to be true. He just tried not to think about it, was all.

"I can see 'em now," Lind said, his face pressed up to the frosted glass of Targa House, the place where all the personnel of the station ate, slept, and lived. "It's Gates, all right, coming in with the SnoCat. Must be bringing those mummies in from the high ridges."

Hayes set down his cup of coffee, scratched his beard, and went up to the window. What he saw out there was winter at the South Geomagnetic Pole . . . sheets of snow whipping and swirling and engulfing. The steeple of the drilling tower, the dome of the meteorology station, the power Quonset, half dozen other structures limned by electric lights and shrouded beneath blankets of white.

Kharkhov Station sat near-center of East Antarctica on the Polar Plateau, some 3500 meters above sea level in what had once been the Soviet sector of the continent. A desolate, godless place that was completely cut off from the world from March until October when spring finally returned. During the long, dark winter, only a small crew of contractors and technicians remained, the others got out before the planes stopped coming and winter set its teeth into that ancient continent.

A burial ground.

That's what it was.

The wind howled and the huts shook and day by day that immense bleak nothingness chewed a hole through your soul and blew through your numbed mind like an October gust through a deserted house. It was the third week of winter and you knew the sun would not rise and break that womb of blackness for another three months. Three long, bitter months that would eat at your belly and your brain, freezing something up inside you that wouldn't thaw until you saw civilization again in the spring. And until then, you waited and you listened and you were never really sure what for.

A graveyard indeed, Hayes thought.

The visibility returned for a few fleeting moments and he could see the lights of the SnoCat bobbing through the dimness. Yeah, it was Gates, all right. Gates and his cargo of goodies that had the entire station on edge. He had radioed in three days before from the tent camp about what he had found up there, what he was cutting from the ice.

And now just about everyone was beside themselves with excitement, just waiting for Gates' return like he was Jesus or Santa Claus.

But it was infectious.

Hayes had been seeing it for days now, that look of raw exhilaration and wonder on those usually dour, bored faces. The faces of children who were on the verge of some great discovery . . . wonder, awe, and something just beneath it akin to superstitious terror. Because it didn't take too much to get the imagination rolling in that awful place and particularly when Gates promised he'd be rolling in with mummies from a pre-human civilization.

Jesus, the very idea was overwhelming.

"He's bringing the 'Cat over to Six," Lind said, fists clenched at his sides, something in his throat bobbing up and down. "Shit, Hayes, we're gonna be in the history books over this one. I was talking to

Cutchen and Cutchen was saying that, come spring when they pull our asses out of here, we're all going to be famous, you know? Famous for discovering those mummies . . . he said this discovery will shake the world to its knees."

Hayes could just imagine Cutchen saying something like that. Cutchen's only pastimes seemed to be sarcasm and toying with lesser minds.

"Cutchen's full of shit," Hayes said.

"I thought you two were friends?"

"We are. That's why I know he's full of shit."

"Sure, but he's right about us being famous."

"Christ, Lind . . . listen to yourself. *Gates* is going to be famous. He's the man who found all that stuff up there. And maybe a couple of the other eggheads like Holm and Bryer who helped him . . . but *you?* Or *me?* Hell no, we're just contractors, were support personnel."

But Lind just shook his head. "No, what they found up there . . . we're part of it."

"Jesus Christ, Lind, you're a plumber. When the Discovery Channel or National Geographic start making their documentaries, they're not going to want to know how you bravely handled the Station's shit or heat-taped two-hundred feet of piss-pipe. They'll be talking to the scientists, the techs, even that NSF hard-on LaHune. But not us. They'll tell you to keep the water running and me to run a couple extra two-twenty lines for all their equipment."

Of course, it was all lost on Lind.

He was so excited by it all he could barely contain himself. He was like a little kid waiting for trick-or-treating to start, tense and shaking, having a hell of a time just keeping his feet on the floor and not jumping for joy. And it was pretty funny to see, Hayes had to admit that. You took a guy like Lind — barely 5'5, just as round as a medicine ball and not much lighter, bad teeth, scraggly beard — and watched him hopping around like he was waiting for the candy store to open, it was absolutely priceless.

Damn, where was the camcorder when you needed it?

If Gates' mummies had been female, they would've wanted to keep their legs crossed in Lind's presence because he was that excited and that in love. Course, those mummies weren't male or female from what Gates said over the set. In fact, he was having a hell of a time deciding whether they were animal or vegetable.

Lind said, "They're unloading the sled now . . . must be bringing those mummies into the hut." He shook his head. "And here I thought this winter was going to be a waste of time. How old he say those mummies were?"

"He's guessing two- to three-hundred million years. Back when dinosaurs ruled the earth."

Lind clucked his tongue. "Imagine that. I didn't even know there *were* mummies back then."

Hayes just looked at him, shook his head. It was a good thing Lind was some kind of plumber, because when you came down to it, he wasn't much smarter that most dingleballs hanging off a camel's ass. A real natural with pipes and venting, but anything else? Forget it.

As Hayes watched, Lind began pulling on his fleece jacket and thermal pants, parka, boots, and wool mittens. "Well aren't you coming, Hayes?"

But Hayes just shook his head. Already he could see people spilling out of shacks and buildings, some of them still pulling on their ECW's even though the wind was shrieking and it was pushing seventy below out there.

"I'll wait until the groupies thin," he told Lind.

But Lind was already going out the door, the frigid breath of Antarctica blowing in until the heaters swallowed it.

Hayes sat down, lit a cigarette and sipped coffee, staring at the game of solitaire on his laptop. Yeah, it was going to be a long goddamn winter. The thought of that set on him wrong for reasons even he wasn't sure of, made him feel like he was bleeding inside.

Outside the compound, the wind rose up, showing its teeth.

3

You had to love Lind, Hayes thought later as he got a look at the mummies over in Hut #6. He was really something, positively good to the last drop. Hayes was standing there with him and two other contractors that knew about as much about evolutionary biology as they did about menstrual cramps . . . and Lind? Oh, he was just going on and on while Gates and Bryer and Holm took notes and photographs, made measurements and scraped ice from one of the mummies.

"Yeah, that's one ugly, prick, Professor," Lind was saying, hovering around them, taking up their light while they continually, and politely, told him to step back. "Damn, look at that thing . . . enough to give you the cold sweats. I bet I have nightmares until spring just looking at it. But, you know, more I look at it, more I'm thinking that what you got there is one of those animals without a spine, you know, an un-vertebrate like a starfish or a jellyfish. Something like that."

"You mean *invertebrate*," Bryer, the paleoclimatologist corrected him.

"Isn't that what I said?"

Bryer chuckled, as did a few of the others.

Outside, the wind pelted the walls with snow just as fine as blown sand. And inside, the air was greasy, warm, close. A funny, acrid stink beginning to make itself known as the thing continued to melt.

"We really made a find here, eh, Professor?" Lind said to Gates.

He looked up over his spectacles, a pencil hanging from his lips. "Yes, we certainly did. The find of the ages, Lind. What we have here is entirely new to science. I'm guessing its neither animal nor plant, but a sort of chimera."

"Yeah, that's what I was thinking," Lind said. "Boy, this is gonna make us famous."

Hayes laughed low in his throat. "Sure, I can already see your picture on the cover of *Newsweek* and *Scientific American*. There's a picture of Professor Gates, too, but it's kind of small, stuck down in the corner."

There were a few laughs over that.

Lind scowled. "You don't have to be a smartass, Hayes. Jesus Christ."

But Hayes figured he did. Here these guys were trying to figure out what this was all about while Lind circled them on his unicycle, pumping his red horn and shaking a rubber chicken at them.

So, *yes*, he had to be a smartass.

Same way Lind had to talk . . . even about things he knew nothing of. These were traits they both practiced month by dark month during the long, grim South Pole winters. But in the hut . . . with that defrosting mummy laid out like something spilled from a freakshow jar . . . well, maybe they were doing it because they *had* to do something. Had to say something. Make some noise, anything to disrupt the malign sound of that nightmare melting, dripping and dripping like blood from a slit throat. Hayes couldn't stand it . . . it made his scalp feel like it wanted to crawl off the back of his head.

And he kept thinking: *What the hell's with you? It's a goddamn fossil, it can't do nothing but wait.*

Wait. Yeah, maybe that wasn't what he'd meant to think, but had thought it all the same. And the more you stared at that goddamn thing, more you started thinking it wasn't a fossil at all, just something ancient . . . *waiting.*

Christ, of all crazy things to be thinking.

The wind shook the hut and that was enough for the other two onlookers — a couple contractors named Rutkowski and St. Ours. They went out the door like something was biting their asses. And maybe something was.

"I'm starting to get the feeling that our friends here don't like what you've found," Holm said, running a hand through his white hair. "I think it's giving them the creeps."

Gates laughed thinly. "Is our pet here bothering you, Hayes?"

"Hell, no, I like it, big ugly sonofabitch," he said. "Got all I can do not to hug it and get it alone somewhere."

They all started laughing at that. But it didn't last long. Not very long at all. Like laughter in a mortuary, good cheer just did not belong in this place. Not now. Not with what was berthed in there.

Hayes did not envy Gates and his people.

Sure, they were scientists. Gates was a paleobiologist and Holm was a geologist, but the very idea of touching that monstrosity in the melting ice, well, it made something in his stomach roll over and then roll over again. He was trying desperately to catalog what it was he was feeling, but it was just beyond him. All he could say for sure is that that creature made his guts roll up like a dirty carpet, made something inside him run both hot and cold. Whatever that thing was, it revolted him on some unknown inner level and he just couldn't get a handle on it.

It was dead.

That's what Gates said, but looking at it, Christ and the saints, you really had to wonder. For the blue ice was getting very clear now and it was like looking through thick glass. It distorted things, but nowhere near enough for Hayes' liking.

The mummy was big. Probably an easy seven feet from end to end, shaped like some great fleshy barrel that tapered at each end and was set with high vertical ridges that ran up and down its length. Its skin was an oily gunmetal gray like that of a shark, set with tiny fissures and minute scars. Midline, there was a pair of appendages that branched out like tree limbs and then branched out again into fine tapering tendrils. At the bottom of the torso, there were five muscular tentacles, each an easy four feet in length. They looked oddly like the trunks of elephants . . . though not wrinkled, but smooth and firm and powerful. They ended in flat triangular spades that might have been called feet on another world.

And the ice kept melting and the water kept dripping and that weird rotten fish-stink began to come off the thing.

"What's that there?" Lind said. "That . . . that a head?"

"Yes," Gates said. "It would seem to meet the criteria."

Maybe for a biologist, but not for Hayes or Lind. They stood around like mourners, just wanting to throw dirt over it. At the top of the thing's torso was a flabby, blunt neck that almost looked like a wrinkled-up scarf or foreskin. On top of it was something like a great five-pointed starfish, dirty yellow in color. The radial arms of the star were made of tapering, saggy tubes and at the end of each, a bulbous red eye.

Hayes thought that it looked like the creature had been frozen very quickly, flash-frozen like one of those mammoths up in Siberia you read about. Because it looked . . . well, almost *startled* like it had been caught by surprise. At least that's what he had been thinking, but the more the ice melted and the more of that head and those five leering red eyes he saw, the more he was thinking it looked pissed-off, arrogant, superior, something. And whatever that look was, it sure as hell was not friendly.

You wouldn't want to meet this fellah on a good day, Hayes thought, let alone with that evil look about it.

And thinking that, he just couldn't imagine how something like it could have walked. For it was debased and degenerate, the sort of thing made to crawl, not walk upright like a man. But according to what Gates told Bryer, it stood and walked, all right.

"That's some sort of wing there I'd bet," Holm said, indicating an arched tubular network like bones on the thing's left side that were folded-in on themselves like an oriental fan. Even folded, you could see the fine webbing of mesh between the tubes. "And another over here. Certainly."

"Jesus, you mean it could fly?" Lind said.

Gates scribbled something in his notebook. "Well, at this point we're opting for some sort of marine adaptation . . . maybe not wings, but possibly fins . . . though until we can actually examine them, I'm only guessing."

In his mind, Hayes could see that thing flying around like some sort of cylindrical gargoyle, dipping down over sharp-peaked roofs. That was the image he had and it was very clear in his mind for some reason as if it was something he had seen once or maybe dreamed about.

"Has LaHune see it yet?"

Gates said he hadn't, but that he was very excited about the prospects of the discovery. And Hayes could almost hear LaHune saying just that, *Gentlemen, I am most excited about the prospects of this monumental discovery.* Yeah, that's exactly how he would have said it. Hayes shook his head. LaHune, he was some kind of guy. Dennis LaHune was the NSF administrator who ran Kharkhov Station, summer and winter. It was his job to keep things running, make certain resources were not wasted, keep everything on the straight and narrow.

Yeah, Hayes thought, resident ballbuster, bean-counter, and NSF ramrod. That was LaHune. The headmaster lording over this clutch of unruly, free-thinking students as it were. LaHune had more personality than your average window dummy, but not much.

Lind said, "I can't believe he hasn't come to see what we have out here. You would think it was his job."

"C'mon, Lind," Hayes said. "He's got more important shit to be doing like counting pencils and making sure we're not using too many paperclips."

Gates chuckled.

The water that melted off that irregular block of ice was being collected in buckets, tagged for later study. Drip, drip, drip.

"Gets under your skin, don't it?" Lind said. "Just like that movie . . . you ever seen that movie, Hayes? Up at the North Pole or maybe it was the South, they got this alien in a block of ice and some dumbfuck throws an electric blanket over it and it unthaws, runs around camp sucking everybody's blood. Think that guy from *Gunsmoke* was in it."

Hayes said, "Yeah, I saw it. Was kind of trying not to think about it."

Gates smiled, set his digital camera aside. With his big shaggy beard he looked more mountain man than paleontologist. "Oh, we're unthawing our friend here, boys, but it won't be by accident. And don't worry, this creature has been dead a long, long time."

"Famous last words," Hayes said and they all had a laugh over that.

Except Lind.

They'd lost him somewhere along the way.

He stood there staring at the thing in the ice, listening to the water dripping and it seemed to have the same effect on him as the call of a siren: his eyes were fixed and wide, his lips moving but no words coming out. He stood there like that for maybe five minutes before anyone seemed to notice and by then it looked much like he was in a trance.

Hayes said, "Lind . . . hey, Lind . . . you okay?"

He just shook his head, his upper lip pulled up into a snarl. "That fucking LaHune . . . thinks he's in charge, but doesn't have the balls to come and look at this . . . this *monster*. Bastard's probably on the line with NSF McMurdo, bragging about this, telling them all about it.

But what does he know about it? Unless you stand here looking at it, feeling it looking *back* at you, how can you know about it?"

Hayes put a hand on his shoulder. "Hey, chill out here, Lind, it's just a fossil."

Lind shrugged off his hand. "Oh, is that all it is? You telling me you don't feel that thing *looking at you?* Jesus, those eyes . . . those awful red eyes . . . they get right inside you, make you feel things, make you want to do things. You telling me you can't feel it up *here?*" He was rubbing his temples, kneading them roughly like dough. "Can't you feel what it's thinking? Can't you feel it getting inside your head, wanting to steal your mind . . . wanting to make you something but what you are? *Oh Christ, Hayes, it's . . . those eyes . . . those fucking eyes . . . they unlock things in your head, they . . . "*

He paused there, breathing very hard now, gasping almost like a fish that was asphyxiating. There was sweat all over his face and his eyes were bulging from his head, cords straining at his neck. He looked to be on the verge of utter hysteria or maybe a good old-fashioned stroke.

"You better get him back to the compound," Gates said.

They were all staring at Lind, thinking things but not saying them. A clot of ice dropped from the mummy and Hayes stiffened at the sound. It was enough, by God, it was more than enough.

He helped Lind with his parka and led him to the door. As Hayes made to open it, Lind turned and looked at the scientists. "I'm not crazy, I don't care what you think. But you better listen to me and you better listen good." He jabbed a shaking finger at the mummy. "Whatever you do, whatever any of you do . . . don't stay in here alone with it, if you know what's good for you, *don't stay in here alone with it . . . "*

Then they were out the door.

"Well," Bryer said. "Well."

The wind clutched the hut like a fist, shook it, made the overhead lights flicker and for barely a second, they were in the dark with the thing.

And by the looks on their faces, they hadn't cared for it much.

There were a lot of camps at the South Pole. Collections of pitted bones scattered over the frozen slopes and lowlands like sores and contusions on the ancient hide of the beast. But only a handful of them were occupied when winter showed its cold, white teeth.

Kharkhov was one of the few.

Just another rawboned research station, its numerous buildings like meatless skeletons rising from the black ice, shivering beneath shrouds of blowing white. A desolate and godforsaken place where the sun never rose and the wind never stopped screaming. The sort of place that made you pull into yourself, roll up like a pillbug and hold on tight, waiting for the night to end and spring to begin. But until that time, there was nothing to do but wait and languish through the days that were nights and keep your mind occupied.

What you didn't want to do was to think about ancient, hideous things that had been exhumed from polar tombs. Things that pre-dated humanity by God knew how many millions of years. Things that would drive you mad if you saw them walk. Things with glaring red eyes that seemed to get inside you and whisper with malevolent voices, filling your mind with reaching, alien shadows.

5

Although he drank a pint of Jim Beam Rye before lights out, Hayes didn't sleep worth a damn that night. He had weird dreams from the moment he closed his eyes to the moment they snapped back open at four a.m. In the darkness he lay there, sweat beading his face.

The dorm room was dark, the readout of a digital clock over on the wall casting a grainy green illumination. There were two beds in there. If you fell out of yours, you stood a good chance of falling into your partner's. They were crowded places, the dorms, but space was limited at the stations. Tonight, the other bed was empty. Lind was sleeping on a cot in the infirmary, shot full of Seconal by Doc Sharkey.

Hayes was alone.

Dreams, just dreams. Nothing to get worked up about.

Maybe it had been what happened to Lind and maybe it was something else, but the dreams had been bad. Real bad. Even now, Hayes was all fuzzy-headed and he couldn't be sure they *were* dreams. He couldn't remember them all, just some tangled skein of nightmares where he was pursued, hiding from terrible shapes with burning eyes.

He could only remember the last one with any clarity.

And that's the one that had yanked him out of sleep, made him sit right up, teeth chattering. In the dream, some grotesque freezing black shadow had fallen over him, bathing him with the cold of tombs and crypts. It had been standing at the foot of his bed, that seething amorphous shape, looking at him . . . and that had done it. He'd woken up, fighting back a scream.

Nerves.

Jesus, that's all it was. Too much weird shit happening lately, his imagination had been cranked. And when you lost control of your imagination during the long Antarctic winter, you could be in real trouble.

Hayes settled back in, deciding to lay off the microwave lasagna before bedtime. Because that was probably the real culprit.

Couldn't be anything else.

By the next afternoon, everyone in camp had heard about Lind's little episode.

At a research station like Kharkhov, there were no secrets. Stories — whether real, imagined, or grossly exaggerated — made the rounds like clap at a convention. Everything was passed around, retold, re-invented, blown out of proportion until it bore little resemblance to the incident that had inspired it.

In the mess hall, trying to eat his grilled cheese sandwich and tomato soup in peace, they were all over Hayes like birds on roadkill, all pecking away to see if there was any good red meat left on the carcass.

"Heard Lind tried to slit his wrists," Meiner, one of the heavy equipment operators was saying, smelling like diesel fuel and hydraulic grease and not doing much for Hayes' appetite. "Sumbitch just went crazy, they're saying, crazier than a red-headed shitbug. Just lost it staring down at that mummy in the ice."

Hayes sighed, set his sandwich down. "He –"

"It's true enough," St. Ours said. "I was there with him for awhile. He was getting a funny look in his eyes the whole time, just staring at the ugly bastard in the ice, that monster just thawing out and that face swimming up clear . . . and it weren't no sort of face I'd want to see again."

Rutkowski jumped in at that point, started saying how Lind had gotten a funny gleam in his eyes like a man ready to jump off a bridge. That none of it surprised him because there was something funny about

Lind and something even funnier about those dead things Gates had dragged back from the camp in the foothills.

They talked on and on non-stop.

Didn't let Hayes get a word in edgewise about any of it. Other than Gates, Holm, and Bryer, he'd been the only one to see Lind's breakdown, if that's what it had been. Both Rutkowski and St. Ours had left the hut maybe fifteen minutes before. Not that the lack of firsthand experience in the matter was slowing them down any.

Meiner was saying how he'd been at the Palmer Station on Anvers Island one lean winter and that three people had committed suicide one week, slit their wrists to a man, one after the other. It was spooky shit, he said. Got so people at Palmer thought there was some sort of insanity bug making the rounds. But that was the Antarctic winter, sometimes people just couldn't take the isolation, the desolation, it got under their skins like scabies. And when that happened, when something slipped a cog upstairs, then that left a person wide open to bad "influences."

"Don't surprise me, not one cunt-hair," St. Ours confessed to them. "We had this man and wife team at McMurdo one winter, funny ducks they were, geologists, studying rocks and corings, always looking for something but real vague as to what it was when you put a question to 'em. Anyway, they were up on Mount Erebus for maybe a week, doing some digging. They come down, come back, and they got this funny look in their eyes . . . kind of a shellshocked look, you know?"

Rutkowski nodded. "Seen it plenty of times."

"Sure enough," St. Ours said. "Sure enough. Only this time it was worse, savvy? They had all these rocks they found up there, but real flat with weird carvings on 'em like hieroglyphics or some of that Egyptian gobbledegook. They was acting damn freaky, hoarding those rocks, getting really scary about 'em. So one day, I was over at their shack and I says to 'em, I ast 'em what in Christ were those rocks about? They said they were artifacts from some ancient civilization, wouldn't let me touch 'em. Said once you touched 'em, your mind went one drop at a time and something else filled it. What? I ast 'em. But they wouldn't say, just grinning and staring like a couple pitch-and-throw carnie dolls. Two days later, yessir, two days later, hand in hand they wandered off into a blizzard, left a note that they was following the 'old voices from under the mountain.' Jesus Christ. But that just goes to show you the kind of horseshitty things that happen down here."

"I believe it," Meiner said.

Hayes pushed his plate away, wondering why they had to choose him as their totem pole to dance around. "Listen, you guys, I was there when Lind dropped his deck. None of *you* were, only me. He didn't try to slit his wrists or anything like that, he just had a bad time of it is all."

They listened intently, nodded, then Rutkowski got that conspiratorial look in his eyes and said, "Slit both his wrists, that's what they're saying. Probably would've made a go of his throat if there were time."

"I don't like it," St. Ours said.

"Listen – " Hayes attempted, but they shut him off like a leaky tap.

"I don't like the idea of three more months up here with a crazy man," Rutkowski said. "They better lock his ass up. That's all I gotta say on the matter."

Meiner said, "It ain't that crazy shit you got to worry about, it's what Gates brought back here. Jesus and Mary, go out there and look at that one he's defrosting . . . it'll make you want to piss down your leg. Looks like some kind of crazy gray cucumber with these yellow worms growing out of the top of its head and big, staring red eyes at the end of each one . . . nothing that looks like that thing can be up to any good. Believe you me."

Gradually, as the shit got deeper and it got difficult to find leg room or draw a breath with the stink, they moved off and Lind was pretty much forgotten. Now it was just the mummies and how word had it they weren't even from this planet. Ghost stories and campfire tales and those three big, seasoned men trying to out-do one another, scaring the shit out of each other in the process.

Hayes ignored it all and sipped his soup, listened to the wind trying to strip Targa House off the frozen tundra as it did day after day, reaching and clawing and howling like something hungry come down out of the mountains to the west.

"Join you?" a voice said.

Hayes looked up and it was Doc Sharkey, the station's physician, a short pretty redhead with bright blue eyes. She was the only woman in camp and all the men were saying how she was too heavy for their liking, but by spring they'd all be trying to get into her pants.

Thing was, she wasn't heavy, not in Hayes' worldview. She was wide in the hips, nicely rounded in that way he'd always found blatantly sexual. No, the men kept their distance (at least for the time being) because she intimidated them. It wasn't anything she actually said or did, but her face more than anything. Those upturned Nordic eyes of hers gave her a cold, detached look that was enhanced by her mouth which had a sort of cruel lilt to it.

Hayes liked her right away when he met her and the reason for that was downright silly and he didn't even like to admit it to himself: she reminded him of Carla Jean Rasper from the third grade, his first serious crush. Same hair, same eyes, same mouth. When he'd first caught sight of Sharkey, he'd been instantly transported back to grade school, speechless and stupid just like he'd been around Carla Jean. *Good Morning, little schoolgirl . . .*

"Earth to Jimmy Hayes . . . what's your frequency?"

"Huh? Oh yeah, Doc, sit down. Please do," Hayes said.

What's your frequency? He liked that. Hadn't that nut who attacked Dan Rather on his way to CBS that time said something like that? Sure. *What's your frequency, Kenneth?* REM had done a song by the same name.

Sharkey sat down and Hayes found himself staring into her eyes a little too long. He wasn't married, but she was. Her husband was an anthropologist on a grant somewhere in Borneo studying monkey semen or something like that.

"How goes it?" Sharkey asked, pouring some dressing on her salad.

Hayes laughed without meaning to do so. "Well, I been thinking that they better take a chance and send a plane down here before all these people go completely mad."

She smiled. "We won't see a plane until September at the earliest and mid-October wouldn't surprise me. Sorry, Jimmy, what we got is what we got and we'll have to live with it."

"They're talking some pretty crazy shit, Doc," Hayes told her. "And not just the contractors either, if what I'm hearing is correct."

The building shook and the lights dimmed momentarily.

Sharkey sighed. "No, it's not just the contractors, it's the scientists, too. I think this is going to be a long winter. Should make for an interesting psychological profile by spring."

"Sure, I don't doubt it a bit. Maybe Gates ought to ship his mummies back up to those caves."

"That won't happen," she laughed.

"I'm serious, Doc. Those goddamn things are like catalysts. These people are already acting goddamn loony and I hate to see what another month will bring."

"I've spent three winters at the Pole, Jimmy, and most of them are just lonely and quiet and boring. But I don't think we'll see that this year. What Gates found has everyone worked up. I'm hoping it'll die down in a week or so, but I have to wonder. Even I have to wonder."

"Why's that?"

She looked at him, her eyes sparkling. "You saw those mummies, Jimmy, and you can't deny that there's something . . . *peculiar* about them. Don't look at me like that, you felt it same as I did. They have to be the most alien-looking creatures I've ever seen, but I don't know if that's what's eating people around here. I'm only going to say, from a very safe medical pedestal, that those . . . *remains* seem to be having a very unusual psychological impact on whoever looks at them."

Hayes didn't doubt that a bit. He'd felt it right away when he'd been in Hut #6 with Lind and the others. He hadn't been able to put a finger on what it was about the thing and still really couldn't, other than to say that there was something extremely *unsettling* about it. Something that got inside you, dug in deep like a burrowing worm looking for a hot, moist place to lay its eggs.

And what had Lind said?

Can't you feel it getting inside your head, wanting to steal your mind . . . ?

Hayes swallowed, something caught in his throat. "There's something . . . *bad* about those things, Doc. We're all feeling it. Maybe not Gates and those other eggheads, but the rest of us are feeling it just fine, thank you. I don't know what to make of it."

"Lind seemed to think it was trying to steal his mind or something?"

Hayes nodded. "That's what he said. It was getting inside his head, unlocking things. You want to take a stab at that?"

She shook her head. "I'm not a therapist, Jimmy. I've given you my learned G.P. speculation, that's all I can do."

"How about off the record?"

She set her fork down. "Off the record? Off the record you couldn't pay me a million dollars to spend the night alone out there with that horror."

7

That evening after dinner, Gates finally left the side of his lover out in Hut #6, and joined the others in the community room at Targa House. At what seemed a prearranged moment — the entire winter crew in attendance, some 20 scientists and contractors — he stood up and tapped a spoon against his water glass. It drew everyone's attention right away, because to a man, they'd been waiting for it.

Waiting patiently.

Now, it was rare to find everyone in the community room. Usually some of the contractors would be out at the power station or working on the vehicles and snowmobiles, maybe down in the shafts checking lines. And the scientists were usually out at the drilling tower or in one of their improvised labs or at their laptops, tapping away.

But not tonight.

Everyone was there, gathered around just waiting for Gates to say something because he hadn't exactly been a social butterfly since he came down from the tent camp. So everyone was in attendance like spooks hanging around the War Room wondering if the president was going to bomb some country.

Hayes was sitting with Doc Sharkey and Cutchen, the meteorologist, playing poker. Rutkowski and most of the other contractors were at the table opposite playing cribbage . . . now and again, one of them would look over at Elaine Sharkey, nod their heads as if to say, yup, she's a woman, all right, knew it first time I saw her.

"I think Dr. Gates would like to say a word or two," LaHune said.

He was sitting alone at a table in the corner looking . . . *efficient.* Sitting there in his fancy *L.L. Bean* sweater and windpants, straight and tall like he had an iron bar shoved up his ass and he wanted to keep it there.

"Ah, the plot thickens," Cutchen said.

Gates smiled to everyone. His eyes were bloodshot with brown half-moons under them. He'd been busy and hadn't been sleeping much. "Hello, everyone," he said. "Tomorrow afternoon I'm going back up to the excavation, but before I do that, I'd like to touch base and tell you what all this is about and what it might mean."

Everyone was watching him now.

"I'm not going to waste a lot of your time talking about the mummies themselves as we've only just completed a preliminary dissection of one of the intact specimens and it'll take time to correlate and interpret all the data Dr. Holm, Dr. Bryer, and myself have compiled. But I don't think I'd be going out on *too* shaky of a limb by saying what we've found out there will certainly revolutionize the field of biology. The creature . . . creatures . . . are of a completely new variety, composed of characteristics of both plant and animal and a few that fit neither pantheon. Let me just say that, in regards to its basal anatomy, it seems to fit nowhere in the fossil record. I'm guessing what we've uncovered up here will keep comparative anatomists and physiologists alike busy for decades to come.

"Anyway . . . let me just mention its nervous system briefly. I have made a pretty extensive examination here and . . . well, I think I can safely say that this creature was almost certainly intelligent. Possibly far in advance of ourselves. I don't want to bore you with anatomy, but I want you to understand a few things. Now, the human brain is double-lobed, as you I'm sure know, left and right hemispheres controlling a variety of functions, depending on whether you are left or right handed. These hemispheres communicate via bundles of axons. Now, let me say that our creature . . . we have, as yet, no good name for it . . . has a *five*-lobed brain which hints at an incredible level of neurophysiologic sophistication. Whereas our brains have but two main types of cells, the creature's brain has no less than five. Microscopic examination of its neurons, brain cells, also indicate a staggering degree of neural specialization and complexity. Human neurons are basically made up of a central cell body, the soma, and branched fibers called dendrites and axons. Neurons share information with other neurons via electrical impulses gathered by the dendrites at connection points which are called synapses. This information is processed by the soma and its output travels down the axons to the synapses of other neurons. Boring? I suppose it is. Regardless, I tell you this only in comparison for the creature's neurons are totally alien, though, I would assume, operate in roughly the same manner. You see, the creatures' neurons are not made up of a single cell body, but a sort of triple soma connected to a highly sophisticated network of dendrites, axons, and a mysterious third plexus of branching fibers that has us simply baffled.

"Why do I tell you all this?" Gates smiled thinly, then frowned. "Because you need to understand the nature of what we're dealing with here, the level of intellect this creature must have possessed in life which must have been limitless. I doubt the human brain will be anywhere near this level of development for several million years. Maybe not even then. So now you know . . . this creature was possessed of something of a hyper-intellect and appears to have sensory adaptations that hint at senses beyond the normal five."

Hayes looked over at Sharkey and she whistled silently. Which was pretty much what he'd been doing in his head. Sure, some of what Gates said was a little heady, but the impact of it was shocking. What he was saying was that these creatures — apparently million of years gone — were intellectually above man as man was above your average toad. Jesus, it was enough to suck the wind out of you.

Gates took a drink of water. "Now I know that there's been a lot of talk about our mummies . . . I'm not sure if that word even applies such is the state of their preservation . . . and a lot of it has been pretty wild. What I keep hearing is that people are saying these creatures might be alien, as in *extraterrestrial*. I won't even hazard a guess as to that, but I will say that, given their level of development and culture, I suppose it's not impossible. We won't even be able to speculate much on things like that until we begin a comprehensive analysis of the creatures' DNA and proteins. As you know, I'm sure, all life on Earth shares the same DNA . . . we're only different from a spider or a fungus because of *how* our DNA synthesizes and replicates proteins. If, say, the DNA breakdown of the creature was to show marked irregularities from our own . . . or even a completely alien structure . . . then, my friends, we would have some very tough questions to ask ourselves."

Hayes wasn't liking any of this.

Gates wasn't definitively saying that those things were from Mars or Altair-6, but he sure as hell wasn't ruling it out either. Christ, Rutkowski and the boys were going to have a field day with this.

Gates took another drink of water. "Okay, time for your history lesson now that you've had your biology lecture." There were a few stifled laughs at that. *"Aliens.* It's sort of a word that's pretty much been worn out, but it's one you hear about from time to time if you've spent any time down here in Antarctica. For years there's been crazy stories circulating about some great pre-human civilization under the ice. I'm sure most of you vets have heard your share of horror stories. But how did all that start? Well, I'll tell you — the Pabodie Expedition and the Starkweather-Moore Expedition. Ah, I saw a few eyes light up at the mention of those names. Some of you might be familiar with them . . . "

He went on to say that both of these expeditions had taken on the characteristics of urban myths over the years to such an extent that most people — even most scientists — were of the mind neither expedition had ever taken place, that it was all some great hoax dredged up by conspiracists and Antarctic field workers with too much damn time on their hands. But, in truth, the expeditions had not only been very real, but serious in intent and staffed by some very bright people. It was all a matter of historical fact.

"The Pabodie expedition of 1930-31 was the first," Gates said. "It was led by William Dyer, a geology professor from Miskatonic University . . . where, heh, heh, I did my undergrad work. Anyway, the purpose of the expedition was to do coring work with a newly-designed drill and shed a little light on the geologic and paleontologic history of the Antarctic continent. Well, the results, at first, were mixed. Then the team's biologist, a fellow named Lake, discovered what appeared to be fossilized prints in Precambrian rock that Lake surmised was from the Archeozoic era . . . "

As it turned out, Gates said, it was the beginning of the end. More prints were discovered and Lake had no doubt by that point that what he was seeing was the fossil evidence of some unknown, but apparently advanced organism that walked upright eons before such a thing could have been possible. It was startling. The fossil record was implicit on the fact that nothing beyond simple algae or very rudimentary worms were extant at the time, roughly 700 million years ago.

Then, drilling northwest of the main camp, Lake and his associates broke into a subterranean cave.

"Now, people, this is where things get strange. Lake discovered the remains of creatures that were, yes, exactly like the ones my team has uncovered. He broadcast some fairly detailed information back to Dyer at the main camp, telling Dyer that he had found more fossilized prints and that he was of the opinion that the specimens he found were, in fact, the individuals that had *made* those prints. Fascinating stuff . . . "

Through the years, he explained, the controversy surrounding Lake's discoveries had become something of a battleground for scientists. No actual specimens were taken back for further study, so all they had was Lake's word on it and some corroborative testimony from Dyer, a few blurry snapshots that were not exactly undeniable proof of anything.

"It seems that at this point, things went bad for the Pabodie Expedition. After they had not heard from Lake for several days, Dyer and a few others flew up into the mountains to Lake's temporary camp. What they found was utter destruction . . . tents flattened, machinery destroyed, sleds gone, and, worse, all eleven men were missing. As were the specimens Lake had found. Curious. Anyway, this is the point where most people believe that Dyer and his people went mad, *dementia Antarctica,* they called it, that he imagined all the awful things that he later freely admitted to . . . "

Dyer apparently radioed back to the world a censored version of what he saw at the devastated camp, saying that a freak wind storm had wiped out the entire party. But he wrote a completely different version that was pretty much kept from the public at large and with good reason. For it wasn't a wind storm, he claimed, that destroyed that camp but something much worse. Something Gates wouldn't even comment on.

"So, Lake and his people were gone. Dyer and the others used the drills to seal the cave entrance shut and then flew higher up into the mountains and discovered the ruins of an incredibly ancient city clinging to the slopes, the remains of an advanced pre-human civilization. Dyer said it looked vaguely like Macchu Picchu in the Andes, but exaggerated to a fantastic extreme. He mentioned, also, the excavated

Sumerian foundations of primal Kish. Basically, then, an immense prehistoric city, much of which was covered by the glaciers. Dyer claimed that the city dated from the Carboniferous Period, some 280 to 350 million years ago, and had been abandoned sometime during the Pliocene, roughly two or three million years ago when our ancestors were little better than manlike apes.

"Well, Dyer returned with what remained of his party and quite of few of them were completely mad and had to be institutionalized. Dyer's findings . . . supported only by those dim photographs . . . were scoffed at. His journal, which went into some impressive detail about the city and culture of what he called the *Old Ones* or *Elder Things,* was shown only to certain scientists, then locked away in the vaults of the Miskatonic. I was allowed to read it about ten years ago, one of a handful that have been granted that opportunity. Well . . . " Gates sighed and shook his head " . . . it's wild stuff, people. Dyer had no doubt that these Old Ones built that city and were of an extraterrestrial origin. Much of Dyer's journal is probably sheer fantasy induced by temporary madness, but there can be no doubt now that Lake did indeed find these Old Ones, for, as you know, we've found them now, too.

"Well, where does any of this leave us? I'm not really sure. I rather doubt we'll be able to corroborate much of what Dyer said, but some of it, yes, a great deal in fact. But what about that city? Is it still up there? Yes and no." Gates looked around at those faces, seeing maybe fascination and curiosity and, yes, maybe fear, too. "What Dyer described, unfortunately, is gone. The area he visited was decimated in the 1930s and '40s by geologic cataclysm and intense glaciation. Those awe-inspiring 'Mountains of Madness' of his were destroyed for the most part . . . the seismic activity and shifting of the glaciers now makes it almost impossible to say *where* his ruins in fact were. The entire area is changed . . . gorges and valleys opened where none existed before and the shattering of those high peaks he spoke of opened up the area to intense snowfall. If any of it's there, it's now buried beneath a mountain of snow and ice."

"What about that other expedition?" someone asked.

"Starkweather-Moore? That was a follow-up to Dyer's in 1931 to '32, but it proved inconclusive. Shortly after the Pabodie Expedition, the first of those geologic upheavals obliterated much of the region.

So it was a bust. They had gone seeking evidence of a pre-human civilization and particularly of that great stone city built by an alien race and found neither. So, as you can imagine, all that Dyer claimed was scoffed at by the scientific community. Another expedition was funded privately in the 1960s but without any success. And since the days of the Pabodie Expedition, the tales down here of aliens and weird civilizations have been ripe and abundant. There has been no proof . . . until now . . . "

Here we go, Hayes was thinking. Now comes the spooky shit as if all of this wasn't spooky enough already. Jesus. He looked over at Sharkey and she looked at him. It was hard to say what exactly passed between them, but it was akin to the look a couple of wide-eyed kids might give each other around a campfire after they were told that, yes, the ghost story they had just heard was really *true*. It was certainly a day of revelations.

Gates was busy sketching out for them his own excavations in a series of naturally-hollowed limestone caves which were far east of Dyer's "Mountains of Madness." The original aim of Gates' team was paleontological and was extremely successful. They discovered Mesozoic theropods and tetrapods, near-complete sauropod dinosaurs. Proto-mammals such as triconodonts and cynodonts as well as Jurassic mosasaurs and plesiosaurs, even more recent fossils of cetacians from the Cenozoic. And not just animals, but plants, cycads and cycadeoids. Vascular pteridophytes from the Devonian which included new species of Lycopods, club mosses, and sphenopsids. Gates went into great, dusty clinical detail concerning Cretaceous angiosperms and gymnosperms, Permian seed ferns.

It almost seemed that maybe he wanted to discuss anything but those "Old Ones" and the ruins he had discovered. But, finally, he came back around.

"So, as you can see, we did not go into this hoping to validate any of Dyer's wild stories, we had plenty of other concrete things to do amongst those ancient fossiliferous rocks. The specimens we found will take months to remove from the strata and years and years to classify properly. But, as you know, we found other things there that immediately diverted our attention. These limestone caves I spoke of is where we found our richest fossil beds. But as we explored deeper into this labyrinth of caverns we discovered something like a burial pit into which our creatures had been interred vertically and then . . . yes, then our caverns grew into immense grottos hundreds and hundreds of feet in height. What we found there easily dwarfs Kentucky's Mammoth Cave . . . some of the caverns were so large you could tuck away entire cities in them . . . "

And somebody had.

For inside those immense caverns they had found the ruins of a cyclopean city from some incredible ancient civilization much like the one Dyer had written about. Gates wasn't ready to put his reputation on the line and say that the Old Ones had built it, but it seemed a pretty fair guess from where he was standing. Within the ruins they had uncovered bas reliefs and hieroglyphics which pictured these creatures and the history of their culture.

"Now understand," Gates pointed out, "that these pictoforms are incredibly weathered and unreadable in parts, but what we're seeing would seem to indicate that the creatures were in fact the architects of that ruined city. The city, if I might call it that, goes on literally for miles underground. Much of it is glaciated and much of it is buried beneath cave-ins . . . but there's enough there for years and years, if not lifetimes, of research. Now, Dyer wrote about these same types of bas reliefs. His interpretations of these same glyphs and pictographs are, I think, utter fantasy. He wrote that they told the story of interstellar wars and the decimation of the Old Ones via some protoplasmic monstrosities they had created . . . but I've seen nothing like that. Now, granted, I'm no archaeologist and neither was Dyer. *But,* before diverging completely into paleontology, I did my undergraduate work in prehistoric archaeology, so I'm not completely ignorant of interpreting some of these things. In the spring, we'll fly in a real team of archaeologists, but until then, my team and I will do what we can, lay some sort of groundwork if possible. But let me just say that what Dyer claimed to have read in those ruins is positively pedestrian in comparison to what we're seeing, the story those glyphs are telling us. For, people, what I'm seeing there is something that might make us re-think *who* we are and *what* we are."

Everyone really started murmuring then, firing off question after question, but Gates would say no more. He told them frankly that he would field no more questions until he and his team had had at least a few more weeks, if not a month, for further study and exploration.

But nobody was satisfied with that. You couldn't drop a bomb like that and just walk away. The crowd was getting ugly, particularly Rutkowski and his band of merry men. They were on their feet demanding to know what the hell it all meant and if those aliens (he wasn't afraid to use the term) were going to wake up and start sucking peoples' brains out. Even the scientists themselves were demanding answers, even crazy speculation.

Finally, Gates said: "You're all asking me to answer questions without having had enough time to even make an educated guess. Are the creatures alien? Unknown. Did they build that city? Possibly. Are they any threat to us? Of course not. C'mon, people, put away your comic books here. That city was abandoned during the Pliocene and the mummies we've found have been dead, I'm guessing, since the Triassic."

Feeling that he had thoroughly chastised them and turning away from them with the sort of distaste he might reserve for torch-bearing villagers and other superstitious idiots, he donned his coat and stomped out into the night.

LaHune, who had been studying it all with his usual detachment, stood up and said, "That's enough now. Dr. Gates has told you all he *can* tell you. Really, people, he has been good enough to share with you some of his findings and you're acting like a bunch of children."

And for once, Hayes was in complete agreement with him. Children? No, more like villagers looking for a witch to burn. Slowly, they settled down, realizing to a man that LaHune had made mental note of their reactions and it would be going into their files. A bad mark on their records would mean any number of them wouldn't be returning to Antarctica. That meant the loss of big money for contractors and the loss of NSF funding for the scientists.

"Well, wasn't that amusing?" Sharkey said.

Hayes grunted.

Amusing? Well, it was certainly something. Ancient civilizations. Pre-human intelligences. Aliens. Then that bit about what they had found up there changing the idea of *who* and *what* the human race was . . . well, how did you walk away from that without your chin dragging on the floor?

"What do you make of that?" Hayes finally asked Sharkey.

"I think I can't wait for spring," was all she would say.

But Cutchen, well, he had an opinion. His specialty was supposedly the weather, but he always seemed to have an opinion on everything. "Tell you two something right now. I heard all about what happened to Lind and, like you, I've drawn a few of my own conclusions. Maybe that thing thawing out in the hut had nothing to do with Lind's breakdown . . . but if it did, just keep in mind we're trapped here until spring and whatever that thing is, we have to live with it all winter."

"It's just a fossil for godsake," Sharkey said.

"Do you think so, Doc? Do you honestly believe that? Great. Then go out to the hut and stare in those red fucking eyes and tell me if something's not staring back at you."

But Sharkey wasn't about to do that.

True to his word, Gates went back up to the tent camp, but left his mummies behind. He had three of them thawing in the shed — which was now locked and bolted, LaHune having the only key — and three more still frozen in their sheaths of ice out back in the cold shed.

People were still talking about it all, but they had calmed somewhat. Even grand revelations became mundane given time. You made some discovery that will alter our view of who and what we are? It might change civilization as we know it? No shit? Ain't that something. You wanna hear something better? Word has it a couple of the techies over at the drilling tower are doing some drilling of a more intimate nature, you catch my drift, sunshine.

Didn't matter what happened at South Pole stations . . . its shelf-life was relatively short.

Besides, truth be told, it was an exciting winter at Kharkhov and there was more on the stove than just Gates' fossils and some dusty old ruins up in the mountains.

There was the lake.

Some three-quarters of a mile beneath the continental ice sheet that the Kharkhov Station sat on, there was a huge subterranean lake roughly the size of Lake Ontario. It had been discovered some five years previously using ice-penetrating radar and radio echo-sounding and promptly named Lake Vordog. This in honor of a Russian seismologist whose early studies in the region led to its discovery.

Vordog was hardly the first lake discovered beneath the ice, there were some seventy others, but Vordog — and a few others — had piqued the curiosity of the world scientific establishment. For here was an underground lake trapped beneath nearly a mile of ice, some 300 miles long and nearly fifty in width, that had been hidden away from the light of day for some forty-million years. No sunlight, no outside atmosphere, no contact with any organisms but those it contained originally. Such isolation, it was thought, may have allowed whatever lived in it to follow an entirely separate path of evolution than that of the outside world.

Imaging had shown that Vordog was over 2,000 feet deep in spots and thermographs proved that instead of being frozen or near-freezing like other sub-glacial lakes, Vordog had a near-constant water temperature of fifty degrees with hot spots up to sixty-five. The only thing that could possibly account for that was some form of subsurface geothermal heat source, possibly hydrothermal vents like those on the ocean floor. In which case, the lake could possibly be teeming with life . . . much of it completely unknown to science and, quite possibly, evolved forms of organisms long extinct elsewhere.

So instead of the usual paleoclimate coring carried out at the drilling tower, this winter there was something truly exciting happening: a group of technicians headed by a CalTech glaciologist named Gundry were drilling down to the lake in order to release robotic probes into those ancient and pristine waters. The entire thing was being funded by NASA, as part of their groundwork for the Europa Ice Clipper mission which would send similar probes to Jupiter's ice-covered moons, Europa and Callisto, which were both thought to contain large subglacial oceans.

Whatever was down there had been undisturbed for forty-million years.

And now that was about to change.

Exactly one day after Gates' big announcement and two days before Gundry's drilling team broke through the ice, the Kharkhov Station was zipped-up tight and locked-down. Communication of any sort, whether radio or satellite or email for that matter, was brought to a screaming halt. They were suddenly alone and more isolated than they had been before. But it wasn't because of a fierce storm or mechanical failure, it was because of LaHune. His directive was quite simple: until further notice, all communication with the outside world was suspended, save emergency beacons.

It didn't go over real big.

When LaHune announced it to the lunch crowd in the community room, it caused a near-riot. For the winter crews at the stations didn't have much else going for them but their satellite Internet and an occasional radio chat with a loved one. These were their only ties with the outside world, the only things that could remind them that, yes, there were other people in the world and they weren't really on the moon or Mars, just down yonder at the bottom of the world.

Later that day, Hayes caught up with Dr. Sharkey at the infirmary. "Did you try to talk sense to that overblown prick?" he asked her.

She nodded. "Oh, I tried, all right. I tried until I was blue in the face, not that it did me any good. This is an NSF facility, he said, as such it's under government jurisdiction same as a military base. We all signed the Official Secrets Act and now he's activating it. Nothing goes out, not until he says so. End of story."

James Bond shit. "Jesus Christ, Doc, I supposed to log in with some of the boys from McMurdo tonight. We've got a poker game going on the web . . . what the hell are they going to think?"

"What's the rest of the world going to think?"

Hayes sat down, sighed.

Sure, there was more than just a poker game in the offing here. There were wives and children, sisters and brothers and parents. When they didn't hear from their people at Kharkhov, they were going to start expecting the very worst.

And Hayes was with them, because he already expected the worse. He'd felt it from the moment he'd stepped off the LC-130 Hercules at Kharkhov Station six weeks ago and, day by day, it had been growing like a tumor in his belly . . . that near-certainty that things were going to get dark and ugly this winter. But he hadn't mentioned that to anyone. They would have thought he was crazy.

Sharkey folded her arms. "I don't use the Internet much and I don't really have anyone I keep in contact with, so I guess I'll survive better than most."

Hayes felt something swell up in his throat. He tried to swallow it down. "What about . . . what about your husband?"

Sharkey looked at him, then looked away. And there it was again, that barely concealed tightening around her mouth and eyes that was akin to bitterness. "We generally don't keep in close contact." She uttered a small laugh. A very small one. "Besides, where he is, out in the jungle, the Internet basically consists of knocking coconuts together."

Hayes did not comment on that.

He was divorced, no children. He had a sister, Liza, in Des Moines who was a Jehovah's Witness. Last winter at the Amundsen-Scott Station they'd started emailing back and forth. But that had come crashing to a halt when he admitted to her that he did not believe in God and never had, asked her point-blank how she'd gotten mixed up in a cult like the Jo-Ho's.

So, like Sharkey, he was pretty much alone.

LaHune had sited security reasons for the blackout. *Security reasons.* That was his explanation and he refused to elaborate on it. And you could count on LaHune to keep his word. No amount of ass-kissing or sweet-talking would thaw him. Better luck trying to get inside a nun's habit than that cast-iron lockbox LaHune called a skull.

"Did he say anything?" Hayes asked her. "I mean, shit, people are already wigged out down here. They don't need this, too. Did you try the medical approach? The psychological benefits and all that shit?"

Sharkey nodded again. "I tried everything short of a lapdance, Jimmy. It's a no-go. He told me that when he receives clearance from the NSF bigwigs, he'll give us our Internet and all the rest back. But not until. The National Science Foundation rules."

"Clearance? Clearance for what?"

She shrugged. "He's very cloak-and-dagger about the whole thing. But I get the feeling it's because of Gates' discovery and the things he was saying. The NSF doesn't want that stuff getting out, not yet. Not until they've had time to think over how they're going to handle all the questions they're going to get barraged with. This is big stuff, Jimmy. You've got to know that."

"I do know it, Doc. But, shit, I'm almost a thousand in the hole with those ringers at McMurdo. I mean, damn."

Sharkey said she thought that part of it might be the flack the NSF was going to take, the intimations that everyone at Kharkhov was cracking up. Cabin fever.

"We *are* cracking up for chrissake," Hayes said. "This whole goddamn winter has a real bad smell to it, Doc. I've had a bad feeling since the planes left and the snow started blowing like hell. A real bad feeling and don't you dare laugh at me."

"I'm not laughing," she said.

He shrugged. "Like I said the other day, those goddamn mummies are like some kind of catalyst here, a big ugly spoon to stir the pot. And now that pot is all stirred-up and the soup is smelling like shit. If that makes any sense."

She smiled, seemed to understand.

"I guess what I'm saying, Doc, is that LaHune cutting us off like this is just plain stupid. What with those weird mummies and Lind's breakdown, the crew down here are thinking funny things, you know? They sit around and do their bit, pretend like none of it's bothering them, but it is. You can see it behind their eyes. They're getting paranoid and scared. They're sensing something and its eating their guts out, only they don't dare admit to it and you can't blame them."

Hayes would never have said any of this to anyone else, but it was true. What you generally had at a station like Kharkhov during the winter was a lot of boredom. There was work to be done, sure, but the pace was nowhere near as frenetic as you saw during the summer. This year the boredom had been replaced by something else . . . a nervous tension, a sense of expectancy, the knowledge that the ball was going to drop. Hayes could feel it. Although the crew wandered around with stupid smiles on their faces and went through the motions, it was all an act. You peeled those smiles off and underneath you were going to see people on the edge, people cringing, people confused and worried and, yes, scared.

The atmosphere at a winter station locked down by the cold and snow and perpetual darkness was never exactly yippy-skippy, let's-have-ourselves-a-parade, but even on bad years when you threw together a group that simply did not get along, it was not like this. There was not this sense of brooding apprehension, that almost spiritual sort of taint hanging in the air.

"What're you thinking, Doc?" Hayes asked, seeing Sharkey's blue eyes focused off into space.

She shrugged. "I'm just wondering if I'm going to have enough happy pills to get these people to spring."

"Pills won't cut it," Hayes told her.

Sharkey smiled, looked into his eyes. "I was just thinking, Jimmy, how easy it would be for the NSF to dump a group of us down here and then throw something odd at us like this, see how we handled it. A sort of feasibility study. A group of people fairly diverse in that they come from the working class right up to the scientific elite. See how we react to certain things."

"You saying they invented those mummies? Those ruins?"

"No, of course not. But it would be an interesting opportunity for the powers that be to take advantage of. Us stranded down here, facing philosophical and psychological challenges brought about by our isolation and the discovery of Gates' mummies."

"Doc, really, don't be feeding my paranoia."

She laughed. "Oh, I'm just speculating here."

"Sure, but it sounds right to me. The bunch of us riding out this fucking winter, our lines of communication severed. Those goddamn mummies out there that are scaring the shit out of everyone . . . whether they're willing to admit it or not."

"Yes, exactly. And with our good Mr. LaHune as the control.

Because, you know, if it wasn't for him I wouldn't be surprised if a mob decided to gather up Gates' mummies and burn them like alien witches."

Sharkey laughed nervously as if to dismiss it all, but Hayes wasn't ready to dismiss it. He wasn't much on conspiracies and the like, but those mummies *were* having a very negative effect on the crew. They were getting under peoples' skins, making them imagine the worst possible things and runaway imaginations were a bad thing when you were trapped down at the bottom of the world. A mass-paranoia becoming a mass-insanity could become savage and devastating at the drop of a hat.

"If LaHune has any brains," Hayes said, "then he'll open this place back up, let these people chat with the outside world. It can't be good for them to be internalizing this shit, chewing on it and swallowing it whole, letting it boil in their bellies."

"It's not," Sharkey said. "Ever since those mummies came I've had people coming to see me wanting sedatives. They can't sleep, Jimmy, and when they do they have nightmares."

Oh, I'll just bet they do. Some real doozies no doubt.

LaHune knew what all this was doing, but he was a company man and he'd toe the line regardless of what it did to these people. Even if the crew started cracking up and going at each other — and themselves — with razors, it wouldn't move him. He'd sit there like some shit-eating weasel atop a heap of turds, simply enjoying the stink, the rot, and the flies.

Because that's the kind of guy he was.

"I tell you what, Doc, LaHune better get his hands out of his fucking shorts already and derail this train because I got me a nasty feeling the track ahead is real dark and real bumpy."

PART TWO

THE MIND-LEECHES

"A voice from other epochs belongs in a graveyard of other epochs."

— H.P. Lovecraft

10

But the train wasn't derailed.

And that night, about two in the morning, there was a fierce pounding at Hayes' door and from the intensity of it, you could be sure it wasn't a social call. Hayes came awake, shaking off some dream about mountains of black ice, and took a pull from his water bottle.

"*Hayes!*" a voice called. "Hayes! Would you fucking wake up already!"

It was Cutchen.

Hayes climbed out of bed, hearing the wind moaning through the darkness of the camp, cold and eternal. It sounded like something hungry that wanted in, something looking for warmth to steal.

"Coming," Hayes said.

He fumbled the lock open — never used to lock his door, but lately he'd gotten in the habit — and pulled the door in. Cutchen was standing out there in the corridor, a small gray-haired man with a matching beard and dark, probing eyes that always seemed to know something you didn't.

"It's Lind," Cutchen said. "Sharkey said to bring you. Lind has really gone over the edge now. C'mon, we better go."

Shit, shit, and *shit.*

Hayes climbed into his Kansas State joggers and sweatshirt, brushed his bushy hair back with the flat of his hand and then he was following Cutchen down the gray corridors to the other side of the building where the infirmary was.

Outside the door, in the hallway, St. Ours, Meiner, Rutkowski and a few of the other Glory Boys were gathered, whispering like little old ladies at a funeral, espousing dirty secrets.

"See, Jimmy?" Rutkowski said to Hayes. "I told you he'd do something like this. Crazy bastard."

"What happened?" Hayes said, his head blown with fuzz from sleep.

"He slit his fucking wrists," St. Ours said. "Got a knife in there and plans on using it."

"He won't let Doc get to him," Cutchen explained. "He's lost a lot of blood and if she can't get to work on him right away, he's going to be toast. She thought you could talk to him."

Hayes sucked in a breath and went in there slowly, heavily, like he was dragging a ball and chain behind him. Before he saw the blood, he could smell it: sharp and metallic. It got right down into his guts. He scoped out the situation pretty quickly because the infirmary just wasn't that big. Lind was sitting in the corner between two cabinets of drugs and instruments, kind of wedged in there like maybe he was stuck. His back was up against the wall and his knees were drawn up to his chin. There was a lot of blood . . . it was scarfed over his shirt and there was a smeared trail of it running across the tiles to his present position. His left arm looked like he'd stuck it in a barrel of red ink.

And, yeah, he had a knife in his hand. A scalpel.

Sharkey was standing next to an examination table, her usually capable and confident face looking pinched and rubbery like she'd been out in the cold. Her blue eyes were wide and helpless.

"Lind," she said in a very soft voice. "Hayes is here. I want you to talk to him."

Lind jerked like maybe he'd been asleep. He held the bloody scalpel out in warning towards Sharkey, droplets of blood dripping from his wrist. "I'm not talking to anyone . . . you're all infected and I goddamn well know it. I know what's going on here . . . I know what those *things* want, I know how they got to you."

Hayes clenched his teeth, unclenched them, willed himself to go loose, to relax. It was not easy. Jesus, Lind looked like shit. And it wasn't just the blood either. He looked like maybe he'd dropped twenty pounds, his once round face seemed to be sagging under his scraggly beard. Just hanging like the jowls of a hound, slack and sallow. His eyes were bulging from their sockets, discolored and shot through with tiny red veins. They gleamed like wet chrome.

Hayes squatted about four feet away from him. "Lind? Look at me. It's me, it's Jimmy. Your old bunkmate . . . just look at me, tell me about it. Tell me how they get to you."

Lind jerked again, seemed to be doing so anytime somebody mentioned his name like he was hooked up to a battery. "Jimmy . . . oh, shit, Jimmy . . . they . . . them out in that fucking hut, you know what they do? You know what they want? They come in your dreams, Jimmy. Those mummies . . . the *Old Ones* . . . hee, hee . . . they come in your dreams, Jimmy, and they start sucking your mind dry because that's all they want: our minds."

"Lind, listen to me," Hayes said. "Those ugly pricks have been dead millions of years – "

"They're not dead, Jimmy! Maybe they can't move their bodies no more, but their *minds,* Jimmy, their minds *are not fucking dead!* You know they're not . . . they've been waiting down here in the ice for us, waiting for us all these millions of years to come and set them free! They knew we would because that's how they planned it!" Lind was breathing real hard, gasping for breath or maybe gasping for something he just couldn't find. "Jimmy . . . oh Jesus, Jimmy, I know you think I'm fucking crazy, you *all* think I'm fucking crazy, but you better listen to me before it's too late."

Hayes held his hands out. "Lind, you're going to bleed to death. Let the Doc patch you up and then we'll talk."

"No." Flat, immovable. "We talk now."

"Okay, okay."

Lind was trying to catch his breath. "They been frozen in the ice, Jimmy, but their minds never died. They just waited . . . waited for us to come. Those minds . . . oh, Jimmy, those awful fucking minds are so cold and evil and patient . . . they've been dreaming about us, waiting until we came for them. And when we did . . . when that limpdick Gates went down in that cave . . . those minds started *waking up,* reaching out to our own . . . that's why everyone's having nightmares . . . the *Old Ones* . . . those minds of theirs are invading ours, getting into our heads one inch at a time and by spring, by spring there won't be any men left down here, but things that *look* like men with poisoned alien minds . . . "

Lind started laughing then, but it was not good laughter. This was stark and black and cutting, a screech of despair and madness echoing from his skull.

"Have . . . have they come in your dreams, too, Lind?" Hayes asked him, feeling Sharkey's eyes burning into him, knowing she did not like him encouraging this delusion. But, fuck it, that's how it had to be handled and he knew it.

"Dreams," Lind sobbed, "oh, all the dreams. Out in the hut, you remember out in the hut, Jimmy? It touched my mind then and it hasn't let go since. Tonight . . . "

"Yes?"

There were tears rolling down Lind's face now. "Tonight I woke up . . . I woke up, Jimmy, and I could feel the cold, oh, the terrible blowing cold . . . and it was there, one of them things . . . *it was standing there at the end of my cot, thinking about me . . . all those terrible red eyes looking at me and ice dropping off it in clots . . .* "

Hayes felt gooseflesh run down his arms and up his spine, thinking that he would have went for the knife, too. But it was just a dream, had to be just a dream.

Lind looked like he wanted to say something else, but his eyes slid shut and he slumped over. Hayes moved quick and pulled the scalpel from his fingers, all that blood, but there was no fight left in Lind. With Sharkey's help they got him on the table and she started swabbing out his slit wrist.

"It's deep, but he pretty much missed the artery," she said, cleaning the blood from his wrist and injecting some antibiotics right into it.

Hayes watched as she stitched him close, saying she was going to have to get an IV going, get some whole blood and plasma into him.

"Then you better dope him up, Doc," Hayes said, "and strap his ass down. Because he might have failed this time, but he's going to try again and we both know it."

Then Hayes went out into the corridor, out to the wolves skulking around there, waiting for him to toss them scraps of bloody meat.

"He dead?" St. Ours said.

"No, he'll be all right."

"He say . . . he say why he did it? Why he slit his wrists?" Meiner wanted, *had* to know.

They were all looking at Hayes now. Even Cutchen was. They were all thinking things, maybe things they'd imagined and maybe things they'd dreamed. You could see it on their faces . . . unspoken fears, stuff they didn't even dare admit to themselves.

"Tell us," Rutkowski said. "Tell us what made him do it."

Hayes grinned like a skull. He was sick of this place, sick of these people and their ghoulish curiosity. "Oh, come on, boys, you know damn well what made him do it . . . the nightmares. The things in his head . . . same things that are going to make you all do it, sooner or later."

11

ayes could remember having to do things that scared him. Could remember how he felt before and how he felt afterwards. He remembered having to call his mother up when he was sixteen from the police station, tell her he'd been busted for selling pot, she had to come and get him. He remembered getting in a car accident when he was nineteen, walking away without a scratch while his best friend, Toby Young, who'd been driving, died in the emergency room. When Toby's parents got there, asking how Toby was, he'd had to tell them, see that look in their eyes — disbelief, shock, then something like anger because he was alive and their son was dead. And, yes, he remembered when his old man was laying in that hospital bed eaten up with the cancer and his sister was out of her head with religious hysteria. He remembered having to tell the doctor to shut the old man off.

All these things had scared him, had stripped away his innocence and made something rot inside him. These were things you had to do, things which you could not walk away from unchanged, but you did them because it was expected of you. It was the right thing and it had to be done.

But none of them, none of those things, as terrible and necessary as they'd been, had gotten inside him like when he'd gone to Hut #6 to look at those mummies, to prove to himself that they were dead and nothing but dead. The temperature had dipped to a bitter seventy below and the wind was shrieking at sixty miles an hour, flinging snow and pulverized ice crystals across the compound. Antarctica at dead-winter: black and unforgiving, that wind wailing around you like wraiths.

Hayes went alone.

He did not ask for the key from LaHune. He took a set of boltcutters, bundled into his ECW — Extreme Cold Weather — gear and started off across the compound, following the guylines through that blasting, sub-zero tempest, knowing that if he let go of the guiding rope and got off the walkway, he'd probably never find his way back. That they'd find him curled up out there come spring, a white and stiffened thing frozen up like meat in a deepfreeze.

The snow was piling up into drifts and he pounded through it with his white bunny boots, gripping the guyline with a wool-mittened hand that was already going numb.

You're crazy to be doing this, he told himself and, hallelujah, wasn't that the goddamned truth? For, Christ, it wasn't as if he *really* believed what Lind had said. But there was something there . . . a grain of sanity, an underlying nugget of truth . . . in what the man had been raving about. Something behind his eyes that was incapable of lying. And Hayes was going to see what that was.

The snow crunched beneath his boots and the wind tried to strip him right out of his Gore-Tex parka. His goggles kept fogging over, but he kept going until he made Hut #6. Outside the door, he just stood there, swaying in the wind like some heavily-swaddled child just learning the fine art of balance.

Just fucking do it.

And he knew he had to, for something both ancient and inexplicable had woken deep in the very pit of his being and it was screaming *danger!* in his head. There was danger here and that half-forgotten sixth sense in him was painfully aware of the fact. And if Hayes didn't get on with it already, that voice was going to make him turn and run.

LaHune or Gates or both had locked the hut with a chain and a Masterlock and the bolt cutter took care of that pretty damn quick. And, holy oh God, it was time for the show.

The wind almost pulled the door out of his hand and his arm out of socket to boot. After a time, he got it closed and went inside, feeling the heat of the hut melting the ice out of his beard. It was only about fifty degrees in there, but that was positively tropical for East Antarctica in the cruel depths of winter.

In that stark and haunted moment before he turned on the lights, he could've almost sworn there was movement in the hut . . . stealthy, secretive.

Then the light was on and he was alone with the dead.

He saw the mummies right away, trying to shake the feeling that they were seeing him, too.

Crazy thinking.

They were stretched out on the tables like shanks of thawing beef.

The shack shook in the wind and Hayes shook with it.

Two of the specimens were gradually defrosting, water dripping from them into collection buckets. For the most part, they were still ice-sheathed and obscured, unless you wanted to get in real close and peer through that clear blue, acrylic-looking ice and see them up close and personal. But that wasn't necessary anyway, for the other mummy was completely unthawed.

Unthawed to the point where it was really starting to smell. Gates had thrown a canvas tarp over it and Hayes knew he had to pull that tarp back, had to pull it back and look at the thing in all its hideous splendor. And the very act took all the guts he had or would ever have. For this was one of those godawful defining moments in life that scared the shit right out of you and made you want to fold-up and hide your head.

And that's exactly how Hayes was feeling . . . terrified, alone, completely vulnerable, his internals filled with a spreading helix of white ice.

He took off his mittens, let his fingers warm, but they refused. He took hold of the tarp, something clenching inside him, and yanked it free . . . and it slid off almost of its own volition. He backed up, uttering a slight gasp.

The mummy was unthawed.

It was still ugly as ugly got and maybe even a little bit worse, because now it had a hacked and slit appearance from Gates and his boys taking their samples and cutting into it with knives and saws.

And the smell . . . terrible, not just rotting fish now, but low tides and decaying seaweed, black mud and something like rotten cabbage. A weird, gassy odor.

Fucking thing is going bad, Hayes was thinking, *like spoiled pork . . . why would Gates want that? Why would he let the find of the ages just rot?*

But there were no answers for that. Maybe the thing turned faster than he anticipated.

Regardless, that wasn't why Hayes had come.

He got in close as he dared to the monstrosity, certain that it was going to move despite that smell. It looked much the same as it had the other day, despite the various incisions: like some bloated, fleshy eggplant. Its shell was a leaden, shiny gray, looked tough like the hide of a crab. Chitinous. Its wings — if that's what they were and not modified fins — were folded-up against its sides like umbrellas, some sticky fluid like tree sap had oozed from them in puddles and runnels, collected on the table. Those branching tentacles at the center of its body now looked like nothing but tree roots, tangled up and vestigal. And those thick, muscular tentacles at its base had blackened, hung limp like dead snakes.

Yes, it was dead, it was surely dead.

Yet . . .

Yet the tapering arms of that bizarre starfish-shaped head were erect like an unclenched, reaching hand. Those globular eyes at each tip wide and blazing a neon red, filled with an impossible, unearthly vitality. They were shiny with tiny black pupils, the gray lids shriveled back, something like pink tears running down the stalks.

Hayes had to remember to breathe.

He could see where one eye had been cut away, the black chasm left in its place. He was trying desperately to be rational, to be lucid and realistic, but it was not easy because once you looked at those eyes it was very difficult to look away. They were not human eyes and there was nothing you might even abstractly call a face, *still* . . . Hayes was looking at those eyes and thinking they were filled with an absolute, almost stupid hatred, a loathing that made him feel weak inside.

Turn away, don't look at it.

But he was looking and inside it felt like he'd popped a hole, everything draining out of him. He had to turn away. Like a vampire, you couldn't stare into its eyes or you were done. But he kept looking, feeling and emoting and sensing and it was there, all right, something in the back of his head. He couldn't put a name to it at first . . . just that it was something invasive, something alien that did not belong in his mind. But it had taken root and was spreading out like fingers, a high and sibilant buzzing, a droning whine like that of a cicada. Growing louder and louder until he was having trouble thinking, remembering anything, remembering who and what he was. There was just that buzzing filling his head and it was coming from the thing, it was being directed into him and he knew it.

Hayes wasn't even aware of how he was shaking or the piss that ran down his leg or the tears that filled his eyes and splashed down his face in warm creeks. There was only the buzzing, stealing him away and . . . and showing him *things.*

Yes, the Old Ones.

Not three like there were in the hut or even ten or twenty, but hundreds, *thousands* of them. A buzzing, trilling swarm of them filling the sky and descending like locusts come to strip a field. They were darting in and out of low places and hollows and over sharp-peaked roofs, rising up into that luminous sky . . . only, *yes,* it was not in the sky, but underwater. Thousands of them, a hive of the Old Ones, swimming through and above some geometrically impossible sunken city in a crystalline green sea with those immense membranous wings spread out so they could glide. He saw their bodies bloat up obscenely as they sucked in water and deflate as they expelled it like squids . . . moving so quickly, so efficiently. There had to be a million of them now, more showing themselves all the time, swimming and leaping and rising and falling –

Hayes went on his ass.

Teetered and fell and it was probably the only thing that indeed saved him, kept his mind from going to sludge. He hit the floor, fell back and cracked his head against a table and that buzzing was gone. Not completely, there was still a suggestion of it there, but its grip had been broken.

And he came to himself and realized that it had taken hold of him, that thing, and nobody would ever make him believe different. He could hear Lind's voice in his head saying, *Can't you feel it getting inside your head, wanting to steal your mind . . . wanting to make you something but what you are?*

Hayes scrambled to his feet, smelling the thing and hating it and knowing it somehow from some past time and the revulsion he felt was learned and instinctual, something carried by the race from a very distant and ancient time. What he did next was what any savage would have done when a monster, a beast was threatening the tribe, invading it, trying to subvert and steal away all that it was: he looked for a weapon.

Panting and half-out of his mind, he stumbled through Gates' makeshift laboratory, past the two thawing horrors and amongst tables of instruments and chemicals. He wanted fire. His simplified brain told him the thing had to be burned, so he sought fire, but there was nothing. Acid, maybe. But he was no chemist, he wouldn't know acid if he saw it.

And in those precious seconds that he stumbled drunkenly through the hut, he could feel that buzzing in his head rising up again and he looked over his shoulder at the Old One, certain now it would be rising up, those bulging red eyes seeking him out with a flat hatred and those branching tentacles reaching out for him –

But no.

It lay there, dreaming meat.

But its mind was alive and he knew that now, could feel it worrying at his will, and that was insane because there was an incision just beneath that starfish-shaped head and he knew without a doubt that Gates had removed its brain. That even now it was sunk in one of those jars around him, a fleshy and alien thing like a pickled monstrosity in a sideshow.

Yet, its mind was alive and vibrant. The idea of that made hysterical laughter bubble up the back of Hayes' throat and then he saw the axe hanging by the fire extinguisher and then his hands were on it, gripping it with a primitive glee. He raced back at the thing, knocking a table of fossils over in his flight. He was going to chop that motherfucker up, hack it to bits.

And he meant to.

He stood over the thing, axe raised and then the buzzing rose up, felt like a fist taking hold of his brain and squeezing until the agony was white-hot and he cried out.

The axe fell from his fingers and he went down to his knees.

Fight or flight.

He crab-crawled to the door, fumbling it open and falling out into the screaming polar night. He got the door shut, those frozen winds slapping him none too gently back into reality. He found his mittens, put them on and pulled himself along the guylines back to Targa House, the door of Hut #6 wide open, hammering back and forth in the wind.

He looked over his shoulder only once, thinking he saw some lurid alien shape moving through the blowing snow at him . . .

12

The next morning, before they started their day, the boys were hanging out in the community room, chewing scrambled eggs and bacon, sipping coffee and smoking cigarettes, doing a lot of talking.

"I'll tell you guys something," Rutkowski said. "LaHune is some kind of fucking nut about all this. No communication, no email . . . I mean, what the hell? What's all this James Bond shit about? Because of those dead things that might be aliens? Jesus H. Christ, so what? What if they are? He can't lock us down here like prisoners. It ain't right and somebody's gotta do something about it."

St. Ours lit another cigarette from the butt of his first, flagrantly ignoring the NO SMOKING sign on the wall and getting hard looks from some of the scientists who were trying to eat. "Yeah, something's gotta be done. And it's up to us to do it. You know those fucking egg-heads won't lift a finger. You lock them in a closet with a microscope and they'd be just fine and dandy with it. Now, way I'm seeing this, LaHune has slipped a cog and he's about six inches from being as crazy as Lind. He's supposed to be in charge? Well, if we were at sea and the captain was crazy . . . "

"Mutiny?" Rutkowski said. "Get the hell out of here."

"You got a better idea?"

If Rutkowski did, he wasn't admitting it.

Meiner sat there watching them, thinking things. He knew these two. He'd wintered over with them half a dozen times. Rutkowski was full of hot air, liked to talk, but was essentially harmless. St. Ours, however, was a hardcase. He liked to talk, too, but he was a big boy and he wasn't above using his hands on someone that pissed him off or got in his way. When he drank, he liked to fight and right now there was whiskey on his breath.

"We can't just go doing shit like that," Meiner said, though part of him liked the idea. "Come spring they'll throw us in the clink."

"Hell we can't," St. Ours said. "Let me do it. I'd like to take that little cockmite LaHune outside and pound the snot out of him."

Meiner didn't even bother commenting on that. The visual of a couple guys out in that sub-zero blackness in their ECW's swinging was hilarious.

"Just simmer down now," Rutkowski said. "LaHune is a pushbutton boy, all company. Push button A, he shits. Push button B, he locks us down. He's just doing what hard-ons like him always do. The mummies is why. He's towing the NSF line and it's because of those fucking mummies."

"That's Gates' fault," St. Ours said.

"Sure, it is. But you can't blame him, finding something like that. Like a kid first discovering his pecker, he can't help but take it out and pull on it. Besides, Gates is not a bad sort. You can talk to the guy. Shit, you can even talk pussy with him. He's all right. Not like some of these other monkeyfucks — " Rutkowski shot a glance over at a few scientists at a nearby table, some of the wonder boys who were drilling down to Lake Vordog " — he's okay. See, boys, the problem here is those mummies. If they were gone, LaHune might be willing to pull an inch or two of that steel rod out of his ass and let us join the freaking world again."

"You plan on stealing 'em?" St. Ours said.

"Well, maybe *losing* them might be a better word for it. Regardless, it's something for us to think about."

"It couldn't happen soon enough for me," Meiner said, his hand shaking as he brought his coffee cup to his lips.

"You . . . you still having those nightmares?"

Meiner nodded weakly. "Every night . . . crazy shit. Even when I do manage to fall asleep, I wake up with the cold sweats."

"Those things out there," St. Ours said, looking a little green around the gills, maybe even blue. "I'm not too big of a man to admit that they're getting to me, too. No, don't you fucking look at me like that, Rutkowski. You're having the dreams, too. We're all having the dreams. Even those eggheads are."

"What . . . what are your dreams about?" Meiner wanted to know.

Rutkowski shifted in his seat, licked his lips. "I can't remember, but their good ones . . . something about colors or shapes, things moving that shouldn't move."

"I remember some of mine," St. Ours said. He pulled off his cigarette, let the smoke drift out through his nostrils and past those wide, blank eyes. "A city . . . I dream of a city . . . except it ain't like no city you've ever seen before. Towers and pyramids and shafts, honeycombs that lead through stone, don't come out anywhere but into themselves. I dream I'm flying above the city, moving fast, and there are others flying with me and they all look like those ugly pricks out in the hut. We . . . we fly and then we dip down, down into those holes and hollow places, then . . . then I wake up. I don't want to remember what happens down in those holes."

"I dream about holes sometimes, too," Meiner admitted. "Like tunnels going up and down and left and right . . . lost in those tunnels and hearing a buzzing like wasps, only that buzzing is like words I understand. I'm scared shitless, in the dream. I know those voices want something from me."

He stopped there. By God, it was enough. He wasn't going any farther with it, he wasn't going to pick at the scabs of his nightmares until all that black blood started flowing again. He wasn't going to tell them about the rest of it. The tunnels and high stone rooms, all those things standing around while Meiner and dozens of others laid on tables. The things . . . oh Jesus . . . those things would be inside their heads and touching them, sticking things into them and cutting into them with blades of light, making things happen to them . . . and the pain, all the pain . . . needles going into him and knives cutting and tubes stuck in his head and oh dear sweet Jesus the agony, the agony while those trilling voices kept talking and talking, hands that were not hands but things like tree branches or twigs taking him apart and putting him back together again . . .

Rutkowski looked gray and old suddenly. "I don't like it, I just don't like it. Those dreams . . . they're so *familiar*, you know? Like I've seen it all before, lived through all that shit years ago. Don't make no sense."

And it didn't. Not on the surface. But they'd all felt it, that sense of familiarity, that déjà vu they couldn't get out from under. It haunted them. Just like the first time they'd seen the mummies — they had all known implicitly that they had seen them before, very long ago, and the fear those things inspired was inbred and ancient, a wisp of memory from a misty, forgotten past.

"Yeah, I remember those things. Somehow, I do," St. Ours said. "Fuck me, but Gates sure opened up a Pandora's box here."

And, God, how true was that.

Meiner knew it was true, just like he knew he was afraid to close his eyes even for an instant. Because when he did the dreams came and the things swam up out of the darkness, those buzzing voices in his head, filling him, breaking him down. And sometimes, yes, sometimes even when he was awake, when he'd come out of the nightmares at three a.m. sweating and shaking, feeling the pain of what they had done to him or someone like him, he would still be hearing those voices. High and trilling and insectile, outside, carried by the winds, calling him out into the storm and sometimes out to the hut where they were waiting for him.

But he wasn't about to admit any of that.

13

O f course, Hayes didn't sleep.

He didn't do much of anything after his return from Hut #6 except drink a lot of coffee laced with whiskey and take a few hot showers, trying to shake that awful feeling of violation, the sense that his mind had been invaded and subverted by something diabolic and dirty. But it was all in vain, for that feeling of invasion persisted. That his most private and intimate place, his mind, had been defiled. He nodded off for maybe thirty minutes just before dawn — what passed for dawn in a place where the sun never rose, that was — and came awake from the mother of all nightmares in which shapeless things had their fingers in his skull, rooting around and touching things, making him think and feel things that were not part of him but part of something else. Something alien.

No, none of it made any real sense.

But what had happened in Hut #6 didn't make any either. It had happened, he was certain it had happened. But what proof was there? Minute by minute it was fading in his head like a bad dream, becoming indistinct and surreal . . . like something viewed through yellowed cellophane.

Hayes knew he had to put it into some kind of perspective, though, had to beat it into submission and stomp it flat. Because if he couldn't do that, if he couldn't bronze his balls and inflate his chest . . . well then, he would start raving like Lind, his mind going to a warm fruiting pulp.

Hut #6, Hut #6, Hut #6.

Jesus, he was starting to think of it as some taboo place, a shunned place like a haunted house filled with evil sprits that oozed from the shattered walls or the cobwebby tomb of some executed witch that had eaten children and called up the dead, was looking for a good reason to rise herself. But that's how he saw it: a bad place. Not a place that was necessarily physically dangerous, but psychologically toxic and spiritually rotten.

Twice since returning from Hut #6, he had marched over to the infirmary, stood outside Doc Sharkey's room, wanting to pound on the door, scratch his way through it, throw himself at her feet and scream out the horrors he had suffered. But each time he got there, the strength, the volition to do anything more than listen to his own feeble, crushed voice shrieking in his head was gone.

He wasn't entirely sure how he felt about Sharkey . . . a married woman, Christ in Heaven . . . but he knew, deep down he knew, that he could have gone to her, any time of day or night and she would have helped him, she would have been there for him. Because the bond between them was there, it was real, it was strong, it was strung tight and sure like cable. Yet, for all that, he just couldn't do it. Couldn't see him dumping this rotting, smelly mess at her feet.

She would want you to.

But Hayes still couldn't do it, just couldn't open up his flank like that. Not yet. That feeling of violation — go ahead and say the word, bucko, *rape*, because that's how it made you feel, like you'd been viciously *raped* — was too real yet and he couldn't put it into perspective. He would need time.

His second trip to the infirmary, he just stood outside Sharkey's door with a breathless, silent sobbing knotted in his throat. Before the sobbing became the real thing, he went into the infirmary itself and beyond to the room where there were a few cots set up for sick people.

Lind was on one of them.

He had been restrained now, pumped full of God-knows-what to keep him calm and quiet, Thorazine or something like that. Hayes stood in the doorway looking at the form of his old roommate lying there, looking wasted and old and fragile like if he fell off the cot he might break into pieces. Hayes could see him fine in the nightlight like some little old man shot through with cancer, his life wheezing out of him in rattling breaths.

It was a hell of a thing, wasn't it? To see him like that?

Hayes felt a lump of something insoluble in his throat that he couldn't seem to swallow down. Fucking Lind. Dumb sonofabitch, but harmless and funny and even sweet in his own way.

Lind, Jesus, poor Lind.

Lind whose vocabulary was severely challenged and thought gonorrhea was one of those boats they used in the canals of Venice and bullocks were a woman's breasts. Claimed he had a maiden aunt named Chlamydia and that his sister married a guy named Harry Greenslit. He used to make Hayes laugh all the time, talking about his shrewish wife and how she rode his ass so hard when he was home he couldn't wait to get back to fucking Antarctica to cool it off. He equated his wife's tirades and foul mouth with being sodomized, as in, Jesus, Hayes, she banged me for three days straight, soon as I walk in the door, she bends me over and pounds the stuffing out of me. My asshole's so fucking loose by the time I get back here, I gotta shove a lemon up there to get it to pucker back up.

Lind. Christ.

Hayes walked into the room, over near Lind's cot and right away Lind started to thrash in his sleep. He began to twitch, his eyelids fluttering. Hayes stepped back in the doorway, a weird thrumming sensation at his temples, and Lind settled back down. What the hell was that about? Hayes walked back over there and the thrumming started again with drumming waves and Lind started jerking again like he could sense Hayes' presence and maybe he could and maybe it was even more than just that.

A voice in Hayes' head was saying: *It isn't your mere presence he's reacting to, you silly bastard, it's what you're carrying. That thing in the hut, that pissing Old One, it touched you, it got inside you, it stained something in you that'll never wash completely clean. That's what Lind's reacting to . . . he can smell it on you same as he can smell it on himself. Violation.*

You bear Their touch.

It was crazy, but it made sense. Like they had planted some seed in his head just as they had done with Lind, woke something up inside them that had been sleeping a long time. Something mystic, something ancient, something unspeakable.

But what? What was it?

For as Hayes neared Lind again, he started twitching and moaning, trembling as if he had come into contact with some sort of energy. Hayes backed away again, all the spit in his mouth dried up, a tension headache starting behind his eyes . . . except it wasn't that, it was something else completely. For he could –

He was seeing inside of Lind's head.

It was crazyass bullshit, but, yes, he was *seeing* what Lind dreamed. It could be nothing else. He was connecting with him, their minds touching, sharing thoughts and brainwaves. The thrumming had gone away now and there was just those grainy, distorted pictures like a broadcast coming in on an old black and white Sylvannia tube set. Hayes felt dizzy, disoriented, those images rushing through his brain and making him want to pass cold out. But he saw, he saw . . .

He saw . . . a landscape . . . valleys and low snow-covered hills, hollows in which great beasts wandered listlessly, gnawing at squat vegetation. The beasts were shaggy things like bison or maybe rhinoceros, but with huge archaic horns. It was tundra mostly, the snowline creeping in from all sides, the world turning to winter. There was an immense lake in the distance or maybe it was part of the sea. It was flanked by mounds about which was built some rolling, immense city that looked to be quarried from stone. The image was wavering, fading, but Hayes could still see those towers and weird skeletal spires, arched domes and scalloped discs . . . an impossible city heaped and clustered and crowded, tangled up in itself like the bones of some gigantic beast . . .

Then it was gone.

Hayes backed away into the infirmary, wide-eyed and shocked. He had not imagined any of it, he had not hallucinated any of it. He sat at Sharkey's desk, trying to catch his breath, wiping the sweat from his face. He was thinking things then, thinking terrible, impossible things that he believed nonetheless. That landscape . . . it was Antarctica as seen maybe in the late Miocene before the glaciers had covered it. When that immense, alien city found first by Pabodie and then later by Gates was not up in the mountains but set atop low mounds that would someday *be* mountains.

Gates had said the ice sheet was roughly forty-million years old.

Hayes went through all the normal channels trying to make sense of it, but there was no getting around what he had seen or *how* he had seen it. Lind was maybe like some sort of receiver picking up broadcasts from the dead and dreaming brains of the Old Ones, images of life in Antarctica forty-million years gone. And Hayes had been able to see what he was seeing.

Telepathy.

Parlor tricks. Psychic bullshit.

But he had it now, at least some rudimentary form.

The Old Ones had touched his mind and given him this. No, no, he couldn't believe that. Maybe it had been in him all along and they just, well, woke it up, brought it to the fore from wherever it had been dreaming away the millennia. Hayes was thinking that maybe all men had it inside them, they'd just forgotten how to use it and now and then somebody would be born with the faculty fully activated and be labeled as a freak . . . or quietly go mad.

It was too much.

LaHune had to hear this shit.

14

LaHune was looking pretty much like he'd bitten into something sour as Hayes told him what had happened out in Hut #6. You could see that he did not want to be hearing shit like this. Whether he believed in any of it or not was immaterial, the idea of those dead minds still being somehow active and animate was really beyond the scope of things as he saw them. What could you do with information like that? You surely couldn't crunch it on your laptop or scribble it on your clipboard or slip it in a folder and file it away. This was buggy stuff, now wasn't it? This kind of thing surely upset the old applecart, threw a wrench into the machine, and put the monkeyshit in the mayo.

But Hayes was going to be heard and that was that. Maybe it was the intensity of his voice or the wild look in his eyes, but LaHune listened, all right. Listened while Hayes went on and on, all of it coming out of him in a tidal flow, running from him like waste.

Hayes hadn't come straight to LaHune from the infirmary. No, he went back to his room, had a few cigarettes and a few more cups of joe, thought it out, took himself down a notch. Leveled a bit. Organized his thoughts, pressed and folded them into orderly rows. And then, maybe a few hours later, went to see LaHune and promptly started raving like a madman.

"You think I'm nuts, don't you?" Hayes said when he'd finished, not needing telepathy to reach that shining conclusion. "You think this is just a bad dream or something?"

LaHune licked his lips. "To be honest with you, I don't know what to make of it. I've been out to the hut several times and have suffered no ill effects from close proximity to the . . . the remains."

Hayes almost started laughing.

He knew it had been a mistake coming here. But he'd thought it was worth a try. LaHune was the NSF administrator, right? As such, he had to be notified of any impending threat to the installation, right? Isn't that what it said in the bylaws? Yes, it certainly did. Sure as dogshit drew bluebottle flies.

"I don't care whether you've suffered any effects or not, LaHune. Maybe you need the right sort of mind and maybe they're not interested in you. Maybe they just go for dumbasses like Lind and me and maybe Peter Pan is hung like a horse, but I don't think so and it don't matter, now does it? Those things are dangerous is what I'm saying to you. Can you at least get on the same page with me on that? You know the way they've been getting to people around here."

"Paranoia, isolation . . . it'll do funny things to people."

"It's more than that and you know it. I've spent a lot of years down here, LaHune, and never, ever once have I felt something like this. These people are threatened, their scared . . . they just aren't sure of what."

"And you are?"

Jesus, what a guy LaHune was. Just about everyone at the station was having crazy nightmares and Doc Sharkey admitted she was handing out sleeping pills like candy at Halloween. Dreams weren't infectious, they didn't spread. Yet everyone was having some real doozies since those ugly bastards had been brought in. Maybe it was wild, fringe thinking, the sort of crazy horseshit you found out on the Internet, but it was true and Hayes — and quite a few others by that point — felt it right down to his toes.

Not that you could ever convince LaHune of it.

He was an automaton, a brainwashed, officious little conservative company man. Hayes talked and LaHune clipped his nails, arranged the pens in his desk by color, sorted paperclips by size. He sat there in his L.L. Bean's, perfectly erect in his seat, never slouching, his teeth even and white, his face freshly shaven, his hair perfectly coiffed. Looking either like a mannequin or the latest Republican wonderboy . . . clean and shiny on the outside and empty as a drum on the inside, just waiting for his puppetmasters to pull his strings.

"I'm telling you they're a danger to the well-being of our group here, LaHune. I'm not shack-happy and I'm not drunk and I haven't smoked a joint in fifteen years. You know me, you know how I am. I come from sturdy stock, LaHune, my people and me in general don't see lights in the sky or read tabloids. What I'm telling you is the truth."

LaHune was buffing his nails with an emery board. "So what, Hayes? You want me to destroy the single most important find in the history of the race?"

Hayes sighed. "Yeah, and if you can't do that, then how about we drag the lot of those things about ten miles out and cut 'em a nice little berth in the ice, let Gates worry about 'em come spring."

"No," LaHune said. "That is utterly ridiculous and I refuse to entertain it."

Hayes was beaten and he knew it. Maybe the campaign had been over before it even began. "What's your thing, LaHune? I mean, c'mon, I know you don't like being here and you don't like us as a group. So why the hell are you here? I don't see you as a team player . . . at least on any team I'd be rooting for. So what's your thing? Are you NSF or are you something else?"

A slight blush of color touched LaHune's cheeks, retreated like a flower deciding it was just too damn frosty to bloom. "I don't know what you mean."

"I think you do," Hayes said. "I think you know exactly what I mean. Why are you here? You don't belong in a place like this and we both know it. You're not the type. I heard you spent a summer at McMurdo, but other than that, nothing. You know, ever since I got here, I've had a bad feeling and when I'm around you it gets worse. What's this all about?"

LaHune closed his day calendar. "It's about what you think it's about or, should I say, what you *should* be thinking it's about. Kharkhov Station is a scientific installation running a variety of projects through the winter under the auspices of the National Science Foundation."

But Hayes didn't believe it.

He tried to reach into LaHune's mind, but there was nothing. Maybe the reawakened telepathy had been temporary and maybe there was just nothing inside LaHune *to* read. He only knew one thing and he knew it deep down in his guts: LaHune had a secret agenda here. He'd suspected it for awhile, but now he was sure of it.

And with that in mind, it was time to go fishing.

"C'mon, LaHune, spill it. Are you really NSF or are you something else? NASA or JPL? Something like that. We all know they got their hands in on that lake drilling project . . . are you part of that?"

"You're spinning conspiracies now, Hayes."

"You're right, I am. Because I can't shake the feeling that there's some subtext here, something under the surface I'm not reading. I was there when Gates told you over the radio about those mummies he found, the ruins . . . you didn't look at all surprised. Did you know they'd be there? And does it all tie in with what's down in that fucking lake? Because, maybe I'm crazy, but this all smells funny. You cutting us off from the world for what you say are security reasons . . . security of what? Jesus, LaHune, you're running this like a covert operation."

"I'm running it the way I'm being told to run it," LaHune said. "The NSF does not want any crank stories about aliens and pre-human cities leaking out before we know more."

"Fuck that, LaHune. I don't care if we found the Ark of the god-damn Covenant or Jesus' piss-stained underwear, there's no reason for a clamp-down like this."

LaHune just stared at him.

His eyes were spooky, Hayes found himself thinking, almost artificial-looking. There was something unnerving about them that made your skin want to crawl. Those eyes were sterile, antiseptic . . . dead and flat and empty. Whatever mind existed behind them must have been rigidly controlled, brainwashed and inhuman. The mind of an ant or a wasp, incapable of thinking beyond the mind-set of its superiors. Yeah, LaHune would shut off the generators if he was ordered to do so, watch the crew freeze to death and not feel a single twinge of guilt. That's the kind of guy he was. Like some asshole robotic general ordering men to their death even when he knew it was wrong. Morally and ethically wrong.

Had LaHune always been like this? Or had he only recently sold his soul to the machine? Hayes had to wonder, just like he wondered how much they had paid him to betray the people at Kharkhov. And was it in silver like Judas Iscariot?

"I'm not going to sit here and entertain your paranoid fantasies, Hayes. But let me make myself clear on one point," he said and seemed to mean it. "You start spreading any of this nonsense around and it'll go bad for you, real bad."

Hayes stood up. "What're you gonna do? Send me to fucking Antarctica?"

LaHune just stared blankly.

15

Maybe mid-afternoon, his guts still tangled in a knot from the whole mess, Hayes stopped by to see Doc Sharkey. He stood in the doorway of the infirmary while she administered a tetanus shot to a welder named Koricki who slit open his palm on a shard of rusty metal.

"There," Sharkey said. "No lockjaw for you, my friend."

Koricki pulled his sleeve down, examined the bandage on his palm. "Shit, I won't be able to use my hand for a week . . . damn, there goes half my love life right down the toilet. Anything you can prescribe for that, Doc?"

She managed a grin. "On your way."

Koricki passed Hayes, dropped him a wink. "Can't blame a guy for trying, eh, Jimmy?"

Hayes stood there for some time, smiling at what Koricki had said and unable to stop. The smile was pretty much skin deep and the muscles refused to pull out of it.

"Well? Are you going to come in or stand there and hold up the door frame?" Sharkey wanted to know.

Hayes went in there and sat across from her at her little desk. He did not say anything.

"You look like hell, Jimmy."

"Thanks."

But it wasn't some offhand smartassed comment like one of the boys would drop at him and neither was it a medical opinion . . . it was something else, maybe something like real concern. Regardless, Hayes knew she was right . . . his face was a fright mask. Eyes bloodshot, skin sallow and loose, a tic in the corner of his lips. His hands were shaking and his heart kept speeding up and slowing like it couldn't find its rhythm. And, oh yeah, he hadn't slept more than an hour in the last twenty-four.

"You were up all night?"

Hayes nodded. "You could say that, all right."

"Why didn't you come see me?" she asked, leaving the suggestion of that maybe lay a little too long. "I . . . I could have given you something . . . I mean, heh, something to help you sleep."

But the thinly-concealed innuendo and numerous Freudian slips were completely lost on Hayes and that was pretty much obvious.

"How's Lind?" he asked.

"He's sleeping. He was up a few hours ago, had breakfast, went back out again. He seemed pretty lucid, though. I'm hopeful."

"Me, too."

She studied him with those flashing blue eyes. "I'm ready to listen anytime you're ready to talk."

And she was and he knew it. But was he ready? That was the question. In all those paperback novels that got passed around the station during the winter the characters always seemed to feel some awful story they had to relate got easier with the re-telling, but Hayes wasn't so sure about that. He'd already told LaHune a good piece of it and as he thought about what he had to say, it only sounded loonier to him. But he did it. He marched straight through it like Sherman through Georgia and even clued her into the telepathy bit, seeing Lind's dreams.

"Okay," he said when he was done, his hands bunched into fists. "Should I just go take the cot next to Lind or what?"

She looked at him for a long time and there was nothing critical in that look, concern, yes, but nothing negative. "Two weeks ago I would have put you under medication."

"But now?"

"Now I'm not sure what to do," she admitted. "Something's happening here and we both know it."

"But do you believe me?"

She sighed, looked unhappy. "Yes . . . yes, I suppose I do."

And maybe it would have been easier if she hadn't. Things like this were so much easier when you could simply dismiss them. You got abducted by an alien and they stuck something up your ass? Yeah, okay. Your house is haunted? Uh-huh, I bet it is. Casual, thoughtless dismissal saved you from a world of hurt. But that was how the human mind worked . . . it was skeptical because it had to be skeptical, it saved itself a lot of fear and torment that way, a lot of sleepless nights. Because when you believed, you honestly believed . . . well, that meant you had to do something about it, right?

"You believe," Hayes said, "but you'd rather not? Is that it?"

"That's it exactly." She drummed her fingers on the desktop, looked like she needed to be doing something with them. "Because in my position, I just can't sit on something like this. The health of the entire crew here is my responsibility. I have to do something, except there really is nothing I *can* do."

"How right you are. I already tried our lord and master, but that was pointless."

"I could go to him, too, but I would need something concrete . . . even then . . . well, you know how LaHune is." She opened her desk and took out a little microcassette recorder. "I wonder if you would go through it all again so we have a record? It might be important to have some documentation and your admission, on tape, that LaHune totally blew you off."

Hayes did not want to do that, but he did. He cleared his throat, brought it all back in his head and said what had to be said. It took about fifteen minutes to get all the facts straight.

"I'm glad you left out the conspiracy bit," Sharkey said. Then she held up a hand to him. "Please don't take that the wrong way, but it just wouldn't sound right on the tape. Maybe LaHune does have some secret agenda. If he does and he's involved in something way over our heads, we'll never get him to admit as such. All we can do is sit back and wait."

It made sense. Hayes believed it, though. He didn't know how he knew it to be fact, but he did and nobody could tell him otherwise.

"Are you still . . . still experiencing the telepathy?"

Hayes shook his head. "No, I think it was a brief surge. But I wouldn't be a bit surprised if other people around here start getting it, too."

"Lind's in there," Sharkey said, pointing to the door that led into the little sick bay. "Do you think if you – "

"I'm not up to it."

They heard someone come hurrying up the corridor and Cutchen appeared, looking somewhat tense, maybe a little out of breath. "You two seen Meiner?" he asked.

They both shook their heads.

"Why? What's up?" Sharkey said.

"He's missing."

"Missing?"

Cutchen nodded. "Last anyone saw him was early this morning, maybe around seven. He had breakfast with Rutkowski and the boys and nobody's seen him since. He never showed for lunch and he isn't the sort to miss a meal."

Hayes felt a little tenseness himself now. "You tell LaHune?"

"I sent St. Ours over there with a couple others," Cutchen said. "We've been looking all over the compound for him."

About that time, LaHune came over the PA that was linked to every building and hut at the station, calling for Meiner to report in immediately. There was silence after that, maybe for two or three minutes while they looked helplessly at one another, then LaHune came back on again. Same message.

"He's gotta be somewhere," Sharkey said.

But Cutchen didn't comment on that. They followed him back down the corridor to the community room where maybe a dozen others were gathered in small groups, speculating on Meiner's fate.

"Anyone look down in the shafts?" Hayes said, referring to the maintenance shafts that ran beneath the station where all the lines and pipes were run from the power station and pumping shacks.

"Rutkowski and some of the contractors are down there now."

Hayes looked over at Sharkey and she was spearing him with those blue eyes of hers and they seemed to be saying to him, *this is probably unrelated.* But already Hayes was thinking otherwise.

He walked over to one of the east windows, peering out into the claustrophobic darkness of an Antarctica winter's day. Sheets of snow lifted, blowing through the compound in whirlwinds and torrents, engulfing the buildings and then retreating, backlit by pole lights and security lights whose illumination trembled and shook, casting wild shadows over the white. As the latest deluge played out, Hayes could see Hut #6 out there all by its lonesome, a tomb shrouded in ice.

"Anybody check the hut?" he said to Cutchen. "Gates' hut?"

Cutchen shook his head. "Why the hell would he be out there?"

But Hayes didn't say.

All he knew for sure was that he had left the door wide open when he left last night and now it looked to be closed.

16

Anybody could have closed it, Hayes was telling himself as they followed the guylines and drifted walkway out to Hut #6. Somebody could have passed, maybe one of the maintenance guys or somebody doing a little plowing early this morning.

Could have happened.

Yet, he didn't believe it for a minute. The weather was bad . . . it hadn't stopped snowing and gusting for three days now and the temperature was hanging low at a near-constant seventy below with wind chills pushing it down near a 100 below. In that kind of weather, you didn't go out of your way looking for extra outside work. And just about everyone was steering clear of Hut #6 and what it contained now. Maybe if it was summer and there was light, but in this perpetual screaming blackness . . . no way. Even if someone saw the door swinging wide they would not have gone over there anymore than you would go into a graveyard at midnight because a vault door was left open and creaking.

Superstitious or not, there were limits to what you'd do.

Hayes was leading the charge, battened down in ECW's, eyes wide behind his plastic goggles. Cutchen and Sharkey were behind him. All of them were gripping the guylines, feeling that wind trying to knock them down and sometimes lift them up, up, and away into the frozen night.

Hayes paused outside the door to the hut.

Yes, it was closed, all right. And he had a pretty good idea that the wind had had nothing to do with it. There was no point in looking in the snow for tracks because the wind erased them every ten minutes. Right now, there was a three-foot drift pushed up against the door and Hayes had to kick it away with his boots so they could get it open.

Then he undid the latch, grinned secretly at the length of chain and Masterlock dangling from it, and pulled it open, feeling that warmth coming out at them.

You step in there and they'll eat your mind down to the bone.

But Hayes stepped in and clicked on the lights and the others came in with him, Cutchen shutting the door behind them. They pulled off their mittens and goggles, smelling that room right away. After the ultra-fresh air on the walk over, the stench in the hut was offensive and roiling. It was a thick and vaporous green odor of rotting marshes and sun-bloated fish.

"God . . . what a smell," Cutchen said. "Why in the hell would Gates let these things decay like this? They're priceless."

"Look," Sharkey said.

Neither Hayes nor Cutchen had seen it, the angle of the wall blocking most of the lab except for that decaying, meaty mass on the table. But now they got a look.

"Meiner," Cutchen said.

Yeah, it was Meiner, all right, missing no more. They would never know exactly what got into his head or what he'd been thinking and that was probably a good thing. For Meiner had decided to pull himself up a chair about four feet away from the thawed — and decaying — specimen and stare at it in the dark. Hayes had some ideas as to why, but he did not voice them. He just looked down at Meiner as the wind blew and the shack trembled and an uneasy silence hung thickly in the air.

"What . . . Jesus, what in the hell happened to him?" Cutchen wondered out loud, the color drained from his face.

Sharkey didn't need to get very close to make her diagnosis. "Dead," she said. "Probably four or five hours, I'd guess."

"Dead," Cutchen said as if it were some surprise. "Oh, Christ, he's dead."

And he was.

Just sitting there in that chair, reclined back in his parka, mittens still on. His big white boots were crossed over each other and his mittened hands laid primly in his lap. He looked rather peaceful until you saw his face, saw the way his mouth was contorted in a silent scream, dried blood running from his lips and nostrils like old wine stains. And his eyes . . . just hollow purple cavities with clots of trailing gelatinous pulp splashed down his cheeks like slimy egg whites.

"Holy fuck," Cutchen said as if he was just now getting it. "That snot . . . those are his *eyes.*"

He turned away and Hayes followed suit.

Sharkey didn't care much for what she was seeing either, but medical curiosity and the upcoming post she would have to perform made it mandatory that she belly up to the bar and drink her fill.

Cutchen looked like he was going to be sick, but had changed his mind. He was looking at the mummy on the table, scowling, not liking it very much. Those glaring red eyes at the ends of the fleshy yellow stalks were still extended and wide open.

"I wouldn't stare at it too long," Hayes warned him. "Give you bad dreams."

Cutchen barked a short laugh and looked away. "Crazy goddamn thing. Looks like it was thrown together by some Hollywood special effects people, you know? Reminds me of those bug-eyed monsters Gary Larson draws."

Hayes was thinking more along the lines of Bernie Wrightson, but he kept that to himself. He was getting good at keeping things to himself. While Sharkey gave Meiner the once over, he stood there trying to fill his head with nonsense so the thing would not try and get at his mind again. Finally, he gave up, opened himself up, but there was nothing. The thing was dead and he had to wonder if he wasn't going insane. There was nothing in his head but the neutral humming of his neurons at low ebb. Nothing else, praise God.

The door opened and LaHune came in with St. Ours and a couple of contractors. He looked from the mummy to Hayes, wrinkled his nose at the stink and stripped his goggles off. As yet, he hadn't seen the body.

He shook a finger at Hayes, casting him a feral look. "What in God's name do you think you're doing out here? This hut was locked and chained, it's off-limits to anyone but myself and Dr. Gates' team. You don't have the authorization to be out here."

St. Ours flashed Hayes a little smile as if saying, yeah, good old LaHune, ain't he just the King Shit himself?

Sharkey looked like she was about to say something, but Hayes stepped forward, something in him beginning to boil, to seethe. "I made my own fucking authorization, LaHune. They're called bolt-cutters. But I'm glad you showed up, because I want your high and mighty white ass to see something."

"Jimmy . . . " Sharkey began.

But Hayes wasn't listening. His eyes were locked with those of LaHune and neither man was breaking the staring contest. They faced off like a couple male rattlesnakes ready to go at it over a juicy female.

"I want you out of here," LaHune said. "Now."

"Kiss my ass, chief," Hayes told him and before anyone could stop him or really even think of doing so, Hayes took two quick steps and grabbed LaHune by the arm. And hard enough to almost yank that arm right off. He took hold of him and yanked him further into the hut until he could see Meiner plain as day.

LaHune shook himself free . . . or tried to. "Meiner . . . good God."

Hayes let out a tortured laugh, pulling LaHune over closer to the corpse and its empty eye sockets. "No, God don't have shit to do with this party, LaHune. See, this is what Gates' pets have done. This is what happens when they get inside your head and overload you. You like it? *You like how that looks?"* he said, shaking the man. "Maybe what we need to do is lock you in here in the dark for a few hours, see if you suffer any ill fucking effects from close proximity to the remains. You want that, LaHune? That what you want? Feel that fucking monster getting inside your mind and bleeding you dry, your fucking brains running out your ears?"

LaHune did get away now. "I want everyone out of here and right goddamn now."

But St. Ours and the other boys were too busy looking from the putrefying husk on the table to Meiner, a guy they'd lived with and drank with, played cards with and laughed with. This was one of their own and when the shock started fading, they put their eyes on LaHune.

"Fuck you gonna do about this, boss?" St. Ours said. "Or should I fucking well guess?"

"Nothing," another said. "He won't do a goddamn thing."

St. Ours was big and he could've smeared a guy like LaHune all over the walls, used what was left to wipe his ass with. "Tell you what, boss. I'll give you a day or two to take care of this business here. You don't get rid of these butt-ugly motherfuckers, we'll dump about two-hundred gallons of hi-test in here and have ourselves a fucking wienie roast."

He meant it and there was no doubt about it.

Hayes and Cutchen followed St. Ours and the others out, leaving Sharkey looking helpess and LaHune trying to find his balls, trying to figure out how he was going to crunch this one on his laptop.

17

I t was the dinner hour and the scientists and contractors began to arrive at the community room in twos and threes, bringing with them the smell of machine oil and sweat and exhaustion. A smell that mixed in with the stink of old beer and older cooking odors, smoke and garbage and musty tarps drying along the wall. It was a hermetic, contained sort of stink that was purely Antarctica.

The room wasn't too big to begin with and it quickly filled, people grumbling and complaining, joking and laughing, dragging in snow and ice that melted into dirty pools on the floor.

"You got any good ideas, Doc, on what can boil a man's eyes right out of his head?" Cutchen was saying, watching the room fill.

Sharkey shrugged. She'd completed the post on Meiner and had listed his death, far as she could tell, due to a massive cerebral hemorrhage. What that had to do with the man's eyes going to jelly and exploding out of their sockets was anyone's guess.

Hayes was watching St. Ours, Rutkowski, and the boys at their usual table near the north wall. They were a grim lot with set faces and weary eyes, in mourning of a sort for Meiner. Other contractors threaded past them, said a word or two and kept right on going.

They looked, Hayes decided, like a bunch of roughnecks looking for a fight.

You could almost smell it building over there, that raw stink of hatred and fear that was smoldering and consuming. It was a big odor that rose above everything else, feeding upon itself and growing geometrically out of control. And if something didn't give at the station pretty goddamn soon, it was going to vent itself and Hayes didn't think he wanted to see that.

But it had to happen, sooner or later.

It had been a bullshit winter so far and it showed no signs of getting any better. The entire place had lost its sense of camaraderie and brotherhood that you usually got from living practically on top of each other, depending on each other and knowing there was no one to turn to but the guy or girl sitting next to you. That was all fading fast and in another week or two, you could probably bury it proper and throw dirt in its face. The entire station was starting to feel like some sort of immense dry cell battery storing up fear and negativity, all that potential energy just looking for a catalyst to set it free. And when that happened, when it finally arced out of control, it was going to have claws and teeth and dark intent.

"It's going to be trouble, Doc," Hayes said, "when that happens."

"When what happens?"

Hayes looked at her and Cutchen. "When these people feel like their necks have been strung as tight as they can go and they decide they've had enough. Because you know it's going to happen, you can *feel* it in the air."

"They're afraid," Sharkey said.

"I am, too. But I'm thinking at least so far, I can see reason . . . but some of them? I don't know. You keep an eye on St. Ours. He's dangerous. There's murder in his eyes and if I was LaHune I'd be sleeping real lightly."

"You think it'll go that far?" Cutchen said.

"Yeah, I do. Look at them over there. They're all having crazy fucking nightmares and they're scared and they're not thinking right. It's coming off of them like poison."

And maybe it was.

Because already it seemed like the crew was forming along class lines . . . the scientists were keeping to themselves, the contractors staying with their own. There was no mixing up like you generally saw most winters. Maybe it was a temporary thing, but maybe it hinted at worse things waiting. Waiting to spring.

"LaHune could stop it or slow it down at least," Hayes said. "Give these people their Internet, radio, and satellite back, let them reach outside of this place to the real world. It would work wonders."

"I don't see that happening anytime soon," Sharkey said.

"No, neither do I. And that's what's so fucked up about all of this. Morale has gone right into the pisser and LaHune doesn't seem to give a shit. He's clamping down, playing it close to the vest and spooky and that isn't helping a thing."

"He's the cloak-and-dagger type," Cutchen added, something behind his eyes pretty much saying that he could elaborate on that, but wasn't about to.

Sharkey sighed. "He . . . well, he just doesn't understand people, I'm afraid. What they need and what they want and what makes them happy."

"See, that's what bugs me about the guy, the fact that he could care less, that he doesn't give a shit about the state of mind at his own goddamn station, the one he's supposed to be running. That just rubs me wrong. But, then again, LaHune has been rubbing me wrong since I got here. He has no business running a place like this." Hayes paused, studying a few contractors leaning against the wall and smoking cigarettes, looking bitter, their eyes dead. "Most of the people down here are vets, they've wintered through before. I know all three of us have and many times. Normally, the NSF picks an administrator with people skills, not a fucking mannequin like LaHune. A guy who's equally at home with the techies and the support personnel. A guy who can talk ice cores and sedimentation, turn around and talk beer and baseball and overhauling a Hemi. The sort of guy who can play both ends, keep people happy and keep the place running, make sure the work gets done and people have what they need, when they need it. That's why I don't get LaHune. He has no business down here."

"Well, somebody thought he did," Sharkey said.

"Yeah, and I'm starting to wonder *who* that might be."

Nobody bit on that one and Hayes was okay with that. He'd already reeled off his conspiracy theories for Sharkey and she had warned him to be careful talking like that. That such things would just feed the blaze that was already smoldering at Kharkhov.

Cutchen wasn't stupid, though. He could read between the lines and the way he looked over at Hayes told him that he was doing just that.

"What I don't get," he said after a time, "is why Gates would leave his mummies in there to decay like that. It just doesn't wash with me. If they're what he's saying . . . or not saying . . . then I can't see this opportunity coming his way again."

Sharkey tensed a bit because she knew what Hayes was going to say.

"Maybe he didn't realize what he was doing," Hayes said, true to form. "Maybe he wasn't in his right mind anymore than Meiner was in his when he decided to keep those things company in the dark. Yeah, maybe, like Meiner, Gates didn't have a choice. Maybe he was doing what those things wanted him to do . . . letting them thaw, letting their minds wake up all the way."

Cutchen just sat there. He grinned at first thinking it was a gag, but the grin disappeared quickly enough. He looked over at Sharkey, his eyes seeming to say, *what in the hell is this guy talking about?*

18

"What we're doing here," Dr. Gundry was saying to Hayes inside the drilling tower the next morning, "is to drill down nearly a mile to Lake Vordog. We'll stop drilling about a hundred feet above it and let the cryobot melt its way down the rest of the way. Why? Why not just drill all the way through? Simple. We don't want to contaminate that lake in any way, shape, or form. Remember, Mr. Hayes –"

"Jimmy's fine, just Jimmy."

"Right. Anyway, Jimmy, Vordog is a pristine body of water, un-contaminated by microorganisms from above and has been for nearly forty-million years. Last thing we want is for some of our bugs to get into that water. The ecosystem down there may be radically different from any other on earth and we can't take the chance of contaminating something like that."

Gundry was pretty excited about the entire thing and particularly since he and his team had high hopes of getting down to the lake by the end of the day. They were damn close now. Hayes was trying to share the enthusiasm, but he was getting that bad feeling in his gut again that was telling him maybe that lake should be left alone.

But there would be no leaving it alone.

These guys would not stop until the lid was kicked off Pandora's Box and all the badness had seeped out. Because it was more than the biology, geology, and chemistry of Lake Vordog these guys were inter-ested in. There was something else, something inexplicable and there-fore intriguing: a magnetic anomaly. Using magnetic imaging, the anomaly was discovered by a SOAR (Support Office for Aerogeophysical Research) fly-over the year before. Although at the South Geomagnetic pole, of course, there was a manifested flux in the earth's electromagnetic field and from time to time small, temporary magnetic anomalies were detected, none of it explained what they were seeing roughly dead center of the lake: a self-perpetuating source of intense magnetic energy.

And there simply was no explanation for it.

At least, none that the scientists were ready to share.

Gundry, a CalTech glaciologist, was the project manager. He had six people working under him and the lot of them barely left the drilling tower. Usually sleeping and taking their meals there as well. Gundry had laid it all out for Hayes, best he could. The project was underwritten by NASA as part of the groundwork for the Europa Ice Clipper and Mars cryobot missions. Known as the ATP, the Active Thermal Probe, the cryobot would melt down through the northern ice cap of Mars . . . and eventually, through the frozen crust of Europa. The cryobot being used for the Lake Vordog probe, Project Deep Drill, would be similar to the ones they'd use on Mars and Jupiter's frozen moons. Basically, it was something of a robotic submersible, a cylindrical probe about ten feet long and six inches in diameter with a heated nose cone designed to melt frozen ground and drill hyperthermally.

"It's, essentially, like a high-tech . . . very high-tech . . . self-propelled drill, Jimmy," Gundry explained. "Melting its way through the ice and passing down through the resulting liquid takes a lot less power than conventional augering. The nose cone melts the ice to liquid and the cryobot is drawn downward via gravity."

Hayes nodded. "But on Mars or Europa, you're not going to have a big drill like you have here to get the cryobot started."

"No, good point. But the cryobot doesn't need any pre-drilling, we've just done that to speed things along, you see. In our latest test — and trust me, Jimmy, there have been lots of tests — the cryobot melted its way though two-hundred feet of ice without any problem."

Gundry explained that from the back of the probe there was a self-unspooling umbilical connecting it to the surface carrying power and fibre-optic video and data cables. What would happen was, after the cryobot began melting its way through the cap above Vordog, the hole would freeze up behind it and that would be perfectly fine in that it would seal Vordog from the outside world.

"So, the probe will melt through the cap and then drop down to the lake itself. It's not solid ice above the lake. There's an arched dome up to half a mile high above it," Gundry said. "So the cryobot will have a splash-down of sorts and then go under where it then will split in two. The mother portion will stay just under the surface, analyzing the water and searching for signs of life. The other portion will descend to the bottom on a cable where it, too, will search for life and examine currents and temperatures, which will then give us a good idea what's keeping that lake warm . . . we're guessing hydrothermal vents, smoker vents."

Hayes just shook his head. "The level of technology you guys come up with is amazing."

"Oh, but we're not done yet," Campbell, the microbiologist, said, looking up from his monitor. "Once the lower portion hits the sediment, it will release the hydrobot . . . a tiny submarine of sorts equipped with sonar and a camera. It'll bounce around down there like a soap bubble, showing us what's above and below."

Jesus, it was incredible.

No wonder these guys never came up for air. Project Deep Drill had begun the summer before, bringing in the equipment and setting it up, getting everything on-line and ready for the drilling. It hadn't been until winter that everything was a go.

Hayes had wintered at other stations and usually the drilling towers were involved in core sampling for the NSF's Antarctic Core Repository project. They drilled down, brought up cores for geochemical anaylsis and paleoclimatology studies. The cores could tell them the history of the world's climate, the chemical composition of its water and air, things like that.

But, this year, it was a little more exciting.

Hayes stepped out of the control booth and stood there in the main room of the drilling tower which was cavernous and loud. The massive EHWD (Enhanced Hot-Water Drill) was channeling deep into the ice beneath the tower, making the floor vibrate. Compressors were thrumming and pumps hissing, hoses snaking every which way. The drill, he knew, pumped jets of ultra-hot water from a heating plant down a hose at high pressure to the drill head far below. The melted water was sucked up from the borehole, reheated up in the tower, and pumped back down in a cyclical process.

Hayes walked around, staying out of the way of the three technicians who were actually running the drill, monitoring its progress and keeping an eye on all that expensive machinery. The cryobot itself was over near the wall, looking like a missile suspended from an immense iron tripod and connected to huge spools of cable. The probe itself was sealed in a sterile vinyl bag that it would melt through once it reached its destination nearly a mile below.

Hayes was just staring at it, that feeling in his guts again like somebody had dug a pit in his belly. He couldn't get beyond it now. It wasn't a momentary thing he could laugh off, accost himself for being silly. No, this feeling was deep and ancient and intense. Staring up at the suspended cryobot he figured he was feeling roughly what Rabi, Oppenheimer, and the boys must have been feeling when they tested the atomic bomb for the first time: that the door had been thrown open and there was no going back.

The noise of the machinery clattering in his ears, Hayes slipped away, making for the far side of the drill room and into the core sampling room. Gundry had turned it into an office of sorts.

He was going through reams of computer printouts, mostly graphs. "Something on your mind, Jimmy?"

Hayes chewed his lip. "You were there when Gates made his announcement, right?"

"Sure. I wouldn't have missed it for the world."

Hayes took a deep breath, considered his words carefully. "What do you think of the mummies? That prehistoric city? I mean, not scientifically, but as a person, a human being, what do you think of them?"

Gundry was a small, almost bird-like man who moved with quick, jerky motions. His face was weathered and craggy like all those who spent too much time in the harshest climate on earth. He looked, if anything, like some hard-rock miner who'd lived a hard, demanding life and probably he had. The only thing that off-set this was his full head of almost luxurious silver hair. But for all his nervous energy, he now relaxed, intertwined his fingers behind his head and leaned back. "Well, I'll tell you, Jimmy. I'll tell you what I think," he said in his smooth Southern drawl. "I grew up in the Bible Belt and though religion and I have had a parting of the ways, I think this could be big trouble for the faith. What Bob Gates has found down here just might throw organized religion on its ass. When Gates said that he has something there that might make us re-think who and what we are, I wouldn't take that lightly. I know the man. He doesn't say squat until he's got something and, son, I'm thinking he's got something here that's going to shake our culture to its roots."

"Do you think . . . do you think those are aliens he has there?"

Gundry winced, then shrugged. "All I'm going to say is that it's probably a pretty good possibility."

"I know you boys have been busy over here," Hayes said. "But I imagine you've heard what's going on."

"I have."

"And as an educated man, what do you make of it? All those dreams everyone's having, all of 'em pretty much along the same line."

"As an educated man and a guy who's spent half his lifetime at the Pole, I'd say isolation can lead to paranoia and paranoia can lead to all manner of terrible things. Particularly when you've got those Old Ones as inspiration." Gundry paused, shrugged again. "That's what I'd say as an *educated* man."

Hayes licked his windburned lips. "And as just a man?"

Gundry shifted uncomfortably. "I'd say I don't particularly care for what those things are going to tell us about ourselves and the history of our little world. I'd say they seem to have a bad influence on our kind in general. And, like you, I'm hoping that influence is not truly still active."

"Do you think we're in trouble here, Doc?"

"No, at least, I hope not. But as to our culture? Our society? Yeah, I'd say that's in jeopardy . . . because after what Gates has found, well, let's face it, Jimmy, you just can't go home again. You can't go back to the way things were."

Gundry was saying a lot of things without actually saying them. Hayes had spent a lot of time around scientists and knew they got very good at that. Had to, if they wanted to survive in the fiercely competitive, cutthroat world of government grants and college departmental politics. Scientists like Gundry did not go out on a limb until it had been shored-up by others. At least, not publicly.

Hayes turned to leave, then stopped. "What about that magnetic energy down in the lake? What do you make of that?"

But Gundry would only shrug, blinking his eyes in rapid succession. "What do you make of it, Jimmy?"

Hayes looked at him for a moment. "I'm no scientist, Doc, but I'm not stupid either. I trust my instincts on things like this."

"And what do your instincts tell you?"

"Same thing they're telling you, Dr. Gundry, that whatever's down there kicking up its heels . . . it sure as fuck isn't by accident."

19

"Well, you missed all the excitement," Sharkey said to Hayes that afternoon in the community room as he sat down with his tray of food.

Hayes felt something wither in him. "God, do I even want to hear this?"

"I think you will. LaHune has put us back online . . . Internet, satellite, the works. He made the announcement about an hour ago and you could almost hear the sigh of relief around here."

Hayes wasn't really surprised.

LaHune had to pacify the collective beast before it took a bite out of him. Looking around the community room which was barely half full, Hayes could almost feel that the tensions of the past week had subsided somewhat. Like a chiropractor with a good set of hands had worked out the kinks and bunched muscles of the station.

"No shit?" he said. "You telling me our fine and randy Mr. LaHune isn't worrying about word of our mummies leaking out? That city?"

Sharkey took a bite of stew, chewed it carefully. "Oh, he covered that base. He directed it at our wallets. Told us it's okay to mention that fossils and artifacts had been found, just not to be perpetuating any of the wild rumors circulating through camp. Said that, if crazy stories like that got out, those who sent them would not be invited back by the NSF . . . meaning they can kiss Antarctica good-bye, along with those juicy contracts and exclusive grants."

Though he didn't care for LaHune anymore than he cared for a woodtick fastened to his left nut, Hayes had to agree that it was the right way to handle things. People didn't pay much attention to threats until you put their livelihood and careers on the chopping block. If LaHune had any sense, he would have done it in the first place.

"Honestly though, Jimmy, I don't think people here are going to talk about any of that. They're barely talking about it amongst themselves. It seems that most of them have accepted my post on Meiner as an embolism."

Hayes studied his food, set his fork down. "Yeah, but do *you* accept it?"

Sharkey looked indifferent. "Down here, with the very limited pathological facilities, it'll have to do. I examined Meiner's brain pretty thoroughly. It was a massive hemorrhage, all right . . . blood vessels popped like ripe grapes just about everywhere. So I accept that. As to cause . . . well, that's a different bag of chips, isn't it?"

"I suppose it is at that."

"Gates radioed us this morning on the HF," Sharkey said. "I was in the radio shack when it came in."

"And?"

"A few items of interest. Gates and his team are still finding the things up there. He was saying *fossils,* but I guess by this point we can read through the lines pretty much. More fossils, more artifacts. According to what he said, they've been spending a lot of time in that subterranean city. I got on the horn and asked him what he was making of the ruins, but he was almost . . . *evasive,* I guess, about what he's seeing."

Hayes thought about that, was thinking that Gates should have dynamited that chasm close while he still could. But maybe it was already too late for that. The cage was open, now wasn't it? And the beast had gotten loose after millions of years. He swallowed. "Did you mention that state of his mummies?"

"I did."

"And his reply?"

She shook her head. "He seemed a little confused about it all . . . like it was some gray area in his head."

"I'll just bet it is."

Sharkey said he managed to cover for himself okay, though, saying that letting his specimens thaw and maybe decompose was part of some experiment he was running. And maybe it was, though she didn't believe it. She said Gates alluded to the fact that he had uncovered a great deal more specimens in some kind of cemetery up there . . . or down there . . . and he wasn't too concerned about the ones in the hut.

"He just said to make sure the hut stayed locked and people stayed out of there." Sharkey was looking into Hayes' eyes now. "I suppose he could be worried about us contaminating something he has going in there, but — "

"But you don't believe it?"

"No, I don't." She took another bite of stew and washed it down with coffee. "There was . . . well, almost an undercurrent to his voice, Jimmy. Maybe it was my imagination, but I don't think so. He was almost guarded, unnecessarily formal. At times it almost seemed like he was speaking really low like he didn't want to be overheard and other times he muttered nonsensical things. But when I asked him to repeat, he changed the subject."

"He's in trouble, Doc. I'm willing to bet they all are."

"Maybe. Thing is, LaHune showed for the last half of our convo and, true to form, he didn't seem to think there was anything out of the ordinary. I don't know. Maybe there isn't."

"Did he say anything else?"

"Gates? Well . . . he said that they found an abandoned Russian camp up there, about ten miles from their location. He said it was pretty much buried in snow, but he was really intrigued by it. I could hear the excitement in his voice, Jimmy. It may mean nothing, but . . . "

"Maybe everything?"

Sharkey didn't bother with her food anymore. "I know Gates as well as anyone, Jimmy. He's completely self-involved and dedicated. He pays no attention to that which doesn't directly concern his project. And I tell you right now that his interest in that camp isn't simple curiosity. He asked me to call my Russian friends down at Vostok, see what they had to say about it."

Sharkey corresponded with a Russian physician at the Vostok Station and was pretty friendly with him. The guy's name was Nikolai Kolich and he had been part of the Russian program since the Soviet days in the 1960s. He knew all the scuttlebutt on just about everything. As it so happened, there was another huge warm-water lake beneath the Vostok Station and plans were in place to drill down to it after Vordog.

"LaHune okay with that? You calling him?"

"He suggested it."

"Anything else?"

Sharkey told him that Gates seemed very interested in the progress that Dr. Gundry's drilling operation was making. He seemed, she said, very excited about what might be found down there. Either excited or scared, it was hard to say.

"What do you think's down there, Jimmy?"

He told her about his convo with Dr. Gundry. "He won't say much, but he's thinking things, Doc. Lots of things. I got a good idea that me and him are pissing in the same bucket here, that we're on the same page. There's something down there creating that magnetic flux and I think it worries him."

20

Hayes was there in the radio shack when Sodermark, the communications tech, established contact with the Vostok Station. Another old Soviet installation, Vostok had existed now for some forty-odd years and was staffed by Russians, Americans, and the French, all of whom were involved in joint projects and independent research. Once Sodermark had them on the HF set, he told Sharkey that it was all hers, he was going to grab a cup of coffee and a cigarette.

The connection wasn't bad, despite the weather, though now and then there was a funny whining sound that would rise and fall. Hayes listened while Sharkey and Nikolai Kolich talked shop for a time.

Finally, Sharkey said, "Nikolai? That excavation I mentioned to you . . . yes, I imagine you've heard about it by now . . . Dr. Gates is up there again. No, I don't know, I don't know . . . lots of strange stories flying around that's for sure."

Sharkey smiled and rolled her eyes while Kolich talked non-stop about what Gates had found. If it was all over the Vostok Station, then it was surely all over McMurdo and Palmer, too.

When Kolich stopped for a breath, Sharkey jumped in: "I have a question for you, Nicky. Dr. Gates needs to know something only you can answer, I think. There's a camp up near him, an abandoned Russian camp up there. Do you know of it?"

The usually gregarious Kolich went silent for a moment or two. That whine rose and fell from the set. They waited a minute, two, three, nothing.

"Nikolai? Nikolai? Are you there?" Sharkey asked. "Vostok? Can you hear me, Vostok?"

"Yes . . . we hear you, Elaine. I've . . . I've been getting properly chastised by the radio officer here . . . he says that I am not following proper procedure. I should be saying 'over' and that nonsense. There. There, he is gone and now we can talk."

"The abandoned camp . . . do you know of it?"

"Yes, Elaine, yes. You speak of the Vradaz Outpost, a coring site. It was abandoned back in 1979 or '80, as I recall. There was a lot of noise about it at the time, lots of wild stories . . . "

"Do you remember what happened?"

Silence, static. "Yes, but it's hardly worth going into. Just crazy talk. There was . . . well how do I say this . . . something of a ghost scare up there. Talk of a haunting of all things. Crazy business. Vradaz was a summer post and they were coring, struck into a cave or chasm or something. Yes. Then . . . I remember things got funny after that."

He paused and Hayes looked at Sharkey, but she wouldn't look at him. She was thinking what he was thinking. He knew it.

"Do you remember the details, Nicky?" she asked.

"Details? Yes. Yes, yes, I was here at Vostok when they brought the last three men in. They were all mad, hopelessly mad. The man in charge here then . . . you know of the sort I speak, Elaine? The political officer was a big Ukranian whom no one liked. He placed those three men in segregation, had me shoot them full of sedatives so they would not disturb the others."

"You said three men? I thought there were ten?"

"There was said, I recall, to be a rash of insanity up there. Men killing each other and committing suicide. We had been getting some very odd communications from Vradaz and then, nothing. Three weeks and nothing. A security force went up there, came back with the three and said the others were all dead. I was one of the few, being a medico, that was allowed to see these men. They were only here for three days, I think, then they were flown out. It was a sad, tragic business. Isolation . . . it can do terrible things to men."

"Those communications . . . do you remember them?"

"Yes." Another long pause and Hayes could almost imagine him mopping sweat from his brow. "Crazy business . . . the men up there, they wanted to get out, said they could not stay up there. These were scientists, Elaine, and they were scared like schoolchildren, yes? Talking rubbish . . . noises and bumps, knocks and tappings, shapes seen flitting about at night . . . madness, that's all it was."

Sharkey chewed her lower lip. "Dr. Gates will find this all interesting."

"It was rubbish, Elaine, make sure you tell him that I did not believe these things!"

"Oh, of course not, Nicky." Sharkey stared at the dials and LEDs on the radio, thumbed the mic again. "Did those three men . . . did they say anything?"

The silence dragged on longer this time, much longer. "Yes, even sedated, they would not stop talking. It was all nonsense, Elaine. Silly stories, all of it. They were raving. Sounds in the night, noises in the walls and on the roofs . . . knocks at the door, scratching at the windows. Things of that nature. There was a ruined house when I was a child and . . . but, no matter. These men were raving about nightmares and voices in their heads . . . weird figures wandering through the compound that were not men . . . ghosts, bogies, I think. They spoke of devils and monsters, figures that walked through walls. It was a terrible business."

Kolich signed off soon after this and seemed to be in a hurry to do so. Maybe he was being overheard or maybe the memory of all that wasn't sitting on him right. Regardless, he had something that needed doing and he went to do it.

"What do you make of that?" Hayes asked.

Sharkey kept staring at the set. She shook her head. "Nikolai is a man who likes to talk, Jimmy. But he was very abrupt about all this. Any other time I would have been on here an hour hearing about his take on that business. It's not like him."

"I got the feeling that maybe he was talking about something he wasn't supposed to be saying."

"Me, too."

"But you saw the familiar pattern there, I take it?"

She nodded. "It's like what we have . . . but worse." She was looking in his eyes now and Hayes saw something like fear in them. "Is this what's going to happen here, Jimmy? Are we all going to go mad and kill each other?"

"I don't know, but I think we better do something here before this gets out of hand."

"Like what?"

He smiled thinly. "Oh, I was thinking about asking you to take a little Sunday drive with me. Up to a place called Vradaz."

PART THREE

THE WINGED DEVILS

"That ultimate, nameless thing beyond the mountains of madness."

— H.P. Lovecraft

21

Zero hour.

Gundry and his people weren't calling it that, but that's how Hayes was seeing it. The cryobot had been launched some twelve hours before. It took nearly eight of those for it to melt through the remaining 100 feet of the ice dome over Lake Vordog and then it dropped to the misty, black waters of the lake far below. Gundry and his people had not slept for over twenty-four hours now and Hayes didn't see that happening anytime soon.

They were all wired.

Hayes had gotten up at like four a.m. because he, too, was excited. Excited and, yes, apprehensive as to what might be found down in that ancient lake. He went about his work, checking in at the drill tower from time to time to see how things were proceeding. Apparently, Gundry and Parks, the project's geophysicist, had been concerned about the possibility of there being some massive methane ice bubble trapped down below the cap. Most permafrost regions have quantities of methane beneath them, they explained to him.

"You see, Jimmy," Gundry explained to him. "There was some anxiety about what we're doing down here. Environmental groups were worried that we would pollute that pristine lake below and among the scientific community, there was some grave concern that we might tap into a dangerous quantity of methane gas . . . which, if released, could prove disastrous to world climate."

When Hayes heard that, his mouth maybe dropped open. "You

mean . . . Jesus, Doc, you saying you guys could've wiped us out just to explore that goddamn lake?"

"That was something of a concern, so to speak," Gundry admitted. "But we took every precaution and all our tests and coring confirmed that, while there certainly were quantities of methane, there was also helium, nitrogen, trace amounts of exotic gases such as xenon . . . but nothing that could affect our atmosphere."

So, Project Deep Drill went ahead.

And now the cryobot had melted its way through the ice cap and dropped into the lake itself. It had been there some three hours now, sending back a wealth of information on the lake's temperature, chemistry, and biology. It had already detected vast quantities of organic molecules and even varieties of archaebacteria, eubacteria, and eukaryotes. So the lake was definitely alive just as they thought and not only alive, but organically rich.

This really got everyone excited and particularly Campbell, the team's microbiologist. He got so excited, in fact, he forgot that Hayes was the guy who ran the generators and boilers and not a brother scientist. In the control booth, as all that wonderful info came up from the cryobot and began appearing on the computer screens, Campbell grabbed Hayes by the arm and started babbling on like a kid talking about presents under the Christmas tree. Except what he was talking about were molecular biology studies, forensic biology, and ancient DNA protein analysis. Hayes acted like he knew all about that stuff, smiling and nodding happily as Campbell filled his head with the specifics of Polymerase Chain Reaction (PCR) using gene-specific and random primers, PCR amplification of evolutionary conservative genes and microbial metabolic activity, and, of course, the wonders of cyanobacteria and paleo-indicators.

An hour after the cryobot had entered the lake, it released the secondary cryobot on a cable which then descended to the bottom, some 900 feet below. Gundry and the others had chosen this location because the lake was over 2000 feet deep in some spots and it was near to that perplexing magnetic anomaly. When Hayes got back to the drill tower again, the secondary cryobot was on the bottom and had been for the past thirty minutes.

"You've come just in time," Gundry told him. "We're about to release the hydrobot. Keep your fingers crossed."

Hayes did. He was keeping a lot of things crossed. He was glad they were finding what they had hoped for . . . more, even . . . but there was still that worming tension in his belly, that almost superstitious dread at probing around down here at something that had been sealed away from the world for almost forty-million years . . . like they were picking the scab off a sore and there was a danger of some infection running rampant as a result. Now and again Gundry would look over at him and something would pass between them, some sense that they were on the verge of big things, things that might crush them.

At least, that's how Hayes was reading it.

When the hydrobot was released successfully, there was just Gundry, Campbell, Hayes, and Parks, the geophysicist, in the booth. People had been coming in all day long to see what was going on, but it was a long process and most left soon after they arrived.

But Hayes, in-between his rounds of the power station and boilers, hung on like a tick and now here it was, the moment they'd all been waiting for. When the hydrobot was released and started to send back data everyone cheered. This was going to work, all those millions of dollars were going to pay off. Today Lake Vordog and tomorrow, Mars and the moons of Jupiter. It really was an incredible moment and Hayes was almost wishing Lind could have been there. He would have appreciated the historical significance of it all . . . and *his* part in it, too.

Campbell and Parks sat before monitors, gathering data, and Gundry and Hayes stood behind them. There was a video screen above, but as yet there had been no video feed. The screen flickered a few times, but nothing. Hayes could sense the heavy hearts of the scientists over that.

"I'm reading water temperatures of sixty degrees, with currents up over a hundred. Wait now . . . okay, okay," Parks was saying as the numbers came in from the hydrobot. "Yeah, picking up chemical signals . . . magnesium and iron smoke . . . manganese, zinc . . . copper sulfides, sulfur dioxides . . . carried on the warm currents. Okay, got a hot plume here . . . almost 200 degrees. We've definitely got ourselves a smoker down here, gentlemen. Hydrothermal vents . . . gotta be . . . yeah, more than one. Several sites, I'm guessing."

Campbell was equally as happy for his bio-sensors were picking up all kinds of goodies from both the secondary cryobot on the bottom and the hydrobot. Analysis of water and sediment were showing bacteria, yeasts, archaea, algae, even grains of pollen.

"Diatoms . . . shit, I'm getting indicators of rich plankton fields here."

"Outstanding," Gundry said.

Parks was nodding his head. "Come to papa . . . oh yeah . . . chemical enrichment of water almost two million times that of normal seawater or fresh water."

"Meaning what?" Hayes asked.

"Meaning," Gundry said, "is that the buffet is surely open. You've got smoker vents down here, Jimmy, spewing chemical nutrients into the water that heat-loving bacteria feast upon. The buffet is open."

Parks started fooling around with the uplink to the hydrobot and the video screen flickered, flickered again, rolled and went black. Then it came on and they were seeing . . . well, huge clots of sediment drifting up from the muddy bottom in the powerful halogen lamps of the hydrobot. They were now seeing what it was seeing.

"Incredible," Hayes said without being aware of it.

It was like some alien world and, in effect, that's exactly what it was. A sunken, ancient plain of murky waters and sediment drifting about like motes of dust. It was thick and grainy on the screen.

Hayes swallowed, struck somehow by the eerie stillness of that place. He was seeing flitting shadows at the edges of the light and it could have been the motion of that suspended sediment or something else entirely.

The hydrobot descended again, closer to the lake bottom and Campbell started getting really excited. "Look there, do you see it?" he said, squinting through the ooze and sediment as if it were his eyes seeing this and not the hydrobot's forward camera. "Right there . . . those marks in the mud, those snaking ruts . . . those are the marks of deep crawlers — maybe shrimp or brittle stars, sea spiders. Hard to tell this deep, could have happened yesterday or two hundred years ago. Really hard to say."

The hydrobot roamed ever forward, the screen almost black at times as it pushed on through clouds of silt.

"Any chance it'll get stuck in all that?" Hayes said.

"No, it has a seriously advanced AI package on board, same sort of stuff we use on space probes and the Martian rover, except better. It's doing most of its own thinking right now. It has sonar to avoid large objects and infrared to hone in on living things, an on-board lab to analyze just about anything."

"Why does it keep pausing?"

"It's using its robotic arms to take samples. It sucks them up, analyzes them and feeds the results to Dr. Campbell here."

Gundry told him the hydrobot worked much like an ROV with a prop at the rear to pull it or push it or turn it around and in any direction. It could rise or hover, do whatever its software package demanded of it.

"Magnometer's picking up some strong fluxes," Parks said. "Jumping a thousand, now two-thousand nanoteslas. Five-thousand. Jesus. Strong and steady."

Gundry explained that a nanotesla was the standard measure of magnetism. That the norm here at the Pole was in the vicinity of 60,000 and now they were getting nearly seventy. The hydrobot was reading it and gradually honing in on its source. If it lost it, it would go back to tracking the hydrothermal vents.

The hydrobot climbed and the silt thinned considerably. It went from a blizzard of flakes the size of quarters to a flurry with flakes the size of beads. The light penetrated better now. Suddenly, there was a storm of bubbles coming at the camera and then the hydrobot was buried in them . . . pulsing membranous bubbles that were purple and blue, sometimes orange and red, indigo and neon green.

"Jellies," Campbell said. "Will you look at that! Like comb jellies . . . ovoid with frilled plates to propel themselves. But I've never seen any like this . . . we seem to be in a massive colony."

"Can they hurt the hydrobot?" Hayes asked.

"No . . . see, the hydrobot has slowed down now. It's concerned about hurting *them* so its passing through their ranks very slowy."

It was a world of jellyfish, thousands of them like champagne bubbles. But pulsing and rippling, veined with brilliant bursts of ever changing color like fibre optic lamps. You could see right through them. It was hard to say how big they were, but maybe the size of softballs with lots of little ones, some no bigger than marbles. They seemed unconcerned about the hydrobot. After about ten minutes the colony passed away and the hydrobot dove down into the sediment again, detecting something interesting.

Hayes saw what looked like a gigantic albino crab picking its way through the mud. Its body was jagged and thorny, about the size of a wash tub — Campbell said — with spidery limbs reaching out three or four feet beyond. It had something like black eyes on two-foot stalks and Hayes pointed it out.

"No, not eyes," Campbell said. "Receptors of some sort. It would be totally blind like everything else down here. A new species, though, without a doubt."

The hydrobot passed over it, deciding wisely not to tangle with it, and darted down into a chasm filled with sea grasses and then up again, scanning the bottom and finding the shells of dead mussels and crustaceans, hundreds of them tangled in a bony carpet. Then a gully spread out, dropping maybe five feet below the level of the lake bottom. It was filled not with grasses, but white bloated things that had to be ten or fifteen feet in length, coiling and writhing. To Hayes they looked like thousands of blunt and fleshy hoses with pink suckers at the end that expanded and deflated.

"Tube worms and like none I've ever seen before," Campbell said.

The hydrobot was interested. It inverted itself above them and slowly passed over them, panning them and giving what information it could on them such as their temperature and what the chemical composition of the water around them was. Hayes had seen tube worms on the Discovery Channel, but not like these . . . not moving and undulating, reacting to maybe both the hydrobot and its light. These didn't look like harmless filter-feeding animals, but things that were hungry and predacious.

"This is simply amazing," Gundry said.

Hayes was speechless. What he was seeing . . . no man had seen before and the impact of it all had quieted that feeling in his belly that there was something terribly wrong about this ancient lake.

"Shit!" Parks cried out. "Did you see that?"

They had. Something gigantic and fluttering that looked roughly like a pond hydra, but grown to nightmare proportions. It had to be twenty or thirty feet in length, looking much like an upended tree with a massive root system . . . a forest of clown-white writhing tentacles. It darted away from the light quickly enough and they only got the briefest glimpse of it. But what they had seen made them pretty sure they wouldn't be taking any dips in Lake Vordog in the near future.

"Incredible . . . a mollusk maybe. Certainly squid-like," Campbell said with a dry voice as if the thing hadn't scared the hell out of him.

But it had. Without really thinking, all the men in the booth had pulled away from the screen involuntarily. Something like that . . . white and ghostly and alien . . . roaming in the darkness, well, it did something to you. Made you think bad thoughts, the kind that could keep you awake at night.

The hydrobot did not go after it, which was a good thing. But Gundry explained that it was programmed to study slow-moving creatures when it could, but not to burn unnecessary energy in any hot pursuits. And that hydra . . . or whatever in the Christ it was . . . had been damned fast. Damned fast and damned spooky.

Another bottom-dweller came onto the screen and Hayes had never seen anything like it, either. It looked sort of like a horseshoe crab, but narrowed and lengthened so that it was maybe ten feet long. It was covered in a chitinous exoskeketon that was fish-belly white like most things down there. There were two pairs of spiny walking legs to either side like those of a lobster and a set of hooked chelicerae, pincers, poised out front like they were looking for something to crush. Its plated tail ended in something like a stinger. Overall, it looked like some kind of massive scorpion, but eyeless with no less than four waving antennae.

"My God," Campbell said. "I don't believe it. Do you know what that is? A Eurypterid . . . a sea scorpion. Obviously an evolved form, but a Eurypterid all the same."

"A new species?" Hayes said.

Campbell laughed. "The Eurypterids are an extinct subclass of arthropods, Jimmy. They died out roughly 200 million years ago . . . or so we thought. God*damn!*"

The hydrobot passed beyond the reach of the sea scorpion. Everyone in the booth kept watching the screen, seeing more exotic aquatic plants, colonies of tube worms, bizarre giant clams, some inching worms, and what might have been a squid that ducked away quickly. Then the terrain began to grow more rugged, slashed by chasms that dropped hundreds of feet and capped with rolling submarine hills that were set with something like pale yellow kelp. The magnometer on the hydrobot was picking up higher levels of magnetism and honing in on them.

For a time it was pretty much business as usual save for a school of transparent fish . . . or what looked like fish . . . and then, Campbell saw something.

"Did you . . . what the hell was that?"

Hayes had seen something like it before.

A murky oblong shape that darted away from the light. Maybe it was nothing and maybe it was everything. Whatever they were seeing, catching glimpses of, there were more than one of them and they were quick, stealthy. That feeling was back on Hayes again and he couldn't shake it this time. Because he was thinking things that he didn't dare say . . . not out loud. For whatever was out there, he had the feeling it or *they* were following the hydrobot, but hiding away from the light. The hydrobot was picking up lots of blips, but that in itself meant nothing except that the sea was very alive . . . which it certainly was.

"I'd like to know what those are," Parks said. "They remind me of . . . "

"What?" Gundry asked him.

He shook his head. "Nothing, nothing. Thinking out loud."

But Hayes knew what he was thinking and he wondered if they *all* weren't thinking the same damn thing, seeing those flitting shapes and remembering them from somewhere else and not liking them one bit.

And then –

And then Gundry gasped. "Did you see that? Looked like . . . well, almost like an arch."

Parks fumbled over his words, relaxed and tried again. "Some weird volcanic structure. Can't be an arch down here, not down here."

But it was gone too quickly before any real guesses could be made. All they could say for sure was that it had *looked* like an arch jutting from the roiling sediment below. And a big one at that . . . the hydrobot had passed through it.

Parks, almost nervously, started rambling on about volcanism and how it could shape ordinary rock into the most peculiar shapes. And particularly underwater where the lava flow would cool quite quickly, twisting into the oddest forms that very often appeared man-made . . . or, in this case, manufactured by an intelligence. For there was no possible way anything down here had ever been touched by man.

The hydrobot continued on, tracking that magnetic anomaly and Parks kept calling out numbers and other than that, there was only the occasional beeping of the computers as they logged what was going on below. The men, other than the geophysicist, were quiet, expectant maybe. Hayes could only speak for himself. His mouth was dry as fireplace soot and he was grinding his teeth and bunching his fists.

The silence was so thick suddenly you could've hung your hat from it.

The hydrobot ventured forward, scanning over clusters of things like anemones and spiny urchins and finally great outcroppings of coral. Here was an ecosystem of clinging sponges, pale worms, and bivalves. Primitive bryozoans encrusted like bee honeycombs. Campbell pointed out that, though marine zoology was not his forte, these were either new species or ones long thought extinct.

But he was talking just to be heard, maybe to be comforted by his own voice, as the hydrobot's magnometer was reading pulses right off the scale. To which Gundry joked offhand that it must be picking up the emissions of some massive electromagnetic generator with the mother of all magnetic cores. But nobody laughed and maybe because they didn't like the idea of what that alluded to. Because at that particular moment nobody would have been surprised at anything. Had they seen a flying saucer jutting from the lake bed and weeds, they would not have been surprised. For whatever was putting out that kind of raw energy almost certainly had to be artificial.

And then they saw it . . . or the hydrobot did.

Another arch. And so perfect in form its design could not have been a simple natural abnormality for just beyond it other shapes . . . rectangular slabs standing upright and others lying flat like ancient tombstones and what might have been a shattered dome rising from the congested weeds. What they saw of it had to have been several hundred feet across, though in fact it was probably quite a bit larger. Jagged cracks were feathered over its surface.

Nobody said anything, not a damn thing because there was more of it all the time, whatever it was they were looking at. Now they were seeing what appeared to be monuments jutting at wild angles like gravestones in some incredibly ancient cemetery. Things like obelisks and monoliths leaning over, wanting to fall . . . they were coated in a pink slime and set with the holes of borer worms and appeared to be of a vast antiquity. But there was more, always more. Crumbling walls encrusted with colonies of sponges and the carbonate skeletons of long-dead marine organisms.

"Jesus H. Christ," Gundry said, sounding like he was hyperventilating. "Would you look at that . . . would you just *look* . . . "

Parks kept shaking his head. "A city . . . something, but down here?"

"Why not?" Hayes said. "Why the hell not?"

Parks couldn't seem to stop shaking his head. "Because . . . *because* this goddamn lake has been cut off from the world, tucked under a glacier for forty-million years, Hayes, that's why."

"What about the ruins Gates found? Hundreds of million years old, pre-human in origin . . . I guess this pretty much supports what he told us."

But you could see the look of disbelief on Parks' face. Maybe he hadn't really believed what Gates had said, maybe in his mind — regardless of the facts staring him dead in the face — he had refused to accept the concept of a civilization predating humanity by half a billion years. Human arrogance had a hard time with that one. It reduced the species' significance considerably. Just another drop in the bucket, hardly the chosen ones.

"A city," Campbell kept saying. "A city."

But "city" wasn't what Hayes was thinking, not at all. What he was seeing was sprawling and wild without any indication of an overall plan, more like a graveyard than a city, something that expanded as necessity required. All those monoliths and shafts, oblong slabs and worm-holed pillars, low stone buildings carpeted in ooze and weeds and marine creepers . . . yes, there was something inexplicably morbid about them like centuried graves and collapsing mausoleums and ivy-choked crypts. A necropolis, a marble-hewn city covered in rot and growth and sediment, falling into itself. The structures were crowded together and overlapping one another like what you might see in a medieval slum . . . crowded, claustrophobic, tangled with what might have been deep-cut lanes snaking amongst them. Hayes was looking upon it all, barely able to breathe, at the complexity and profusion. Everything jutting and leaning and rising and falling, like some litter pile of worm-holed bones heaped atop each other for uncounted millennia . . . pyramids and domes, shafts and cones and arches. Yes, like broken skulls and rib staves green with moss, pillared femurs and stove-pipe ulnas and ladders of eroding vertebrae. All dusted by a perpetual rain of silt that was blown and drifting like dandelion fuzz.

The hydrobot was rising as the city or graveyard itself began to rise up a sloping hill and then they saw it, the city. The *real* city. Not this rotting collection of debris and artifacts, but the city itself rising higher and higher up a submarine mountain . . . or maybe the city *was* the mountain. The silt began to thin and they saw the colossal, dead immensity of it as the hydrobot rose up, showing them something that had been hid from the light for forty million years.

Hayes just stood there, something fused inside of him.

A cyclopean, eon-dead city of towers and spires rising up to an incredible height and looking much like some fantastic crystalline growth ballooning up from its base . . . if it really had a base, for much of it seemed to be sunken in a forest of weeds and kelp. The structures were honeycombed with doorways that were like mossy cave mouths from which spilled a limitless blackness. It was a vast, shadow-enshrouded metropolis of perverse geometric architecture. The ruins of some primordial alien city deposited here on this muddy, weedy lake bottom . . . and still the hydrobot rose, its lights splashing over great galleries and domes and spirals of cubes that gravity should have pulled down, but didn't.

It looked to Hayes like some gigantic calliope set with the naked, tubular pipes of a cathedral organ rising above to unknown heights . . . deserted and derelict and tomb-like, shot through with vaults and hollows. He saw panes of crystal and arches and spires and spheres crowded together and built, it seemed, right through one another as if the entire thing had been dropped and had shattered like this, collecting in some irregular pattern of razor-backed shards. And all of it encrusted with an amazing variety of sponges and barnacles and flowering anemones, pale slimy mosses and gardens of thick weeds that seemed to grow right out of the lurching walls, swaying gracefully in some unseen current.

"The . . . the magnetic anomaly," Parks said. "It must be centered in there somewhere, somewhere."

"Yeah," Hayes heard himself say. "Like some engine, some generator that's still running after all this time."

The hydrobot was still rising, panning the city and trying to pull back as far as it could to give a broader view of what it was seeing, put it in some kind of perspective, but its lights simply wouldn't penetrate far enough and all it could show them was more of that weird architecture, that morbid gigantism. Shadows darted and jumped and danced amongst the structures and the effect of it was disconcerting to say the least, making the city appear to be in motion, to be creeping and reaching out at them, those doorways shifting . . . vomiting storms of silt, weeds swaying and undulating.

Hayes was thinking the entire thing looked like some enormous and hideous alien skull, articulated and grinning, punctured with holes and narrow crevices.

But the total effect made him realize how far he was from home and how very alone they were. In a place so distant and remote, a place of echoes and ghosts and lost voices. A place where the sun never rose and the chill never lifted.

No, even for Parks, there was nothing but acceptance now. Bare, stark acceptance of things they now knew and all those things they did not. For no human brain could have conceived of such a city. The very insane geometry of the place made you want to vent your mind in a single rending and wet scream.

The hydrobot had been steadily rising for nearly an hour now and it told them that it had come up over five-hundred feet, but finally they were reaching the pinnacle of the city. From above it looked like a maze-like, congested forest of dead trees . . . all spires and shafts and what looked like the intersecting steeples of a thousand churches. All of which seemed to be connected by a spider-webbing of filaments like ropes. Hayes caught sight of something like gargoyles perched near the tops on flat, see-sawing widow's walks. But they were not gargoyles as such, but slime-covered things like immense horned grasshoppers with too many limbs. Something about them made his guts suck into themselves.

But maybe he hadn't seen them at all.

Maybe it was a trick of the light or darkness, for everything was obscured and encrusted with polyp colonies, gorgonians, whip corals, and the corrugated helixes of bryozoans.

The hydrobot hung over the top of the city, within spitting distance of a tangle of skeletal spires. It just hovered, apparently interested in something. Hayes and the others didn't see what it was, not right away. But for Hayes, he could *feel* it. Feel that something was coming, something terrible and overwhelming, something that crushed him and sucked the juice from his soul. Oh, yes, it was coming, it was coming now. Hayes felt weak and dizzy like some low-grade flu was chewing at his guts. And in his head, there was a low, constant humming like high-power lines at midsummer or a transformer cycling at a low ebb.

"What the hell is that?"

Somebody said that and nobody seemed to know who it was. They were all staring at the screen, at what the hydrobot had been tracking long before it became visual. Except it wasn't an *it*, but a *they*. Everyone in the booth saw them . . . those streamlined, cylindrical forms that looked impossible and ungainly laying on, say, a dissection table, but down here were fluid and free and fast-moving. They rose up above the city, like a swarm of vampire bats come to drain the world dry. Gliding up and forward, filling the ether above the city, their bodies pulsed as they rocketed forward, expelling water like squids and octopi, moving easily with those great outstretched fin-like wings.

Hayes felt like he was going to pass out or throw-up or maybe both. Alive, dear Christ, they were alive. The Old Ones. And what was even worse is that what he was seeing, that swarm rising like locusts, was exactly the image he had gotten from Lind's mind.

Exactly.

The creatures came on, incredibly obscene as they bloated up and narrowed with their bastard propulsion. There was no doubt what was attracting them.

When they were maybe twenty feet away, the screen flickered, rolled, and went black. Everyone stood in shocked silence for a moment or two, not sure what to say or what to do.

Parks started hammering on his keyboard. "Dead," he said. "Dead. Primary and secondary cryobots have lost contact with the hydrobot. It's off-line, I guess."

Well, thank God for small favors, Hayes thought, feeling numb and ungainly. He was glad. If he had had to see those things any closer, he would have lost his mind. If those globular red eyes had filled the screen they would have wiped his brain clean and he didn't think that was an exaggeration.

"They're still down there, still active," he said, almost mumbling. "All these millions of years they've been waiting down there . . . waiting for us."

Parks stood up, something like rage burning in his eyes. He went right after Hayes and Gundry had to stop him from going right over the top of him and maybe stomping him down in the process. "You can't know that!" he said, drool hanging from his lower lip in a ribbon. "There's no way you could possibly know that! You're imagining things and making up things and acting like a scared little boy!"

Hayes laughed and walked straight past him, wanting badly to curl up in a dark corner somewhere. "You got that right, Doc, because I *am* scared. And I think you are, too. We all are and we have a real fucking good reason to be."

22

Sure, Elaine Sharkey was iron. All hard edges and cutting corners sharp enough to slit your throat, you got too close, but when she was with Hayes? Maybe melted butter, something soft and warm and liquid and they both knew it and it was getting to the point that they didn't bother pretending otherwise. Maybe to the other men her eyes were blazing and cold, blue diamonds in a deep-freeze and her scowling mouth was hard and bitter. But to Hayes it was anything but that. It was a mouth to desire and want and feel. Yes, there was a connection between them and it was electric and real and that was the secret they coveted. Which was no secret at all.

When he was done telling her his story, he said simply, "I saw them, Doc . . . *Elaine,* I saw them. They're down there and they have been for millions of years, breeding and living and waiting in that warm darkness. Waiting for us . . . I know they've been waiting for us. It doesn't make sense or maybe it does, but I know it's true. Jesus, I know it's true."

"I wish I really thought you made all this up," was all she could say.

"Me, too. But we all saw that city, those things down there. Christ." He paused, trying to catch his breath just like he'd been trying to catch it ever since he'd seen *them.* Trying to catch his breath and trying to plane his world flat before it went too far askew and pitched him on his ass. "It's all on tape, though. Wait until LaHune gets his hands on this . . . we'll have a blackout like never before. I bet he won't even let anyone see it."

Sharkey fed him whiskey and soft words, gave him a shoulder to lean on. It was enough. It had to be enough. They were in her room, sitting on the bed and maybe it was the best possible place to be and maybe it was the worse. For what came next was the result of chemistry. Later, they could not say who started it. Just that it happened. That they fell into each other and lost themselves in the warmth and necessity of the act. The foreplay had been the telling of Hayes' story, no sweet nothings, but a great and voluminous blackness that had to be covered, had to be shut away somewhere and so it was. Like dread or mourning, the impact of what they knew to be true and what they guessed to be true threw them into each other's arms and the connection was made whole, potential energy gone kinetic, and the power was real. Foreplay abandoned, there was the act, there was motion and breathing and moaning and hot skin, limbs entwined and heat shared and maybe hearts touched and filled. All that Hayes could remember later was that he had never felt so strong or so weak. When he was inside Elaine Sharkey and she was wrapped around him, her eyes glowing like azure flames, he had never felt so completely alive and so utterly pure.

There was an excitement, he knew, in bedding another man's wife. The illicit thrill, the taboo. But it was far beyond that. The hunger had been growing for weeks and it was only a matter of time before the beast showed its teeth and filled its belly. And then, afterwards, the afterglow, a secret and a memory they shared and held deep inside themselves in a special place other hands could not touch or hope to sully. It was theirs and theirs alone and this was enough. This was all and everything and it was not spoken of. They could no more frame it with words than they could hold one another's souls in the palms of their hands. And that was the beauty of it, the thrill and joy and the magic.

And later, wrapped in each other's arms and touching and never wanting to let go, there were soft voices in the darkness.

"What . . . what are we going to do, Elaine?"

"I don't know, Jimmy, I just don't know."

And he didn't either, so he laid there, feeling her, and loving the tactile sensation of her flesh, smelling that perfume coming off her which didn't come out of any bottle, but was just her inner beauty announcing itself as sweet honey, jasmine, and musk.

There were no answers, there was only the two of them in the darkness, feeling and being felt. Listening to the wind scraping across the compound and the blood rushing at their temples. What they had at that moment was the memory of their seduction and it was secret.

23

So LaHune had been feeding them a straight ration of shit for too long now, expecting them to chew and swallow, maybe ask for seconds, fill their bellies and smile and shove back empty plates, my compliments to the fucking cook. But day by day that was getting harder and you could see it behind their eyes and just under their smiles, like there was something pissed-off and randy waiting to show itself and when it did, my dearly beloved, cover your heads and hold onto your privates, this is going to be ugly and fierce and *loud.*

Sure, LaHune, Christian saint that he was, had given them back their Internet and SAT TV and maybe everyone should have been happier than a penis on a Playboy shoot . . . but it wasn't that simple. The TV, the radio, the Internet . . . when you were locked down and nailed shut for five months in the coffin of Antarctica, got so you needed these things. Like clean air to breath. And when someone shoved a pillow over your face and cut off your wind, you didn't exactly thank 'em when they pulled it off, let you breathe. What you did was kick them in the nuts so hard their little gonads rang off the inside of their skulls like ball bearings in a pinball game. Didn't matter how many sweet nothings about the Official Secrets Act they hummed in your ear, you kicked 'em hard and sure so maybe next time they'd keep that in mind.

At least, that's how the Glory Boys — Rutkowski, St. Ours, and a few others — were seeing this little scenario.

"We can sit here and hold each other's dicks while we piss," St. Ours told them. "Or we can zip our flies shut and do something. We can show that fucking monkey-skull LaHune which side his bread is buttered on."

Maybe it was the loss of Meiner and too much whiskey and maybe it was just plain poor sense combined with isolation and confinement and that frustration they'd been gathering up like wool, but it made sense. St. Ours talked and the others listened with an almost religious rapture and plans were laid and not a one of them questioned any of it. Like a swift-rushing river they let it flow and carry them along, never once thinking of damming it.

At the far north end of Targa House, at the end of the corridor that split off the community room, you could find the radio room and supply lockers. You kept going, just around the bend, you'd find an Emergency Supplies Room that held extra radio parts, survival gear, freeze-dried food, ECWs, just about anything you'd need if the going got tough. You'd also find a weapon's locker there.

And if you wanted to get into it, then it was only a matter of kicking through LaHune's door across the hallway. Maybe going in there with three, four tough boys with liquor in their bellies and taking the keys.

LaHune never really saw them come in.

He was sleeping and about the time his eyes started to flicker open and register a vague shape standing over him, a fist had already collided with his temple. There was about enough time to cry out and then another fist caught him just above the eye and the lights went out. LaHune fell into blackness and his last sensory input was of pain and the stink of cheap whiskey, body odor, and machine oil . . . a very working man kind of smell.

"Tie that fucking puke up," St. Ours said, toying with a flap of skin at his knuckle that he'd torn on LaHune's head.

Rutkowski and the others — a couple maintenance jocks named Biggs and Stotts — just stood there like toys waiting to be wound, maybe considering for the first time that they were involving themselves in some real deep shit here. The sort of shit you could and would drown in when the whiskey left your brain.

"With what?" Rutkowski said.

"Cut up some of those bed sheets," St. Ours said. "Tie and gag him, then we'll get some guns and kerosene and have ourselves a wienie roast with Gates' pets out in the hut."

And maybe the others weren't crazy about the idea of hurting LaHune or being an accomplice to an assault, but they liked the idea of torching the mummies. Yeah, they liked that just fine. Using pocket knives, Stotts and Biggs trussed LaHune up and that poor boy was out cold as a salmon steak in a freezer. When they were done, they were sweaty and maybe even a little confused.

"C'mon," St. Ours told them.

In LaHune's desk, they found keys for every lock at the station, but all they wanted were the keys to the Emergency Supplies Room and the gun locker in there. When they had them, they went across the corridor and let themselves in. The room was about the size of a two-car garage. Crates and boxes, medical supplies and laboratory equipment marked fragile, drums of fuel, just about everything else. Because down there at the South Pole during winter, if you didn't have it and you needed it, you had to make it.

In the gun locker they found flare guns, .22 caliber survival rifles. They were hoping for some bigger hardware, but they figured the rifles would be enough. They found the shells easily enough and loaded the guns. Then they stood in a tight little circle, holding up those guns and liking the feel of them . . . their weight and solidity, the way weapons always made a man feel somehow more like a man. A hunter. A warrior. They stood there looking at each other, seeing the lights in each other's eyes, but not knowing what it was, only that it was strong and necessary and good.

It was all up to St. Ours now.

They would do what he said.

"All right," he told them. "We're going to get ourselves some kerosene in the Equipment Garage . . . maybe gas or even diesel fuel, then we're going over to Hut Six and you know what we're going to do then. Anyone gets in our way . . . "

They seemed eager a moment before, but now something in them was weakening and wavering and St. Ours didn't care for it. "What? What the hell is it?" he put to them.

Rutkowski opened his mouth to say something, but the words didn't want to come. He'd been feeling something the past few minutes, but he wasn't really sure what it was. Only that it was in his head.

Biggs was rubbing his temples. "Damnedest thing . . . got me a headache, I'm thinking."

"A headache? So take a fucking aspirin already. Jesus." But St. Ours was looking at the other two and seeing it on them as well. Something was afoot. "Well? Are we going to do this or sit around pissing about our heads?"

Stotts, tall and angular and lantern-jawed like some stock New Englander, kept licking his lips. "It's in the back of my head . . . I can feel it back there."

"Oh, for chrissake."

Rutkowski shook his head, too. There was something there and it wasn't to be denied. The more he tried to ignore it, the more it raged, the more pain it brought with it. Maybe this wasn't a migraine coming on him, but it lived next door.

"Fuck is with you people?" St. Ours wanted to know.

But they couldn't really say because they were having trouble stringing words together and the pain was uniform and disorienting. Like something had woken up in their heads. Woken and stretched and started clawing up things. Rifles were lowered and then dropped and eyes went from being confused to being dark and shifting like simmering oil. Those eyes stared and rarely blinked and there was something very strange about it all.

St. Ours had been thinking maybe these boys had been affected by a leaky gas furnace or something because headaches were sure as hell not catchy. But what he was seeing in their eyes and beginning to feel along the nape of his neck was not gas, it was . . . it was a sense of *visitation.* Something was in that room with them, something unseen and nameless and malefic was filling the empty spaces between them, making everything and everyone just go bad to their cores.

Rutkowski kept trying to talk, but his mouth wouldn't seem to open and his head was filled with a thick, black down and he couldn't seem to think around it. His belly was filled with spiders and he could feel them in there, crawling up his spine and along his nerve ganglia making him want to fold-up or scream and –

"Fuck's with you people?" St. Ours was saying, flat-out scared now. What was in their heads wasn't in his, but he had enough other bad stuff going on to make up for it.

About then, they all became aware of the most peculiar vibration that seemed to be traveling through the floor beneath their feet and up into their bones, making their teeth ache. It was subtle at first, but growing, rising up now like some generator amping into life, that rhythmic thrumming passing through all of them and making them tremble and shake. And, Jesus, it was getting louder all the time like having your ear up against the metal casing of a hydraulic pump.

St. Ours tried to say something, but that thrumming drowned out his voice and the others were completely in thrall to it now, lost in a fog, their bodies moving now in cadence with that awful vibration. Noises began echoing around them . . . pinging sounds, whispering sounds, metallic sounds echoing down long pipes and brief squeals that almost sounded like human screams inverted or played in reverse.

And then there was a crackling like static electricity, a discharge of energy that made the hairs stand up on their arms and St. Ours wanted to cry out, but he couldn't. He still had the .22 in his hands and he wanted to open up on something, drill something, anything to make it stop before his head flew apart. Maybe the others didn't see what he saw then . . . and it was hard to say because they looked empty and dumb like window dummies . . . but it made him want to run.

Except, he didn't think he could.

The far outside wall of the room was getting fuzzy. It was made of bare concrete blocks, except now it looked like it was made of smoke. Something almost diaphanous and insubstantial. It was fluttering and glowing now as if it were backlit by some enormous burst of energy and you could see the mortaring between the blocks standing out lividly.

Yes, St. Ours wanted to run away, but all he did was stumble forward, a weird sucking feeling in the pit of his stomach. But he still had the .22 and he was going to use it . . . use it when whatever was out there melting through the wall made its appearance.

Because it would.

And then it did.

It came through the wall as easily as smoke through a window grating, insubstantial and ghostly, yet gradually gaining solidity. And at that point, a ghost carrying its head tucked under its arm would have been welcome. Because this . . . well, this was something else.

St. Ours knew it was one of those things from Hut #6 and the sight of it filled him with a terror that was dream-like and blank.

It was obscene to see it in motion, to see it gliding forth on those thick and muscular snakelike tentacles at its base. It should have been sluggish, but it moved with a marked fluidity, grace, and ease. Its body was like some oblong barrel, the flesh gray and oily and ribbed, some sort of wriggling parasitic podia hanging from the lower quadrant. When it got within five feet of St. Ours, it opened up its wings, almost seeming to inflate them, fanning them out like the collar of a frilled lizard. It sounded like wet umbrellas being snapped open.

St. Ours could see a black vein networking in those wings. They looked membranous and rubbery. He tried to scream and could not. He was horrified and sickened, knowing it was not truly there physically, could not possibly be, yet smelling its stink which was like a poisoned carcass slowly decaying on a hot beach.

It stood before him, towering over him, wings fanned out like the sails of a hang-glider, stinking and evil and offensive. Those appendages at its middle were reaching out for him, quivering, looking much like branching dendrites and synapses of a brain cell. But the worst part was that starfish-shaped head with those glaring eyes like red glass. These, more than anything, are what made St. Ours start shooting, seeing those slugs pass harmlessly through the creature and punch into the concrete wall behind it.

The thing allowed him this one act of defiance and then those eyes stood out at the end of their stalks, looked at him and *in* him, showing him the pain of refusal, of raging against its kind. He heard a high, shrill, almost musical piping in his head like some distorted and trilling antique harmonium. And suddenly he was nothing and no one. His mind was bleached white and he was just a doll forged from warm plastic with a beating heart and staring eyes. He fell down before the thing, whimpering and giggling, and there was an intense wave of agony in his skull as his brain went to bubbling hot wax and his eyes exploded from their sockets and splashed down his face like wet vomit.

And then the thing began to fade, pulling away from the broken and sightless creature before it.

And back near the door, the spell broken, Rutkowski and the remaining Glory Boys began to scream.

24

Like the wreckage left by some horrendous traffic accident, just about everyone at the station came by to look upon the remains of Tommy St. Ours. They bustled in the corridor, poking their noses through the doorway and asking questions and whispering and then leaving as quick as they could get away. St. Ours was like some horror kept in a jar at a roadside carnival and people had to see what was left just to say that they had, that such a thing could be. Because most of them had never gotten a good look at Meiner sitting in that chair out in Hut #6 with his eyes sprayed over his face like slime, but they weren't going to miss this.

Few actually saw St. Ours, though.

After five, then six and seven people circled in like turkey buzzards, Dr. Sharkey threw a white sheet over him like a corpse in an old movie. What more could really be done? Later, they would wrap him up in a tarp and ship him out to join Meiner in the cold house where was also kept the station's meat and perishables, but for now at least they didn't need to look upon him. So, yes, only a handful saw his grim cadaver, but to listen to them later, you wouldn't have thought so. For they all had stories to tell that seemed to get more gruesome with the re-telling.

And then, after a time, there was only Sharkey and Hayes and LaHune.

"What're you going to log as the cause of death?" LaHune said, gently touching a great red knob over his left eye where St. Ours had hit him.

She looked over at him like maybe he was kidding, making some sick joke, but she saw he was dead serious. "Well, I'll have to do a post, won't I? But, chances are, I'll be writing it up as another cerebral hemorrhage."

"Yes," LaHune said. "Yes."

Hayes felt sorry for the guy . . . a little bit anyway, because nobody should've had to put up with being slugged and then tied up, but the guy just didn't seem to be in touch with mother reality here. He knew what killed St. Ours, just as they all knew it, but he wouldn't admit it.

Christ. An hour ago, Hayes had been sleeping alongside Sharkey and then Cutchen was at her door saying there had been another death and now he was here, looking at this and listening to LaHune.

Which was worse?

Of course, this death had a lot of drama tied to it. Rutkowski and the boys had gone screaming into the community room and the dorms beyond, banging their fists against doors, wanting help or salvation. Maybe both. That was how Cutchen and some of the others had un-tied LaHune and got a look at St. Ours. Now Rutkowski and his Glory Boys were sedated, because none of them were sure what had happened. They were raving about ghosts and monsters, saying that one of the Old Ones was traipsing about camp.

"I don't think, at this point, that we need to be so concerned with *how* St. Ours died, but with *what* killed him," Sharkey said. "Can we agree on that?"

"Well, yes, we need to know that. If you have any ideas, I'm listening."

Sharkey just stared at him like he was an idiot.

Hayes said, "Doc's right, chief. Don't matter what happened, so much as *who* did it."

"If you have any ideas . . . "

"Oh for chrissake, LaHune, what the fuck's wrong with you?" he wanted to know. "You know same as me what happened. Those things out there . . . Gates' fucking fossils . . . they aren't exactly dead as you and I understand dead. Their minds are still active and if we don't do something about shutting those minds down again, then who knows how many of us'll be left come spring."

LaHune swallowed. "I'm not about to accept any of that nonsense. There's simply no real proof. I expect that from Rutkowski . . . he's hysterical, but not you, Hayes."

"Oh, really? You think because they've been frozen a million years or whatever that they can't wake up again?"

"No, I don't."

"All right, then. We'll say it's not the frozen ones, okay? Maybe it was them down in that lake, LaHune, because I can tell you that those bastards are not anywhere near dead. So let's not fuck around here, all right? I know you saw the videotape by now. You know what's down there."

LaHune looked uncomfortable. "Yes, I've seen the tape. But I tend to think what's down in that lake and what's up here are two different situations."

Before Sharkey could hope to stop him, Hayes grabbed LaHune and slammed him up against the wall and with enough force to knock a few things off their shelves. "Listen to me, you pretentious fucking fool," Hayes said. "Those things are physically dead, but psychically very much *alive.* They killed St. Ours because he was going to burn those bodies up and those things don't want that yet. He was dangerous to them, so they squashed him. Those minds out there . . . I don't think they've cycled up all the way yet, but when they do, when they fucking do, we're all toast and you know it. If anybody's left in this camp by spring, I can guarantee you of one thing, they might look like men, but what's going to be in their heads will be anything but."

"**H**e said he would be online at six. That's what his email said," Sharkey was saying. "Let's give it a little longer."

They were sitting in the infirmary, Sharkey and Cutchen and Hayes, staring at her laptop like it was some oracle that would divine their future when it decided the time was right. Nobody was speaking and it was pretty much like that all over camp: just go about your duties and lose yourselves in your work and when you had to talk to others, keep it light and filled with fluff. Talk about how long the winter was and how this was your last one, what you were going to do when you got back to the world. Regardless, don't talk about what was happening and what was still to come.

So they sat and waited, waited for Gates to come online. He was still up at the tent camp, at the excavation, and he had emailed Sharkey that he wanted to talk to her, but not on the radio. Hayes thought that was funny, odd . . . but then again, he was seeing everything a little off-kilter these days. For him, there were spooks and conspiracies behind every tree.

Good healthy paranoia, he liked to tell himself, sometimes it's all that can save your bacon.

When he thought about it, tried to get a handle on things and balance them out in his mind, he could not be sure anymore just when the knowledge that things were fucked up at Kharkhov Station had come to him. True, he had had a bad feeling in his gut from the first moment he had arrived at the camp. And there had been no real reason for it, none whatsoever. But it had lingered on like a summer cold, annoying him and, at times, making him think that he was losing his mind. It wasn't until word had come about Gates finding those mummies and those ruins, that whatever was in his belly really started chewing at him and when he'd seen those awful things in Hut #6 that day —the day Lind had gone mad — he somehow knew they were all in dreadful danger. And that was the funny part of it all, the things he knew. Sometimes when he started talking, he said things that he did not know to be true, but was certain of nonetheless. For example, he did not know that there was a direct link between the mummies and the living ones down in Lake Vordog, yet he was *sure* there was. Just as he was sure that the Old Ones wanted their minds and that men knew them from the dim past, that the hatred and terror they inspired was carried inside him and the others as some sort of race memory.

Christ, a therapist would have had a field day with him and he knew it, yet the certainty of these things remained.

Hayes was having the dreams like everyone else, but it was more than that for him. He had had that thing out in the hut invade his mind and nearly destroy him, but unlike Meiner and St. Ours, he had survived the invasion. Maybe this gave him an edge and maybe some of that telepathy was still cooking in his head. Regardless, he knew there were connections here between all these things and they were the sort you could hang yourself from.

"Getting something," Sharkey said.

Her laptop beeped, letting her know she had incoming.

> Paleodoc: gates here you there elaine?
>
> Sharkey: I'm here. How goes it up there?
>
> Paleodoc: we're making progress finding out about things that maybe we'd be better off not knowing about but don't mind me I'm tired

Hayes could just bet that he was. Up there in those ruins with all the dead Old Ones. Jesus, they must've been having some kind of dreams up there. It was a wonder they hadn't cut their own throats by now and maybe some of them had.

Sharkey: Lots of things happening here. I found out from my Russian friend about that abandoned camp. What he knew about it. Apparently, it was a coring outpost and the crew up there got a little shack happy. Started seeing ghosts and killing themselves.

Paleodoc: any survivors?

Sharkey: None that were sane. They flew them out. The station was called Vradaz Outpost and it's been deserted since the trouble, over twenty years now.

Paleodoc: did he say what the nature of the trouble was?

Sharkey: Just the usual haunted house stuff. Apparitions and sounds. Knockings and rappings. Things of that nature. Is any of that important?

Paleodoc: how did the lake project make out?

Sharkey: The cryobot was a success. Hayes was there when they released the hydrobot. They found a city down there. A gigantic city on the lake bed.

Paleodoc: still there then? I thought it might be

Sharkey: You knew about it?

Paleodoc: I've been studying the pictographs up in the city they tell some pretty wild tales if I'm reading them right think I am there was something I interpreted as a mass exodus down into the lake when the glaciers began to move in

Sharkey: Hayes saw them, Dr. Gates, from the hydrobot's feed. There were hundreds if not thousands of those Old Ones still living down there. They were swarming. They lost contact with the hydrobot about that time.

Paleodoc: yes, I imagine they did

Sharkey: what does it all mean?

Paleodoc: I'm not sure just yet but soon the fact that they're still alive down there is bad though if I'm reading these gylphs correctly the old ones have plans for us they want to exploit us

Sharkey: Are they terrestrial? Can you tell me that?

Paleodoc: no, I don't see how they could be there are evidences in the glyphs etchings on the walls of our star system and others I'm reading it to be evidence of interplanetary and possibly inter-stellar travel I believe these things existed as a race long before our planet cooled I'm guessing if we could visit mars and the outer planets we'd find evidence of their colonization they've been with us since the beginning

Sharkey: Can you be more specific about that?

Paleodoc: the winged devils elaine they've been with us since the beginning all our tales of winged demons and devils have a single source do you follow

Sharkey: What do they want?

Paleodoc: I can't be sure but I believe they've been waiting many millions of years for us to find them.

Sharkey: Why?

Paleodoc: listen to me elaine these things are dangerous in ways I can't even tell you I believe they have seeded hundreds of worlds in the galaxy with life and directed the evolution of that life they have an agenda and I believe it is the subjugation of the races they developed

Sharkey: We've had two deaths here.

Paleodoc: you'll have more they will harvest certain minds and crush the others listen to me elaine I think you should get out of there get in the snocat and make for vostok station you are in danger

Sharkey: You had better come down first.

Paleodoc: can't too much to do up here too many clues to fol-low up on if I or others return watch us close very close some-thing not right with Holm I think they have his mind now they want mine and yours too elaine get out get out while you can

  Sharkey did everything she could do to bring Gates back up, but he was gone. He had gone off-line according to her messenger. Finally, she gave up and shut her computer down and was forced to look at those two dour faces.

Cutchen spoke first. "Well," he said. "Well . . . either our good Doctor Gates has lost his mind or we're in terrible danger."

"I don't believe he's lost his mind," Sharkey said, but would not elaborate on it. "I don't believe that at all."

"Neither do I," Hayes said. He looked over at Cutchen. "I don't think you do either. What Gates said . . . what he's been reading from those hieroglyphs or whatever he found in that old city . . . it's nothing I haven't suspected or felt. A lot of us have been dreaming crazy shit and feeling worse things, but none of it really made sense. We all maybe connected it up with those mummies out there, but was that because we were sure they were the culprit or because we were scared and we needed a scapegoat, a witch to burn? But now –"

"You left out something," Cutchen said. "Gates' little chat the night before he left. People were feeling funny about those fossils of his and Lind's nervous breakdown, but the things he said to us in the community room were pretty wild. I don't think there's a one of us who didn't come out of that with an inflamed imagination."

"Sure. I'll admit to that. But it's more than imagination, Cutchy, let's get fucking real here. We didn't imagine the dreams or Lind's nervous breakdown or Meiner and St. Ours having their brains boiled to jelly. There's a common cause for these happenings and it's right out in Hut Six, like it or not. Because those things are not dead the way we know dead, their minds are still active and maybe that has something to do with the *living* ones down in the lake, I don't know, but Gates is right: we're in terrible danger here. You heard what he said. Those things . . . they've been waiting for us down here, they want to use us. They have plans for us."

"It's pretty wild shit, Hayes," was all Cutchen would say and yet, just behind his eyes, you could see an acceptance of it all.

"Sure, it's the wildest thing in our history, without a doubt." There was a big NO SMOKING sign on the wall and Hayes lit up anyway, completely carried away by what he was saying and maybe just happy to be letting it all out of his head. "Imagine them, Cutchy. Try and imagine a race like theirs that is so fucking patient they can wait for us millions of years. And so intelligent, they know that sooner or later, we'll come down here because we have to."

"How could they know that?"

"You saw what Gates said . . . other worlds, other stars . . . God only knows how many times they've watched beings like us evolve until they reached a state where they might be useful to them. No, Gates is right. They *knew* we'd come. It's our nature to come down here and they were completely aware of the fact. They're ancient and they know things we'll never know. Who knows how many races like ours they've cultivated?"

"You make me feel like a potato," Cutchen said.

"To them, you're not much more," Sharkey said.

Hayes didn't say anything for a time. Maybe he was afraid of *what* he might say if he opened his mouth. "Rats in a maze, that's what we are. Just rats running the maze," he said finally, laughing at something he didn't seem to find very funny at all. "It's perfect, isn't it? We're trapped down here and they know it. It's exactly what they wanted. It's been some time, I think, since they've had an ample opportunity to pick away at human minds. But now here we are and here they are. This camp is a great living laboratory and they've got months to do whatever it is they want to do."

"Which is?" Cutchen said

Hayes swallowed. "To harvest our minds."

PART FOUR

THE HAUNTED
AND THE POSSESSED

"The nethermost caverns . . . are not for the fathoming of eyes that see; for their marvels are strange and terrific. Cursed the ground where dead thoughts live new and oddly bodied, and evil the mind that is held by no head."

— H.P. Lovecraft

26

fter he got out of the infirmary, it began to occur to Hayes just how apt his rats in a maze analogy was. It was so apt that he wanted to run screaming out of the compound . . . except, of course, there was nowhere really to run *to*. He kept imagining the lot of them there like microbes on a slide while some huge, horrible eye peered down on them gauging their reactions. It was very unsettling.

So, since he couldn't run, he did the next best thing: he got rid of some snow.

It was something Biggs and Stotts generally did, but after what happened to St. Ours and what they had seen . . . or not . . . they weren't in much shape to do much but hide in their rooms. Rutkowski was doing the same. None of them were as bad off as Lind, but they'd been broken on some essential level.

So Hayes decided he would pick up the slack.

The snow blower they used to keep the walkways clear was basically a big garden tractor with a blower attachment on it and a little cab that kept the wind off you. Hayes was tucked down in his heated ECW's, so the cold that was hovering around sixty below wasn't bothering him. The night was black and blowing, broken only by the security lights of the buildings themselves. Hayes moved the tractor along at a slow clip, clearing the walkways that led from Targa House to the drill tower and power station. The secondary paths that connected them with the numerous garages and outbuildings and huts, some of which held equipment and some of which had become makeshift labs. He banked the snow up against the walls of the buildings to help keep them insulated and most, by that point in the long winter, no longer had walls as such, just drifts of snow that sloped from the roofs to the hardpack on the ground. Doorways were cut and windows kept clear, beyond that everything looked like igloos.

He cleared a path to the meteorology dome — Cutchen would appreciate that — and tried to sort out what was in his head. The things Gates had said were exactly the sorts of things Hayes did not want to hear. Just affirmations that all the crazy shit he'd been thinking and feeling were not out and out bullshit, but fact. That was hard to take.

But, then again, everything down here this year was hard to take.

There was so much ugliness, it was hard to take it all in, keep it down. Sharkey said that Lind was getting no better. He no longer was any danger as such and didn't need to be restrained, but he did need to be watched. She said she considered him to be clinically depressed now. He wouldn't leave the little sick bay. He sat in there and watched TV, most of which was routed through American Forces Antarctic Network-McMurdo. Sometimes he read magazines. But most of the time he just sat on his cot with his head cocked to the side like a puppy listening for his master's approach.

And maybe that's exactly what he's doing, Hayes thought.

And maybe it was what they were all doing without realizing it. Waiting and waiting. Because, when he thought about it, didn't that seem almost right? That maybe what he'd been feeling since he stepped onto the frozen crust of Kharkhov Station was a sense of expectancy? Sure, underlying dread and fear and rampant nerves, but mostly expectancy. Like maybe somehow, some way, he'd known what was coming, that they were going to make contact with *something.*

Sounded like some pretty ripe bullshit when you actually thought about it, framed it into words, but it almost seemed to fit. And maybe, when you got down to it, there was no true way of knowing what was going on in that great soundless vacuum of the human psyche and its subcellar, the subconscious mind. There were things there, imperatives and memories and scenarios, you just didn't want to know about. In fact, you –

Jesus, what in the hell was that?

Hayes stopped the tractor dead.

Terror punched into him like a poison dart. He was breathing hard, thinking things and not wanting to think them at all. He swallowed. Swallowed again. He thought . . . Christ, he was almost sure he had seen something over near Hut #6, something the tractor lights splashed over for just an instant. Looked like some shape, some figure pulling away, moving off into the darkness. And it wasn't a human shape. He peered through the clear plastic shield of the cab. Didn't see anything now and maybe he hadn't in the first place.

Fuck that horse, there was something there. I know something was there.

But whatever it had been, it was gone now.

Hayes sat there for a few more minutes and then started throwing snow again. A storm was on them and the snow was flying thick as goose down, filling the shaking security lights of the compound with white clots that seemed busy as static on a TV screen. Snow was drifting and whipping, powdering the cab of the tractor like sand. The wind and blackness were sculpting it into huge, flying shapes that danced through the night.

Hayes stopped the tractor again.

That wind was funny, the way it howled and screamed and then dropped off to a steady buzzing whisper. You listened long enough, you started not only seeing things, but hearing voices . . . sweet, seductive voices that were pulled out long and hollow by the wind. The voices of women and lovers lost to time. Voices that wanted you to run off out into those bleak, frozen plains where you could lose yourself forever and maybe, just maybe, you wouldn't mind being lost, those blizzard winds wrapping you up tight and cooing in your ear until it was just too late. And by then, you would recognize the voice of the wind for what it was: death. Lonely, hungry death and maybe something else, maybe something diabolic and secret that was older than death.

Stop it for the life of Pete, Hayes warned himself.

But it could get to you, the wind and the snow and perpetual night. So many men had gone glaring mad with it that the medicos had coined a term to explain something that was perhaps not explainable at all: *Dementia Antarctica.* They saw it as a disease born of loneliness and isolation and maybe they were half right, but the ugly and bitter truth was that it was also a condition of the soul and its dark, destructive poetry that seemed to cry in your head: *I am your soul and I am beautiful, I am a lover's sonnet and silver rain, now destroy me . . . if you love me, destroy me and yourself, too.*

Hayes figured if he kept up like this, he would run off into the silent devastation of the polar night. So he put his mind on other things, things he could get his hands on and wrap his brain around, make work for him. And what he started to think about was not something you could really touch or ever know: the city. That great sunken, cyclopean city which lay dreaming on the bottom of Lake Vordog. Sheathed in weeds and morbid aquatic growths, time and madness, it was like some grotesque and moss-covered alien skeleton down there.

Remembering it now, it seemed like seeing it had been some nightmare, but Hayes had seen it all right and it had seen him. At the time he had not been able to truly understand the way it made him feel, it was just too shocking and overwhelming, but now he thought he understood: that city was taboo, shunned. He . . . and all men, he supposed . . . retained a vestigal memory of the place. It was some awful archetype electroplated onto the human soul from the race's infancy that would later re-channel itself as haunted houses and cursed castles and the like. Evil places. Places of malignancy and disembodied horror. Maybe something about the angles and the sense of desertion, but it had persisted and it always would, that memory. The first true dream of supernal terror humankind had known.

Here again, Hayes was thinking things he had no right to think. Maybe it was like Cutchen said, maybe part of it was Gates' disturbing little talk coupled with all the badness those mummies emanated. But he honestly thought it was something more. He truly believed that the Old Ones and their phantasmal, eldritch city were locked down in the minds of all men in the form of primal memory.

We interacted with those things, he found himself thinking, *in our distant past. We must have. And probably not out of choice. That's the only thing that can explain our instinctual terror of them and that nameless city . . .*

Without realizing it, Hayes had stopped the tractor.

Most of the job was done, but with that blizzard pounding down on them, he could pretty much start again for already the walkways were drifting over. But the thing was, he had stopped the tractor on its way to Hut #6 and he did not know why. He just sat there, feeling cold and hot, looking around desperately for the reason and not coming up with a thing. The night was alive with viscid shadows and creeping shapes and the wind was full of voices. He could hear them calling to him through that blowing white death: *There's no hurry, Jimmy. You just sit tight and wait and all will be revealed to you. Because you're waiting for something as you've been waiting from day one and maybe all your life and that something is coming, Jimmy. It's coming out of the darkness of the polar graveyard and, like a chameleon, it's about to show itself . . .*

And then it did.

About the time he was ready to call himself a fucking lunatic, it did.

But before he saw it, he heard it.

Heard that weird, high musical piping that he knew was a voice. Heard it in his head and outside the cab, and in the pit of his mind he remembered that voice as one of authority, as the voice of a master and such was its dominance, he did not dare try to get away from it. He could feel the ice of Antarctica breathing in his belly, sending out breaths of frost that shut him down and made him watch.

Then he saw it.

It came drifting out of the shadows, a ghostly alien form with outspread wings and trembling tentacles and leering red eyes that opened up his brain like a tin can and reached in there with cold fingers. He screamed, he supposed he screamed, for something came ripping out of him that slapped him sure and hard across the face.

The thing came closer and Hayes pressed down on the accelerator of the tractor, those chained balloon tires catching and vaulting Hayes forward and right at the thing. And he felt something snap in his brain like a tree branch and the pain was immense. But then the tractor rammed into that thing and it broke apart into a thousand luminous fragments.

Then he was alone.

And the wind was just the wind and the snow was just the snow.

But in his mind, there were shadows. Ancient shadows that called him by name.

27

There were things in life that could destroy you an inch at a time. Booze, drugs, depression, tobacco. Hayes knew all about the tobacco-thing, because he'd been smoking for nearly thirty years now. So he knew that one and understood it and realized like anyone else that you lost a minute or five or whatever it was every time you lit up.

But he never saw it that way.

He looked on it by the months and years. That he was buying himself a plot of cemetery earth, shovelful by shovelful. But it didn't stop him and it didn't slow him down. The nicotine had him and it was a pure and senseless thing that was more than just a simple physical addiction, but something destructive in the soul that saw its own end and welcomed it.

So, he understood there were things that took your life slowly. But there were also things that ate away your life in big chunks, in heaping spoonfuls. And what was laying on the cot in the sick bay the next morning was definitely one of them.

Lind.

Or maybe not Lind at all.

Sharkey had him strapped down and he was sweating and feverish and his skin was bubbling like hot fat. Actually *bubbling*. You could say in your mind that they were blood blisters or water blisters, but that didn't cut it and you knew it. Just as Hayes knew it. What he was looking at, what Lind had become, was something akin to the little girl in that old scary movie. The one who puked up green slime and had the Devil in her.

"What the hell's wrong with him?" Hayes asked.

"You tell me," Sharkey said. "I can't explain the lesions any more than I can really explain his state of mind. I would guess this is something psychosomatic, but –"

"Yes?"

"But to this degree? This is out of my league, Jimmy."

She had wisely shut the door now to the sick bay and the outer door to the infirmary itself. Lind was just laying there, staring up at the ceiling, his mouth opening and closing. He was making a gulping sound in his throat like a beached fish.

Hayes swallowed down whatever was in him that made him want to turn and run. He swallowed it down and went over to Lind. He looked terrible. His flesh was white as a toad's belly and the oddest smell was coming off him . . . a sharp chemical odor like turpentine.

"Lind? Can you hear me? It's Hayes."

The eyes blinked, the pupils hugely dilated, but nothing else. There was no sense of recognition. Anything. Lind's mouth snapped close and then his lips parted slowly. The voice that came out was windy and echoing, unearthly . . . almost like Lind was speaking from the bottom of a very deep well. "Hayes . . . *Jimmy* . . . oh, Christ, help me Jimmy, don't let them . . . ."

He stopped, making that gulping noise again. Although he was restrained, his hands were flopping madly about, looking for something to grasp. Horrified as he was by all of it, Hayes was seeing another human being in a terrible plight and he put his hand in Lind's own. He almost immediately pulled away . . . touching Lind was like laying your hands on an electric cow fence. Hayes could feel the energy, the electricity thrumming through the man. It seemed to be moving in waves and he could feel it crawling over the back of his hand.

Lind took a deep breath and that energy died away. Thankfully.

Now all Hayes was aware of was the actual *feel* of Lind's flesh against his own. It was hot and moist and repulsive. Like handling some reptilian fetus that had been expelled from its mother's womb in a breath of fevers. Lind's hand was like that . . . smooth, warm, sweating toxins and bile. It took everything Hayes had in him not to pull away.

"Lind . . . c'mon, old buddy, you can't go on like this, you –"

"I can hear you, Jimmy, but I can't see you, I can't see anything but this place, this awful place . . . oh, where am I, where am I?"

That voice was making a rushing, hollow sound that human lungs were simply incapable of. Hayes couldn't get past the notion that it was coming from very far away. It sounded like it was being accelerated across great distances.

Hayes looked over at Sharkey and she chewed her lip.

"You're in the infirmary, Lind."

Lind's hand played in his own, felt pliant like warm clay, something that might melt away from body heat. "I can't see you, Jimmy . . . Jesus Christ, *but I can't fucking see you,*" he whimpered. "I . . . I can't see the infirmary either . . . I see . . . oh I see . . . "

"What do you see?" Hayes asked him, thinking it might be important. "Tell me."

Lind just lay there, staring holes through the ceiling. "I see, I see . . . " He began to thrash, a wet and tortured scream coming from his mouth. And it almost seemed more like a shout of surprise or terror. "The sea . . . there's only the sea . . . that big, big sea . . . the steaming, boiling sea . . . and the sky above . . . misty, misty. It's . . . it's not blue anymore . . . it's green, Jimmy, shimmering and glowing and full of sparkling mist. Do you smell it? That bad air . . . like bleach, like ammonia." He started to gag and cough, moving in boneless gyrations like a snake, sweat rolling down his blistered face. He was madly gulping air. "Can't . . . breathe . . . *I can't fucking breathe, Jimmy, I can't fucking breathe!*"

Hayes held onto him, trying to talk him down. "Yes, you can, Lind! You're not really there, only your eyes are there! Only your eyes!"

Lind calmed a bit, but kept gulping air. His eyes were huge and filled with tears and madness. His breath smelled unnatural, like creosote.

"Take it easy now," Hayes told him. "Now just relax and tell me what you see. I'll help you find your way out."

And Hayes figured maybe he could, if he could find out just where the hell this place *was.* Sharkey was watching him, neither approving nor disapproving of what he was doing. Just standing by with a hypo if it came to that.

"It's hot, Jimmy, it's hot here . . . everything is smoking and misting and those, those great jagged sheets of glass . . . sheets of broken glass rising up from the sea and shattering into light . . . that green, green, green sky . . . purple clouds and pink clouds and shadows . . . those shadows coil like snakes, look how they do that . . . do you see? Do you see? Shadows with . . . veins, veins . . . living shadows in the green misting sky . . . "

"Yes," Hayes said. "I see them. They can't hurt us, though."

"I'm sinking, Jimmy, don't let me go, *don't let me go down there!* I'm sinking down into the sea and the water is warm, so very warm and thick . . . like jelly . . . how can it feel like that? The depths, oh those glittering emerald depths. The sea lights itself up and it shows you things . . . and . . . and *I'm not alone, Jimmy.* There are others here, many others. Do you see them? They swim with me . . . swimming and gliding and rising and falling. Yes, yes! Them things, them things like in the hut . . . but alive, all of them alive, gathering at the city!"

It could have been the city beneath Lake Vordog, but Hayes seriously doubted it by that point. Wherever this was, it was no place man had ever trod. Some awful, alien world with a poison atmosphere. And the crazy thing was, although Hayes could not see it and was glad of the fact, he could *feel* it. He could feel the heat of the place, that thick and turgid heat. Sweat was running down his face and the air was suddenly close and gagging, like trying to suck air through a hot oven mitt.

Jesus.

Hayes was nearly swooning now.

He could see the heat and it was coming from Lind, rolling off him like shimmering heat waves from August pavement. Hayes looked over at Sharkey and, yes, her face was beaded with sweat. It was incredible, but it was happening.

Lind was like some weird portal, some doorway to those seething alien wastes. He was there, his mind was there, and he was bringing some of it back with him. Because now it was more than just the heat, it was the smell, too. Hayes was gagging, coughing, his head reeling, the room saturated with an unbearable stench of ammoniated ice. Steam was rising from Lind now and bringing the smell of that toxic atmosphere with him. It reminded Hayes of wash day back home when he was a kid. That eye-watering, nose-burning stink of Hilex bleach.

Sharkey wisely opened the door to the infirmary and started a fan going. It cleared the air a bit, at least enough where Hayes wasn't ready to pass out.

Lind was talking on through it all: " . . . seeing it, Jimmy? You seeing it? Oh, that's a city, a gigantic city . . . a floating city . . . look how it bobs and sways? How can it do that? All them high towers and deep holes, honeycombs . . . like bee honeycombs, all them cells and chambers . . . "

"Are you still with them, Lind? Those others?"

Lind chattered his teeth, shook his head. "No, no, no . . . I'm not me anymore, Jimmy, *I'm one of them!* One of them spreading my wings and swimming and diving through those pink honeycombs and knowing what they think like they know what I think . . . we . . . we're going to . . . *yes!* That's the plan, isn't it? That's always, always, always been the plan . . . "

"What's the plan?" Hayes asked. "Tell me the plan, Lind."

But Lind was just shaking his head, a funny light in his eyes now like a reflection from a mirror. "We're rising now . . . the hive is rising now . . . through the water and ice into the green glowing sky . . . thousands of us into the sky on buzzing wings, thousands and thousands of wings. We are the hive and the hive is us. We are the swarm, the ancient swarm that fills the skies . . . "

"Where are you going?"

"Above, up and up and up into them clouds and thickness, sure, that's where we go . . . up beyond into the cold and blackness and empty spaces. The long, hollow spaces, long, long . . . "

"Where are you going? Can you see where you are going?"

Lind's breathing had slowed now to barely a rustle. His eyes were glazed and sleepy and lost. The air in the room no longer stank like bleach. It was cold, very cold suddenly. The temperature plummeting until a bone-deep chill settled into Hayes. Sharkey killed the fan and cranked the heat up, but it was barely keeping an edge on that glacial cold. Hayes could see his breath coming out in frosty plumes.

"There are winds," Lind said in a squeaky whisper. "We drift on the winds that carry the hive and we dream together . . . we all dream together through the long, black night that goes on and on and on . . . nothingness . . . emptiness . . . only the long, empty blackness . . . "

Lind stopped talking. In fact, his eyes drifted shut and it seemed he had gone out cold. He was sleeping very peacefully. He stayed that way for ten or fifteen minutes while Hayes and Sharkey could do nothing but wait. About the time Hayes decided to pull his hand free, Lind gripped it and his eyes came open.

HIVE

"The world . . . the blue world . . . the empty blue world . . . this is where we come, this is where the hive goes now. Oceans, great oceans . . . black, blasted lands . . . mountains and valleys and yellow mist."

Hayes knew where they were now. They could be nowhere else. "Is there anything alive there, Lind? Is there any life?"

But Lind was shaking his head back and forth. "Dead . . . dead . . . nothing. But the hive, the hive can seed it . . . create organic molecules and proteins and the helix, we are the makers of the helix . . . *we are the farmers, we seed and then we harvest. The primal white jelly . . . the architect of life . . . we are and have always been the farmers of the helix, the hive mind, the great white space, the thought and the being and the structure and . . . the helix . . . the perpetuation of the helix, the surety and plan and the conquest and the harvest . . . the makers and unmakers . . . the cosmic lord of the helix . . . the continuation of the code the helix the code vessels of flesh exist to perpetuate the helix only exist to perpetuate and renew the helix the spiral of being . . . the primal white jelly . . . the color out of space . . .* "

Hayes tried to pull away now, because something was happening.

Lind's eyes were now black and soulless and malevolent, filled with a dire alien malignancy. They were black and oily, yet shining brightly like tensor lamps. They found Hayes and held him. And those eyes, those bleeding alien cancers, they did not just look through him, they looked straight into the center of his being, his soul, coldly appraising what they found there and contemplating how it could be crushed and contained and converted into something else. Something not human, something barren and blank, something that was part of the hive.

Hayes screamed . . . feeling *them,* those ancient minds coming at him like a million yellowjacket wasps in a wind tunnel, punching through him and melting away his soul and individuality, making him part of the greater hole, the swarm, the swarm-mind. He tried vainly to pull his hand out of Lind's grasp, but his muscles had gone to rubber and his bones were elastic. And Lind was like some incredible generator, arcing and crackling, electric flows of energy dancing over his skin in pale blue eddies and whirlpools.

And that energy was kinetic. It had motion and direction.

The glass face of a clock on the wall shattered like a hammer had struck it. Papers and pencils and folders were scattered from Sharkey's desk and blown through the air in a wild, ripping cyclone. Shelves were emptied of bottles and instruments and the floor was vibrating, the walls pounding like the beat of some incredible heart. The infirmary and sickbay were a tempest of anti-gravity, things spinning and jumping and whirling in mid-air, but never falling. Sharkey was thrown against the wall and then to the floor where she was pushed by a wave of invisible force right against the door leading out into the corridor. That awful vibration was thrumming and thrumming, the air filled with weird squeals and echoes and pinging sounds. Hayes lost gravity . . . he was lifted up into the air, Lind still clutching his hand, tethering him to the world. Cracks fanned out in the wall, ceiling tiles broke loose and went madly spinning through the vortex and then –

And then Lind sat up.

The straps holding him down sheared open, wavering and snapping about like confetti in a tornado. His face was contorted and bulging, tears of blood running from his eyes and nose. He seized up, went rigid, and then collapsed back on the bed.

Everything stopped.

All those papers and pens and vials of pills and drugs and books and charts and paperclips . . . all of it suddenly crashed to the floor and Hayes with it. He sat there on his ass, stunned and shocked and not sure where he was for a moment or what he was doing. Sharkey was pulling herself up the wall, trying to speak and only making weird grunting sounds. The force of that wind, or whatever in the Christ it had been, had actually blown the tight pony tail ring from her hair and her locks hung over her face in wild plaits. She brushed them away.

Then she was helping Hayes up. "Are you okay, Jimmy?"

He nodded dumbly. "Yeah . . . I don't even know what happened."

Sharkey went to Lind. She pulled open one of his eyelids, checked his pulse. She picked her stethoscope up from where it was dangling from the top of the door. She listened for Lind's heart, shook her head. "Dead," she said. "He's dead."

Hayes was not surprised.

He looked down at Lind and knew that if the man's heart had not given out or his brain exploded in his head, if whatever had not killed him, then both Sharkey and himself would probably be dead now. That energy had been lethal and wild and destructive.

"Elaine," he said. "Should we . . . "

"Let's just clean this mess up."

So they did.

They had barely begun when people were coming down the corridor, demanding to know what all the racket had been and why the goddamn infirmary smelled like bleach or chemicals. But then they saw Lind and they didn't ask any more questions. They politely tucked their tails between their legs and got out while the getting was good.

After they had put things back in order and swept up the rest, Hayes and Sharkey sat down and she got out a bottle of wine she'd been saving. It was expensive stuff and they drank it from plastic Dixie cups.

"How am I going to log this one?" Sharkey said. "That Lind was possessed? That he exhibited telepathy and telekinesis? That something had taken over his mind and it was something extraterrestrial? Or should I just say that he died from some unexplainable dementia?"

Hayes sighed. "He wasn't possessed or insane. At least, not at first. He was in *contact* with them somehow, with those dreaming minds out in the hut or maybe the living ones down in the lake. Probably the former, I'm guessing." Hayes lit a cigarette and his hand shook. "What he was telling us, Doc, was a memory. A memory of an alien world where those Old Ones had come from . . . it was a memory of colonization. Of them leaving that planet and drifting here through space, I think."

"Drifting through space?" she said. "It must have taken ages, eons."

"Time means nothing to them."

Sharkey just shook her head. "Jimmy . . . that's pretty wild."

He knew it was, but he believed it. Completely. "You have a better explanation? I didn't think so. You felt the heat, smelled that ammonia . . . it was probably one of the outer planets they came from. Maybe not originally, but that was their starting point when they came here. Jesus, they must have drifted for thousands of years, dormant and dreaming, waiting to come here, to this blue world."

"But the outer planets . . . Uranus, Neptune . . . they're cold, aren't they?" she said. "Even a billion years ago, they would have been ice cold . . . "

Hayes pulled off his cigarette. "No, not at all. I'm no scientist, Doc, but I've been hanging around with them for years . . . I knew this one astronomer at McMurdo. We used to hang out at the observatory and he'd tell me things about the planets, the stars. Neptune and Uranus, for example, because of their size have immense atmospheric pressures, so the liquid on them can't freeze or turn to vapor, it's held in liquid form in massive seas of water, methane, and ammonia."

"All right," Sharkey said. "But for them to drift here . . . you have any idea how long that would take?"

"Again, time only means something to creatures like you and me with finite life spans and I think the Old Ones are nearly immortal. They'd have to be. Sure, they may die by accident or design, but not from old age. No, Doc, they *drifted* here like pollen on the wind."

Hayes said he figured it was how they worked. Maybe drifting from one star system to the next, something that probably took millions of years. Then establishing themselves on worlds, hopping from planet to planet, seeding them with life.

Sharkey didn't want to believe any of it, but slowly the logic of it took hold of her despite herself. "Yes . . . I suppose that's how it must've been. It's just incredible, is all."

"Of course it is."

"You heard what Lind said? That business about the helix and organic molecules, proteins . . . the conquest and the harvest . . . the perpetuation of the helix?"

"I heard."

"And . . . "

"They created life here, they are the engineers of our DNA," Hayes said. "They created it. Maybe out of themselves or from scratch, who knows? Jesus, this is outrageous. This is really going to throw the creationists firmly on their ass. So much for religion."

"So much for everything."

"I guess we've seen the face of God down here," Hayes said. "And it's an ugly one."

Sharkey started laughing. Was having trouble stopping. "Gates . . . that's what Gates was saying. That they might have seeded hundreds of worlds, directed evolution, that their ultimate agenda was harvesting those minds they had created . . . "

And this was the very thing Hayes was having trouble with. "But why? What do they want with them? What could it be?"

"To bring them into the hive, subjugate them . . . who knows?" Sharkey swallowed. "Down in the lake . . . those things down there . . . they've been waiting for us all this time. Waiting to harvest what we are. Fucking Christ, Jimmy . . . the patience of those *monsters.*"

What Hayes was trying to figure out is why they took total possession of Lind like they had. He'd been in the hut that day with Lind and those mummies had freaked him out, made him feel bad inside, but they hadn't taken over his mind. Was it that Lind was just a sensitive of some sort? A natural receiver, a *medium* for lack of a better word?

And what about Meiner and St. Ours?

Those things had leeched their minds dry and destroyed their brains. And Hayes himself had been psychically attacked twice by the Old Ones . . . once in the hut alone and last night out on the tractor . . . why hadn't they killed him, too? Why did he have the strength to fight? And Sharkey? She had had the dreams, too, as they all had. What in the hell were those things saving them for? What was the ultimate plan here?

"You feel up to that drive I was talking about?" he asked her.

"Vradaz?"

He nodded. "I don't think we have much time left, Elaine. If we can learn something up there, maybe we might make it out of this yet."

"Okay," she said, but didn't sound too hopeful. "Jimmy? Lind said 'The Color Out of Space'. I've heard him say it before while he was heavily sedated. I thought it meant nothing . . . but I'm not so sure now. What is this *Color Out of Space?*"

"I don't know. Maybe it's the Old Ones themselves," he speculated. "And maybe it's something a lot worse."

28

"Tell me again why I'm doing this," Cutchen said.

"For the good of humanity," Hayes told him. "What more reason do you need?"

Maybe Cutchen needed some reassurance here, some encouragement, but Hayes didn't really have a lot to offer up in that department. Why were they going up to Vradaz Outpost, the abandoned Russian camp? Even he wasn't sure, not really. But something bad, something truly terrible had happened there and he felt it was important that they find out what. Maybe they'd find nothing but a snowed-in empty camp, but Hayes was thinking there had to be evidence of what came down. If even some of what Nikolai Kolich said was true, then the outpost had undergone pretty much the same sort of shit that Kharkhov Station was currently undergoing.

Hayes could remember very well what Kolich had said.

Vradaz was a summer post and they were coring, struck into a cave or chasm or something. Yes. Then . . . I remember things got funny after that.

And didn't that just sound familiar?

"Storm's picking up pretty good out there," Sharkey said.

Hayes worked the stick of the SnoCat, pressing in the clutch, and bringing it up to high gear as they came over a rise and moved across a barren ice plain. He figured they'd make Vradaz in thirty or forty minutes if the storm didn't swallow them alive. They were plunging through Condition Two weather, sheets of wind-driven snow blasting the SnoCat and making it tremble. It was dark out, of course, and the only lights came from the 'Cat itself. All you could see in the high beams was the white, uneven tundra broken occasionally by knobs of black rock and the swirling, blowing snow.

"You're not going to get us lost are you?" Cutchen said.

"No, I don't think so. I have a roll of kite twine on the back of the 'Cat and I tied the other end to Targa House." He glanced out his window at the huge rectangular mirror out there. "Shit . . . must have run out of string."

"Ha, ha, you so funny," Cutchen said.

"Relax. GPS knows the way and I took a bearing on Vradaz before we left. If we get lost, the beacon from Kharkhov will bring us back home."

"If worse comes to worse," Sharkey said, "we can gather up some wood and start a signal fire."

"Boy, you guys are good. I'll book you in Vegas when we get back . . . unless we don't get back." Cutchen thought about that a moment. "You think these Old Ones have much of a sense of humor, Hayes?"

"Yeah, I think they do. Look-it all the gags they've pulled on us. They're some really silly bastards, you get to know 'em."

The SnoCat began to jump and lurch as it passed over a field of sastrugi, frozen ridges of snow and ice that looked like waves heading ashore at a beach. Except these never moved and they were tough as granite. But the SnoCat handled them just fine, jarring and bouncing, but handling it better on its twin sets of caterpillar tracks than an ordinary wheeled vehicle would have.

Hayes swung the 'Cat around a glacial valley, the storm getting worse, beginning to howl and screech, filling its lungs full of frost and white death and letting it back out in a wild, whipping tempest. The cab of the 'Cat was warm even without their ECW's on, but outside? They wouldn't have lasted long. Hayes had followed the ice road that Gates and his people had flagged for some thirty miles before the GPS told him it was time to trail blaze. It was dangerous work on an Antarctic night, but he had plotted a course on the contour map so he didn't drive them into a fissure or crevice. It was lumpy and bumpy rolling over serrated ice ridges and steering around weathered black outcroppings of stone, but they were going to make it.

Hayes had already decided that.

He just wasn't giving much thought to whether or not they'd make it back again.

One heartbreak at a time.

The wastelands to either side were dead white with canopies of ice that jutted like mountain peaks. You caught them out of the glare of the lights and out of the corner of your eye, they looked like monuments and gravestones sometimes. The landscape became very hilly as they approached the Dominion Range, full of sudden gullies and ice-pilings, horns of wind-blasted rock rising up like church spires. Rough, dangerous country. The Dominion Range was located along the edge of the East Antarctic ice sheet, where the massive Beardmore and Mill Glaciers came together. Had it been daylight, Hayes knew, they would have been able to see the rugged cones of the Transantarctic Mountains rising before them.

The SnoCat plodded along, plowing through waist-high drift and over ridges of ice. The wind kept blowing and the snow kept pushing from the high elevations, threatening to bury them at times.

"Hey! You see that!" Cutchen said, almost choking on his words.

Sharkey tensed next to him and Hayes tried to swallow. "What? What did you see?"

"I . . . well, I saw a shape . . . I thought I saw a shape," Cutchen said. "Off to the right. It passed right by us . . . then I lost it in the snow."

"Probably some rocks," Sharkey pointed out.

"No, it was moving . . . I think it was moving away from us." Cutchen let that hang a moment, then added, "I thought I saw eyes reflected."

"Eyes?" Hayes said. "How many?"

Sharkey crossed her arms almost defiantly. "Stop it. Both of you."

"Just a shape," Cutchen said. "That's all."

Hayes was going to tell him he was crazy, that there was nothing moving out there but them, but the spit had dried up in his mouth. It felt like something was spinning a web at the base of his spine, a chill stealthily creeping up his back.

"It was probably nothing," Cutchen said like he was trying to convince himself of the fact.

Ten minutes passed while Hayes hoped they'd see nothing else. He checked the GPS. "Okay, we should be right on top of Vradaz . . . gotta be right in this area somewhere."

But it was dead winter in Antarctica, the perpetual night billowing and consuming like black satin. Hayes downshifted the 'Cat and cranked up the headlights, put the spots on. Shafts of light cut across the glacial plane, making it no more than twenty or thirty feet before they reflected back the blizzard. It looked and sounded like a sandstorm out there.

They kept going, Hayes bringing the 'Cat around in a loose circle, staying within the perimeters of the GPS field. Cutchen splayed the spots around. The snowfall died down a bit and they could see a huge ice barrier just beyond them that must have been seventy or eighty feet high.

"There," Cutchen said. "There's something over there."

He was right.

A cluster of irregular shapes thrust from the snow, right at the foot of the barrier. Hayes could see what might have been roofs, an aerial, the rusted sheet metal of a wall blown clean of drift. Much of it was lost beneath an ice fall. The glaciers were pushing that barrier down from the mountains, a few feet a year. Sooner or later, Vradaz Outpost would be crushed beneath it.

Hayes pulled the SnoCat in closer, pushing through the night. Waves of snow like breakers at sea were spread across what must have been the compound at one time, gathering here at the foot of the ice barrier.

"A few more weeks and the camp would have been buried," Cutchen said. "I think we should have waited."

Hayes pulled the 'Cat to a stop and killed the engine. Suddenly then, there was only that immense and eerie stillness, that ominous sense of desertion and lifelessness all abandoned camps seemed to have. The wind was blowing and that great ice barrier was cracking and popping.

They sat there in the cab, waiting, thinking.

Hayes didn't know about the others, but the sight of Vradaz entombed in snow and ice made something in his belly stir like gravy. There was a tenseness to his limbs, a tightening of his ligaments and a quickness to his pulse. He found himself involuntarily reaching out for Sharkey's hand just as she reached for his and for Cutchen's. And there they sat, in that windy darkness, listening to the snow glance off the windshield and pepper the sides of the SnoCat. Nobody was moving. They were barely breathing.

Like standing outside a haunted house on a chill October night, Hayes found himself thinking. *Listening to the leaves blow and the shutters creak and wondering if we have the balls to see this through.*

"Okay, I've had enough," Cutchen said. "Either we do this or turn around. I say we turn around. The brochure clearly said this place had a pool. I don't see any pool."

Hayes broke his grip with Sharkey's gloved hands. "I suppose we can't sit here like this being all girly."

He opened his door and the cold blasted in.

And outside, the snow piled up and the wind screeched their names.

Well, it was no easy bit getting into the Vradaz Outpost.

It was a small camp, but the buildings — those that weren't crushed beneath the ice barrier — were pretty much drifted from roof to ground. Hayes and his compatriots had to fight through snow that came up above their hips at times and then was blown clean five feet away. Hayes had brought lanterns, ice-axes, and shovels and they put them to good use. They chose a squat, central structure that appeared to be connected to the others and got to work. The sight of the place had filled them all with an unknown terror, but after thirty minutes spent shoveling and cutting their way through the heaped snow, that passed.

It was just a dead camp.

That was all it was and the exertion helped them see it. Their nerves were still sharpened, but Hayes figured that was only natural. Jesus, this was the South Pole at the dead of winter. Wind screaming and snow flying and the temperature hanging in at a steady fifty below. If their imaginations got a little worked up, it was to be expected.

When they found the door, it was sheathed in blue ice, buckled in its frame and Hayes had a mad desire to plow right through it with the SnoCat, but he didn't want to take the chance of destroying anything in there. Anything that might remain. So they took their turns chopping through the ice by lantern-light, the snow whipping and creating jumping, distorted shadows around them.

And then the door was free. One good kick and it fell in.

"You first," Cutchen said. "I'm the intellectual type . . . you're the brave, stupid type."

"Shit," Hayes said, ducking in through the doorway and turning on his flashlight, something pulling up inside of him as he entered the abandoned structure. There was a smell of age and dust and wreckage.

The place was made of wood and prefab metal like most of the buildings at the South Pole. Concrete didn't hold up too well with the abrasive wind and extreme temperature changes, it tended to flake away and crack wide open.

Looking around in there with his flashlight, Hayes was seeing debris everywhere like a cyclone went ripping through. The floor planking was ruptured, the roof sagging, great holes punched into the walls. Snow had drifted into the corners. He supposed the place was held mainly together by frost and ice. Seams of it necklaced the walls.

"Look," Sharkey said. "Even the back of the door."

"Jesus," Cutchen said.

There were crude crosses etched into just about any available surface. Hex signs, really, to ward off evil. You could almost breathe in the madness that must have overtaken the place. Those scientists losing their minds when their science could not explain what appeared to be some sort of malefic haunting . . . in their desperation they had turned to the oldest of apotropaics: the cross.

But it had failed them.

Hayes, Sharkey, and Cutchen stood there maybe five minutes, sucking in the memory of evil and insanity that seemed to ooze from those bowed, ice-slicked walls.

"Looks like a bomb went off in here," Cutchen finally said.

"Maybe one did."

They were in some sort of entry, what Hayes' mom had called a Mud Room back in Kansas. The sort of place you stowed your boots and coats and work clothes when you came in out of the fields. They passed through another doorway into a larger room. There were some old fuel oil barrels in there and a stove over in the corner. Everything else was in shambles . . . camp chairs overturned, video equipment shattered, papers spread in the dusting of snow. What looked like a desk had been reduced to kindling. A light fixture overhead was dangling by wires. The rungs of a red fireman's ladder against the wall were hung with icicles.

Sharkey was examining some of the papers with her lantern.

"Make anything of it?" Hayes asked her.

She dropped them. "My Cyrillic is a little rusty."

They passed into another room in which the ceiling was caved in, stalactites of ice hung down and pooled on the floor. The walls were charred and bowed. There was a lot of electronic equipment in there, most of it destroyed and locked in flows of ice.

"Looks like they had a fire," Cutchen said. "I wonder if it was an accident."

They kept going, moving down a short corridor past some cramped sleeping quarters and then into another room which had been a laboratory once. There was still equipment in there . . . microscopes and racks of test tubes, antique computers and file cabinets whose drawers had been yanked open and left that way. The floor was a down of broken glass and instruments and papers. Hayes found a couple drills and an electric saw they must have used to slice up their ice core samples. There was a small ell off the room with a handle like a freezer on it. Inside were the core samples themselves, dated and tagged.

Sharkey almost went on her ass on a flow of ice on the floor. "Look at this," she said, indicating a room just off the lab. The walls in there had great, blackened holes ripped into them through which you could see a maze of snow, ice, and lumber . . . the portion of the outpost crushed beneath the ice fall. There were a series of smaller holes drilled into the walls, too.

"Bullet holes," Hayes said. "And those bigger ones . . . "

"Grenades?" Cutchen said, panning his light over them.

Sharkey was on her hands and knees studying some ancient stains on the walls, others spread over some folders caught in the ice flow. "This . . . well, this could be blood. It sure looks like it. I guess it could be ink or tomato sauce or something."

Hayes felt something sink in him. *Yeah, and maybe the center of the universe has creamy white filling, but I don't think so. You were right the first time, Doc. That ain't the blood of tomatoes, it's the blood of people.*

"Must've had themselves a showdown here," Cutchen said. "Or a slaughter."

Hayes was wondering how much truth there was in what Kolich had told them. There was more to this mess than just men going mad and seeing ghosts and what not. You could almost feel the agony and suffering in the air. Those holes . . . there was no doubt about them. Somebody had opened up with an automatic weapon in here.

What had Kolich said?

A security force went up there, came back with the three and said the others were all dead.

Or been killed.

Hayes was picturing some security force, maybe something more along the lines of a hit squad coming in here and killing everyone. Saving those three others for interrogation or study. Whatever had happened it had been violent and harsh and ugly. The outpost had been under Soviet jurisdiction at the time. The Soviets knew how to handle little problems like hauntings and alien minds trying to take over their men.

"So what does it tell us?" Sharkey said.

Cutchen shook his head. "Nothing we want to know about."

There was a set of double doors against the far wall. They were encased in twining, thick roots of ice. Summer melt-water from the barrier that had frozen up come winter. Desks and furniture and battered file cabinets had been piled up against it. They had to use the ice-axes to free the wreckage.

"What do you suppose the point of this was?" Cutchen said.

Sharkey started hammering ice away from the doors. "Only two possibilities, isn't there? They were either trying to keep something in or something out."

Cutchen paused, resting his axe on the shoulder of his red parka. "I was thinking that and, you know, I wonder if certain doors shouldn't be opened."

"You scared?" Hayes asked him, because he knew he was.

Cutchen tittered. "I don't know the meaning of the word. Still . . . I think I might have left my electric blanket on. Maybe I should pop back to camp, come back for you two wide-eyed intrepids later on."

"Chop," Sharkey told him.

But it was really getting them nowhere, for the ice had puddled beneath the door and locked it tight as a bank vault. Hayes dashed out to the 'Cat and came back with a propane torch. He ran the flame along the bottom of the door until it loosened. Then he hit the hinges and the seam where the two doors came together.

"Okay," he said.

Cutchen looked from one to the other, then pushed his way through, stepping out into a larger room that held a variety of equipment, mostly portable ice drills, corers, and air tools. The far wall was collapsed and a foot of snow had blown over the floor.

"Looks harmless enough," Cutchen said. "You two coming in or —"

There was an instantaneous cracking and ripping sound and Cutchen let out a cry and disappeared from view. They heard him land below, swearing and calling the Russians everything but white Christians.

Hayes and Sharkey crept forward. They put their lights down there and saw Cutchen sitting in a drift of snow, a gleaming wall of blue ice behind him.

"Are you all right?" Sharkey asked him.

"Peachy. Why do you ask?"

Hayes went for the ladder they'd seen when they first came in. Sharkey stayed there, hanging her lantern over the edge of the hole. "Looks pretty big down there. Must have been their cold storage," she said. "I bet you stepped on the trap door."

"Do you really think so?"

Cutchen dug his flashlight out of the snow, stood up, slipped and dropped it farther away. He cursed under his breath and dug it out from a drift. "Hey, what the hell?" he said, down on his knees, digging through the snow. He was uncovering something with mittened hands, brushing a dusting of white away from it.

"What is it?" Sharkey said from above.

"I'm not sure," Cutchen said, his voice echoing out in the cavernous hollows below. "Looks like a . . . oh Jesus, yuck." He stumbled away from whatever it was, breathing hard. "Where's that goddamn ladder? Tell your boyfriend to hurry."

"What?" Sharkey said.

Cutchen put his light on it.

Even from where she was, Sharkey could see it just fine. It was sculpted in ice, but there was no doubt what it was: a human death mask. A face peeled down nearly to the skull beneath and frosted white.

Cutchen wasn't liking it much. "I'm hoping this is just evidence of a Halloween party that got out of hand."

He stepped away from that leering, hollow-eyed face and made it maybe two or three steps and cried out. His leg had sank nearly up to the knee. His flashlight took another ride, this time landing about ten feet away, just under the trapdoor. It spun in circles, casting a magic lantern show of vast and twisted shadows over the ice walls. Cutchen went down on his hands and knees, struggling away from whatever he'd gotten himself stuck in. His knee sank once and his hand dropped down a foot another time. But he got out of there.

Whatever it was he'd been on . . . it was not made for walking.

Hayes came back with the ladder, banging it into walls and getting it hung up on the door. He saw the look on Sharkey's face, said, "What? What now?"

"Never mind, Rapunzel," Cutchen said, an odd edge to his voice. "Let down you fucking hair already."

Hayes fed it down into the hole and he'd barely gotten it balanced before Cutchen came scrambling up it like a monkey up grapevine. His foot slipped once and he banged his chin, but he never slowed down. He lay in the snow on his back, breathing hard, looking like he'd been inflated in his bulky ECW's.

"I found out where they keep the Halloween decorations," he said to Hayes.

Sharkey started down the ladder and Hayes went after her, taking the flashlights and leaving Cutchen the lantern.

The room they found themselves in was about twenty feet in width, maybe thirty in length. The floor was hard-packed snow and the walls were ice and you could clearly see the chopping and hacking marks in it. The Russians had cut it right down into the ice.

Hayes played his light around.

There were crates of food and barrels of gasoline along the walls. One barrel was tipped over and ruptured as if somebody had opened it with an axe. A small room off to the left held a small Honda gasoline-powered generator that was now hopelessly ruined, covered in frozen melt-water. Huge stalactites hung from the ceiling and Hayes had to duck under them. Some reached right to the floor.

Sharkey was on her hands and knees, brushing snow away from what Cutchen had found.

Hayes helped her.

It took some time, but before they were done they had uncovered a roughly circular pit filled with frozen cadavers. It looked like a winter scene from Treblinka: skulls with yawning jaws and hollowed orbits, jutting femurs and ulnas, the barrel staves of ribcages. He figured there were probably twenty bodies in there, all tangled in a central heap of limbs and skull-faces and spirals of vertebrae that were fused together in a pool of ice. Some had the rags of clothes wrapped around them and others went to their maker naked. They weren't exactly skeletons, but damn close. They all looked blackened and melted, knitted with sinew and wasted quilts of muscle.

And they'd all been shot.

Skulls had bullet holes in them. As did iliums and sternums and clavicles. Arm and leg bones were snapped. Jaws blasted away and pelvic wings shattered. No, this hadn't been a careful cleansing here, this had been a wild murder spree carried out with submachine guns and automatic rifles. These bodies had taken an incredible volume of fire and at close range.

Hayes just stood there, breathlessly, staring down into that bone pit and almost sensing the terror and madness that had brought an atrocity like this into being. He stepped back and away, having trouble being clinical about it all like Sharkey. To him, it looked like those cadavers were trying to crawl out of the ice. All those staring faces and reaching, cremated hands. Like something from a waxworks or a spookshow, but certainly nothing real.

He ducked away beneath the ceiling of icicles and saw another irregular shape in the snow. For some reason, it caught his eye. Motes of dust and crystals of ice hung in the air. His breath frosted from his lips in great clouds. Using his boot, he scattered the snow away from that shape beneath. He was looking down at a shriveled, conical form maybe six or seven feet long that had been incinerated right down to a husk. Looking now like something that had been pulled from an alien crematory.

Hayes knew what it was, of course.

He recognized that shape and it filled his belly with fluttering wings. Another one of those things. Probably chopped from the ice and then burned when they realized what it was doing to them. Or maybe the security force had burned it. Not that it mattered.

"You better come over here," he said to Sharkey, using a hush and quiet voice. The kind you used when you didn't want to wake an infant . . . or something sleeping in a coffin.

"What now?" Cutchen said from above. "Can you guys hurry this up? I'm . . . I'm starting to lose it up here."

Sharkey came over, saying, "Some of those bodies are wearing fatigues, Jimmy. Some of Kolich's security people must have went in there, too."

And Hayes didn't doubt it.

. . . a rash of insanity up there. Men killing each other and committing suicide . . . weird figures wandering through the compound that were not men . . . ghosts, bogies, I think . . . they spoke of devils and monsters, figures that walked through walls . . .

Yes, he could hear Nikolai Kolich saying it.

Except Kolich had left out the meat of the matter. These men at the outpost had drilled into a chasm, yes, but it hadn't been just any chasm, but maybe a burial chamber of the Old Ones. And opening it had been like cutting the scab off some primordial, invidious wound. And the pus that leaked out was infectious and evil, a wasting pestilence in the form of alien memories and undead essences, a decayed intelligence that was still virulent after all those uncounted eons, a spiritual contamination that took their minds one by one by one. Making them something less than human, something ageless and undying, a cosmic horror.

"Another one," Sharkey said. "Their tombs must be all over these mountains and rifts."

Hayes kicked it with his boot to prove to himself that it was dead. A piece of its leathery, burnt hide fell off like tree bark. It was hollow inside, that alien machinery boiled to ash. Even its ghost was dead now. Or what Hayes would have called a ghost, because nothing else seemed to fit. That diabolic power, the vestiges of those remorseless minds that seemed to cling on after death like a negative charge in a dry cell battery . . . just waiting to come into contact with living mental energies they could twist and subvert.

"You wanna guess what happened here?" Sharkey said.

"Oh, you know as well as I do. They dug up some of these ugly pricks and those minds woke up, became active. The Russians started having bad dreams and seeing ghosts and hearing things . . . and by the time they realized what was happening, they weren't even men anymore. Just . . . vessels for dead, alien minds that maybe wanted to fulfill some perverse plan set into motion millions of years ago." He put a cigarette in his lips and lit. "Then the people at Vostok got worried, so they sent in soldiers. Some of the soldiers got contaminated by those minds . . . but not enough. Those that weren't, killed everyone except those three Kolich mentioned, those drooling and insane things that had once been men. The soldiers burned the rest and the Old Ones, too."

"That's why they abandoned this camp, Jimmy. To stop the spread of the infection."

Cutchen said, "C'mon already, I . . . " He paused like his throat had seized up. "I'm hearing things up here, people. Sounds. I don't know . . . like things moving, sliding . . . "

Hayes walked over to the ladder.

He heard a thump up there, followed by another. Then a scraping sound like nails dragged over ice. Then there was silence. Cutchen came barreling down the ladder, missing the last three rungs and landing on his ass.

He looked up at Hayes with wild, unblinking eyes. His face was white as kidskin. "There's . . . there's something up there, something *moving* in the other room."

They were all tensed and waiting, just as still as the ice around them.

A floorboard overhead creaked. There was a weird and low vibration followed by a crackling sound. A pounding like a fist at the door above. A sliding, whispering noise. They were all crouched down low with Cutchen now, holding onto one another. A shrill, echoing peal sounded out above.

"What the hell is it?" Cutchen said.

"Shut up," Hayes whispered. "For the love of God, be quiet . . . "

They waited there, hearing sounds . . . thumpings and knockings, scratching noises and that unearthly crackling. Hayes held onto them, never having felt this absolutely vulnerable in his life. His thoughts had gone liquid in his head. His soul felt like some whirlpool sucking down into fathomless blackness. He felt something catch in his throat, a cry or a scream, and Sharkey made a muted whimpering sound.

No, they hadn't seen anything, but they had *heard* things.

The things that probably drove the Russians insane. And they were feeling something, too . . . something electric and rising and palpable.

Those vibrations started again, making the entire building tremble. The walls above sounded like hammers were beating into them.

There were other sounds above . . . like whispering, distorted voices and hollow pipings, a buzzing noise. And then –

Then Sharkey gasped and a huge, amorphous shadow passed over the trap door as if some grotesque figure had passed before the lantern, making a sound like forks scraped over blackboards and then fading away.

They stayed together like that maybe five or ten minutes, then Hayes went up the ladder, expecting to see something that would leech his mind dry. But there was nothing, nothing at all. The others came up and not a one of them remarked on those weird spade-like prints in the snow.

The wind was whipping and the snow coming at them in sheets as they found the SnoCat and Hayes started it up. He brought it around and bulldozed through a few drifts. Cutchen was staring into his rear-view mirror, seeing things darting in and out of the blizzard that he would not comment on.

"Just drive," he said when Hayes asked him. "For the love of Christ, get us out of here . . . "

So in the days following the successful probe of Lake Vordog, Professor Gundry found himself wishing that he had stayed at CalTech working on his glaciological models. Wishing he had never come down to Antarctica and opened Pandora's Box, got a good look at what was inside. For though it made absolutely no scientific sense, he now knew there were things a man was better off not seeing, not knowing. Things that could get down inside a man, unlocking old doors and rattling primal skeletons from moldering closets, making him feel things and remember things that could poison him to his marrow.

Gundry was no longer the man Hayes had gotten to know, however briefly.

He was not a bundle of nervous energy and inexhaustible drive and ambition. He was no longer a perpetual motion machine that seemed to move in all directions simultaneously, constantly thinking and emoting and reacting. No, now he was a worn, weathered man in his mid-sixties whose blood ran cold and who felt the weight and pull of each of those years dragging him down, compressing him, squashing him flat. His mind was like some incredibly rare and tragic orchid whose petals no longer sought tropical mists and the heat of the sun, but had folded up and withered, pulled into itself and sought the dark, dank depths of cellars and crawlspaces. Cobwebbed, moist, rotting places where the soul could go to mulch and fungus in secret. There were such places in Gundry, crevices and mildewed corners where he could lose himself.

Away from prying eyes and questioning tongues, a man could face the truth of who and what he was, the ultimate destiny of his race. For these were weighty, soul-scarring issues that would crush any man just as they were crushing Gundry.

Gundry was a Southerner.

He was from the Bible Belt and his old man had been something of a lay-preacher. When he wasn't raising sugar beets, melons, and sweet corn, the elder Gundry did his share of preaching at county fairs and carnival booths. He had no earthly patience with such higher realms of thought as organic evolution and cosmic generation. He believed what the Bible taught and was happy within those narrow confines.

Gundry had always thought his father ignorant and parochial, a fly trapped in amber, a man in a constant state of denial as science and technology slowly ate away the foundations of conservative belief and tradition. The way Gundry saw it, science and enlightenment were the only true cure for dim centuries of religious bigotry and hypocrisy.

But now, all these many years later, Gundry finally understood his father.

Though he could not honestly believe in some invisible, mythical god, he could understand religion now. He could understand that it was a security blanket men wrapped around themselves. Maybe it was dark and close under that blanket and you couldn't see more than a few inches in any direction, but it was safe. God created Heaven and Earth and there was a serenity to that, now wasn't there? It was simple and reassuring. And if religion was indeed a sheltering blanket, then science was the cold hand which yanked it away, showing man his ultimate insignificance in the greater scheme of things, the truth about his origins and destiny. The very things man had tried for so many millennia to walk away from, to forget. A cage he had liberated himself from slowly and, even if a candle of truth still burned in the depths of his being, if he did not look at it, then it did not exist. But now man had been thrown back into that cage, had the door slammed shut in his face. And the truth, the real truth of who and what man was and where he'd come from, was staring him dead in the eye.

And, with that in mind, Gundry knew now that enlightenment was the lamp that would burn mens' souls to cinders and the truth was the beast that would devour him and swallow him alive.

For if those things down in the lake had their way, men would never be men again, but just appendages of a cold and cosmic hive-intelligence as it had been intended from the very beginning.

The idea of that terrified Gundry.

It shook him to his roots and filled his soul with venom. All these years, all these thousands upon thousands of years, man had been running from his origins. And now the world was poised on an event that would throw him right back into those very arms. Culture, society, philosophy, religion, poetry, art, music . . . it would all be rendered meaningless beneath the burning, dominating eye of that dire alien intellect.

There was something very offensive and even obscene about that.

So very late in life, Gundry finally, ultimately embraced the insular teachings of organized religion and came to accept that, yes, there indeed was a serpent in Eden . . . and it had come from another star.

Gundry was sitting in the old core sampling room, his head in his hands, whimpering, mourning at the grave of humanity.

Jesus, oh Lord, if you exist, stop this, stop Them before it's too late. Before everything we are is lost to Their memory, swallowed by it.

Nobody had been to the drilling tower in several days now.

Oh, they knew what had been found in the lake and mainly because Hayes had been blabbing about it, but they preferred to leave it alone. Even the scientists themselves had not asked to see the video feed. And wasn't that interesting? Yes, but not surprising with what was going on. Mankind was going full circle and they all felt it and it scared the shit out of them.

Scared? Gundry thought. *They think its bad over at the compound, they should try it over here for a few days.*

Gundry refused to go into the control booth anymore.

Campbell and Parks had pretty much been in there since the day they launched the cryobot. Though the hydrobot was dead, the primary and secondary cryobots were still operating. Still operating and passing reams of information to the surface.

But that wasn't all they were passing.

They were picking up a series of vibrations down there that were steady and organized, a constant stream of pulses that repeated every five minutes to the second. Gundy knew it was not due to some natural phenomena. This was purposeful and directed and he knew it was coming from the archaic city down below. These vibrations were very much like Morse code. The computers could crunch those pulses into mathematical symbols, attach to them a numerical value . . . but it would take months if not years to accurately decipher what the Old Ones were sending.

Or maybe not.

Because maybe on the surface those pulses sounded like noise, but inside, deep inside your mind, you recognized them and understood them. Something long dormant in the human brain was receiving them and waking up. That's why Parks and Campbell would not leave the booth — they were in tune with it. Gaunt, haggard zombies with eyes like staring glass was all they were now, listening and listening as the Old Ones imposed their will upon them and stripped away their humanity inch by inch.

Gundry could not go in there now.

Those pulses made something in his head ache and something in his belly recoil. The three techs who had operated the drill were gone now. Gundry didn't know what had happened to them exactly. Just that one afternoon they stood over the drill hole, staring down into it with blank looks on their faces. And by evening, they were gone. Gundry figured they had wandered off into the Antarctic night just as they were told to.

There was a sudden vibration in the drill tower that Gundry could feel coming up through his feet. It was a constant, electronic humming that rose and fell. Made him want to chatter his teeth and scream his mind away. But it was more than that, for it got inside his head and made something hurt in there. And he knew if he would only stop fighting against it, the pain would recede and a black wave of acceptance would carry him off to eon-dead worlds.

Pray for us sinners, now and at the hour of our death.

The pain was so intense in his head now, thrumming in cutting, tearing waves, that Gundry's vision blurred and tears were squeezed from his eyes. His molars ached and drool fell from his lips. But he was still a man and he would remain one. Digging frantically into his desk drawer, he pulled out his little .38 and put the barrel in his mouth. There was an explosion and an impact, a shattering and a sense of falling.

Gundry's corpse slid from the chair to the floor.

Denying the intellect of the hive, he died as a man with freedom on his tongue and defiance in his soul.

"'m all out of answers. I'm empty and finished and just going through the motions now," Hayes said the morning after they returned from the Vradaz Outpost. "I don't know what to think and what to feel. Like a rat in a fucking maze. Once again."

"Least you're not alone in the maze," Sharkey told him.

Why did that seem precious little consolation?

No, he would not have been able to handle any of this alone. It would have stripped his gears. But at least alone he could have sought the oblivion of suicide, but now that was out of the question. For he felt a sense of responsibility here. Maybe to his race and the world, but certainly to those that were still alive at Kharkhov Station.

Maybe he was inflating his own importance, but he didn't think so. For he had an odd and unwavering sense of *necessity*.

Looking back, he was the only who had felt the badness coming and seen it for what it was. More or less. Maybe the others had, too, in some sense, but just refused to admit it. He felt somehow that he was the guiding hand in this shitfuck and if there was going to be any closure to it, he would be the one to shut the door.

Maybe because those things had tried to infect his mind several times now and had failed. Maybe it was this that gave him such a feeling of self-importance. Sharkey was on the same page with him and so was Cutchen . . . most of the time . . . but the others?

No, from LaHune on down they were mice.

Just going about their mindless business and nibbling their cheese, pretending they were not in incredible danger. St. Ours had been an asshole. Hayes would be the first to admit to that. But good or bad, St. Ours had had enough gumption to sense danger and fight against it.

But what now? What came next?

Hayes just wasn't sure.

Sharkey had just finished telling him two disturbing pearls of knowledge. First that Gates and his people had not been heard from in nearly thirty-six hours now. And secondly, that she'd been on the radio with Nikolai Kolich at the Vostok Station and he had pulled a complete 360 on them, acting like he had never said a word about anything odd happening at Vradaz. Completely denying it all like somebody had a gun to his head. If they'd had an ally there, they'd lost him now.

"We have to decide what we're going to do, Jimmy. Do we try and sit this out? I don't think so. Something has to be done and it's up to us to do it. We can't expect LaHune to help us and probably nobody else either." She appraised Hayes with those crystal blue eyes of hers that always made something seize up inside him. "What I'm thinking is we first . . . *neuter* those mummies out in the hut. A little exposure to our lovely air down here ought to put them back to sleep. Also, how do you feel about me sending a message to the NSF that we're in serious trouble here?"

Hayes didn't know if that was such a good idea. "I'm willing to bet the NSF will ignore it. Because, chances are, LaHune is sending in his glowing daily reports, fiddling while Rome burns to fucking toast."

"You're probably right."

He figured he was. "We'll look like a couple crackpots. Besides, Cutchy says we're heading into a full-blown Polar cyclonic storm within twelve hours. We're going to be looking at white-out conditions when those winds start sweeping down from the mountains, picking up everything in their path. No way in hell a rescue team can get in here . . . even if they wanted to."

Sharkey didn't dispute any of that.

Winter on the Antarctica continent was savage and relentless, marked by screaming subzero winds, perpetual darkness, and wild blizzards that buried camps almost overnight. Planes did not fly to the South Pole even on good days, let alone what they were facing a Condition 3 blizzard with zero visibility and 80 mile-an-hour winds that would lock Kharkhov down for days if not weeks. So whatever was going to happen here, they were going to face it alone.

"There's more here at work than the weather, Elaine, and I think we both know it." Hayes lit a cigarette, seemed to find revelation in the glowing tip. "We've all been sensing a lot of things, some of it coming in dreams and some of it coming just as feelings we can't honestly explain. I'm probably the worst of the lot, spouting out reams of bullshit that I have no way of explaining or proving. Most of what I've been . . . what word should I use here? . . . *intuiting* has been about those dead ones out in the hut, the others down in the lake. But not all of it's been about that. I told you I had a bad feeling about LaHune and I still do. And now, with our good buddy Nikolai Kolich turning his pink tail on us . . . I'm getting an even worse feeling."

Sharkey just watched him, far beyond the stage where she would even consider trying to talk him out of his conspiracy theories . . . because piece by awful piece, the puzzle he'd been prophesizing was slowly coming together. "You think . . . " She swallowed, paused. "You still think that LaHune is sitting atop a conspiracy, don't you?"

He shrugged. "Yes, even more than I did before. I'm seeing him as the big old mother hen sitting on a brood of eggs that are going rotten and wormy, but he's so fucking brainwashed that he don't have the sense to climb off . . . until he's told to. You like that, darling? Well, I got more. You wanna hear more?"

"Yes, I suppose I do."

Hayes grinned. "Well, sweetheart, it's your quarter so you might as well get your money's worth." He pulled off his cigarette. "LaHune. I told you once he doesn't belong here and that's the truth. But I think he was *selected* for this post by certain high-ranking assholes. Maybe he's NASA or JPL, shit maybe he's NSA or Cee-Eye-Aye, baby, I don't know. But I think Uncle Sugar sent him down here. I think LaHune is some kind of spook. There, I said it. I felt it pretty much all along and now I'm admitting it. You've pulled a few tours down here, Elaine, and I'm willing to bet you've heard the same tired old stories I have. Crazy, fringe-shit about the government sending certain security types down here on occasion, undercover, just to keep an eye on things."

Sharkey couldn't lie. "Yeah, I've heard it. And it was probably true during the Cold War . . . but now?"

"Yes, *particularly* now. I'm not even saying for one mad moment that the NSF is even aware that these types are crawling through their organization like worms in shit, but I'll bet they are. My guess is that some people on the highest rung of the dirtiest ladder we got . . . or sitting on the biggest turd, take your pick . . . arranged to have LaHune come down here. Why? Because I think they had an inkling of what we were going to find. Maybe that nonsense you hear about Area 57 and Roswell isn't as crazy as you think. Maybe there are things like that and maybe our government knows about 'em. Maybe. And just maybe they knew about what was down here. Maybe they took the Pabodie Expedition a lot more seriously than people imagined . . . and, hell, maybe the same sort of people who quashed that back in the thirties are active now, sterilizing things for public consumption. Yeah, I know. That's a whole big peck of pickled peppers I'm balancing on the top of my pointy head, but it all makes sense to me."

Sharkey smiled. "I like the peppers analogy, because all of this is giving me an upset stomach."

"Don't blame you. Maybe I'm crazy, maybe I have cabin fever and maybe my dick is made of yellow sponge cake, but I don't think so. LaHune is dirty and he has an agenda. I think the people who yank his strings knew about that ruined city and had suspicions about what was down in the lake . . . and that magnetic anomaly? Well, that was the icing on the cake, so to speak."

Sharkey leaned back in her chair, locking her fingers together behind her head. "Oh, Jimmy," she said, looking like a bad headache was coming over her. "I'm not saying you're wrong . . . but it's pretty spooky thinking, you know? If it is true, then why did LaHune lift the ban on communications, email?"

"I think he had to . . . or he was told to so things didn't get too randy down here." Hayes finished his cigarette. "Listen to me, Elaine. I'm not saying I'm completely right here, but I think I'm on the right path. And I think you know I am. I don't know what LaHune's people might want . . . maybe they want the technology, maybe they want to seize it before anyone else does. I don't know. I don't believe they realized the level of power that was still active down here, but maybe they did. Again, maybe they had some kind of half-ass inkling of it. But I don't really think they meant to put us in any sort of real danger. I'm not that much of a conspiracist. No, whoever these people are, they only wanted us to do our jobs and gather intelligence for them . . . I don't think they meant to hurt us."

Sharkey just sat there for a time, not looking at Hayes, but the papers on her desk, a few framed snapshots of friends from other Antarctic camps. "You know what pisses me off, Jimmy?"

"No, but I have a feeling you'll tell me."

"*You* do."

"Me?"

"Yes. And you piss me off because I think you're right. Maybe not completely, but I think you're pretty close. What I saw at Vradaz pretty much confirms that. But where does any of it get us? Nowhere. Even if it's true, so what? It's out of our hands. LaHune will do what he's told to do and maybe some of us will walk out of this come spring. And I'm willing to bet if we do, we're never invited back."

"I agree," he said. "But I think it's beyond just that now. Regardless of what LaHune's puppet masters decide or don't decide, these things, these Old Ones, are the immediate threat. They're the ones in power now. If we want to get out of here alive, we better start thinking of how we're going to cut their balls off . . . if they have any."

Sharkey got out of her chair and walked around behind Hayes. She stroked his hair and then kissed him on the cheek. "Why don't you go accidentally knock Hut Six down . . . that's a start. That might shut them down or at least set them back."

Hayes stood up and took her into his arms. And maybe he didn't really take her, because she seemed to fall right in place like a cog. He kissed her and she kissed him back and that kiss was in no hurry, it held on, pressed them together and only ended when it was on the verge of bigger things.

"I think I'll go do just that. Have a little accident with the 'dozer. A big fucking oops," he said, his insides filled with a warmth that quickly sought lower regions. "And then we'll see. We'll just see. You know, lady, I got me this crazy idea of us walking out of here together."

"Me, too," she said.

Hayes turned away and started down the corridor.

"Be careful, Jimmy," she said, not sure if he heard her or not.

PART FIVE

THE SWARM

"Nor is it to be thought...that man is either the oldest or the last of earth's masters, or that the common bulk of life and substances walks alone. The Old Ones were, the Old Ones are, and the Old Ones shall be. Not in the spaces we know, but between them, They walk serene and primal, undimensioned and to us unseen."

— H.P. Lovecraft

A few hours after Hayes went out on his mission, Cutchen appeared at the door to the infirmary. "Knock, knock," he said.

"It's open," Sharkey said. She was staring into the screen of her laptop, glasses balanced on the end of her nose. "If you want drugs, the answer is no."

But Cutchen didn't want that.

He had an almost rakish smile on his face. And his eyes had that typical I-know-something-you-don't-know gleam in them. "How's things? Anything going on I should know about?"

Sharkey still hadn't looked up from her laptop. "Go ahead, Cutchy. I know you want to. You look like a little boy trying to sneak a snake into the schoolhouse. Spill it."

"It concerns our Mr. Hayes."

"Really?"

"Yeah, about an hour ago I was coming back from the dome and I saw the craziest damn thing. I saw the camp bulldozer suddenly roar into life, come plowing through the compound and smash through the wall of Hut Six. Now isn't that astounding?"

Sharkey was still reading off her screen. "Yup. Crazy things happen. Hard to see out there."

"You know what I saw then? Oh, this is even better. I saw Hayes hop out of the 'dozer and elbow his way through a group of people at Targa House, ignoring their questions as to what the hell he thought he was doing. Those people kept asking and he kept ignoring them and they were all smiling, some were even clapping."

"Really?" Sharkey was looking up now, smiling herself. "Sounds like Hayes did a pretty careless thing . . . but it certainly perked up morale, didn't it?"

"I would say so. Jesus, everyone's been wandering around here like a bunch of goddamn zombies. All of them afraid of their own shadows . . . and now this. Yeah, they needed it. It was a real big boost, kicked them out of their shells. Maybe even gave them the sort of hope they've been lacking." Cutchen laughed. "It certainly gave me a charge. Hayes is like our very own rebel leader now, our own Pancho Villa, our Robin Hood. But you already knew about this, didn't you?"

"Yes."

"And did you put him up to it?"

Sharkey shrugged. "I suggested it. Our Mr. Hayes is a very impulsive fellow, you know."

"Oh, I know. Everyone seems to look to him now, like he's in charge and not LaHune. I would tend to agree. Hayes is now our spiritual leader." Cutchen sat down across from her. "LaHune didn't care for any of it, of course."

Cutchen explained that LaHune came storming into the community room, demanding to know what Hayes thought he was doing and Hayes told him that he was preserving Gates' specimens before they rotted away completely. That he'd taken down that wall purely out of scientific concern for the mummies.

"LaHune, of course, started threatening Hayes with all sorts of repercussions."

"Really?"

"Yeah. Hayes then told him to go promptly fuck himself." Cutchen laughed about this. "As you might expect there was more applause."

"I imagine so."

Cutchen sat there for a time watching Sharkey who seemed to be pretty enrapt with what was on her laptop. "Tell you the truth, Elaine, I didn't just come here to tell you about that, though."

"No?"

"Nope. For some time now, both you and Hayes have been pulling me into this scenario of yours and I'll be the first to admit, I'm not seeing the big picture in this conspiracy. I know what I've been dreaming about and what I've been feeling and the things I've seen here . . . and at Vradaz. But you two have yet to feed me more than scraps. So let's have it. Tell me everything."

"Funny you should be asking these things, because I think I'm in a position, finally, where I can tell you. What I've been studying here on my laptop are Dr. Gates' files. I hacked into his system because I had a pretty good feeling that everything he hadn't told us that day in the community room was locked up on his computer and I was right." Using her mouse, she scrolled through a few pages. "You see, not only was all of it there, but more. Gates has been sending written reports from his laptop up at the excavation to his desktop here. The last one was dated two days ago . . . "

"You're a sneaky devil, Madam."

"Yes, I am."

"And? What did you find?"

"Where do I begin?" She sat back in her chair. "What we saw at that Russian camp, Cutchy . . . how would you classify that business?"

He shrugged. "Ghosts, I guess. Memories locked up in those dead husks like Hayes said. Sensitive minds come into contact with them . . . or maybe any minds at all . . . and out pop these memories: noises and apparitions and that sort of business. I never believed in any of that bull before, but I don't have much of a choice now."

"You'd call them ghosts?"

"Yes." He leaned forward. "Unless you have a better term . . . maybe one that would help me sleep better at night."

Sharkey shook her head. "I don't. 'Ghosts' will have to do. Because, essentially, that's what they are. Gates wrote in some detail about psychic manifestations occurring in proximity to the Old Ones. People have been seeing spooks down here a long time, having bad dreams and weird experiences . . . and I guess you can figure out why. *Reflections,* are what Gates calls these phenomena, projections from those dead husks, from minds that never truly died in the way we understand death . . . just waited. Maybe not conscious really or sentient, but dreaming. And what we're picking up are the ethereal projections of those dead minds . . . intellects, a mass-consciousness that was so very powerful in life that even death couldn't crush it. Not completely. Gates isn't certain about a lot of that . . . just that those minds are active in a way, not really alive but functioning pretty much on auto like a radio station, broadcasting and broadcasting. Our minds come into contact with them and we pick up those signals, then the trouble starts."

Cutchen nodded. "I'll buy that. Makes sense. And maybe as they unthaw, those minds become stronger. Maybe that's what got to Meiner and St. Ours."

"They may have been more sensitive to it than others. Same way I think Hayes is. Gates had another theory on that. He thought that maybe those dead minds were being energized not only by us, but amplified by that huge and overpowering central consciousness down in the lake. That the living ones might be acting as sort of a generator."

"He's guessing, though."

"Of course he's guessing. There's no way to know." Sharkey scrolled through a few pages on the screen. "Did Hayes tell you about his experiences? Out in the hut and on the tractor?"

"Yeah. Those minds almost did to him what they did to Meiner and St. Ours," Cutchen said.

"Did he tell you about his telepathic link with Lind after the events in the hut?" She could see that he hadn't, so she filled him in on it. "Lind was seeing things millions of years old. A city here at the Pole before the glaciers swallowed the continent. And just before he died, well . . . "

"Possessed." Cutchen said the word so she didn't have to. "That's what everyone's saying. That Lind was possessed by those things."

"Yes, at least what we could call diabolical possession. He manifested all the signs you hear about in those cases . . . telepathy and telekinesis, that sort of thing. He described to us the original colonization of this world and we were able to smell and feel what he was smelling and feeling. The thick poisonous atmosphere of another world, the heat there, then the freezing cold of deep space."

"Did Gates confirm that they are alien? I mean we've all been tossing the word around, but — "

"Yes, he was certain. You see, he unlocked the code of their writings, their glyphs and bas-reliefs. That ancient city he found, it was scrawled with writings which were essentially a written history of who the Old Ones were, where they came from, what they planned to do . . . and had done."

"He unlocked all that? In just a month or so?"

Sharkey nodded. "Yes, because he found something akin to the Rosetta Stone, except this one was a key to their language and symbols. He called it the Dyer Stone after Professor Dyer of the Pabodie Expedition. A soapstone about the size of a tabletop . . . with it, he was able to translate those writings."

"And . . . and what did he find out?"

"There are carvings in those ruins, Cutchy. Ancient maps of our solar system and other systems as well. Dozens and dozens of them. Firm evidence, Gates said, of interplanetary and interstellar travel and this probably before our planet was even cool. Dyer mentioned certain ancient books and legends that hinted at Pluto as the Old Ones' first outpost in this star system, but according to the maps Gates found, they came here from either Uranus or Neptune . . . but before that, who can say?"

"Uranus? Neptune?" Cutchen shook his head. "Those are dead worlds, Elaine."

"Sure, now they are . . . but what about 500 million years ago? A billion? Maybe that's why they came here, because they knew their world . . . Uranus or Neptune . . . was doomed. And maybe they just came seeking our warm oceans. Gates thinks that they are originally marine organisms, but given their durability, they can adapt themselves to just about any environment. Gates thinks that myths and legends concerning winged demons and flying monsters might be race memories of them, impressions from the dawn of our race that survived in the form of folktale and legend. Regardless, they've been here since the beginning. *Our* beginning and the beginning of all life on this world."

"I was hoping you weren't going to go there," Cutchen said.

"I have to. Because that's what this is all about: life. The creation of it, the continuation of it, the modification of it. When Lind was . . . well, *possessed,* he started ranting on about the *helix.* There was no doubt he was talking about DNA . . . the plan of all life on this planet. He was uplinked with those dead minds and telling us about the helix, that they were the farmers of the helix. That they created the helix and seeded it, world to world to world."

"That's kind of what Hayes was saying," Cutchen said, looking beaten and cramped from the weight of it all. "That they started life here, they started it and they would harvest it."

"Yes. It almost sounded like to the Old Ones, the helix was God. Which, I suppose, fits in with what certain evolutionary biologists have been saying. That life, all life, is merely a host, a vessel to ensure the propagation and continuation of the genetic material."

"That's pleasant."

Sharkey nodded. "Remember what Gates told us that day? Lake, the biologist in the Pabodie Expedition, had found fossilized prints in Precambrian rock that had to be at least a billion years old. The prints of the Old Ones. Probably from one of the earliest of their earth colonies. Some time later, Gates wrote, there would have been a mass migration that went on for millions of years. Their original outposts were doomed and unsuitable, so they came here. They came to earth en masse to colonize and found our planet to be dead, so they engineered a highly ambitious blueprint to bring forth not only life on this world, but *intelligent* life."

"But that's insane," Cutchen said. "I'm sorry, but it is. That the human race is the end result of something they started into motion a billion years ago. That's crazy."

"Is it? Think about it. These things have been seeding life on dozens and dozens of planets probably since before our sun was born. And they've been doing it with a very specific agenda: to bring forth intelligence. Intelligent minds that they could master, that they could modify and subvert. And since none existed here, they created them. God knows how many colonies they've created. Maybe hundreds if not thousands spread across space, outposts on countless alien worlds. Out in our own solar system there are probably ruins of ancient cities much like the ones Gates found. And probably on the planets orbiting a hundred stars, if not a thousand." She stopped, maybe to catch her own mental breath or to let Cutchen catch his. "It's fantastic, heady stuff, I know. That city Gates found . . . it was probably on a plain or in a valley originally that became a mountain millions upon millions of years later. Gates said that, according to ancient legend, there were other cities . . . in Asia, the Australian desert, a certain sunken continent in the Pacific. Maybe our tales of Atlantis, Lemuria, and Mu are, again, just ancestral memories of these places . . . "

Cutchen was looking for a hole in her logic . . . or Gates' . . . and Sharkey knew it. He was looking at it from all sides and trying to find the hole in it. Either he couldn't find one or it was so big he'd already been sucked down into it without knowing. "Okay," he said. "How is it these things got here? Not in ships as we understand them, I'm guessing."

"No, they did not possess a material, mechanistic technology, according to Gates. Not in the way we do. He said they would have possessed an *organic* technology if you can wrap your brain around that one. A living technology maybe supported by a certain level of instrumentation . . . but not gadgets like we have. Not exactly. They would have been light years beyond us to the point that their minds might have been strong enough to manipulate matter and energy and maybe even time as they saw fit.

"But as to your question, they *drifted* here. They went into a dormant state, according to Gates, and drifted on what he called the solar winds. I suppose it's the same way they drifted into this solar system. Gates mentioned them possibly manipulating fourth-dimensional space. You might remember that bit if you ever had any quantum physics . . . you jump into the fourth dimension at Point A and jump out at Point B. A to B could be ten feet away or ten million miles, it wouldn't matter. You could transverse incalculable distances easily as a man stepping off his porch. Maybe that's how they crossed interstellar voids. But if Lind's *memory* of them was correct — and I tend to think it was — then, yes, they went into a sort of dormancy and drifted here."

"Shit, Elaine, that would have taken eons," Cutchen pointed out.

"So what? It wouldn't have mattered to things like them. A thousand years or a hundred-thousand would be all the same to something that was essentially immortal and endless. Lind was in contact with that memory, Cutchy, a memory a billion years old and probably even two or three. And he experienced it . . . the dormancy, the drifting. Even the cold and lack of atmosphere were no deterrent to them. Nothing would be."

"I'm still having trouble with this," Cutchen admitted. "I mean, listen to what you're saying here. Something like this . . . to put forth a plan, a grand design for this planet that wouldn't see fruition for hundreds and hundreds of millions of years. It's just too incredible. That amount of time . . . "

"You're looking at this as any being with a finite lifespan would. But time means nothing to them, nothing at all," Sharkey said, realizing she was using the same arguments on him that Hayes had used on her.

Cutchen sighed. The bigness, the longevity of such an operation, the huge scale it must have been carried out on . . . all of this was flooring him. Not to mention that everything she said completely dwarfed man's history, his importance, his very culture. It made the human race no more significant in the greater scheme of things than protozoans on a laboratory slide. It was very . . . sobering. "All right. So these Old Ones drifted here, started life with some master plan behind it all . . . then what? Just hoped for the best?"

"Hardly. Our evolutionary development would have been carefully monitored through the ages," Sharkey told him, glancing back to her screen from time to time. "Remember, they colonized this world and they had no intention of leaving and still haven't. They would not have left anything to mere chance. Gates wrote that there are great gaps in our own fossil record, times when our evolution jumped eons ahead for no apparent reason. 500,000 years ago, for example, the brains of our ancestors suddenly doubled in size if not tripled. It happened more than once, Gates said. These were the times, Cutchy, when those ancestors of ours were carefully manipulated by the Old Ones. Through selective breeding, genetic engineering, molecular biology, methods we can't even guess at."

"And . . . and they've been waiting for us . . . their children . . . all this time?"

Sharkey nodded. "Yes, waiting and watching through unimaginable gulfs of time while the continents shifted and the glaciers arrived, while the Paleozoic Era became the Mesozoic and finally the Cenzoic. While our ancestors evolved along lines already laid out for them. And at times, I would think, entire populations would have been taken to their cities and altered, then placed back again with selective mutations installed. They've waited and watched and now, if Gates is right, we're ready for harvesting. Our intellects are sufficiently advanced to be of use to them. Down there in that warm lake, Cutchy, is the last relict population of a race as old as the stars."

"And now we've come," he said. "Just as they knew we would."

"Exactly. Men have always been drawn down here to the Pole, haven't they? And if what Gates is saying is correct, then it's been more than a sense of exploration. As a race we would be drawn to those places where our memory was strongest."

Cutchen was sweating now and couldn't help himself. The idea of it all was terrifying. Like the human race had never, ever been in command of its own destiny. It was shocking. "It's like we're . . . what? A seed planted in a fucking garden? Cultivated, cross-bred, enhanced . . . until they got the proper strain, the proper hybrid they desired." He just shook his head. "But what do they want, Elaine? What do they have in mind? To conquer us? What?"

She shrugged. "I'm not sure and neither is Gates. But one thing's for sure, it's our minds that they want, our intellects they need. They are of a single mind, a single consciousness, a hive mentality. That is exactly what they intend for us to be. For us to be *them* but in human form." She scrolled through a few pages on her laptop. "According to Gates, they've bred certain characteristics into us. There are probably latent gifts we all carry in our minds, our carefully engineered minds, that they will now exploit. They'll reawaken faculties that we've long forgotten about, but have been buried in us all along . . . "

"Like what?"

"Abilities they planted in us long ago. Abilities that would make us *like* them. Mechanisms seeded in our brains, special adaptations that have been passed on through our genes . . . wild talents that occasionally make themselves known like telepathy, telekinesis, prophecy . . . talents that, when the time was right, would make us like them — a single, ominous hive mind. That coupled with an overriding instinct, a blind compulsion to serve them. An all important seed they would have planted in our primitive brains and is still there today."

Cutchen said, "So everything we are, our entire history and even our destiny . . . these Old Ones were the architects of it? We're . . . *synthetic?*"

"Yes and no. Our culture, our civilization is our own, I think. Though much of it might be based upon archetypes imprinted upon our brains eons ago. Even our conception of a god, a superior being, a creator . . . it's no doubt based upon some aboriginal image of them placed into our subconscious minds. They would have seen themselves as our gods, our masters . . . then and now . . . and we, in essence, were designed to be their tools, an extension of their organic technology, to be used for what plans we could never even guess at. But it might be in us, that knowledge, lying dormant in our brains until they decide to wake it up. And when that happens . . . when that happens, there will be no more human race, Cutchy."

Cutchen's face was beaded with sweat, his eyes were wide and tormented. "We have to stop this, Elaine. We have to stop this madness."

"If we can. *If* we can," she said, her voice filled with a bitter hopelessness, a dire inevitability. "Lord knows what they planted in us, what buried imperatives and controls that they might be, right now, getting ready to unlock on a global scale to bring us to our ultimate destiny."

"Which is?"

But Sharkey could just shake her head. "I don't know and I don't think I want to find out."

"We're fucked, Elaine. If Gates is right, we're fucked." Cutchen kept trying to moisten his weathered lips, but he was all out of spit. "I really hope Gates is a lunatic. I'm really hoping for that."

"I don't think he is," Sharkey told him. "And the scary part is, nobody's heard from him in over forty-eight hours now."

33

The way Hayes was seeing it, he'd paid for this dance and LaHune was going to have a cheek-to-cheek waltz with him whether he liked the idea of it or not. And LaHune most certainly did not like the idea. But he knew Hayes. Knew trying to get rid of the guy was like trying to shake a stain out of your shorts.

Hayes was tenacious.

Hayes was relentless.

Hayes would hang like a tattoo on your backside until he got exactly what he wanted. No more. No less. But LaHune, of course, had had his merry fill of Jimmy Hayes and his paranoid bullshit. Had it right up to his left eyeball and this is what he told Hayes, not bothering to spare his feelings one iota. In his opinion, Hayes was the rotten apple in the storied barrel. The bee in the bonnet. And the cat piss in the punch.

"I've had my fill of you, Hayes," LaHune told him. "I'm so sick of you I could spit. Just the sight of you roils my stomach."

Hayes was sitting in the administrator's office, his feet up on his desk even though he'd been warned a half dozen times to get his dirty, stinking boots off of there. "Are you trying to tell me something, Mr. LaHune? Because I'm getting this funny feeling in my gut that you just don't like me. But maybe it's just gas."

LaHune sat there, really trying to be patient. Really trying to hang onto his dignity which had been chewed up, swallowed, and shit on by this man from day one. Yes, he was trying to hang onto his dignity and not come right over the desk at Hayes, that smarmy, bearded dirtball.

"No, you're reading me fine, Hayes. Just fine. And get your goddamn feet off my desk."

Hayes crossed one boot atop the other. "You saying it's over between us, then? No more quickies behind the oil tanks in the generator shack?"

"You're not funny, Hayes."

"Sure I am. Ask anybody."

LaHune sat there, sighing heavily. Yes, Hayes had pissed all over his dignity, his authority, and his self-respect. But that would come screaming to an end one way or another. LaHune wasn't used to dealing with working class hardcases like Hayes. Guys like him buttered their bread on the wrong side and spawned in a different pond. Maybe he was good at his job, but he was also smartassed, disrespectful, and insubordinate.

"I'll tell you what you are, Hayes," LaHune finally said. "You're reckless and childish and paranoid. A man like you has no business down here. You're not up to it. And when spring comes . . . and it will come and no aliens, flying saucers, or abominable snowmen will stop it . . . when it comes, I'll see to it that you never get another contract down here. And if you think I'm joking, you just fucking try me."

"Hey, hey, easy with the profanity! Remember my virgin ears, you fucking prick."

"That's enough!"

Hayes pulled his feet off the desk. "No, it's not, LaHune. And it won't be until you pull your over-inflated head out of your ass and start seeing things as they are. We're in trouble here and you better start accepting that. You're in charge of this installation and the lives of these people are in your hands. And until you accept that responsibility, I'll be riding you like a French whore. Count on it."

LaHune said nothing. "I don't what to hear about your paranoid fantasies, Hayes."

"That's all it is? Paranoia?"

"What else could it be?"

Hayes laughed thinly. "Where do they put your batteries, LaHune? I think they're running low." He sat back in his chair, totally frustrated, folding his arms over his chest. "Those goddamn mummies are making people go insane. You've got three men from the drilling tower, that Deep Drill Project, that are missing. You've got three dead men . . . what more do you need?"

"I'll need something factual, Hayes. St. Ours, Meiner, and, yes, Lind have died from cerebral hemorrhages. If you don't believe me, ask Dr. Sharkey. Dammit, man."

Hayes uttered that laugh again. "Cerebral hemorrhages? No shit? Three of 'em in a row? I didn't know they were catchy. C'mon, LaHune, don't you think that three exploded brains pretty much tweaks the tit of chance a little too hard?"

"I'm not a medico here. It's not my job to engage in forensics."

Hayes just shook his head. "All right, let me try again. Remember that day we called Nikolai Kolich over at Vostok? Sure you do. Well, old Nikolai, boy, he told us some kind of fucking yarn. You remember that derelict camp Gates and his boys found? Yeah? Well, that there was a Russian camp from the old Soviet red scare days of yore. Joint called the Vradaz Outpost. Yup. Now this part here, boyo, it's going to sound just whackier than Mother Teresa working the pole in a thong and pasties. But Kolich told us they all went mad at Vradaz. Yup. Crazier'n bugs in bat shit. You know what drove 'em crazy? *Spooks.* Sure. Now I know this is all going to sound real fantastic to you, real far-out and nutty, because you've never heard of nothing like this, but I'm willing to bet you can wrap your spooky little brain right around it, you try hard enough.

"See, how it started at Vradaz was that those scientists up there, they drilled into a chasm, found some things in there. We'll call 'em *mummies,* okay? Well, not long after, all those commy scientists started having real weird dreams and before you could say Jesus in drag, they started hearing things. Knockings and poundings. Funny sounds. Then they started seeing apparitions, ghosts that walked through walls and the like. Well, the Soviets said that's enough of this horseshit, so they sent in a team to take care of those boys, root out the infection so to speak. So, those silly communists, they killed everyone there. Isn't that a funny story?"

LaHune was unmoved. "That's some pretty high speculation, isn't it?"

"Oh, not at all. See, the other day when Sharkey and I went with Cutchen to check his remote weather stations, we went out to Vradaz instead. Took a look around there."

LaHune just shook his head. "You are so very out of control, Hayes. That installation, abandoned or not, is property of the Russian Federation."

"No, they disowned it years back, LaHune. Some twenty-odd years back to be exact." Hayes had him and he knew it. He had LaHune hooked and he was now going to play him for all it was worth. "Okay, so we dug our way in there and, lo and behold, we found bullet holes and blood, crosses cut into the walls to keep the haunts away. Then, down below, we found a pit with bodies in there. All them scientists but the three insane ones the Ruskies took away with 'em. All those bodies, LaHune, they'd been gunned down and then *burned.* Yeah, you heard me right. We also found one of those alien carcasses down there that had been toasted like a marshmallow at Camp Cockalotta. And Ivan did these things because he realized the very thing that you're afraid of: that those aliens are dangerous. They get in men's mind and destroy them, same way they're doing here. The Russians killed those men and burned them along with My Favorite Martian because those dead, alien minds are a contagion that spreads and devours healthy human minds just as they always have. It was quite a scene there, LaHune. There were even a few Russian soldiers in that pit and you know why? Because those alien minds got them, too."

LaHune said nothing.

There was nothing he could say.

But Hayes could see that he believed him. Completely believed him. But he wasn't really shocked or surprised by any of it and Hayes figured that was because their grand NSF administrator knew all about what happened at Vradaz.

"Now, while back, LaHune, you asked me why in the hell I knocked in that wall on Hut Six. Well, I did it to freeze those fucking Martians back up before this entire goddamn station is destroyed. Before we all have our minds sucked out or blown up. See, I don't think those dead minds are completely unthawed yet, but when that happens . . . well, you get the picture, don't you?"

"You're completely mad, Hayes."

"Oh, but let me share one more thing with you. We gave old Nikolai a jingle at Vostok and you know what? He denies ever telling us any of that business. His puppet masters have yanked his strings and now he's dancing to their tune same way you're dancing to yours."

Hayes stood up. "But that's okay, LaHune, I'm just shit-tired of argu-ing with you. What happened to the Russians will happen to us. Those minds will eat us alive. But you just sit there on your shiny white ass and do nothing. That's fine. Your mind already belongs to some ass-fucking suits back in Washington. But as for me? I'm going to fight this tooth and nail and if you want to get in my way, I'll fucking step on you. And that, sonny, is a promise."

With that, Hayes offered him a courtly bow and left LaHune's office.

The next two days passed with a measured, languid slowness . . . drawn out, elastic, and mordantly unreal. A claustrophobic, evil shadow had fallen over the station, breeding a tension and a fear that was barely concealed like a moldering skull seen through a funeral veil. It was an almost palpable thing, a suffocating sense of malevolence and you could feel it wherever you went . . . bunching in the shadows, scratching at the frosted windows, oozing from the ice like contaminated bile. You could tell yourself it was imagination and nerves and isolation, but you never believed it, because it was everywhere, hanging over the camp in a frightful pall, patient and waiting and acutely sentient. It was behind you and to either side, giggling and chattering its teeth and reaching out for your throat with cold, white fingers. And like your soul, you could not put a finger on it, but it was there, alive and breathing and namelessly destructive. It was in your blood and bones like a disease germ and just beneath your thoughts like a dire memory. And whatever it was, it was something born to darkness like worms in a grave.

The personnel at Kharkhov did not speak of it.

Like a cluster of little old ladies at a church luncheon who refused to discuss disquieting things like cancer or the boy next door who came back from the war in a body bag, it was a taboo subject, one their minds burdened under, but one that never got past their lips.

Such things did not make for polite company.

They stirred up bad odors and opened dank cellars that were best left bolted and chained. So the scientists carried on with their research and experiments. The contract personnel kept things humming. People gathered in the community room for lunch and dinner and talked sports and current events and went out of their way not to look one another in the eye because it was better that way. And the subject of Gates and the ruined city, the mummies and those down in Lake Vordog, were never brought up.

A psychologist would have called it *avoidance* and he or she would have been right. When you did not openly discuss things, they seemed all the less real . . . even if said things *did* make your skin crawl. But you ingested them, tucked them away into the scarred and secret landscape of your subconscious where you ultimately knew they would boil and fester and one day fill you with a seething poison. Like being touched in a private place by a child molester, you purged it and pretended such things could not have happened.

But later? Well, yes, later it would show its teeth, but that was later. And this is how it was at Kharkhov Station.

This was how the population kept their sanity . . . by sheer deception and willpower born of self-preservation and desperation. But it was there, of course, that gnawing and pervasive sense of violation. The feeling that maybe your mind and your thoughts were not entirely your own and maybe never had been. But such ideas were venomous and infective, so the small colony refused them and went about being industrious and ignorant even while that ancient web was spun around them thickly. What they were feeling and how they were dealing with those feelings was exactly how they were supposed to deal with them. Exactly how the architects of their minds had intended it so very long ago.

Hayes, of course, was not among them.

He freely admitted the danger to any and all who would listen. But therein lie the twist: they *refused* to listen. They nodded when he spoke to them, but not a word of what he said got past their ears. He had put a stop to it by bulldozing down the wall of Hut #6. If there ever was a danger — and they were not certain of this — then it was over now. Back to reality. But Hayes didn't believe them because he was feeling what they were feeling and was seeing that barely-disguised terror in their eyes.

"You see that's what kills me," he said to Sharkey on the evening of that second day while they lay in the warm darkness of her bed. "That's what really fucking tears me a new asshole, Doc. These people *know* they're screwed, but they won't admit to it now. Not a one of them."

"It's herd instinct, Jimmy. That's all it is. They cope by losing themselves in the mundane politics of day to day living. They submerge themselves into the body of the herd and pretend that there is no tiger hiding in the shadows," Sharkey told him. "This is how they stay alive, how they stay sane. It's human nature. If something is so immense and terrible that it threatens to peel your mind bare, you exorcise it and pretend everything is hunky-dory."

"I suppose," he said.

"No, really. How do you think people survived those concentration camps? Do you think they dwelled on their imminent deaths or what that smoke coming out of the chimneys was from? The fact that they could be going to the showers next? Of course not. If they had, not a single sane mind would have come out of that horror. But a surprising amount did."

"There's a parallel there, Doc, and a good one, but I'm just too pissed-off at them to see it. I hate complacency. I hate people sitting around and pretending the world isn't falling apart around them. That's what's wrong with us Americans as a whole . . . we've gotten too goddamn selfish and too goddamn good at putting our blinders on. Millions are being slaughtered in Rwanda? We just accidentally bombed a schoolhouse in Iraq . . . oh, that's just terrible, isn't it? Well, not my affair. Praise the Lord and pass the gravy, mom."

Sharkey said, "I never realized you were a political activist at heart."

He relaxed a bit, chuckled. "I do get on my soapbox now and again." He lit a cigarette and blew smoke into the darkness. "My old man was a dire-hard conservative republican. Anything the government told him, he believed. He thought they were incapable of lying. The sort of guy politicians thrive on. Salt of the earth, but mindless. I had a teacher in high school . . . a real 1960s radical who was big on confrontation with those in power . . . I think a lot of him rubbed off on me. Because he didn't just sit there and take it. He demanded that our government be held responsible for anything it fucked up or lied about. I agreed then and I agree now. My old man and me had some real rows over our conflicting viewpoints. But to this day, I feel exactly the same. I do not trust people with money and power and I despise the little guy who looks the other way while these fat cats fuck up the world as they always have."

"And you're seeing a microcosm of that here, aren't you?"

"Yeah, definitely. I have to ask myself if those people deserve saving . . . are they worth it?"

"And?"

"And I'm not honestly sure. Complacency deserves what its gets."

Sharkey didn't say anything for a time.

Neither of them did.

Hayes wasn't sure what she was thinking. Maybe it was something good and maybe it was something bad. Regardless, she just didn't say. The silence between them was heavy, but not uncomfortable. It seemed perfectly fine, perfectly acceptable, and that's how Hayes knew this wasn't what you might call a winter-camp fling. It was something more. Something with weight and volume and substance and he was almost glad that things were too crazy, too spooky for him to sit and think about the absolute truth of their relationship. Because, he figured, it might just have scared the shit out of him and sent him running into a hole like a rabbit with a hawk descending.

"Tell me something, Doc," he said, pulling off his cigarette. "Be honest here. Do you think I'm losing it? No, don't answer that too quickly. Ponder it. Do that for me. Because sometimes . . . I can't read you. You no doubt know that some of the boys around here see you as some sort of ice-princess, a freezer for a heart and ice cubes for eyes. I think it's some kind of wall you put up. A sort of protective barrier. I figure a woman like you that spends a lot of time marooned in camps full of men has to distance herself some way. So, really, I'm not judging you or insulting you in any way. But, like I say, I can't read you sometimes. I wonder if maybe you're thinking I'm a whacko or something, but are too polite to say so."

He felt her hand slide into his, felt her long fingers find his own and grip them like they never wanted to let go. But she didn't say anything. He could hear her breathing, hear the clock ticking on the shelf, the wind moaning through the compound. But nothing else.

So he said, "Sometimes I say things, I start spouting off about things, theories of mine, and you just don't say anything. And I start to wonder why not. Start to wonder if maybe this all isn't in my head and I'm having one of those . . . what do you call them?"

"Hysterical pregnancies?"

"Yeah, that's it."

"No, I don't think you're crazy. Not in the least. Sometimes I just don't say anything because I need time to think things over and other times, well, I'm just amazed by a man like you. You're so . . . intuitive, so impulsive, so instinctual. You're not like other men I've known. I think that's why even when we had no real proof about those aliens, I believed what you said. I didn't doubt any of it for a moment."

Hayes was flattered and embarrassed . . . he'd never realized he was those things. But, shit, she was right. He was a seat-of-the-pants kind of guy. Trusting his heart over his brain every time. Go figure.

"Tell me something, Jimmy," she said then. "Nothing's happened really since you plowed in that wall. Nobody's been coming to me for sedatives, so I'm guessing our contagion of nightmares has dwindled in direct proportion to you freezing those things back up. But what about you? Have you had any dreams?"

"No. Not a one. I shut my eyes and I sleep like I'm drugged. There's nothing. I don't think I can remember having such deep sleep . . . least since I quit smoking dope."

"That's a good thing, isn't it? Not having dreams? It's a good indicator?"

He shrugged. "I don't know. My brain tells me we're in the clear, maybe. But my guts are telling me that this is the calm before the storm. Whenever I try to talk to anybody here, I don't know, I get a bad feeling from them. Something that goes beyond their avoidance of all this . . . something worse. I'm getting weird vibes from them that weren't there before, Elaine. And it makes me feel . . . kind of freaky inside."

He was having trouble putting it into words, but the feeling was always there. Like maybe the lot of them had already been assimilated into the communal mind of those things. That they were already lost to him. Whatever it was, it made his guts roll over, made him feel like he could vomit out his liver.

"Good. I've been feeling that way all day . . . like there's nothing behind their eyes," she admitted. "And all over camp . . . well, something's making my skin crawl and I'm not sure what it is."

Hayes stubbed out his cigarette. "I'm willing to bet we're going to find out real soon. Because this isn't over. I know it isn't over. And I'm just waiting for the ball to drop."

35

When the ball did in fact drop the next afternoon, Hayes was lucky enough . . . or unlucky enough . . . to have it pretty much drop at his feet. He and Sharkey and Cutchen had decided on a plan of attack which was to do absolutely nothing. Just to go about their jobs and to not even mention what had happened before and what might be happening now.

But to keep their eyes open and their minds, too.

For Hayes, there was always work to be done. The energy supply at the Kharkhov Station was supplied by no less than five diesel generators, two wind-turbine generators, grid reactive boilers, and fuel-fired boilers. All of which were run through a central power station control system. Most days he pretty much sat at his computer in a booth at the power station and studied read-outs, crunched numbers, and made sure everything was operating at peak efficiency. But then there were the other days that demanded physical maintenance. And today was one of those.

He was glad for it.

Glad to climb into his heated coveralls and get some tools in his hands. Get dirty and sweaty and cold, anything to be doing something other than letting his imagination have full reign.

He shut the diesel generators down in sequence, changing their oil and putting in new fuel and air filters. He tested fuel injection nozzles and drained cooling systems. Inspected air cleaners and flame arrestors, checked the governors. When he had the generators back on-line, he went after the boilers. He checked fuel systems and feed pumps, he reconditioned safety valves and inspected mercury switches, recorded gas and oil pressures, checked the cams and limit controls. Then he shut down the wind turbines and made physical inspections of their alternators and regulators. He spent most of the day at it.

It was demanding, time-consuming work.

And when he was done, he was sore and aching and pleased as always after putting in a hard day's work. There was something about a day of manual labor that steadied something in the human beast. Got it on an even plane. Maybe when the muscles woke up, the intellect shut down and that always wasn't a bad thing.

Especially at the South Pole.

And especially that winter.

Finally, though, Hayes called it a day and climbed into his ECW's, which consisted of a polar fleece jacket and wool pants, wool hat and mittens, balaclava and goggles. As soon as he stepped out into the winter darkness, the winds found him. Did their damnedest to either carry him into that black, brooding sky or knock him flat. He took hold of the guylines and never let go.

Cutchen's prediction of a Condition One storm became a reality. The wind was rumbling and howling and moaning, making the structures of Kharkhov Station shake and creak. The snow came whipping through the compound, obscuring everything, knocking visibility down to less than ten feet at times. Three-foot drifts were blown over the walkways. Snow-devils funneled along the hard-pack.

Hayes struggled along, the wind pulling at him, finely ground ice particles blasting into him. He could see the security lights outside the buildings and huts and the blizzard made them look like searchlights coming through thick fog. They glowed orange and yellow and murky, trembling on their poles.

As he followed the guylines to Targa House, he suddenly became aware that faces were pressed up against the windows. He wasn't sure at first, but the nearer he got, yeah, those were faces pressed up to the frosty windows.

Was his plight that entertaining?

The wind shifted and he heard what he first took to be the muted growl of some beast echoing across the ice-fields, then he realized it was an engine. He stopped and looked into the wind, snow spraying into his face. He could see the lights of the compound . . . the far-flung huts and even the meteorology dome . . . but nothing else. The blizzard hammered into him and nearly knocked him over like a post . . . and then it died out some, still howling and screeching, but sounding like it was old and tired now and in need of a rest.

And that's when Hayes saw those other lights, four of them in fact. Two below and two above coming out of the storm, coming down the ice-road past the meteorology dome. He was hearing the engine now, too . . . noisy, rattling diesel being down-shifted. The roar of the engine, the grinding of gears.

Jesus, it was the Spryte from Gates' camp. It had to be.

The Spryte was a small, tracked utility vehicle for ferrying men and supplies back and forth. It looked roughly like a bright red box sitting on caterpillar treads.

What in the hell?

The storm was taking a momentary breather, but the wind was still strong, but not strong enough to stay Hayes' curiosity. They hadn't heard from Gates in days and now here came the Spryte. Hayes stepped over the guylines and walked out into the compound. The sound of that approaching engine was getting louder, the lights brighter.

People were coming out of Targa House now, wearing goggles and parkas, straining into the wind. They were carrying lanterns and flashlights. Looked like a mob of angry villagers from an old Frankenstein movie.

Rutkowski came up behind Hayes. "What the fuck's going on, Jimmy?"

"Hell if I know."

He stood there in the wind, watching the Spryte coming on. The others were circled behind him in a loose knot. It took a lot to get people out on a night like that, but something like this, well, it drew them like metal filings to a magnet.

"Sodermark tried to raise 'em on the radio, but they're not responding," Sharkey said as she joined the group out there.

Hayes stared off into the night through his goggles. His beard was already stiff and frozen. His breath and that of the others billowing out in great, frosty clouds that turned on the wind. Cold-pinched faces waited and wondered. A light snow was coming down now, just as fine and white as beach sand.

"Look!" somebody cried out. "You see that?"

Hayes didn't at first, but now he did.

And seeing it, he had to stop and blink, brush snow from his goggles because he couldn't really be seeing what he thought he was seeing. His heart caught in his chest, held painfully there for a moment like an animal caught in tar. *This can't be good,* a voice in his head was telling him. *As far as developments go, this is next door to shitty.*

Somebody behind him gasped and somebody else swore under their breath.

What they were looking at was a lone form out there, running and stumbling before the Spryte, managing to keep just ahead of it, but barely. At first Hayes thought the Spryte was chasing the figure to catch up with it, but now it didn't look like that at all.

It looked like they were trying to run him over.

"Holy shit," somebody said.

"Rutkowski? Go get me one of those rifles," Hayes snapped. "And make sure it's fucking loaded."

Then he was running, the wind propelling him forward and then doing its damnedest to pitch him sideways. He pounded through drifts, slipping on his ass only once. The others were coming, too, but staying behind him like they wanted him to see it first.

"Hey!" Hayes called out as he got in closer. "Hey! Duck behind that hut! Duck behind that fucking hut . . . it's almost on you!"

The figure drunkenly zigged and zagged, went face down in the snow and crab-crawled frantically forward like a kid in gym class doing barrel crawls. But no kid ever had to plow through three- and four-foot drifts, keep his footing on pack-ice while the wind screamed into him at fifty and sixty miles an hour. And no kid ever had to do this in a bulky parka with the wind chill dipping down to seventy below zero.

Hayes was shouting at the lone man *and* at the driver of the Spryte, but it was doing him no good. With a sickening realization, he knew that the Spryte was going to overtake the man and was going to crush him beneath its treads. The figure got to his feet, moved off to the left and the Spryte compensated, its treads creaking as it came around. The Spryte was bearing down on him and Hayes was just too damn far away to do anything. People were shouting out behind him and he made one last valiant dash, but he lost his footing and went down in a drift, coming back up with his face covered in snow. He frantically pawed it away.

The man fell.

But he saw Hayes.

He was shaking his head back and forth, shouting something, but Hayes couldn't hear what it was in the racket of the Spryte's engine. The lights of the Spryte were glaring and intense, snow swirling in their beams. Hayes could just make out a dim figure in the cab.

Where in the fuck was Rutkowski with that gun?

He heard Sharkey scream his name and then the Spryte rolled right over that lone figure in the snow, those jointed tracks crushing him with a popping, wet sound that was meaty, organic, and brutal. The Spryte lurched as it went over him, leaving nothing but a red and ripped heap in its wake.

And then it was coming at Hayes.

"Oh, shit," he said under his breath, backing away now, preparing to break into a run.

But the Spryte stopped dead. Downshifted, started in reverse with a jerk as whoever was in that cab worked the stick roughly. There was no doubt what was happening: this crazy bastard was going to roll right over the body again.

The Spryte backed up and did just that and suddenly Rutkowski was there with the rifle in his hands, just standing there, speechless.

"Shoot that motherfucker!" Hayes told him.

But Rutkowski stood there, seeing that spreading red stain in the snow, smelling the blood and macerated flesh and he could not move.

Hayes took the rifle from his hands.

It was just a little bolt-action .22 survival rifle. He brought it up and popped a round through the cab. Worked the bolt and put another through there. He saw the bullet holes in the wide, sloping windshield. Saw the second bullet make the form in there throw its hands up and fall over.

The Spryte stopped.

Right on top of the body.

Hayes scrambled around the side of the cab and brought the rifle up, ready to finish the job and knowing that if anybody even so much as got in his way they were going to get a rifle-butt upside the head.

But nobody did.

They came up, but stayed a good distance away. Cutchen was there with Sharkey. Koricki and Sodermark. Stotts, Biggs, and Rutkowski. A few of the scientists. Nobody was saying a thing. The engine died on the Spryte and the door to the cab swung open and then shut again as the wind took it. Then it slammed open again and whoever was in there stepped out and onto the treads.

It was Holm.

The geologist from Gates' team. He just stood up on the treads like a politician preparing to make a speech. He wore a parka, but no hat. His white hair rustled in the wind. His face was the color of boiled bone.

"Holm?" Hayes said to him, wondering if he'd really hit him with the .22 or not. For he seemed perfectly healthy. "Holm? Goddammit, Holm, what the fuck do you think you're doing?"

"Watch it, Jimmy," Rutkowski said. "There's something funny here."

Oh yeah, there definitely was.

Holm hopped off the treads, down into the snow and stepped forward even as Hayes stepped back. Holm was a skinny old guy in his sixties and Hayes could have broke him over his knee without working up a sweat . . . yet, at that moment it would have been hard to picture a more dangerous man than Holm. There was something cold and remorseless about him.

"Holm . . . " Hayes said.

Holm was looking at him and his eyes were filled with a chill blankness. There was nothing in them. Nothing human at any rate. He surveyed Hayes with a flat indifference, that pallid face punched with two black eyes that made something go liquid in Hayes' belly. You didn't want to spend too much time looking into those eyes. They were like windows looking through into some godless, dead-end of space. You could see yourself there, suffocating in that deranged, airless void.

Hayes swallowed.

Those eyes drilled into him, sucking him dry.

There was power in those eyes, something immense and malignant and ancient. The way Hayes was feeling at that moment was how he felt looking into those glassy red orbs of the aliens in Hut #6. They got inside you, owned you, crushed your free will like a spider under a boot. At some primary level, they consumed and swallowed you. And you could feel all that you were sliding down into some black, soundless gullet.

Hayes made a squeaking sound in his throat, but that was it.

What he was feeling was awful . . . gut-deep and bone-cold and he was powerless to refuse it. It was like waking up in a coffin and hearing dirt thud against the lid . . . but having no voice with which to scream.

"Jimmy," Sharkey said. "Get away from him . . . *get away from him right now.*"

Her voice was like a slap across the face. Hayes blinked and stumbled backward, almost fell as his feet skated out in opposite directions. But his mind came back and the world swam into view. And as it did, he was remembering the night they chatted with Gates on the Internet. He could still see those threatening words on the screen:

you are in danger if I or others return watch us close very close something not right with holm I think they have his mind now

This was how Hayes knew the ball had dropped.

He brought the gun up. "All right, Holm, no closer. Next one goes between your eyes. Where's Gates? Bryer? The others? What have you done with them?"

Holm cocked his head slightly to one side like a puppy, but the effect was hardly cute . . . it was offensive and loathsome like feeling a spider unfurling its legs in your palm. It gave Hayes the same sense of atavistic revulsion. It actually made him take a step backward. His breath caught in his throat.

"Where's Gates?" he said again, noticing how weak and puny his voice seemed in the icy blackness of the night.

"Shoot him," Rutkowski said. "Put that fucking animal down. Look what he did . . . just look at what he did . . . "

But Hayes wasn't going to look.

He did not dare take his eyes away from Holm. Not for an instant. He was not looking *at* his eyes, but lower where the collar of his parka nestled against his chin. To look in those eyes was to see graveyards and misting hollows choked with bones. To look in those eyes was to feel the sweet poison of death pulling you down to sterile plains.

Holm stepped forward, paused, looked at Hayes with an arcane sort of amusement. The way you might look at a dog that had learned to sit up and beg or one of those cute monkeys that could turn the crank of an organ grinder. It was something like that. No fear or concern about Hayes and the rifle in his hands, but just a profound and boundless amusement at it all.

"Well somebody do something," another voice said. "Before I lose my fucking mind here."

The night was bunched around them, huge and black and freezing. The wind was still blowing and that powder of snow was still falling, blowing over those gathered there, dancing in the beams of the lights they held and the dimming beams of the Spryte. Holm was breathing very fast, the sound of it like somebody drawing air through crackling, dry hay. Each time he exhaled a cloud of frost gathered and dissipated.

Hayes could hear that wind moaning around the buildings, the sound of boots rocking uneasily on the hardpack snow.

Holm took another bold step forward, as if daring Hayes to put him down. He moved quickly with an almost fluidic motion, a vitality an old man had no right to possess. Hayes figured that, even though there was six feet separating them, Holm would have been on him before he even pulled the trigger. He was staring at Hayes and his eyes were wet and glistening, horribly dilated so that the iris and sclera of both eyes were swallowed by those fixed and expansive pupils. They were glassy and reflective.

Holm opened his mouth in something like a snarl, showing those even white teeth that were probably dentures. A sibilant hissing came from his throat, gaining volume and scratching up into a voice: *"Gates? Gates is dead . . . we're all dead . . . "*

Hayes almost shot him right then.

That voice was just too much. It was utterly inhuman, like the echo of subterranean water trying to form words. Holm smiled at what he had said and made a lunge at Hayes. He wasn't as quick as he seemed at first and Hayes sidestepped him and brought the rifle butt down on his temple. Holm went to his knees immediately, but did not make a sound. Unless the howling wind was his voice, echoing off into the night, sweeping across that lonesome and ancient polar plain.

"All right," Hayes said. "Somebody get some rope or chain or something. We'll tie him up and bring him inside."

"Just kill him, Jimmy," Stotts said. "Do it, Jimmy . . . look at those eyes . . . nothing sane has eyes like that."

Rutkowski and Biggs came over, as did Sodermark and one of the scientists, a seismologist named Hinks, who spent most of his time out at remote tracking stations and was not privy to the majority of the madness at Kharkhov Station. Carefully then, Hayes handing off his rifle to Sharkey, they surrounded Holm.

"Get up," Rutkowski told him. "While you still fucking can."

Holm looked up at them with that same almost insipid blankness. His black eyes like those of a grasshopper considering a stalk of grass. That's how they looked . . . unintelligent, completely vacant. At least at that moment. But Hayes knew those eyes and what they could do. One minute they were dead and empty, the next overflowing with all the knowledge of the cosmos.

Rutkowski and Hinks were looking pissed-off.

Looked like what they had here was just some offensive drunk and they were going to pitch him out into the alley, maybe bang his head off a dumpster for good measure. They both reached down and yanked Holm to his feet. Hayes took hold of him, too, as did Biggs. They got him standing and then he started moving, fighting and writhing and twitching almost like he had no bones, was made of liquid rubber. He fought and struck out. He knocked Hinks aside and sent Rutkowski scrambling. Hayes darted in and gave him a quick shot to the jaw that snapped his head back and then something happened.

Hayes felt it coming . . . an energy, a building momentum like static electricity generating before lightning strikes. And then that thumping vibration started up, seeming to come from the ice below them. They could all feel it coming up through their boots and traveling along their bones in waves. It was the same sound Rutkowski had heard the night St. Ours died and the same sound Hayes, Cutchen, and Sharkey had heard at Vradaz . . . a rhythmic pulsating that rose up around them, getting louder and louder. Like the humming of some great machine. Then there was that crackling, electric sound that made the hairs stand up on the back of their necks. Thumpings and echoing knocks, a high and weird whistling sound.

Then Biggs and Stotts were suddenly knocked flat.

The window in the door of the Spryte's cab shattered as did the windshield. Hayes felt a rolling wave of heat pass right before him — so warm in fact that it melted the ice from his beard — and hit Rutkowski and Hinks, lifting them up and throwing them back five or six feet onto their asses.

Somebody screamed.

Somebody shouted.

And Holm stood there, his face almost luminous. The vibrating and crackling sounds grew louder and then there was a piercing, shrieking wail that made everyone cover their ears and grit their teeth. It broke up around them into a shrill piping. An almost musical piping like Hayes had heard the night in Hut #6 when the things had almost gotten his mind. It rose up all around them, strident and keening and Hayes saw forms out in the darkness . . . oblong shadows coming at them.

And then there was an explosion.

An echoing report and Sharkey was standing there with the .22 in her hands. All the noise suddenly stopped and there were no shadows mulling around them. There was nothing. Just those shocked faces and Holm standing there with a neat hole in his forehead about the size of a dime. Blood had spattered over his face from the impact and it looked like black ink in the semi-darkness. He tottered and fell over, striking his head on the treads of the Spryte.

People started getting out of there right away.

Hayes stood there, watching them leave. They all knew it was over with and they were rushing away.

"No, don't worry," Hayes called after them. "I'll drive the Spryte off this stiff . . . don't worry your heads none about it. Let me take care of it."

Then it was just him and Cutchen and Sharkey standing there, not saying a thing. The wind kept blowing and the snow kept drifting and the polar night wrapped around them like it would never let them go.

Finally, Sharkey dropped the rifle. "I . . . I guess I just killed a man," she said, seeming confused as to how she should feel about this.

But Cutchen just shook his head. "I don't know what it was you killed, Elaine. But it sure as hell was not a man."

36

Two hours later, they were all in the community room and LaHune was holding court. For once, he didn't have to tell everyone to pipe down so he could be heard. Nobody was talking. They were all looking at the floor, their hands, the tables before them. Anything but at each other and LaHune standing up there in front.

"For some time now," LaHune said, looking oddly uncomfortable up there, "Mr. Hayes has been warning me and most of you, I would imagine, that we are in danger here. That those . . . *relics* Dr. Gates and his team brought in are somehow hazardous to us. Mr. Hayes believes . . . as some of you do, no doubt . . . that those creatures are not entirely dead. That there is activity in them. A sort of psychic energy, if you will, that they emanate. Up until tonight, I was not ready to accept any of that. But now, after what happened out in the compound, I'm not so sure."

Hayes sat there with his arms folded, looking indignant. He wasn't sure what LaHune was up to, but he didn't care for it. The idea of having the man on his side suddenly was even worse than having him against him. He wasn't sure why, but it irked him.

"Now, Mr. Hayes has taken care of those creatures out in the hut . . . put them back to sleep so to speak . . . "

Somebody tittered at that.

" . . . but that's hardly the end of the problem. It's been five days now since we've heard from Dr. Gates' party. I don't care for it and neither do any of you. In fact, the only thing we've learned about them came in the form of that particularly ugly incident this evening."

Ugly? Hayes liked that. No, *ugly* didn't cut it. That business was a nightmare, a goddamn tragedy.

LaHune went on: "The bottom line is, people, we are very much alone out here. We can't look for help from the outside world until spring and spring is a long way off. We have to send a party up to Gates' camp to look for survivors. They may already be dead or worse. I don't know. But somebody has to go up there, so I'm – "

"I'll go," Hayes said. "I think Dr. Sharkey and Cutchen will come with me. Anyone else that wants to tag along, well, I'd welcome your help."

Hayes stood up and looked around.

Nobody would meet his eyes.

It seemed that for a moment maybe Rutkowski and Hinks were considering it, but they lowered their heads one after the other.

"Didn't expect any of you would," Hayes said.

LaHune cleared his throat. "Now, I can't order you three to go up there."

"You don't have to," Sharkey said.

She stood up with Cutchen and Hayes. The three of them scanned those dour, frightened faces in the room.

"I guess that's it then," Hayes said. "We leave in an hour. Any of you happen to grow a pair of balls by then, meet us out at the SnoCat."

The three of them left and the gathering broke up. Broke up quietly. Nobody had a thing to say. They plodded back to the dark corners of their lives and looked for a convenient pile of sand to stick their heads into.

37

Two or three times on the way up to the tent camp, Hayes found himself wondering what in the hell LaHune was up to. His sudden about-face was worrisome. Troubling. There was no sense of satisfaction attached to it; none whatsoever. No, *thank God you're with us now, Mister LaHune, things is going to be better now, yessum.* For LaHune, as far as Hayes was concerned, was a man with an agenda and Hayes had to wonder just how this abrupt turn of face might possibly serve the administrator and his masters.

There had to be something there.

And maybe had he been more awake, not so worn and squeezed dry, he might have seen it. But as things stood, he was having trouble thinking about little else but the storm and the darkness and the incredible danger they were all in.

They had not been able to honestly identify who the body that Holm ran over belonged to. There was no ID on the corpse and its physical state was appalling. Like 150 pounds of bloody meat poured into a parka and thermal wind pants. But they had answered one little question. They'd been wondering what the scenario of all that was. They found it hard to believe their John Doe had made it all the way from Gates' encampment to Kharkhov on foot and in a Condition One blizzard yet. But about two miles from the station they'd found a Ski-Doo snowmobile abandoned on the ice road. Their John Doe had escaped on the sled and Holm had come after him on the Spryte.

And what would have happened, Hayes wondered, if Holm had gotten him out on the road? What then?

He kept picturing Holm returning and doing the most awful things once they'd invited him amongst them. Because, of course, they would have. Like a disease germ he would have circulated freely and then –

"What are we going to do," Cutchen said then, "if we find no one at the camp? Or worse, what if they're all dead or . . . *possessed* like Holm? What then?"

"We'll do whatever feels right," Sharkey said.

"Regardless of what that might be," Hayes added.

And that was it in a nutshell, wasn't it? *Regardless of what that might be.* Because honestly he had no idea what they were going into, only that the idea of it gave him about the same sense of apprehension as sticking his hands into a nest of rattlesnakes sidled up in a desert crevice. The idea of getting bit wasn't what bothered him, it was the idea of the venom itself. And the sort of venom he might get stuck with in those blasphemous ruins was the sort that could erase who and what he was and birth something invidious and primal implanted in his genes a hundred-thousand millennia before.

You don't know that, you really don't.

Yet, he did.

Maybe whatever it was had hid itself in the primal depths of the human psyche, but it was there, all right. Waiting. Biding its time. A ghost, a memory, a revenant hiding in the dank and dripping crypt of the human condition like a pestilence waiting to overtake and infect. A cursed tomb waiting to be violated, waiting to loose some eldritch horror upon the world. An in-bred plague that festered in the wormy charnel depths of the subconscious, waiting to be woken, activated by the discordant piping of alien minds.

Dear Christ, there could be nothing as horrible as this.

Nothing.

He did not and could not know the ultimate aim of awakening the sleeping dragon the Old Ones had planted in the minds of men . . . but it would be colossal, it would be immense, it would be the end of history as they knew it and the beginning of something else entirely. The continuation of that primordial seeding, the vast outer extremity of that tree, the ultimate objective.

The final fruit.

It made Hayes weak just to think of it, whatever it might be.

So he did not think about it. Not much, anyway.

He kept an eye on what the blazing lights of the SnoCat showed him. Which was just snow and whiteness, ragged ridges of black rock. The terrain was rough and hilly as they plied the foothills of the Dominion Range, moving up frozen slopes and down through rivers of drift, bouncing madly over crests of volcanic rock. Moving ever higher and higher along the ice road.

"Jesus," Cutchen said as the SnoCat shook like a wet tabby, "this is worse than I thought. We have no business out here . . . those winds are sweeping down from the mountains and picking up everything in their path, peeling this fucking continent right down to the bare rock."

"We'll make it," Hayes said. "Unless the GPS goes to hell."

"You can't trust anything in a blow like this."

The storm.

Hayes could see it out there in that haunted blackness, the headlights clotted with snow thick as a fall of flower petals, thick as dust blowing through the decayed corridors of a ghost town. It was more than just a Condition One storm with near-zero visibility and winds approaching a hundred miles an hour and snow falling by the bails, pushed into frozen crests and waves. No, this was bigger than that. This was every storm that had ever scraped across the Geomagnetic graveyard of that white, dead continent. Pacific typhoons and Atlantic hurricanes, Midwestern tornadoes and oceanic white squalls, tempests and blizzards and violent gales . . . all of them converging here, bled dry of their force and suction and devastation, reborn at the South Pole in a screaming glacial white-out that was sculpting the rugged landscape in canopies of frost, leeching warmth, driving blood to freon, and pushing anything alive down into a polar tomb, a necropolis of black, cracking ice.

And, just maybe, it was more than that even.

The winds were cyclonic and whipping, making the SnoCat shake and feel like it was going to be vacuumed right up into that Arctic maelstrom or maybe be entombed beneath a mountain of drifting now. But these were physical things . . . palpable things you could feel and know, things with limitations despite their intensity.

But there were other things on the storm.

Things funneling and raging in that vortex that you could only feel in your soul, things like pain and insanity and fear. Maybe wraiths and ghosts and all those demented minds lost in storms and whirlwinds, creeping things from beyond death or nameless evils that had never been born . . . the gathered malignancies and earthbound toxins of that which was human and that which was not, writhing shadows blown from pole to pole since antiquity. Yes, all of that and more, the collected horrors of the race and the sheared veil of the grave, coming together at once, breathing in frost and exhaling blight, a deranged elemental sentience that howled and screeched and cackled in the shrill and broken voices of a million, a million-million lost and tormented souls . . .

Hayes was feeling them out there on that moaning storm-wind, enclosing the SnoCat in a frozen winding sheet. Death. Unseen, unspeakable, and unstoppable, filling its lungs with a savage whiteness and his head with a scratching black madness. He kept his eyes fixed on the windshield, what the headlights could show him: snow and wind and night, everything all wrapped and twined together, coming at them and drowning them in darkness. He kept blinking his eyes, telling himself he wasn't seeing death out there. Wasn't seeing spinning cloven skulls and the blowing, rent shrouds of deathless cadavers flapping like high masts. Boiling storms of sightless eyes and ragged cornhusk figures flitting about. Couldn't hear them calling his name or scraping at the windows with white skeletal fingers.

It was imagination.

It was stress and terror and fatigue.

Too many things.

He could feel Sharkey next to him, her leg against his own and both separated by inches of fleece and wool and vinyl. He wondered if she saw what he was seeing and if she did . . . why didn't she scream? Why didn't they both scream? What held them together and why were those seams sewn so tightly, so strongly that not even this could tear them?

My God, but Hayes felt alone.

Maybe there were people in the cab with him and maybe he had only willed them to be there so he didn't go stark, screaming insane. That viscid, living blackness was pressing down upon the SnoCat, inhuming it beneath layers of frozen graveyard soil. And he could feel it happening. Could sense the weight and pressure, the eternal suffocation of that oblong box. His throat was scratchy. The air thin and dusty. His breath was being sucked away and his brain was dissolving into a firmament of rot. Nothing but worms and time and clotted soil. Oh, dear God, he could *really* feel it now, that claustrophobic sense of entombment, of burial, of moist darkness. He could really hear the sounds of rats pawing at his box and the scratching requiem of a tuneless violin, time filtering out into dusty eternity. And his own voice, frantic and terrified: *Who did you think you were to flex your muscle against this land? To raise your fist in defiance against those who created you and everything else? The dark lords of organic profusion? What worming disobedience made you think for one shivering instant you could fight against those minds that already own you and have owned your kind since you first crawled from the protoplasmic slime?*

Oh, dear Christ, what had he been thinking? What had he –

"Are you all right?" Sharkey suddenly asked him.

And the answer to that was something he did not know.

He'd been thinking about what the Old Ones had buried at the core of humanity. He'd been talking about the weather with Cutchen and then . . . and then he wasn't sure. Hallucinations. Fears. Insecurities. Everything coming at him at once. But none of it had been real. None of it.

He swallowed. "Yeah, I'm fine."

"Really fine?" she said.

"Hell no," he said honestly.

"We're close," Cutchen suddenly said. His voice was calm, yet full of the apprehension a doctor might use when he told you your belly was full of cancer. "According to the GPS, we're practically there."

But Hayes knew that without looking. He could feel it in his balls, his guts, along the back of his spine. It was an ancient sensory network and in the worst of times, it was rarely wrong.

Hayes slowed the SnoCat, downshifted, said, "Yippy-fucking-skippy."

When Hayes stepped out of the SnoCat, first thing he became aware of was that silence. The wind was still blowing and the snow was still falling, but they were protected here in the lower ranges of the Transantarctic Mountains. You could hear the wind howling still, but it was distant now. Here, in the little valley where Gates had set up his tent camp, it was silent and lonely and forever. All he could hear around them was an odd sighing sound like respiration. Like something was breathing. Some weird atmospheric condition produced by the rocky peaks around them, no doubt.

The sky above was pink and you could see fairly-well in the semi-darkness. Here the glacial sheet had been stopped by the Dominion Range, had piled up into breathtaking bluffs of crystal blue ice like sheets of broken glass several hundred feet in height. The snow had been stripped down to the glossy black volcanic rock beneath, a terrain full of sudden dips and craggy draws. And above, standing sentinel were those rolling Archaean hills and the high towers of the mountains themselves, like the cones of witch hats rising grimly up into the polar wastes. Rolling clouds of ice-fog blew down from them in a breath of mist.

Standing there, taking in that primeval vista all around him and feeling its haunted aura, Hayes was struck how the landscape looked like something plucked from some dead, alien world light years distant. High and jagged and surreal, a phantasmal netherworld of sharp and spiky summits that reminded him of monuments, of obelisks, of menhirs . . . as if they were not merely geological features, but the craggy and towering steeples of ancient, weathered tombstones. That what he saw was nothing so simple as a mountain range, but the narrow and leaning masonry of the world's oldest cemetery.

Yes, this is where the gods came to bury their own . . . here in this polar mortuary at the bottom of the world. A shunned place like a graveyard of alien witches.

And, Jesus, hadn't he seen these mountains in his dreams? In dozens of nightmares since earliest childhood? Weren't they imprinted on the mind and soul of every man and woman? That deranged geography of sharp-peaked cones, that unwavering line of warning beacons?

Hayes stood there, his beard frosted white, shaking, seeing those mountains and feeling certain that they were seeing him, too. They inspired a terror so pure, so infinite, so aged, that he literally could not move. Those peaks and pinnacles were somehow very *wrong*. They were desolate and godless and spiritually toxic, a perverse geometry that reached inside the human mind and squeezed the blood out of what they found there. Literally wrung out the human soul like a sponge, draining it, leeching it. Yes, there was something ethereal and spatially demented about those aboriginal hills and they were like a siren song of destruction to the human mind. Geometrically grotesque, here was the place where time and space, dimension and madness came together, mating into something that fractured the human mind.

So Hayes stood there, letting it fill him as he knew it must.

The cones had an uncanny hypnotic effect on him, a morphic pull that made him want to do nothing but stare. Just stand there and watch them, trace them with his eyes, feel their soaring height and antiquity. And he would have stood there for an hour or five, mesmerized by them, until he froze up and fell over. Because the more you watched them, the more you wanted to. And the more you began to see almost a funny sort of light arcing off the crests and narrow tips, a jumping and glowing emission like electricity or stolen moonlight. It made Hayes' heart pound and his head reel, made his fingertips tingle and filled the black pot of his belly with a spreading heat like coals being fanned up into a blaze. He had felt nothing like it in years, maybe never: an exhilaration, a vitality, a preternatural sense of awe that just emptied his mind of anything but those rising, primal cones.

Pabodie had called them the "Mountains of Madness" and, dear

God, how very apt that was.

For Hayes felt practically hysterical looking upon them.

But more than that he felt a budding, burgeoning sense of wonder and purpose and necessity. The import and magnitude of this place . . . yes, it was enough to drive any man insane. Insane with a knowledge of exactly who and what he was. Destiny. The sense that he had come full circle.

"Jimmy?" Sharkey said and it almost sounded like she was calling to him from one of those conic apexes. "Jimmy? Jimmy, are you all right?"

"Yeah," he said.

He looked away from those peaks that had snagged his mind. Looked at Sharkey and then at Cutchen. In the glow of Cutchen's lantern their faces were drawn with concern. With fright and apprehension and too goddamn many things to catalog.

"I'm okay," he said. "Really."

He had only felt something like that once in his life. Just after high school he'd worked at a transformer substation where the juice traveling down high-tension wires was stepped down, dampened, for household and industrial consumption. He'd quit after three weeks. Those transformers had been pissing out an energy that only he seemed to be aware of. When he got too close to them, his teeth ached and his spine crawled like it was covered with hundreds of ants. But there was a mental effect, too. It amped him up. Made him feel nervous and antsy and wired like he was full of caffeine or coked-up. Later on, one of the engineers told him that the high-tension lines and their attendant transformers put out moderate alternating electrical and magnetic fields and some people were just more susceptible to them.

Those high peaks were doing that to him, he knew. Creating a negative charge of energy that maybe only he was feeling.

Sharkey put her gloved hand on his arm. "You can feel it, can't you?" she said, touching her chest and her head. "In *here* and *here* . . . an attraction to this place, a magnetism or something. The secret life of these mountains and what they hide."

"Yes," he said. "It's strong."

Even turned away from those spires and cones he was feeling it right down to his marrow. A dizzy sense of deja-vu, deja-vu squared. A dark and misty recognition of something long-forgotten and rediscovered. But it was more that, it was much more. He was feeling something else, too, something huge that seemed to blot out his rational mind. He was in touch with some ancient network and he could feel the legacy of his race, the twisted and shadowy ancestral heritage that had been passed down from impossibly ancient and forgotten days. The race memory of this place and others like it, the creatures who occupied them . . . all of it was rushing up at him, sinking him in a mire of atavism and primal terror. These things had been written and remembered, he knew, in the form of folktale and legend and myth. Channeled through the ages into tales of winged demons and devils, night-haunts and the Wild Hunt itself.

But if those were just tales, then what inspired them was bleak and real.

"Okay, let's go take a peak before I start beating my sacrificial drum and chanting about the Old Ones," he said.

They both looked at him.

"Never mind."

"I suppose we might see things," Cutchen said, maybe just to himself. "I suppose we might hear things."

As they climbed down away from the SnoCat and deeper into the valley towards Gates' camp, Hayes concentrated only on each step. He pressed one boot down into the snow and followed it with another. Kept doing this, disconnecting himself from the aura of this place and what it could do to him. He saw nothing and he heard nothing and that was just fine.

When they reached the periphery of Gates' encampment, they just stopped like they met a wall. They stopped and panned their lights around. Everything was quiet and still like sleeping marble. It could have been a midnight cemetery they were in and the atmosphere felt about the same . . . hush, breathless, uninviting. The camp was grim and cold and bleak, crawling with black, hooded shadows. It had all the atmosphere of a mausoleum. Just the gentle moan of the wind, tent flaps rustling in the breeze.

Hayes knew it was empty long before he entered.

Not so much as a single light was lit and the place just felt dead, deserted.

They could see a couple Ski-Doo snowmobiles dusted with white, the hulk of Gates' SnoCat. A wall of snow blocks surrounded the actual camp as a wind-shelter, with secondary walls to protect the cooking area and give some privacy to the latrine. There were a series of rugged Scott tents and bright red mountaineering tents that were anchored down with nylon lines and ice-screws, dead man bolts. Snow had been heaped around them to guard against the fierce Antarctic gusts. A couple fish huts had been set up and there was a Polar Haven for storage.

Just a typical research camp.

Except it was completely lifeless.

Lifeless, yes, but far from unoccupied.

Hayes led the way into one of the fish huts. It was being used as sort of a community living area. There was nothing out of the ordinary. Cots and sleepmats, sleeping bags and vinyl duffels of personal items. Some boots and ECW's hanging along the wall. A couple MSR stoves near the wall. Boxes of canned and dehydrated foods, propane stoves, water jugs. A field radio and INMARSAT system for voice and data transmission and retrieval. A corkboard was hanging above it with notes and telnet numbers. Somebody had tacked a photo of Godzilla up and pencilled in a smile on his face

Cutchen swallowed. "Nothing out of the ordinary."

"Except everything's down," Sharkey said. "Generator's quit, Ethernet is off. Like it was abandoned."

"C'mon," Hayes said.

He went into the other fish hut. It was being used as a field lab by Gates and his people. A table was heaped with fossil specimens, others were bagged and tagged in crates and boxes. There were a pair of portable Nikon binocular microscopes, a few boxes of slides and trays of instruments. Hand-drills and chippers. Some bottles of chemicals and acids, piles of cribbed notes with an ammonite fossil used as a paperweight. A curtain separated a cramped dark room with cameras and a photomacroscope.

Sharkey paged through the notes. "Nothing interesting," she said. "Geologic and paleontologic stuff . . . measurements and classifications, sketches and stratigraphy and the like. Stuff about brachiopods, crinoids . . . fossil-bearing stratas."

"Geo one-oh-one," Cutchen said.

Sharkey kept looking.

There were squat shelves crowded with spiral-bound notebooks, rolled-up maps, ledgers, boxes of writeable CDs. A few odd books. Down on her hands and knees, Sharkey checked it all out with her flashlight. She pulled out manila folders, hand-written field logs.

"Are you doing inventory?" Cutchen finally said.

"Yes, I am," she said, still searching. "I just have to find out how many rolls of toilet paper they've used up."

Hayes giggled.

Cutchen flipped her off.

Hayes didn't interfere because she wasn't just wasting their time. If she was bothering to look through those heaping stacks then she was hot on the trail of something. Something relevant.

Hayes leaned against the doorway, thinking about the cold.

They were each wearing an easy thirty-odd pounds of cold weather gear: long underwear, sweaters, wool socks, insulated nylon overalls, Gore Tex down parkas, mittens, ski gloves, and bunny boots . . . those big white moon boots that were inflated with air to provide insulation. But even so, prolonged exposure to the Antarctic winter night was not recommended. The trough of glacial air was sweeping over the top of the valley and screaming across the ice-plain at an easy seventy miles an hour . . . driving a temperature of eighty below zero somewhere into the range of 120 below. They were protected from that here, but it was still damnably cold. The sooner they could wind this up the better. Hayes was keeping an eye on both Cutchen and Sharkey, as well as himself. Looking for the signs that they needed to get out of the cold right away . . . stupor, fatigue, disorientation. So far, so good.

But it would happen out here.

Sooner or later.

"Nothing," Sharkey said. "Nothing at all."

"What were you looking for?" Cutchen asked her.

"I don't know . . . something belonging to Gates. A personal journal or something. Maybe it's in the 'Cat."

Outside again, the cold seemed worse . . . bitter, unrelenting. They could hear the distant sounds of the glaciers cracking and snapping, the crackling sound their own breath made as the moisture in it froze and drifted down as they walked.

They stopped by the Polar Haven and there wasn't much of interest in there either. Just the usual: shovels and ice-axes, sledge hammers and ice drills, spare parts for the coring rig, cots and tarps. Sharkey steered them back towards Gates' SnoCat. There was nothing in it either. Nothing resembling a journal, at any rate.

Sharkey found something beneath the seat, though. It looked like a TV remote. "What's this?"

"Detonator," Cutchen said.

Hayes took it away from her, studied it in his light. "Yeah . . . it's armed, too."

They were all looking around now. The proximity of high explosives was the sort of immediate threat that could make you forget very quickly about aliens that could suck your mind away. Hayes set the detonator on the seat.

"Are we in danger here?" Sharkey asked him.

"No . . . I don't think so." Hayes looked around. "My guess is somebody has a charge rigged around here somewhere, maybe doing some seismic echo work. Maybe."

But that wasn't what he was thinking at all. Given what must have happened here, Hayes would not have been surprised to learn that the entire camp was rigged to blow-up.

They moved back down beyond the snow-block walls, away from the structures and to a wall of black sandstone that rose up maybe two-hundred feet. Situated at the base of it was Gates' corer, a portable shot-hole drilling system. The drill tripod, compressor, and hose spool were sled-mounted and had been pulled away from a yawning black fissure that led down into the earth. It was roughly elliptical in shape, maybe twenty feet at its widest point. A winch was set up near it so supplies could be lowered and specimens could be brought up and swung out.

"The famous chasm," Cutchen said. You could hear the bitterness in his voice and nobody blamed him for it. "If they would have drilled somewhere else, we might not be in this fix now."

"Oh, yes we would," Hayes said. "What's happening down here has been *meant* to happen."

Gates' team had set up an emergency ladder for people to climb down with. Using his light, Hayes saw that the drop was maybe twenty feet. But it was just as black as a mineshaft down there and the idea of descending made something seize up in his chest. But there was no real choice. He went down first and it was no easy bit in his ballooned-out bunny boots, like walking a tight rope in hip waders. He went down slowly, while Sharkey kept her flashlight beam on him. Tiny crystals of ice floated in it, clouds of his steaming breath.

Finally, he made it.

The floor was uneven, rocky, veined with frost and ice. Hayes played his light around and saw that he was in a passage that gradually sloped deeper into that frozen earth. "Okay," he called out. "Next."

Sharkey's turn. She moved fairly quickly down the ladder. Cutchen followed, bitching the entire way that the last time he'd followed them down into a hole he'd had to squeeze out his long johns when they'd gotten back to the station. But, finally, he was down, too.

"Looks like the set from an old B-movie," he said, holding his lantern high. "A natural cavern, I'd say. I don't see any signs of chipping or toolwork on the walls."

Hayes didn't either. "Limestone," he said, studying the striations, the layers pressing down upon one another.

"Sure, a natural limestone cavern. Probably hollowed out by ground water over millions of years," Cutchen said.

Sharkey chortled. "Now who's talking Geo one-oh-one?"

The passage was about eight or nine feet in height, maybe five in width. Hayes leading, they started down its sloping path. It would angle to the left, then to the right, had more twists and turns to it than a water snake. And they were going deeper into the mountain with each step. Ten minutes into it, Hayes began to notice that things were warming up. It still wasn't time for a bikini wax and a thong, but it was certainly warmer. Cutchen noticed it, too, saying that it had to be due to a volcanic vent or geothermal action.

"Least we won't freeze down here," Sharkey said.

Cutchen nodded. "You know, I was wondering how Gates and the boys were handling this so well. Being down here hour after hour. If it wasn't for the warmth they would have froze their balls off – "

Sharkey put a gloved finger to her lips. "Quiet."

"What?"

"Shut the hell up," she whispered.

Hayes was listening with her now, too.

He didn't know what for and part of him honestly did not want to know, but he listened nonetheless. Then he heard an echo from somewhere below . . . just a quick, furtive scratching sound that disappeared so quickly he wasn't sure he had heard it at all. Then he heard it again not five seconds later . . . like a stick being scratched along a subterranean wall.

And down there in that underworld, going to a place that was as storied and terrible in their imaginations as some vampire's castle, it was probably the worse possible thing to be hearing. For a scratching implied motion and motion implied something *alive* . . .

Hayes was thinking: *Could be a man, could be one of the team . . . and it could be something else entirely.*

They stood there, looking at each other and at those limestone walls, an ice-mist tangling through their legs like groundfog. In the glow of Cutchen's lantern, there was only their frosting breath, suspended ice crystals and drifting motes of dust. And shadows. Because down in that creeping murk, the lights were casting huge and distorted shadows.

Hayes took a few more steps, his belly feeling hollow and feathery. He played his light farther down into the stygian depths of that channel which, from where he was sitting, might as well have led right down to the lower regions of Hell itself.

He heard the sound again and started.

A distant scraping that seemed to be moving up the passage at them and then a few seconds later, sounded impossibly far-off. It would pause for a moment or two, then start up again . . . closer then farther, that same scratching, dragging sound. Hayes felt a trickle of sweat run down his spine. Something in his bowels tensed. He could hear his own breathing in his ears and it seemed impossibly loud. Then, suddenly, the scratching was much closer, so very close in fact that Hayes almost turned and ran. Because it seemed that whatever was making it would show itself at any moment, something spidery with scraping twigs for fingers.

Then it abruptly ceased.

"What in Christ was that?" Sharkey said behind him, edging closer to him now.

And he was going to tell her that it was probably nothing. Sound would carry funny down in the hollowed earth. That's all it was. Nothing to get excited about. But he never did say that, for less than a minute after the scratching stopped, something else took its place . . . a strident, squeaky piping like an out-of-tune recording of a church organ played on an old Victrola. It rose up high and shrieking, gaining volume and insistence. No wind blowing through no underground passage could have created something like that. The sound of it was eerie and disturbing, the auditory equivalent of a knife blade pressed against your spine and slowly drawn upwards.

Hayes suddenly felt very numb, rubbery and uncoordinated.

So much so that if he moved, he figured he would have fallen flat on his face. So he didn't move. He stood there like a statue in a park waiting for a pigeon to shit on him. That still, that motionless. His tongue felt like it was glued to the roof of his mouth. The sound died out for maybe a second or two. But then it came again, shrill and piercing and somehow malevolent. It was reedy and cacophonous and something about it made you want to scream. But what really was bothering Hayes about it was that it was not neutral in the least . . . it sounded almost hysterical or demented.

And then it died out for good, ending it mid-squeal, shattering into a dozen resounding and tinny echoes that bounced around through caves and hollows and openings. But the memory of it was still there.

And what Hayes was thinking was something he did not dare say:

That's what they sound like . . . I heard it that night on the tractor and I heard it out in the hut . . . that was a voice of a living Old One . . .

But he kept that to himself.

He stood there, teetering from foot to foot, feeling like something had evaporated inside of him. Maybe it was courage and maybe it was just common sense.

"Okay," Cutchen said, his voice barely audible. He cleared his throat. "I'm for getting the hell out right now."

"I'm for that," Sharkey said.

Which dumped the whole stinking mess at Hayes' doorstep. He shook his head. "We want answers? We want to know what happened to Gates and the others? Then those answers are down there."

Cutchen looked at him with anger that slowly subsided. "All right, Jimmy, if that's what you want. But this is the last fucking date I go on with you."

It was a pale attempt at humor, but it made them all smile. Hayes knew it was not intended to be funny, however, it was just how Cutchen responded to terror and uncertainty: with funny lines born out of contempt.

They started down again.

After another five or ten minutes in that passage, it narrowed to a hole that was perfectly circular like the shaft of a sewer. Its circumference was about ten feet, but so perfectly symmetrical it could not possibly have been cut by ancient floodwaters. Hayes stepped through first and found himself in a room that was again uniform, but rectangular in shape. At the far end, another passage dropped away into darkness. He examined it with his light and saw a set of carved stone steps dropping away into the blackness. They were long, low steps, more like slabs, each large enough, it seemed, to set a dining table and chairs on.

Whatever walked them, Hayes got to thinking, did not have the same tread as a man.

It took time to navigate them because each was about five feet wide. They were set with faults and cracks, the edges falling away. There were lots of tiny pebbles and bits of rock strewn over them as if some ancient subterranean river had deposited them there. Now and again, Hayes saw little protrusions like bumps or knobs that had been almost completely worn away. So maybe they weren't steps at all.

On they went, their lights bobbing and their footfalls loud and scraping.

As they descended, Hayes was filled with an exhilaration much like Gates and his people must have felt originally coming down there. A sense of discovery, of anticipation, of great revelations laying ahead. As he moved ever downward, some smartass voice in his head kept saying things like, *who do you suppose built all this? Is there life on Mars and in outer space?* But it was not funny. It left a bad taste in his mouth like he'd been chewing on spiders.

Finally, he paused. "Everyone okay?"

Cutchen just grunted.

Sharkey said, "Peachy."

Down they went and by the time they hit bottom, Hayes figured they had descended at least a hundred feet if not more. And now they entered a grotto that was absolutely immense. The floor was littered with fallen shelves of sedimentary rock, loose stones, the pillars of gigantic stalagmites that had been smoothed into near-perfect cones probably by those same long-gone floodwaters.

"Christ," Sharkey said and her voice echoed out, breaking up and pulled away into fantastic heights above them.

They stepped farther into the grotto.

It was so huge that their lights literally would not penetrate up to the roof or the surrounding walls. Everything echoed. Somewhere, water was dripping. Faint, distant, but dripping all the same. They spread out in a rough circle, trying to find something in there. Overhead, what had to be at least a hundred feet straight up they could see the tips of stalactites. They kept in sight because it would have been just too easy to get lost in there and never find your way out again. The flashlight and lantern beams picked out a cloistered haze in the air, motes of dust. It smelled dirty and dry in there like relics pulled from an Egyptian tomb.

"You'd need a spotlight in here to see anything," Cutchen said.

They kept fanning out, stepping over rock outcroppings, the occasional vein of ice. There were crevices cut into the floor. Some were no more than a few feet deep and a few inches wide, but others were big enough to swallow a car and had no bottom that the lights could find. They moved on, trying to follow what they thought was a path through that colossal underworld. Everything echoed and bounced around them. It was like an amphitheater in there . . . one exaggerated to a tremendous scope. Now and again, a light rain of ice crystals would fall on them. The air was oddly rarefied like they were on a mountaintop and not far below the surface.

Then suddenly, maybe a full city block into the grotto, they stopped.

Before them was a gigantic gully about as wide as a football field choked with debris . . . much of it was nothing but huge boulders, some of them as big as two-story houses, lots of loose rocks and stacked wedges of sandstone. But not all of it was of natural origin, for there were other shapes down there, ovals and pillars, assorted masonry that had been cut into those shapes.

And there was no doubting where it had come from.

For to either side of the gully, they could see the remains of the ancient city climbing up sharp slopes into the murk above. It was enormous, what they could see of it, for it climbed much higher than their lights could reach. A sleeping fossil, a mammoth city from nightmare antiquity.

Looking upon it, Hayes was instantly reminded of Ansazi cliff-dwellings and pit houses . . . but those were primitive and pedestrian compared to this. For the city they were seeing had been a metropolis carved from solid rock — clusters of rising cubes and crumbling arches, cones and pyramids and immense rectangular towers honeycombed with passages. At one time, both halves of the city must have been joined together until that deep chasm opened up and the center collapsed beneath into that grave of bones.

"Oh my God," Sharkey said and that pretty much summed it up.

Cutchen was too busy ooing and ahhing to feel the atavistic terror that was thrumming through Hayes. Part of it was that he had seen this before, except that it was at the bottom of Lake Vordog . . . and part of it was that just the sight of that cyclopean prehistoric city made something inside him recoil.

He finally had to look away.

It was just too much.

Like everything about the Old Ones, this city . . . it lived in the race memories of all men. And there was nothing remotely good associated with it. Just horror and pain and madness.

"C'mon," Hayes said, a little harsher than he had intended. "You can sightsee later."

He edged around the gully to the right until he was at the foot of the city itself. He could feel its height and weight towering over him. There was a flat table of stone to walk on and then a haphazard collection of trenches and deep-hewn vaults, megaliths and conical monuments, the city itself set some distance back. It had been the same beneath the lake, that irregular borderland of bizarre masonry, only now Hayes was walking amongst that jutting profusion. There seemed to be no plan, no blueprint, just a crazy-quilt of shattered domes and rising menhirs, narrow obelisk and great flat slabs, a twisting and confused lane cut through it all like the path through a maze. There were patches of frozen lichen growing on some of the shapes, arteries of blue ice.

"What is all this?" Cutchen said, panning his lantern around, throwing wild and creeping shadows. "Did all this fall from up there? Parts of the city?"

But Hayes didn't think so.

He wasn't certain what he was thinking, but all of this was no accident. He knew that much. They climbed over low walls and edged around towering monoliths, ever aware of those vault-like trenches cut here and there without any plan. It was positively claustrophobic, monuments towering above and to either side, long and low, high and narrow. Everywhere it was rising and falling, busy and confusing, uprisings of stone clustered like toadstools. They had to turn sideways to pass between some of them.

Sharkey suddenly stopped.

She leaned against a squat stone chamber with a multi-peaked roof. She swept her light around, taking in those broken domes like fossilized craniums, the crumbling and pitted columns rising above them, those squared off vaults below . . . many of which were clogged with pools of black ice. She squatted down, peering into one of those chasms. "Have you guys ever been to Paris?" she asked them. "To Pere Lachaise? It's like this there . . . just a crowded tangle of marble . . . stones and markers and crypts with very little egress."

Cutchen said, "But Pere Lachaise . . . that's a cemetery."

"And so is this," she said.

Hayes stood there, something like madness scratching at the pan of his brain. An alien graveyard. Well, yes, certainly. A necropolis. That's what this was . . . a network of graves and tombs, headstones and sepulchers. A funerary grounds as envisioned by those cold and insectile minds of the Old Ones. The disorientating geometry was apparent in everything they built.

Cutchen turned and looked at him and it was hard to say what he was thinking. There was a vacancy in that look, an emptiness threatening to fill up with something impossibly bad. His face was blotchy, maybe from the cold and maybe from something else. He kept looking at Hayes like he was looking for a denial, looking for Hayes to reassure him that, yes, Sharkey was fucking crazy, so just relax. Nothing to worry about here.

But Sharkey wasn't crazy and she certainly wasn't wrong, so he said nothing and Cutchen just looked at him, his eyes moist and rubbery like eggs floating in dirty brine.

Sharkey was leading now, the other two slowly deflating behind her. Maybe the idea of an alien graveyard was setting on them wrong, but she found it all simply incredible and you could see it. She led them in circles, paying little to no attention to Hayes telling her that they had to move this along and Cutchen telling her he was leaving. With or without them, he was leaving.

Finally, she crouched down. "Hand me that lantern, Cutchy," she said.

He grumbled under his breath, but did so.

She was crouching before one of those vault-like chambers cut into the stone. She got down on her belly and lowered the lantern down. She didn't need to alert them to what she had found. About twelve feet down, maybe fifteen, they could see the shriveled conical tops of alien corpses protruding from a pool of ice. They were corrugated, dehydrated-looking. Those starfish-shaped heads and attendant eyes were terribly withered, looking much like flaccid clusters of shriveled grapes.

"Well, they bury their dead," Cutchen said. "And vertically. So what?"

His scientific interest had waned considerably, been replaced pretty much by an I-don't-give-a high-hairy-shit sort of attitude.

"Why not vertically?" Sharkey said. "We bury our dead at rest, laying down. These things rest upright, so it's perfectly natural, isn't it?"

Cutchen grunted. "Yeah, this whole place is perfectly fucking natural."

Sharkey led them away, peering here and peering there. Nodding her head at things that interested her, speculating freely under her breath. Finally she came to one of those rectangular buildings and paused. This one had a long horizontal opening that you could look through. And, of course, she did just that.

"Look," she said. "Just look at this."

Cutchen refused, but Hayes did and mainly because he respected this woman and maybe even loved her. Otherwise he would have told her that enough was enough. His nerves were wearing thin as was his patience.

What he was looking into was a mausoleum of sorts. Arranged against the walls in there like Mexican mummies in a catacomb, were maybe a dozen or so Old Ones. Their oblong bodies were leaning against each other, many badly decomposed and rotted into hollowed husks like blackened cucumbers falling into themselves. Their append-ages and eyestalks were nothing but dead, drooping worms. Many of the bodies had disintegrated down to wiry barrel frames that might have been some sort of primitive skeleton, but looked more like leath-ery networks of sinew and tendon.

Like some dead alien forest, is what Hayes found himself thinking. Some dead, mutated forest of distorted and cadaverous tree trunks that had grown into one another, sprouting narrow skeletal pipes and branching twigs, looping desiccated root systems and downs of snak-ing vines like threads of moonflax.

It was hard to get over the idea that they were lifeless things, an-cient mummies far older than the ones Gates had brought in. These had decayed and mummified before the glaciers arrived making them positive relics. They were hideous in life, but maybe more so in death . . . shrunken and wrinkled and leathery, tangled in their own limbs. Alien zombies.

And they were not powerless, Hayes thought.

Not in the least.

Maybe their great age had something to do with it, but those pruned eyes dangling from corded stalks still seemed to glimmer and shine with a blasphemous vitality.

Enough.

They started again, moving as quickly as they could through that labyrinth that probably made perfect sense from above, but at ground level was positively insane. Sharkey kept pausing to look at things, growing increasingly agitated at the other two for their lack of scientific curiosity. The graveyard alone, she told them, would have kept legions of archaeologists and anthropologists busy for years and years. The Old Ones had reverence for their dead, they had no doubt developed complex funerary rites and death customs.

"So what?" Cutchen said.

She looked like she was going to either call his mother an unflattering name or kick his ass, but she just sighed and stalked off with Hayes in tow. At least until they were nearly out of that charnel grounds and then something else caught her interest. On an elevated platform there was a huge sarcophagus cut from some unknown black stone and highly-ornamented with carven vines and bizarre squid-like creatures, things like clusters of bubbles and countless staring eyes. At the head, there was a lavish five-pointed mound of some tarnished metal like platinum. Inside, there was an Old One held in a rippling shroud of ice. Though blackened with immense age, it had not rotted like the others.

"This one's important," Sharkey said. She tapped the mummy with her ice-axe. "I'll bet it's some kind of chief or maybe even one of the original colonists. Who can say? But I'll bet it was preserved somehow for future generations."

"Why is it laying flat?" Cutchen asked.

"Looks like it fell over," Hayes said.

He was staring down at that regal monstrosity and hating it instinctively as he hated them all. Maybe this one was a king or a chief or one of the first to make the journey and just maybe it was the very architect of all life on earth, but he could not respect it. You could wrap a bloated, vile spider in gold ribbons and fancy lace and it still repulsed you. Still made you want to step on it. And a spider, when you came down to it, was much more attractive to the human mind than what was laying in that stylized box.

Hayes thought: *Christ, look at that old ice and what it holds. Like every dark and nameless secret of antiquity is locked up in that frozen sarcophagus. All of mankind's primal fears, cabalistic myths, and evil sorceries given flesh. The archetype that inspired every nightmare and twisted racial memory, every witch-tale and every legend of winged demons. All the awful, unthinkable things the race had bred and purged from the black cauldron of collective memory, all the obscene things it could not acknowledge nor dare admit to . . . it was here. This horror. The engineer of the race and of all races. And it had been waiting down here in the eon-old ice. Waiting and waiting, dead but dreaming, consciously forgotten but grimly remembered in the subconscious and dark lore of humankind. But all along, they were dreaming of us just as we dreamed of them . . . because they were us and we were them and now, dear God, millions upon millions of years later, they were waking up, they were rising to claim their children and their childrens' intellect . . .*

Thinking this and wanting to believe it was utter fantasy, but knowing it was dire and inescapable truth, Hayes felt like some savage standing before the grave of a fallen and cruel god. He had a mad desire to whip out his dick and piss on this thing. To show it his defiance that was innate and human and something he knew they had not foreseen developing in their carefully-manipulated progeny.

Enough.

They were stalling with all this and he knew it.

"Let's go," he said and meant it. "We're not here for this and we all know it."

So he took the lead and clambered over slabs and low walls, ignoring everything but that dead city rising above them. He got no arguments on this. Sharkey and Cutchen followed him and he figured they would have followed him just about anywhere at that moment.

"Oh, look," Sharkey said, panning her light at the foot of some crumbled masonry.

It was Gates.

He was pressed into an alcove between shattered blocks of stone that had no doubt fallen from above. He was curled up in sort of a fetal position, knees to chin, his face white as new snow and contorted into a grimace of absolute horror. Blood had trickled from the rictus of his mouth. His eyes were spilled down his cheeks in gelatinous trails like squashed jellyfish.

It was horrible. Just like all the others.

But worse somehow, because you could almost feel the agonal convulsions that Gates had suffered before he died. There was no getting around the fact that he looked like he'd been literally scared to death. And that death had been a dark matter, mindless and perverse and ghastly. No man should have had to go like Gates did . . . alone and mad in that suffocating darkness, dying a crazy and hopeless death like a rat stuck in a drainpipe. Screaming as his eyes boiled to soup and splashed down his face. As his brain went to sauce and his soul was burnt to ash.

Gates had paid the final price for his curiosity.

But Hayes knew it was more than just scientific interest . . . Gates had been trying to unravel the mystery of the ages. He had been trying to put it all together so he could maybe save his own race. He was a hero. He was one of the greatest of great men.

Sharkey kneeled before him. She dug into his coat and found his field journal. "There's a funny odor about him . . . not a death smell, something else. Sharp, acidic."

Hayes had smelled it, too: a caustic, acrid stench like monkey urine.

The tenseness feeding between the three of them was electric and cutting. It lay in each of their bellies, a twisted knot of nausea.

"All right, all right, goddammit," Hayes said, starting up into the city. "Let's go see what did this, let's go see what scared Gates to death."

40

"N o," Cutchen said then, holding his lantern up. "Wait a minute now . . . what's that over there?"

Hayes stepped down off some broken stones.

Sharkey was already over there, checking it out. Collapsible tables had been set out, half a dozen of them upon which were stone artifacts taken from the city, hammers and drills, cases of instruments, lanterns. There were piles of notebooks and a couple digital cameras. Microscopes. There was a crate full of rolled-up maps that turned out to be rubbings made from the walls inside . . . figures, glyphs, strange characters.

Cutchen grabbed a folding chair and sat down. There was a thermometer on the table. "It's almost ten degrees in here. Balmy."

Sharkey and Hayes looked around, found a flare pistol which she took and a twelve-gauge Remington pump that he took. They did not comment on these things. The men who had brought them down here had had their reasons and nobody dared question what those might have been.

Bottom line was, they felt better being armed.

"Look," Hayes said. "A generator."

It was. A Honda industrial job on a rolling cart. A spiderweb of power cords ran off of it, all of them leading up into the city itself. As Hayes followed them with his light he could see that there were cords hanging from the face of the city. There were several five-gallon cans of gasoline. He went to the generator. It had a 3800 watt capacity, so it could've lit up most of the entire city if you had enough light bulbs and judging from what he had seen, Gates and the boys certainly had enough of those.

"Will it work?" Sharkey asked.

"I think so." Hayes checked the tank. It held ten gallons and was about half full. He took one of the cans and filled it up. Then he threw the circuit breaker and hit the electronic ignition. It roared to life immediately, finding a happy idle and sticking with it.

"Where's the light?" Cutchen said.

"Just a minute. Let it warm up." Hayes stood there, lighting a cigarette and waiting for the engine to push the coldness from itself. It didn't take long. He turned the circuit breaker back on and suddenly, the cavern was bright.

"Damn," Cutchen said. "That's better."

With all those bulbs netting the first thirty or so feet of the city, Hayes finally got a good look at that ancient structure. It was simply incredible. The sight of it literally sucked the breath from his lungs and the blood from his veins. That old, ugly familiarity was there, of course, the sense that these aged ruins were something long-hidden in the depths of all men's minds. But looking up at it, canceled all that out. On TV, ancient cities always looked too neat, too tidy, too planned in their obsolescence, but not this one. It rose up incredibly high, yet sagging and leaning and crumbling away in too many places. Hayes could see that it went up at least two-hundred feet until it met the grotto's domed roof . . . and even then, it simply disappeared into solid rock. As if the mountain had grown up around it and engulfed it through the ages. Such incredible antiquity was mind-boggling. But Gates had reiterated what Professor Dyer of the Pabodie Expedition had said: the ruins were at least 350 million years old and that was a conservative estimate.

These ruins were from an amazingly advanced pre-human civilization.

Hayes knew that, but the words had meant little to him until now. Pre-human city. Pre-human intelligence.

"God, look at that will you?" Cutchen finally said. "You can . . . you can almost feel how ancient it is . . . right up your spine."

Ancient? No, the sphinx and the Acropolis were ancient, this was *primordial*. This predated man's oldest works by hundreds of millions of years. It was a dawn city. A nightmare exercise in diverging geometrical association, a relic from some depraved and evil elder world. It did not look so much like a city, but like some immense and derelict machine, some dreadful mechanism from a Medieval torture chamber. A profoundly synergistic and yet nonsensical device made of pistons and pipes, wires and cylinders, vents and cogs. Something rising and leaning, squat yet narrow and tall, diverging at impossible right angles to itself. The human mind was not prepared to look upon such a thing . . . it automatically sought an overall structural plan, a uniformity, and found nothing it could pull in and make sense of. This was a perverse and godless architecture born of minds reared in some multi-dimensional reality.

"Christ, it gives me a headache," Sharkey said.

And that was very apt, for it did tax the brain . . . it was too busy, too profuse, too multitudinous in design. It was formed of arches and cubes, rectangular slabs set on their ends, a lunatic labyrinth of cones and pyramids, octagons and hexagons, spheres and towers, radiating spirals and bifurcating masts. Like the forking, tangled skeleton of some primal beast, some sideshow sea serpent tacked together out of dozens of unrelated skeletons into a single gangly whole, a mad bone sculpture. An insane and precarious armature that should have fallen, but didn't. It balanced upon itself like some surreal experiment in abstract geometry and unearthly symmetry.

Hayes thought it looked impossibly random like something formed by nature, the hollowed remains of deep-sea organisms heaped upon one another . . . corals and sponges, anemones and sea cucumbers, crab carapaces and ghost pipes. Just an odd and conflicting collection of dead things that had boiled and rotted into a single mass, grown into one another and out of each other until there was no beginning and no true end. Standing back and taking it in, he was envisioning it as the black and glossy endoskeleton of some massive alien insect rising from the earth . . . a deranged biomechanical hybrid of girders and ribs, vertebrae and pelvic disks, conduits and hollow tubes held together by spiraling ladders of ligament. A chitinous and scaly ossuary, a jutting cyclopean honeycomb capped by rising narrow protrusions like the chimneys of a foundry or the smoker vents of hydrothermal ovens.

But even that wasn't right, for as haphazard and conflicting as the city was, you could not get by the disturbing feeling that there was a purpose here, that the structure was highly mechanistic and practical to its owners, a symbiotic union of steel and flesh, rock and bone. It had an odd industrial look to it. Even the stone it was cut from was not smooth nor polished, but ribbed and knobby and oddly crystalline, set with saw-toothed ridges and jutting teeth and the threads of screws. Almost like there was some dire machinery inside attempting to burst through those bowing, scalloped walls.

To call it a city was an oversimplification.

For this was not a city as humans understood a city. No human mind could have dreamed of this and no human brain had the engineering skill to make it stand and not fall into itself. This was not a city as such, a place of homes and lives, this was harsh and hostile, utilitarian and machined, something brought forth by hopelessly cold and automated minds. An anthill.

A hive.

Hayes felt that just seeing it, just letting his eyes roam that obscene geometrical matrix, made him somehow less than human. It evaporated the sweet and fine milk of the human condition drop by drop. It was evil and unholy and sacrilegious. Words engendered by a weak, superstitious mind, but Hayes was proud of that mind. Because it made him human. He was warm and emotional, not a machine like the things that had reared this awful place.

"Just like Gates said, it seems to go for miles," Cutchen pointed out.

There was no way to know just how far into the belly of the mountains the city reached. For as Gates said, it went on as far as the eye could see and as far as their lights could reach, though in the distance you could see that parts of it were covered by cave-ins and swallowed in frozen rivers of glacial ice.

A paleozoic megalopolis.

The sort of place that might have inspired the wild tales of mythical places like Thule and Hyperborea, Lemuria and the Mountains of the Moon. Mystical Commoriom and veiled Atlantis. This was the prototype of countless prehuman blasphemies such as the Nameless City and eldritch Kadath in the Cold Wastes beyond Leng. You could see plainly how it had been scarred and scraped by the movement of the glaciers, carried up and pressed down, ground between massive ice flows like corn meal.

"You don't honestly expect us to go into that bone pile, do you?"

Cutchen said in a dry, cracking voice. "I mean . . . c'mon, Jimmy, it doesn't look safe. And, Jesus Christ, I'm not afraid to admit that it scares the shit out of me just looking at it."

It scared Hayes, too.

Scared him in fundamental ways he was not even aware of. It offended him as it offended all men, whether savage or rational, and he had an overwhelming compulsion to come back here with all the dynamite he could fit in the SnoCat and bring that fucking mountain down right on top of it.

"It's safe enough," he said. "Gates and the others were crawling through it, so can we."

"Bullshit. I don't care what those fucking labcoat Johnnies were doing, I'm not going in there. That's it. That's all there goddamn well is to it." He stood there, breathing hard, looking like he wanted to scream or cry. "C'mon, Jimmy, don't do this to me . . . lookit that fucking thing, will ya? I'm having bad dreams just seeing it. But going in there . . . it's like a tomb, like a big rotting casket with the lid thrown open . . . I . . . I'm sorry, Jimmy . . . I'm just not up to it."

Hayes went over to him, clapped him on the shoulder. "Just wait out here for us. We shouldn't be long. Keep an eye on that generator."

"Hell, I can't even change the oil in my goddamn car," Cutchen said.

He stood there, hands on his hips, watching them scramble up shattered stone columns and through an oval opening, one of hundreds if not thousands set into the weathered face of that city.

"You two would really leave me alone out here, wouldn't you?" they heard him call. "Boy, isn't that just great? Assholes. Your both assholes."

They were barely inside and Cutchen came stumbling in after them, calling them every name he could think of and some that made absolutely no sense whatsoever.

Maybe the city did look like a casket, but at least inside it, he wouldn't be alone with the bleak, antehuman memory of the place.

41

Inside, the city was no less amazing.

No less insane.

There were endless hexagonal mazes of corridors that seemed to lead into nothing but other corridors that branched to either side, above and below like jungle gym tangles of hollow pipes that had been welded at right angles to one another. Some were quadrilateral and others were triangularly obtuse. Circular passages began and ended with solid walls or sphere-shaped apartments. Rooms simply opened into other rooms like dozens of narrow cubes strung together or stacked atop one another. They were either massive and vault-like or cramped like the cells of monks or honeybees. Arched doorways were set halfway up fifteen foot walls. Sometimes they led into cylindrical channels that went on for hundreds of feet before narrowing to tiny, cubelike alcoves or sometimes they opened into gargantuan amphitheaters with madly curving walls that were set, sloping floor to fifty-foot ceiling, with ovoid cells. Some rooms had no ceilings, just immense shafts that led into a grainy fathomless blackness above and others had no floors, just narrow walkways spanning the great depths below. There was nothing that might have been called stairways, but now and again ribbed helixes rose to the floors above or far below.

The building plan was chaotic at the very least.

The floors were not necessarily distinct nor differentiated from one another. There was no first floor, second floor, third floor etc. The stories converged into one another, rooms and chambers dropping from above or rising up from below, tangled in lattices like diamond crystals.

Five minutes into it, the three of them were sweating and shaking and having trouble catching their breath. The marrow of that damnable city was claustrophobic, profuse, and intersecting. The angles were wildly exaggerated, roofs becoming floors and floors arching up into roofs that were walls. Chambers were never perfectly square but slightly off-kilter and set off-center. Corridors were never exactly linear, but convoluted and sloping, tall then squat and then enormous. There was something geometrically perverse about any brain that could make sense of such a thing without backing itself into some jagged, narrow corner and screaming itself insane. Moving through there was like navigating through the tangled, surreal gutters of a lunatic's mind, looking for reason that did not exist . . . for reason here was swallowed by amorphous shadows, the shattered wreckage of paranoia as imagined by German expressionists.

They followed the electrical cords that had been attached to walls and strung over black depths below. Even so, it was not long before they had to rest. This place was not engineered for the ease of mobility of the human race. And moving through it was not only psychologically exhausting, it was physically fatiguing as well. Constantly climbing through those tomblike hollows, scuttling down threaded tunnels, and crawling over the litter and debris of collapsed partitions.

They finally paused amidst a line of rooms that were not rooms at all, but sunken chambers with translucent concave floors made of some transparent glass or plastic. If you rubbed very hard, you could clean the grit off the material just enough to make out structures lying far beneath.

"This is a fucking madhouse," Cutchen said. "What the hell was wrong with Gates? This should have been pulled down. You know? Just fucking pulled down."

Sharkey said, "It seems mad, but I think it's all very carefully systematic if you happen to have a brain that can understand the system. I'm afraid our simple mammalian brains are not up to the task . . . maybe not for another couple million years anyway."

"Can we just get out?" Cutchen said. "Christ, I've never felt like this before . . . half the time I'm so nervous and depressed I want to slit my wrists, the other half I feel like I could vomit my intestines out."

"Just a little while longer, then we'll call it quits," Hayes said.

Cutchen rested his head on his knees, squeezing his eyes very tightly shut.

Hayes felt for the guy, for he knew exactly how he felt.

The way this place opened up a can of something creeping and ugly inside of you and shook it around. Tied your belly in knots and made your head ache and your eyes bulge. The human mind was designed to consider regularities, straight lines and simple angles, forms and shapes that were consistent with themselves. But this place . . . it was mathematically distorted, a fourth-dimensional madness. Like being inside some alien wasp hive. It was just too much.

After a brief rest, they moved on and suddenly discovered themselves in an immense courtyard set between rising blocks of that nightmare city. They moved between colossal seventy-foot walls and around towering spires that seemed to serve no earthly purpose. The courtyard was tiled and roofless, nothing above but empty blackness reaching to dizzying heights. Now and again there were domes like buildings set about, but the only way of getting into them was scaling the smooth walls and entering from apertures at the top. There were also high blank facades lacking egress that were set with jutting rectangles fifty and sixty feet above that looked like nothing but perches for rooks or hawks.

They had left the strings of lights behind and were moving with flashlight and lantern again. They came to another of those crazy domes and this one was honeycombed with oval passages that seemed to lead down.

"Give me the lantern, Cutchy," Hayes said. "I'm going in there."

Sharkey shook her head. "No, Jimmy . . . it's too dangerous."

He took the lantern. "I'm going. I'll be careful."

He chose a passage and entered it.

It was about five feet in diameter at the opening and he had to move downwards at a crouch. It was like being inside a funhouse twisty slide, just a hollowed tube that moved this way, then that, ever downward. But the walls and floor were set with tiny bumps so there was no chance of losing your footing or sliding away into darkness. Hayes kept going, his throat constricting and sweat beading his face. Finally, the passage opened into a series of massive rooms with hooded ceilings.

He stood there in that shrouded darkness, panning the lantern around. He instantly did not like the place. That terrible sense of deja-vu was haunting him again, clawing and worming at the pit of his mind.

"Yeah," he whispered. "I remember this place, too, but why?"

He moved on, passing beneath archways and steering himself around accumulated heaps of detritus. He came into a room that seemed to be nothing but an ossuary, a collection of aged bones . . . skulls set into little cells in the walls, the skeletons of men and extinct animals fully articulated, great birds dangling from above with nothing seeming to hold them. The floor was a litter of bones as if most of the displays here — and there must have been thousands at one time — had collapsed through the ages, maybe from their own weight or seismic activity shaking them loose. It was tough going climbing over those heaped bones, the lantern casting flying and grotesque shadows, the air swimming with clots of dust. But it was necessary. For as much as this place disturbed him, he knew it was no simple natural history collection.

This was much more.

At the far end, there were cylindrical plastic cases that he had to scrape the grit off. Inside were more human skeletons . . . but most were small and hunched, not quite erect, the craniums set with great brow ridges that sloped ever backward to braincases much smaller than those of modern men. Some of those skulls had exaggerated canines and incisors, heavy jaws. None of them were anatomically the same. These were the skeletons of manlike apes and quasi-human types — *Afropithecus* and *Australopithecus* — and their proto-primate ancestors and primitive forms of anthropoids, homo erectus and Neanderthal man, and something like an archaic form of homo sapien.

Hayes scraped the gunk from a dozen of those cylinders, but there must have been hundreds.

You know what this is, don't you? he thought. *You know what kind of awful, gruesome place this.*

And he did.

The very idea of what he was seeing and feeling and thinking and remembering made the sap of his race run cold and poisoned.

In the next room, more skulls and more bones.

They were all carefully arranged on tables and hung from the walls, set into recesses . . . they were all human or proto-human and they had to span millions of years. A paleoanthropologist's wonderland.

But as Hayes examined many of the skulls, they fell apart like delicate crockery, but he did notice that a great many of them had what appeared to be holes in their craniums that had either been drilled into them or burned through. There were several tables upon which the articulated skeletons of prehistoric men had been strapped down with what appeared to be some sort of plastic wire . . . and the fact that they had been bound so, made Hayes think that they had not been skeletons when they were brought in here.

The next of those gigantic vaults was piled floor to ceiling with more plastic tubes, but these were much smaller like laboratory vats. Once he'd used his knife to scrape them clean, Hayes could see pale, fleshy things floating in solidified serum like flies trapped in amber. They were all anatomical specimens . . . glands and muscles, ligaments and spinal columns, brains and sexual organs, eyes drifting like olives in ancient plasma and hundreds of things Hayes simply could not identify.

The next room held more tables made of some unknown quartz-like mineral, perhaps fifty or sixty of them. There were weird spirals of discolored plastic tubing and spidery nets of hoses and conduits leading from spheres overhead that must have been some sort of bio-medical machinery. There were racks of instruments . . . at least what he thought were instruments . . . some were made of a transparent glassy material that might have been some alien mineral. There were great assemblages of these things . . . hooks and blades and probes and others that were flat and hollow like magician's wands. Hundreds of varieties and everywhere, those spiraling tubes and things sprouting from the walls like fiber optic threads. Great convex mirrors and plate-like lenses set upon tripods. There were other things that had gone to dust and wreckage and a great part of the room had been buried in a cave-in.

Another massive chamber led off from it, but debris blocked the doorway. Hayes climbed up it and could see through a three-inch slit at the top of the door that it was cavernous inside and set with dusty helixes of alien machinery, things that looked like black, fibrous skeletons with thousands of appendages and reaching whip-like protrusions. Other things like giant gray oblong blocks, the faces of which were profuse with biomechanical knobs and ribs and scaled ridges, fluted poles and serpentine coils and interlocking disks. All of them were set with recesses that were shaped like human beings into which subjects could be placed. There were other tables and the framework of some huge glass wheel that seemed to be made of mirrors and dusty lenses. And coming from overhead was a triple cylinder like that of a compound microscope, except where the optical mechanisms would have been there were a protruding series of glass blades . . . some short and serrated, others long and forked like snake tongues, and still others composed of thousands of tiny shards each of a different shape and texture. There were other machines in there that left Hayes cold and gasping, but he could look no more.

This entire place was some arcane biomedical laboratory and he knew it.

The sort of place and the level of specialized technology that man would not be able to guess at for ten-thousand generations.

Hayes slid down the heap of debris, pressing his hands to his head, trying to shut out the memories of this place . . . the torment and the torture, the cutting and burning and severing, the draining of fluids and the samples of blood, marrow, and brain tissue extracted. The graftings and injections and metabolic manipulation.

Yes, this is where it all happened.

This was where the true origin of species was to be found.

This was the factory of the helix and the primal white jelly Lind had raved about. This was where the evolution of terrestrial life was studied and cataloged by extraterrestrial minds. This was the place that man was born and modified. This is where Hayes' own ancestors were bagged and tagged and classified, stuck on pins like rare insects, bottled and dissected. Yes, throughout prehistory, possibly every fifty thousand years or so, populations of men and the anthropoids that would become men, were scooped up, brought down into this hideous catacomb and altered, enhanced via microsurgery and vivisection, eugenics and genetic engineering, forced mutation and special adaptation, careful and meticulous modification at the atomic and molecular levels. And all with one ultimate ambition: to bring forth an intelligence that the Old Ones could harvest.

Hayes laid there, at the bottom of that debris heap, his mind racing in a thousand different directions leaving him confused and numb and maybe even slightly insane. There was too much coming at him, way too much. Seeing his origins and knowing it all to be horribly true, he felt . . . artificial, synthetic. Not a man at all, but cold plastic protoplasm squeezed and worked into the *shape* of a man. He felt that his soul had withered, crumbled, gone to ash. He lay there, staring, in that tenebrous, diabolic workshop, feeling the ghosts of his ancestors haunting him, invading his mind and screaming in his face.

He was emptied out now. Used up and gutted, nothing inside but bones and blood and a heart that beat with a hollow cadence. And outside, just a reflection of a man, a grim set of mouth and eyes dead as grimy pennies staring up at you from a dirty gutter.

All those voices and shrill cries, misty race memory and screeching long-dead minds finally boiled down into a flux of gray, running mud. And a single voice spoke from the bottom of his mind: *Isn't revelation something, Jimmy? All these years people were wondering who they were and what they were and where they came from and what their destiny might be and you were one of them . . . but now you know the truth and there's no joy in knowing, is there? There's only madness and horror. The collective consciousness of the human race is not ready for any of this. Men and women are still primarily savages, superstitious gourd-rattling, spell-casting yahoos . . . and the knowledge of this will utterly destroy them, won't it? That all that we are and ever can be can be reduced to an equation, a test tube, chemicals and atoms worked by forbidding alien hands, an ambitious experiment in molecular biology. This will kill the race. This will crush our simple, pagan minds and leave nothing behind. All those years creationists and evolutionists have been battling it out and now, it turns, they're both wrong and they're both right . . . life can arise just about anywhere from a fixed set of variables and there is such a thing as the Creator. Only those variables were manipulated by cold and noxious minds and the Creator is something alien and grisly from some invidious, cosmic gutter out of space and out of time.*

Kind of funny, ain't it?

Life probably would have happened here without them, but men probably wouldn't have. Not as we understand them. And what a serene and peaceful place this would have been. Eden. Only, Jimmy, you know who that slithering serpent was and what it brought to being: your race.

Hayes scrambled to his feet, started running, half out of his mind. He was whimpering and shaking and his heart was palpitating. His mind was strewn with cobwebs. He fled drunkenly from room to room, falling and getting up, tipping over skeletons and rawboned machinery and things that were both and neither. Finally vaulting over a table heaped with a pyramid of subhuman skulls and picking his way through those ancient remains like a rat through a bone pile.

And then there was the tunnel and he was climbing, breathing hard and crying out, feeling those dire and primal memories scratching their way up behind him. Then he fell out at Sharkey's feet.

She went to him, holding him in her arms, tears in her eyes as she soothed him and calmed him and slowly, that contorted grimace left his face and his eyes stopped staring sightlessly.

"Christ, Jimmy," Cutchen said. "What did you see down there? What in Christ did you see?"

So he told them.

42

Thirty minutes later, Hayes came to accept a very disturbing truth: they were lost. Oh, the generator was still running out there and the lights were still glowing, but regardless of what path they took, they couldn't seem to get near them. There was a passage somewhere that would lead them back into the city proper and out of these primeval relics. Problem was, they couldn't find it.

"You know what," Cutchen said when Hayes admitted he was lost, "I've put up with a lot of shit. I've helped you two do things I should never have fucking gotten involved in. And now here we are . . . this is bullshit. You two do whatever in the fuck you want, but I'm getting out. I'm not waiting for you, Jimmy, to get us more lost. I've had it."

If they had an argument to stay him, they couldn't remember what is was.

They stood there stupidly with their flashlights as Cutchen stomped away, his lantern light bobbing and weaving, shining off ice crystals set into the masonry.

"We can't let him go, Jimmy," Sharkey said.

"No, just give him a minute or two. He'll settle down. If not, I'll cold-cock him and drag him behind us."

It was meant as a joke, but humor was lost in this place and particularly with what they had seen and experienced thus far. Hayes tucked his flashlight into the pocket of his parka and kissed Sharkey hard. She responded, their tongues tasting each other and remembering each other and wanting this to last.

Finally Sharkey broke it off. "What's this all about?"

"Just an urge."

"An urge?"

"Yeah . . . I guess I needed to remind myself I was still human."

She smiled. "We'll discuss it later. What about Cutchy?"

"We better go get him –"

There was a sudden rending cry that they first took to be a scream. But it wasn't a scream, it was just Cutchen yelling to them, angry and hysterical and just plain pissed-off.

They ran along behind the wall he'd disappeared around, sighting his light in the distance. They dodged around some towering rectangles and a broken dome, some piled debris. Cutchen was there, standing in a great open courtyard that must have been easily two hundred yards in circumference, flanked on all sides by the city itself which rose up above, overhanging and gradually coming together somewhere overhead. With his flashlight, Hayes could see a narrow passage up there maybe fifty feet across. But right before Cutchen, there was circular hole cut into the stone that was three times that big.

Cutchen held the lantern over the rim and the light was gradually swallowed up by dusty darkness.

"We didn't come this way," Hayes said. "I never saw this before."

"Let's backtrack," Sharkey suggested. "Make for those lights."

Hayes could see them back there. They backlit the honeycombed openings set in that terraced architectural monstrosity like ghost lights, made the city look even more eerie and haunted than it already was.

They turned and Hayes thought he heard something . . . that scratching sound again, but it was gone before anyone else picked up on it. He didn't bother mentioning it.

Because right then, the lights from the generator dimmed and went out completely.

The blackness was absolute. Like being nailed shut in a casket.

"Oh, shit," Sharkey said, bumping right into Hayes.

And then the ground beneath them began to shudder with a weird rhythmic vibration that they could feel coming right up through their boots. There was a deep and jarring reverberation that seemed to come from the bowels of the city itself as if some titanic alien machine had been switched on and was gearing up with pounding cycles and thrumming vibrations. Hayes had felt this before and always just before or during one of those hauntings . . . but this was bigger, this was huge and loud and violent. The vibrations almost knocked them off their feet. They had trouble standing or staying in one place. Flashlight beams were bobbing madly. The city was shaking like it was riding a seismic wave . . . parts of it falling and crashing, flaking away like dead skin.

Cutchen's lantern light framed three white and desperate faces, three sets of staring, terror-filled eyes.

The city was in motion, thumping and rattling and cracking apart. Sharp crackling sounds and metallic grinding noises were echoing up out of the pit, getting louder and louder. The air seemed heavy and busy, whipped into a whirlwind by the intrusion of surging energy. Bits of rock and crystals of ice were pelting into Hayes and the others as they clung to one another. There was a low humming coming up out of the pit now, weird squealing noises and thumps, mad scratchings and the sound of radio static rising and falling in waves.

Cutchen screamed and broke away, dropping his lantern. His face in Hayes' light was rigid and set, lips pulled back from bared and clenched teeth. Drool was hanging from his mouth. His eyes were wide and savage. He looked like he suddenly had gone insane. "*Coming, coming, coming,*" he cried over the volume of the city. "*They're coming, they're all coming . . . the swarm is coming out of the sky . . . no hide there, no hide there . . . seek you out . . . they find you . . . they find your mind and they find your thoughts . . . they come . . . oh, the buzzing, the buzzing, the buzzing, the coming of the swarm . . . the ancient hive . . . the swarm that fills the sky . . .*"

He let out another scream, hands pressed to his ears. He was drooling and delusional and mad, running this way and then that, falling to his hands and knees and creeping like a mouse. Then rising up and hopping along, spinning around, arms swinging limp at his sides like an ape. He made growling sounds, then grunts and weird keening noises.

Hayes was on his ass from the palpitations of the city, cracks fanning out under his legs. But he was seeing Cutchen and knowing what he was feeling, catching momentary glimpses of what he was seeing. *Dear God, he's living it, he's living the terror of it,* Hayes was thinking, trying to hold onto Sharkey. *This place has soaked up so much terror and pain and madness in its existence from so many manic, fevered minds that it can no longer hold it all.*

And that's what was happening to Cutchen.

Those memories . . . not the memories of aliens, but the memories of humans . . . were bleeding out and filling him and he was remembering what they remembered, living through them *as* them. Yes, he was recalling an ancient ritual practiced by the Old Ones when they filled the skies in swarms of winged devils and collected specimens and sometimes entire populations to be brought here for experimentation and modification. He was a primitive man and then an ape and then something between and something not even remotely human, knowing the terror of all species for the swarm, the invading swarm of aliens.

Hopping about madly and gnashing his teeth, Cutchen threw himself over the edge of the pit.

Somebody screamed.

Maybe it was Hayes and maybe it was Sharkey and maybe it was both of them. But then as if it had received a sacrifice, the pit seemed to come alive with a flurry of vibrations and squeals and electric cracklings. And then it began to glow with a rising luminous mist. Whatever it was, a field of phosphorescent energy or just electrified mist, it was boiling up out of the pit like steam from a witch's cauldron. Snaking tendrils and white ropes of it overflowed the lip of the pit and spread over the floor in a shimmering ground mist. Hayes could feel it moving over his legs and arms, swirling and consuming, making his skin crawl like he'd been dipped into an anthill. It was alive and vital and kinetic, like some sentient lifeforce that had come to devour them.

He couldn't seem to move and neither could Sharkey.

And then from far below, but getting closer, rising on that plexus of supercharged mist, there came the sound they had heard earlier: the mad and discordant piping, the frenzied voices of the Old Ones echoing up from the pit. It billowed up, unfolding, becoming a cacophonous shrill whining that sounded more like thousands of droning cicadas than the melodic piping he could remember. It grew louder and louder, a screeching reedy fluting of perhaps hundreds of those things, the rising swarm. They were coming up from beneath, bleating and whistling with squeaking off-key stridulations, a lunatic susurration that rose to an ear-splitting volume like having your head stuck in a hive of hornets.

They were coming, Hayes knew.

The swarm.

Yes, from deep below through nighted and moldering passageways they were coming, just as they had come in those ancient days to reap and collect, to gather specimens for their morbid experiments. But this time they were not coming from the sky, but moving along subterranean networks that probably connected with Lake Vordog under the ice cap.

The spell was broken.

Hayes and Sharkey fought to their feet and that weird fog came up to their waists, perfectly white and shining. And just behind them there came a sound, a single high-pitched squeal of that macabre piping like bellows and pan flutes blown with hurricane winds. They saw one of the things there, one of the Old Ones, those red eyes high and wide on their fleshy stalks, its wings spread and its appendages scratching together.

Then there was another and another.

But they were not real . . . they were ghosts.

Reflections.

Memories loosed from that tombyard below by the influx of human psychic energy and maybe the minds of those coming from below. They dipped and drifted, piping and flapping their wings, trailing wisps of white vapor, ethereal things, insubstantial but lurid and frightening, those eyestalks writhing like flaccid white worms. They bled from the hollows of the city like glowing serpents from burrows, passing through each other and through Hayes and Sharkey in cold breaths. Harmless now as will-of-the-wisps.

Hayes refused to be scared of them, scared of things dead millions of years.

He took Sharkey by the hand and she grabbed Cutchen's lantern and they began moving away from the pit and its attendant phantoms. The city was haunted, it was rife with spirits and drifting spectral intelligences that were only dangerous if you made them so, if you let those bleak minds touch your own, power themselves on your fears and aimless psychic energy. But if that happened, there was enough undirected, potential energy lying in wait to rip a hole in your mind and gut the world.

Hayes and Sharkey would not empower those decayed intellects. They simply refused.

But then there was something coming. Something else.

And it was no ghost.

Hayes felt something heavy glide over his head, felt the wind it created and the evil that exuded from it in a toxic sap.

An Old One. An elder thing.

Not dead and transparent, but tall and full and resilient. In the lantern light, its flesh was a bright, oily gray and its eyes were like shining rubies. Its wings were spread, great membranous kites seeking wind and it flapped them in a blur of motion, creating a high, horrible buzzing sound that rose up and mated with the whining drone of its piping, becoming a solid wall of noise that stripped your nerves raw. It stood atop a shattered pillar, clinging with those coiling and tentacular legs. The branching appendages at its breast scraped against each other like roofing nails.

Yes, it was alive, maybe eight feet in height, grotesque and alien and oddly regal as it towered over Hayes. Its piping fell to a series of chirping squeaks and squeals like it was speaking and it probably was. There was something questioning about those noises, but Hayes could only stand there like a mindless savage staring up at his messiah. A revolting, chemical stink of formalin wafted off it, a stench of pickled things and things white and puckered floating in laboratory jars.

Hayes felt its mind touch his own in a cold invasion.

The flashlight fell from his hands, then the shotgun.

The way it looked at him was devastating . . . it seemed to take him apart at some basal level. Things like defiance and free will writhed briefly in the glaring crimson suns of its eyes, then curled up brown and withered to fragments. There was an unquestioning superiority about the creature. No anger or rage or simple hatred, for such things were by-products of humanity and not within its natural rhythms. It looked down upon Hayes with a neutral passivity, maybe slightly amused even or playfully annoyed the way an owner will look down upon a beloved puppy that has shit on the carpet. *Yes, I've come now, master is here, little one. You've made a mess of things, haven't you? No matter, I'll sweep it up, you precocious and empty-headed little beast.* Maybe that's how it was seeing him. As something stupid and messy and foolish that needed a higher guidance, a taste of discipline to set it right. That's what Hayes was feeling in his head, the sense that this thing thought he and his kind had shit all over the world, but that was at an end now for daddy was here and he would soon set things to right. *We made you what you are and as we made you, little one, we can un-make you.*

And that was it.

Those were the thoughts that blossomed in the whistling vacuum of Hayes' mind. That this horror saw itself as a parent looking down at a child . . . not hate there, just a touch of disappointment.

It was in his head now, easily mastering his thoughts, picking through his memories and emotions and subconscious urges almost by accident. Their minds were so dominating and supreme, they did this almost as an afterthought. Like everything else with them, a mind, a psyche, was just something else to be dissected and rendered down to its base anatomy.

Hayes felt something building in him.

Maybe the creature truly did not dislike him, but it also held no warm thoughts for him or his race, either. It was alien and cold and arrogant. Hayes was warm and weak and idiotic. But there was something in him they had not counted on and that something bubbled up from his core and he charged the Old One with murder in his eyes.

He surprised the old master.

It could not comprehend such out and out rebellion, for revolt against their makers was not something they programmed into the human animal. And as such, it was taken by surprise. Shouting a rebel yell, Hayes dove at it, actually grabbed its wavering stick-like appendages in his gloved hands and it was like touching a high-power line or a white-hot bar of smoldering steel. He was instantly knocked on his ass, his gloves melted and smoking.

But the creature *had* recoiled from him, maybe out of shock or fear. Yes, just like old Doc Frankenstein had recoiled from that shambling monstrosity he created. This thing was appalled by Hayes. He was white and bloated, a hairy and gas-filled fungus . . . symmetrically and anatomically obscene, a disgusting lower order. He had no love for Hayes no more than a scientist has a love for a large spider he toys with . . . but when that spider revolts, it must be crushed as a lesson.

Hayes felt all his hatred drain away.

The Old One was in charge again as must be. Its brilliant and globular red eyes stood stiffly erect at the end of their stalks. The prismatic cilia atop its starfish-shaped head glowed a feral purple, then orange, and then the same color as its eyes. It was pissed. It reached out and took Hayes, a wave of irresistible force slamming into his mind. His eyes went wide and his mouth ripped open in a scream as it took his brain, twisted it in its hands and began to squeeze the juice from it.

And then there was an explosion.

A gout of sparks and fire burst just below the thing's head and it fell back, flapping its wings, making a high and keening sound that was either pain or terror. Sharkey had fired her flare gun at it point blank.

It was enough.

Hayes found the shotgun and brought it up.

And just as he felt a hot wave of searing energy come barreling from the thing's mind, he pulled the trigger and the gun boomed. The buckshot struck the thing right in the head, shattering its eyestalks and eyeballs into a splatter of mucilage. It screamed and it squealed, rising up on those fanning wings and disappearing into the darkness, wailing in torment.

Yes, this is how the dog bites the hand that feeds, you prick, Hayes thought at it. *You may have owned us once. You may have held our squirming destiny in your paws, but no more. Not now.*

As if in answer to the creature's agony, the swarm from below began to shrill with a screeching decibel that almost blew Hayes' eardrums out.

Or was it from below?

Because standing there, leaning against Sharkey, he could see that high above the pit, up in that unfathomed blackness there were dozens of Old Ones drifting about, but looking distorted as if through a bad TV monitor.

"It's not real, Jimmy!" Sharkey shouted. "It's not at all real!"

And it wasn't.

What they were seeing up there was a transmission of sorts. Like looking through a window into a distant room or peering through the looking glass into the crawling madness on the other side. Up there, those images were blurred and fluttering, a vision of some unknown and nameless dead-end of space that was populated by the Old Ones, maybe their home system and maybe some anti-world caught in-between. Another dimension, another reality, some pestilent graveyard beyond the bleeding rim of the universe. Only a glistening and transparent bubble separated the material of this dimension from that godless other.

But it must have been more than a bubble, for it was clear that they were not coming through. Just hanging there, circling that window like moths attracted by light. And Hayes knew they could see him, feel him there. Just as he knew they wanted through, that they needed through, but they were trapped, unable to swing open the door.

There were thousands of them there, hundreds of thousands, millions. They filled that vaporous window and the charnel depths beyond, a raging and droning hive trying to force their way through to consume and devour, to drain the minds of men dry, to turn the green hills into one immense alien hive. Hayes could feel them, even across those infinite distances, those trans-galactic gulfs of limitless space . . . he could feel their chewing, voracious appetites needing to gorge themselves on the latent psychic energies of mankind. For they needed what the human race had. But the barrier held them at bay and even those withering, ravenous minds could not tear through it . . . at least not by themselves.

So they gathered in a writhing, industrious mass, a living and boiling incarnate cloud of sibilance, an alien infestation. A million piping voices built up, a clangorous explosion of noise like scratching metal and broken glass and scraping forks.

If they got through, they'd leech the collective mind of humanity dry in a matter of days. Such a thing could not be allowed. It would be hideous beyond imagination.

And just as Hayes thought that this, the horde waiting on the other side, was the most horrible thing the human mind could conceive of, it got suddenly worse. For that hive began to part and something came oozing and worming from out of that entombed, cryptic blackness . . . a roiling atomic putrescence, a living nuclear chaos, a surging and verminous plasma that was gigantic and alive and crystalline. Yes, an extra-dimensional polychromatic abomination that filled space and filled the mind and sucked the marrow from the souls of men even as it burned their flesh to cinders. It was surging forward, its crystal anatomy flickering and pulsing with colors and brilliance and liquid fire.

Seeing it made Hayes' stomach roll in queasy, peristaltic waves. If such loathsome and wicked beings as the Old Ones could possibly have a god, this was it. The ultimate horror. Hayes had to look away because this thing was burning a hole through his head. It was malignant and noxious and sinister, the enemy of all living things with any purity in their souls.

Its mind was a smoldering reactor and its flesh was not flesh but light and smoke and melting crystals of filth, a crawling fourth-dimensional helix of radioactive plasma. This was the crystallized devil, the incandescent pestilence that crept in the dark and twisted corridors between the spaces men understood, the deranged color out of space that Lind had raved about.

This was it.

The Color Out of Space.

And if the Old Ones ever got through in numbers, that wasting cancer would come with them and it wouldn't be just the earth in jeopardy and the minds of men, because that thing, that sentient cosmic virus, would chew a hole through time and space and matter, yanking the guts out of the universe in moist, noisome coils and feeding on them.

Hayes was understanding a lot of things finally.

He took hold of Sharkey's hand and together they ran from it all, because human eyes were never intended to look upon these things. And as they ran, as their minds got out of range of that dimensional window or mirror or whatever in Christ it was, the image of that terrible place faded and went to static and then darkness. They both saw it go blank like a TV that had been shut off and they both knew that it had been powered by their minds and that made them think things they did not have time to properly consider.

For even though that cosmic TV had been shut off, that insane piping was still rising, reaching fever-pitch, a jarring and disharmonic storm of noise that was like hot needles puncturing their ears. And there was no doubt why, because the Old Ones, the hive from down in the lake were rising up out of the mouth of the pit in a chirring, buzzing cloud like giant palmetto bugs with great whirring wings, that dissonant and vociferous piping sharp as razors. They were gliding and dipping, gathering and dispersing, filling the city as they had millions of years before. The hive. The colony. Like a swarm of locusts they were coming to strip and rend and eat, coming to collect two more minds.

This is the swarm, Hayes thought, *the memory of this is what reverted Cutchen to a frightened beast. The sound, the sight, the smell of them flocking like nightmare birds.*

But there was no more time to think.

They were running, trying to find their way by flashlight and instinct and it seemed an impossible thing. There was no time to consider where they were going or what they would do when they got there. They passed between those cyclopean walls and dozens of the Old Ones gathered atop them like raptors readying to feed. Each time those things got close, Hayes and Sharkey put their lights on them and they scattered. At first Hayes thought it was some rhythmic pattern of flight they were employing, collecting in profuse throngs then scattering away in buzzing pairs. But that wasn't it at all.

The Old One Sharkey had pegged with the flare gun was not afraid of the heat so much, but the *light*. Maybe their ancestors had walked by the light of day, but these evolved versions were strictly nocturnal and had been for countless millions of years. Even when the swarm came to collect specimens in those ancient days, it came in the dead of night filtering up from holes in the earth and the sleeping tangles of their cities, probably up through the ice cap, too. And this particular swarm had been living down in that dark lake for eons.

As Hayes and Sharkey entered the city proper, the Old Ones were done playing, they descended in a droning mob, piping and squealing. Hayes took the flare gun from Sharkey, loaded it, and fired a flare into those seething masses. It exploded into a blazing red ball, throwing orange and red plumes of flame. And the Old Ones scattered immediately.

Then Hayes knew what had to be done.

He and Sharkey moved through the city at a breakneck pace, letting their instinct guide them through those cubes and cylinders and tubes and within twenty minutes they came to one of the honeycombed openings. They were ten feet off the ground and much farther down than where they entered. But close enough. They jumped down, panting and sweating, their lungs aching. They scrambled over to the generator and Hayes kicked into life. The face of the city erupted with light and brilliance that sent the Old Ones scurrying and buzzing back into the shadows.

This was it.

This was their chance.

With the grotto lit . . . or their part of it . . . it was easy enough to make a run back to the archway. They did so, vaulting debris and slipping around stalagmites and climbing over rocks. When they got inside the archway, Hayes tripped and went flat on his face. And if he hadn't, they would not have seen. His light went spinning, revealing the dark corners of the arch they had not originally noticed.

"What is that stuff?" Sharkey asked.

Hayes didn't answer, not right away. What he was seeing were a series of thin plastic tubes wrapped around rocks and the frame of the arch itself. It was detcord hooked to electric blasting caps and their had to be seventy or eighty feet of it. Enough to cause a massive explosion.

That's why the remote control detonator was up in the SnoCat. Somebody was planning on sealing this place off for an eternity. Gates. Must have been Gates.

"Don't touch it," Hayes warned Sharkey. "That's detcord . . . C-8 plastic explosive shaped into a cord."

"The detonator . . . "

"You got it."

The lights were holding the swarm at bay, but they wouldn't for long. Already Hayes could feel those minds out there collecting themselves, gathering their energies, charging their batteries as it were. And when they turned that force at the generator . . .

Hayes and Sharkey started up the steps.

They moved as fast as they could, running and climbing, falling down and getting back up again until they found the original passage. Behind them, echoing and reverberating, came that piping. It was building now. Angry and resolute and directed.

Hayes and Sharkey found the rope ladder, climbed up out of the chasm into the subzero polar night. The storm had passed and there were stars out above. Auroras were flickering and expanding in swaths of cold white light over the mountain peaks.

"Get that 'Cat warmed up!" Hayes called to Sharkey as he ran through Gates' deserted encampment.

He ran one way and she ran the other.

He palmed the detonator from Gates' SnoCat and climbed the slope to his own. Sharkey had it running. He climbed into the warming cab and brought the 'Cat around so its nose was pointing back down the drifted ice road. Then he hit the firing button on the detonator.

At first there was nothing and he thought it hadn't worked or they were out of range, but then it came: a great rumbling from below that set-up a chain reaction of destruction down there. The ground shook and the hills trembled and Gates' camp suddenly disappeared into a smoking crevice.

That's all there was to it.

"Drive," Sharkey said.

Hayes did.

43

On the way back, Sharkey read Gates' field journal, breezing through things she knew. She said nothing for a long time and Hayes just drove. He couldn't think of a single intelligent thing to say after what they'd been through. Nothing. He couldn't even work up the strength to mourn Cutchen. Poor, goddamn Cutchen.

Finally, thirty minutes later, Sharkey said, "Gates had some interesting theories here concerning what this is all about. You up to hearing them?"

He reached over and held her hand. "I'm up to it."

"According to Gates, there's a method to the madness of the Old Ones. They're harvesting minds in a very selective pattern. Some will be harvested to be used, but most . . . most of us will be culled, drained dry, and purged." She clicked off her flashlight and closed Gates' notebook. "They've waited a long time, Jimmy, for their seeds to bear fruit. Again, according to Gates, they'll seek minds much like their own — cold, militaristic intellects that they can easily take hold of, brains that are ready to be awakened and, in some ways, are already awake, receptive. These will be the cells by which they'll contaminate and conquer the entire race . . . reaching out and infecting us mind by mind by mind, spreading out like a plague and waking up those buried imperatives they planted in us so very long ago until we're essentially a hive of bees or wasps, a colony with a single relentless inhuman intelligence, one that can be bent to their will, harvested, and used for their grand plan."

Hayes lit a cigarette. "Which is?"

"Gates is a little vague on that."

"So they don't really want all our minds, just certain ones?"

"Yes. They will infect us all, then purge off those that are what they might consider mutants . . . defiant wills, individualistic minds. They cannot allow such disease germs in the greater whole. But even those that are purged, killed off . . . their psychic energies will be reaped."

"Jesus," Hayes said. "They develop us only to harvest. Like farmers. We're nothing but a crop for them."

Hayes was remembering what Gates had said when they chatted with him. He could see it in his mind now: *I believe they have seeded hundreds of worlds in the galaxy with life and directed the evolution of that life they have an agenda and I believe it is the subjugation of the races they developed . . .*

Sure, the great cosmic farmers spreading out star by star, selecting suitable worlds to be colonized and seeded. Waiting millions of years means nothing to them. For in the end, they always possess the races they engineer and the limitless power of their intellects.

"Gates believed that in every population there were what he refers to as Type-A personalities . . . dutiful, methodical, more machine than man. Minds much like their own. People who place duty and allegiance to a higher cause above all else. And particularly such trifling, human things as love, family, individuality –"

"LaHune," Hayes said, his heart sinking like a brick.

"Yes, exactly. Minds like his may be accidental, but probably not. A small minority the Old Ones engineered in advance to be used like viruses with which to contaminate us all. The end result will be . . . well, I think you can guess."

"A world filled with LaHunes." Hayes looked like he needed to be sick. He pulled off his cigarette, feeling angry and nauseated. "None of us human . . . just cold and brainwashed. Worker ants, drones."

Sharkey nodded. "Yes, but far, far worse, Jimmy. LaHune times ten, LaHune squared. LaHune sucked dry of even his most basal human characteristics . . . automatons with a single directed mind that those aliens can lord over." She paused, slapping the notebook against her knee. "But to what end? I don't know."

But Hayes thought he did.

At least one or two of the reasons, though he suspected there were many of them. They had set a blueprint into motion on this planet as they had probably done on hundreds of others. They sent out colonists that would drift from star to star, planet to planet, seeding them for future harvest just as Gates thought. This would take billions of years but, ultimately, that wouldn't matter to creatures like them that were potentially immortal anyway. And the end result was to establish thousands of outposts, a network of dominance. Using those minds they had engineered, they would have unlimited psychic energy to wield. The sort of energy that was far beyond such simple things as nuclear fusion, it was the very electricity and milk of creation itself.

Oh, it was very simple when you thought about it.

They had known it would work because they had been doing it for trillions of years. They knew how it would happen. All along, they'd known the human race would multiply and spread over the earth. That our engineered neurophysiology would make that quite simple, that we would reason our way out of darkness just as they had. They knew we would over-populate into the billions and that when our numbers reached critical mass we would find them again and they would be waiting, waiting to harness what we had . . . the limitless, pure kinetic psychic force of the human mind. They would harvest it. They would unite us into a single devastating mind. A new mind, a fresh hive, not ancient and jaded like theirs, but fresh and unborn and indestructible, eternal and infinite and immortal. They would direct the cosmic purity of our thoughts and those thoughts would be energy and matter and focus. They would punch a hole through the dark spaces between the stars and bring their race here, the legions, the swarms that would fill the seas and cover the lands and darken the skies and in doing so, would suck humanity dry.

Organic technology. A pure and unmechanistic science.

Yes, we were the ultimate tool, the technology that would summon them and destroy us. And that's what it was all about. Those colonists spreading out, seeding and manipulating, bringing forth a great intelligence that could be absorbed and directed to open doorways between distant gulfs of space. When their plan reached fruition, there would be no million-year migrations, but a simple jump through wormholes tunneled with pure psychic force. They would have the universe, star by star.

It would take forever, but they were patient.

But when they brought the real swarm through, they would also bring that cremating atomic pestilence, the Color Out of Space. That extradimensional horror which curved space and dissolved matter as it slithered along, subverting time and reality and suckling the blood of the cosmos itself. Hayes couldn't pretend to know what it really was, but if the Old Ones could conceivably have a devil, then this was it.

And they were devil-worshippers.

Hayes told Sharkey about this and she agreed with him.

"Doesn't this fucking thing go any faster?" she finally said.

Kharkhov Station.

It came at you out of the whipping, black polar night like some football stadium in the dead center of that glacial white nothingness . . . a sudden oasis of lights and machinery and civilization. Targa House and the meteorology dome. The power station and the drilling tower. Observatories and storage garages. Most of it connected by a webbing of conduits and flagged pathways and security lights. All of it capped by antennas and wind turbines and radar dishes. Outbuildings and huts scattered in all directions. And, off to the far left, the drifted-over runway that would bring the planes come spring. A self-contained community locked down in this eternal deep freeze. And as far as outside help went, it might as well have been sitting dead center of the Martian desert. Because if you were thinking evacuation or rescue, you'd get it about as fast as you would have on the red planet.

He brought the SnoCat in slow, happy to have made it back and, yet, haunted by what he was seeing before him as if it wasn't an Antarctic research station, but some forbidden burial ground, a glacial cemetery that had risen from the ancient ice field, gates swung wide open. Just the sight of it made dread rise in him like flood waters, drowning him in his own sweet-hot fear. By that point in the game he wasn't bothering to talk himself out of such feelings. His guts were telling him that he was going into something bad here and he did not doubt, he accepted that prophecy.

Hayes brought the 'Cat to a stop before Targa House and did not move, feeling the station and letting it tell him things. He couldn't get past the idea that Kharkhov Station had the same atmosphere shrouded over it as the ruined city of the Old Ones now . . . toxic and spiritually rancid.

Sharkey and Hayes stepped from the 'Cat and, although they did not admit it to one another, they could sense the fear and agony and paranoia of the place gathering up into a single venting primal scream that they could hear only in their minds.

But it was real. It was raw. It was palpable.

They could hear it on the wind and feel it in their souls. So they were prepared for the worst when they entered Targa House. What came first was the stink . . . of blood and meat and voided bowels. Death. A stench of death so thick and so complete it nearly emptied their minds just smelling it.

"No," Sharkey said. "Oh, dear God no . . . "

But there was no god at the South Pole. Only the cold and the wind and the whiteness, a ravening ancient intelligence that was always hungry, whose belly was never full.

And here, in the community room, it had feasted.

Everyone was sitting at tables like they'd been called in for a group meeting. And maybe they had been. All of them had their eyes blown from their sockets, their brains boiled to stew. Their white faces were spattered with blood and fluid, carved into shrieking masks of pain and terror. All of them. Like a single diabolic mind had seized them at once and drained their minds in one communal swoop. They were all there in that morgue lit by electric lights: Rutkowski and Koricki, Sodermark and Stotts, even Parks and Campbell from the drilling tower, a dozen others, scientists and contractors alike.

Yes, everyone was there but LaHune.

"We . . . we have to find him," Sharkey said, swallowing, then swallowing again. "We have to get him before he gets out of here. He'll make for another station . . . maybe Vostok or Amundsen. He won't stop until he does and they won't let him."

She came into Hayes' arms and he came into hers and they joined together there in that stinking, ghastly mortuary. Needing to touch and be held, needing to remind one another that they were still alive and still human. There was strength in that. Strength in who and what they were, not in what those fucking Old Ones *wanted* them to be. They had each other and they had feelings and those feelings were real and strong, had greased their skids and fed their engines and got them through all this badness up until now. They figured they could squeeze a few more hours out of them.

"LaHune sent us away on purpose, Elaine," Hayes said. "He wanted us out of the way when he did this, when he made his run. He may have been contaminated for days or a week or who in the hell knows?"

"He didn't think we'd come out of the city alive." She looked around, studying the night pressing up against the windows and frosting the panes with its subzero breath. "They haven't been dead long . . . he might still be here."

Hayes was counting on it.

If LaHune had already made his run, it would mean they would have to go after him. Out onto the polar plateau, racing after him, trying to catch him before he reached the Amundsen-Scott Station or Vostok, the Russian camp. Both were hundreds and hundreds of miles distant. If they caught him, it would be dangerous and if they didn't catch him? Even worse. A break down out there in temperatures dipping down towards a hundred below meant death in two hours regardless of how you were dressed or how hot your little hands were.

It was a simple fact.

So they either stopped him now or let the race begin. Hayes had this mental image of them arriving just behind him at Amundsen, shooting at him, trying to kill him like those Norwegians in *The Thing*, trying to kill that infected dog. He had a pretty good idea that what had happened to the supposed attackers in the movie would play out pretty much the same in real life: LaHune would be rescued and Hayes and Sharkey would be cut down like mad dogs.

So they started searching the station and until you did, you forgot just how big and how spread out Kharkhov was. How many of those orange-striped buildings there were. How many goddamn places there were to hide. You just didn't have your main buildings like the power station or Targa House or the meteorology dome, you had dozens and dozens of little fish huts and storage sheds and warm-up shacks. You had the fuel depo and the garage and the service Quonsets, the man-sized conduits that connected them like arteries beneath the ice. In the summer with twenty men you could have done it in an hour.

In the middle of that endless polar night, it would have taken all day.

Particularly if your quarry didn't want to be found.

So they checked the most obvious places first. They went through Targa House top to bottom, even looking in closets and under beds, in showers and even cupboards in the kitchen. They took no chances. They checked the power station and even the drilling tower. Only good thing they found there was that the hole leading down to Lake Vordog had frozen back up. Hayes made sure of that by turning off the heat and breaking open the windows. Then he opened the drill reservoirs and flooded the hole. Wouldn't take long before it was an ice rink. They also found Gundry...he'd blown his brains out.

He had balls, Hayes got to thinking, covering him with a parka and a tarp. *He wasn't going to let them fucking things have his mind. He went to his grave, middle-finger extended to the Old Ones. God bless you, Gundry. You were the real thing.*

Back on the trail, Hayes and Sharkey huffed it out to the observatory and meteorology dome. Both were empty. The garage was pretty much snowed shut, so they went in the back way and checked everything out, every dark corner and vestibule. They made sure no vehicles were absent. There weren't. They checked the cabs of the Spryte and D-6 Cat, a few four-wheel drive trucks with balloon tires that were used mainly in the summer. Nothing.

"I wonder if he's here at all," Sharkey said, thinking out loud. "I know it's wishful thinking, Jimmy, but what if his mind went, too, and he just wandered out into the night. Got covered by the blizzard."

"If that's true, then sooner or later the wind will dig him back out," Hayes said, knowing the old Antarctic saying was true: Nothing stays buried forever at the pole.

"Do you think it's possible?"

"Sure, Doc, just not probable. For all we know, that crazy fuck is dogging us, staying behind us all the time or ahead of us, just out of sight. We could play tag like this for weeks."

Sharkey brushed a strand of red hair from her forehead. "Is he here, Jimmy? Can you feel him?"

Hayes stood there, leaning up against the Cat dozer and pulling from his cigarette. He thought over her question and when he answered it was not his mind talking, but his heart. "Yeah, he's here. I can feel that bastard out there . . . "

The fuel depo.

If there was any place on the station you could hide, it was here. It was basically a reinforced sheet metal tunnel with tanks of fuel to each side, predominately diesel which ran most of the vehicles and the generators which fired the boilers and kept the lights lit and the systems working and the people warm and fed and the wheels on the bus go 'round and 'round. Even though it was lit by a string of lights, it was shadowy and dank, stinking of oil and diesel fuel.

Carefully then, the Remington pump in his hands, Hayes led the way down the steel catwalk that ran the length of the building. Their footsteps echoed off the steel drums and their hearts pounded, that ominous feeling of expectancy was almost physically sickening. It would have been so easy to hide behind one of the giant drums, springing out and taking them by surprise. But they walked the entire length, peered behind every drum and there was nothing. They walked back towards the doorway.

Hayes suddenly froze.

"What?" Sharkey whispered, sounding like a petrified little girl.

"Well," Hayes said in a blatantly loud voice. "He ain't here." Then he dragged her over near the doorway. "I know where he is. He's down under our feet. He's hiding in the conduit that runs from here to the garage."

Sharkey did not argue with him.

She could see that almost electric look of certainty in his eyes and knew it was fed not by a hunch, but by a deeper knowledge that was inescapably right. If Hayes said he was down there, then LaHune was down there, all right. Hiding like a rat snake in a rabbit hole. And somebody was going to have to flush him out.

He racked the pump on the Remington and put it in Sharkey's hands. "Run over to the garage. Just behind the dozer there's an access panel, a grating set into the floor. He'll try and come up through it when I flush him out. When he comes up . . . blast him. You've got three rounds in there."

"And you?"

Hayes took her ice-axe. He stepped outside with her. "Go, Elaine. Run over there. I won't go down until I see that you made it."

She shook her head, sighed, then ran off into the night, her bunny boots crunching through the crust of snow. The garage was about a hundred feet away. He saw her pause near the back door to it, standing under the light and waving. He waved back.

As quiet as could be, Hayes tip-toed back in . . . if you could realistically tip-toe in those big, cumbersome boots. But he did it quietly. As quietly as he could. By the time he got to the grating, his heart was hammering so hard his fingertips were throbbing. He crouched near the grating.

Elaine should be in place now, let's do the dirty deed and get this done with.

There was no way to be quiet lifting off the metal grating, so he didn't bother. He flipped it off there, letting it clang onto the catwalk. He made a big show of it, talking out loud like he was carrying on a conversation with someone so that LaHune would think he wasn't coming down alone.

Then he dropped down into the conduit.

It was like an escape tunnel from some old war movie, except it was cut through the ice and squared-off perfectly. You could stand upright in there if you were an elf or a pixie, but other than that you had to stoop. Hayes tucked his flashlight into his parka and popped an emergency flare. It threw just as much light if not more and unlike a flashlight, somebody came at you, you could always jam the burning end into their face.

Okay.

Hayes started creeping his way down the length of the conduit.

Fuel lines ran overhead and to either side. The flare was hissing and the smoke was gagging, but bright. Great, slinking shadows mocked his movements. He could hear the flare hissing and just about everything else . . . ice cracking, water dripping as the flare heated the ice overhead, his bones growing, his eyes watering. Yeah, he could hear just about everything, but what might be lurking just ahead of him. His gloved hand was gripping the ice-axe so tightly, he thought he might snap the metal shaft.

C'mon, you asshole, show yourself, daddy wants to cut your fucking head open.

But LaHune did not show himself and Hayes was already half way down the conduit. He was starting to get nervous. Real nervous that LaHune had led him on a merry chase, trapping him down here, getting him out of the way so he could get Sharkey. Yet . . . he still had that feeling itching at the back of his brain that LaHune *was* down here. Somewhere.

And then, two thirds of the way down, it came to him in a flash.

Was down here, you idiot. Past tense. Now he's up in the garage and –

He heard the grating clang open and somebody scramble up and out. Then he heard the shotgun go off. Just once. Sharkey screamed and there rose an instantaneous shrill piping of feral rage and pain. There was a crash and somebody cried out. Hayes started moving as fast as he could, just seconds behind LaHune . . . or the thing he now was. The conduit began to tremble as that deep, thrumming vibration started, rattling down chunks of ice on Hayes.

And then there was the grating.

It was shut, but he hit it like a rocket, swinging it up and open and the first thing he saw as he rolled across the snowy floor was blood. It was splattered everywhere in translucent whorls that looked purple under those sodium lights. Hayes thought madly that it looked like somebody had been shaking a sprinkler can of red ink around in there.

Then he saw Elaine.

She was spread-eagled near the Spryte, face down. The shotgun was a few feet from her and you could smell the smoke and cordite from the blast. Hayes started going to her, but then felt motion behind him and then off to the side.

LaHune.

He hopped off one of the truck hoods and landed very gracefully as if he were held aloft by invisible wings. He kept his knees bent and his hands open like claws against his breast. He was imitating the Old Ones, because he *was* them now. Anything human in him had been squeezed out now. He was just a sponge that was saturated with their minds and powered by the psychic energies of those dead men in Targa House.

He looked hideous.

Being the avatar, the disease cell, of the aliens had not only warped him psychologically, but physically. His head looked unnaturally huge, great patches of hair missing from it. His balding cranium was bulging from what was inside, set with a blue tracery of veins that seemed to throb and wiggle . . . as if there were fat indigo worms just beneath his skin. His face was convoluted and terribly wrinkled, mummified, hollow-cheeked, gray as corpse-flesh. His lips had withered back and his gums were jutting and mottled, the teeth pushed out like fangs.

Hayes brought up the ice-axe, his guts tangled in knots.

LaHune just stood there, his eyes just as red as spilled blood. He glared at Hayes with an almost insane hatred, a blind and consuming wrath. And that was all bad enough. Bad enough to make Hayes take one stumbling step backwards, but what was worse was that Sharkey had not missed.

She had hit LaHune with the twelve-gauge.

It was a glancing shot that had blasted away most of the side of his head, ear included. The flesh around that grisly crater was blackened and burnt from contact burns and inside that jagged chasm of shattered skull, you could see LaHune's brain . . . how it was swollen and fleshy pink, the convolutions rising like bread dough, arteries as thick and loathsome as red pond leeches clutching the gray matter like fingers.

He could not be alive.

And maybe he wasn't. But the parasites living in his head most certainly were.

"Stay back, LaHune," Hayes said, inching his way over to that shotgun.

The administrator was possessed . . . biologically and spiritually. He was not a man any longer. He was like some living monolith, a flesh and blood tombstone erected to the dark memory of those noxious things. They were in him like maggots in rancid meat and no physiology could withstand such an invasion without mutating, becoming a horror itself.

"Just stay back, LaHune, or I swear to God I'll split your fucking head open and piss on what runs out."

But could he? Could he really swing the ice-axe at that hulking alien malignance? Yes, he knew he could. Same as he could step on a juicy spider bloated on blood. Yet, the idea of that ice-axe sinking into that brain and it popping like a water blister or a fleshy balloon and spraying him with filth, it was almost more than he could bear to take.

LaHune came forward in a perverse hopping motion.

He cocked that bulbous head to the side and pink intercranial fluid ran from his gaping wound. His lips were distended and puckered like he wanted a goodnight kiss. The skin there was wrinkled like that of an eighty year-old woman. He made a hollow whistling sound that steadily rose up to that keening, lunatic piping that was loud and piercing and beyond the volume of human lungs to produce.

Hayes felt those blazing red eyes spear into him, but he was already in motion. Be the time LaHune's possessed mind knocked him flat the ice-axe was already in motion. It caught him right between the eyes, the blade splitting his face open lengthwise. Something like blood came squirting out, but this was bluish-green like the juice of a crushed grasshopper and muddy.

Still, LaHune did not die.

He let out a wailing, tormented squealing and fell back and at that very moment the windshields of every vehicle in the garage shattered. A great wind swept through there, knocking Hayes down and then rolling him away. Then LaHune was coming at him, those eyes filled with arcing electricity . . . bleeding red tears and filled with an unearthly fury.

Hayes knew he was done.

This was how cheaters died, this is how revolutionaries were executed by those violating, demented alien minds. Already they were entering his head and crushing his will and sending white-hot jolts of pain through his nerve endings.

But in their arrogance, they forgot Sharkey.

And they didn't remember her until she sat up with the shotgun in her hands. LaHune's huge, grotesque head pivoted on his neck, those eyes smoldered crimson, and those fissured lips came together in a shrill, piping scream of intense malevolence.

Then the shotgun went off, splashing that lewd face from the bone beneath and tossing LaHune up against the dozer. The last round of buckshot nearly tore him in half. And then Hayes was on that writhing, repulsive thing, swinging the ice-axe down on it again and again, sectioning it like a worm. Those vibrations rose up, followed by the crackling of energy, but it was pathetic and weak and soon faded. Yet, he kept bringing the axe down, feeling those invidious minds still trying to worm into his own. The LaHune-thing crawled and inched and slithered, pissing that blue-green mud. It howled and twisted with boneless gyrations.

Hayes jumped up into the Cat dozer and it roared to life.

The LaHune-thing screeching and bleeding and hissing and steaming, the dozer rolled over it, those caterpillar tracks grinding up what was left like bad meat. When it stopped moving, Hayes scraped up what was left with the dozer's blade and pushed it out the door.

And that's when those minds really died.

For they vented themselves with a final cacophonous tornado wind that shattered the windows in the garage and blew all the doors off.

But that was it.

The infection had been stopped.

Hayes stumbled out of the cab and Sharkey was there waiting for him. Leaning against each other, they walked back through the blowing polar night to Targa House.

EPILOGUE

The coming days were busy ones as were the coming weeks.

There were things that had to be done and there was no one but them to do it, so they screwed up their courage and clenched their teeth and got their peckers out of their pants, and did what had to be done.

Hayes bulldozed down the drill tower and reduced all that multi-million dollar equipment to twisted metal and shattered plastic and wiring that the wind and ice claimed immediately. He took down Hut #6 completely and then pushed the frozen mummies into an ice trench. Then he dumped about two-hundred gallons of diesel fuel in there and had a little wienie roast. The Old Ones were reduced to burned out husks. To finish the job, Hayes pushed a two ton slab of concrete in after them which crushed their remains to cinders. Then he pushed snow over the hole and within a day or two, the winter had done its job and you could not see where the grave was.

Sharkey was no less busy.

She wrote out a detailed report of all they had seen and all they had witnessed. Hayes and she spent long nights debating about what they should tell the NSF and what they shouldn't tell them. They decided on a severely truncated version of events. In the report, they would say that LaHune had sent them up to Gates' encampment after he had not been heard from for days. That was essentially true. They would leave out their journey below, saying that the camp was already destroyed when they got there. And that when they returned from the camp, everyone in the station was dead. Again, essentially true. This was the sort of story that would cause the NSF some sleepless nights, but in the long run, they could live with it.

Then came the dirty work.

They photographed the bodies in the community room for evidence and then carried them out into the snow, dragging them off one by one with a snowmobile to one of the storage sheds.

After that, they sent their report and the NSF began besieging them with emails and radio calls. They got more of the same from bigwigs at McMurdo and the Amundsen-Scott Station. But there was nothing to be done. An investigation would begin in the spring.

A month after the death of the LaHune-thing, Hayes and Sharkey were actually beginning to relax. They sat in her bed, drinking cognac and still trying to sort it all out. Whatever came out of all this, they knew, they would always have each other.

"After this is wound-up," Sharkey said, a tangle of red hair falling over one pale shoulder, "they'll start again, you know. Even if they can't dig down to Gates' ruins, they'll be hot to get down to that lake again."

Hayes knew it. He sipped his cognac, listening to the lonesome voice of the wind that no longer sounded haunted. "I know. Those things are still down there and as long as they are, they won't stop until they bring their scheme to an end. Not after all this time. They might be as patient as bricks in a wall, but they're going to want payback."

Sharkey looked over at him. "If it comes down to it, if they push us into a corner, we better tell the truth. I have Gates' notes, his laptop. Gundry's notes. A lot of evidence . . . whether they want to believe it or not is another thing."

They set their glasses aside and hunkered down into the warmth of the bed. "We'll do what we have to do," Hayes said. "I keep thinking about that global warming business. If these caps ever melt all the way, the world is going to have much bigger problems than flooded cities."

"One day at a time," Sharkey said.

And in each other's arms, they did not feel the loneliness and solitude. They only felt each other and in the endless polar winter of the South Pole, that was enough.

Printed in the United States
107684LV00002B/52-78/A